Born and brought up in Islington, London, Susan Oudot worked in publishing for eleven years before becoming a literary agent. From there she was tempted into the world of journalism, where she worked for various newspapers and magazines, before turning freelance. *Real Women*, her first novel, was made into a highly successful BBC series. *All That I Am* is currently in production. She lives in North London with her husband and four daughters and is at work on her next novel.

All That I Am

SUSAN OUDOT

POCKET
BOOKS

LONDON · SYDNEY · NEW YORK · TOKYO · SINGAPORE · TORONTO

First published in Great Britain
by Simon & Schuster UK Ltd, 1998
This edition first published by Pocket Books, 1999
An imprint of Simon & Schuster UK Ltd
A Viacom Company

Simon & Schuster UK Ltd
Africa House
64–78 Kingsway
London WC2B 6AH

Simon & Schuster Australia
Sydney

A CIP catalogue record for this book is available from the
British Library

ISBN 0-671-01568-0

1 3 5 7 9 10 8 6 4 2

Typeset in Goudy Modern by
Palimpsest Book Production Limited, Polmont, Stirlingshire
Printed and bound in Great Britain by
Caledonian International Book Manufacturing, Glasgow

For my friends —
They know who they are
And without whom . . .

Part One

- *Mid-June* -

'Oh, my God! Aaahh . . .'

The swing doors flapped open as the midwife hurried into the labour suite, her face tight with concentration as she slid the long metal poles into the slots at the foot of the bed.

'Hokay, my darlin',' she coaxed, in a strong Trinidadian accent, 'slip your feet into these for me.'

Wearily, Susie raised one foot at a time into the stirrups, feeling peculiarly vulnerable as her knees parted in mid-air. Not that she could give a damn any more who saw her like this. She was beyond that.

She'd arrived twelve hours ago, since when she had learned that the customary greeting in a labour ward was not a handshake but half an arm shoved unceremoniously up one's fanny. The doctor, the anaesthetist, two midwives, three students, anyone, in fact . . . the cleaner, the cab driver, the little old man selling newspapers and Kit-Kats . . .

Having deep-breathed her way through two hours of contractions at home she'd felt more than a little pleased with herself. People had made too much of this birth business, she'd decided. All those horror stories friends had delighted in relating – the two-day labour, the unbearable pain, likened to having your bottom lip pulled up and over your head like a balaclava – had, she decided, been greatly exaggerated. She had coped perfectly well *and* without so much as a whiff of a painkiller. So that when she'd informed Jo she was ready to go to the hospital, she'd envisaged a quick examination on arrival and then straight into second stage with the baby shooting out like a bullet. There'd be a bit of bonding, a clean-up, and then straight on to the phone calls and presents.

The disappointment she'd felt at being told she was barely two centimetres dilated was beyond description. Especially when immediately followed by an overstretched doctor suggesting she might be better off returning home for a while. She had felt a failure, a fraud, but most of all she'd felt . . . fear. Her smug confidence had dissipated into sheer, blind terror. The only way they were going to get her out of that maternity suite was to carry her out, and that, thankfully, was no easy task.

'Listen, mate. If you think I'm leaving this room now, you gotta be kidding.' The last words were squeezed out as Susie's mouth closed in an effort to contain the contraction welling up inside her.

'But you may be some considerable time yet, Mrs . . . er, Ball.' Oblivious to her suffering, the doctor scrawled illegibly on the wad of hospital notes before looking up at her, his tight smile full of insincerity. 'And we shall probably need the bed. So it really wouldn't be fair—'

'Fuck what's fair!' Susie spat, in a manner that defied contradiction. Placing a hand on Jo's shoulder, she hoisted one cheek, then the other, up on to the birthing bed, slumped back against the headrest and pulled up her voluminous T-shirt to reveal a hugely swollen belly. 'Just wire me up to the monitor and get some drugs in here, as quick as you like.'

Half an hour after the second epidural had been administered there was still no sign of even mild relief from the pain. The duty doctor (who, in any case, looked too young to know what he was doing) and the anaesthetist faced one another across the mound of purple-veined flesh, staring at it as though expecting divine inspiration to spring from Susie's stretched and flattened navel.

'It's just one of those things, I'm afraid,' the older man announced unhelpfully, shaking his head. 'It happens in very few women. The drug just doesn't pass across the body . . .'

Susie stopped listening halfway through his first sentence at the onset of a fresh contraction, and began to breathe deeply through her nose, her mouth closing tightly as she prepared for her womb to be dragged up through her liver.

'In fact, you're a rare specimen!' the doctor finished, laughing and looking across at his young colleague, who joined in the joke, the two of them grinning inanely at one another as their patient writhed in agony.

'Listen!' Susie hissed, clutching at the anaesthetist's wrist as the pain subsided and the power of speech was returned. 'I don't give a monkey's arsehole what you give me. Just give me *something*. I'm dying here!'

He smiled indulgently. 'I think you'll find that if you just relax . . .'

Susie gripped further up his arm, a handful of slack muscle firmly in her grasp. She pulled him closer, so that he could feel her stale breath on his neck. 'Don't patronise me, you git! Have you ever had a fucking baby? No! So just bugger off and do what you're paid to do. I want something to knock me out!'

He made a half-hearted and consequently unsuccessful attempt to pull away. But then, feeling her grip tighten about his arm, glanced at the monitor to see signs of increasing activity. Bollocks to another bruised bicep! he thought. And with one quick yank he extricated himself, moving quickly to the end of the bed and safely out of Susie's reach.

'Give me something! Oh . . . Jesus . . . Christ!'

The anaesthetist made a quick note on Susie's chart, muttered something to the young doctor about a good slap being one solution, before calling over his shoulder to Millicent: 'Try gas and air!'

By the time Susie regained her senses and found her tongue, they had disappeared.

'And how's da farver?' Millicent asked kindly, glancing over to Jo as he fidgeted in the chair beside Susie's bed.

'I've got a bit of a backache, actually,' Jo complained pathetically, his face creasing like corrugated paper into a mask of exaggerated discomfort. 'It feels like I've been sitting here for *days*.'

'Here ya are, dahlin',' she said to Jo with apparent sincerity, as she swiped a pillow from the bed. 'Put dis behind you, for a bit of support.'

In spite of the pain growing inside her, Susie looked on in disbelief as he allowed Millicent to plump the pillow and wedge it between his back and the chair, a weak smile of gratitude playing over his lips as Millicent beamed down at him with motherly indulgence.

Jo looked to Susie, whose eyes had narrowed in disdain.

'You prat!' And she snatched her hand from beneath his where it lay at the edge of the bed.

'*What?*' There was a genuine look of bewilderment on his face. 'I was only saying that it gets a bit uncomfortable . . .'

Across the room Millicent cringed, silently willing him to stop right there – for his own sake.

'*Uncomfortable!*' Susie pounced on the word like a hungry lioness. 'All you've done is sit there and stuff your bloody face, drink cups of tea and yawn. Well I'm sorry if I'm keeping you up but I 'appen to be laying here in fucking agony.'

'Susie. Darling.'

'Don't you darling me. Aaahh . . .'

Jo dare not admit, even to himself, that at that moment he had been grateful for the wave of pain surging through his wife's body.

'Look!' she screeched suddenly. 'My legs! I'm having a fit!' she wailed, her legs shaking uncontrollably like some absurd Elvis impersonator on speed.

But even as she stared in horror at the quivering lumps of meat dancing in the stirrups, she congratulated herself on the full leg wax – with bikini line – she'd had the forethought to organise just the day before.

Suddenly businesslike, Millicent gave a brief, reassuring smile as she moved to the end of the bed. 'Everything's fine,' she said before inserting a hand between Susie's legs. 'I'll just have a leetle feel.' Removing her plump fingers, she beamed up into Susie's anxious face.

'Hokay, dahlin'. We're in second stage now. You're doin' marvellous. Just marvellous.'

Momentary elation was replaced by deep dread as Susie watched the room become a hive of activity, with Millicent's short round figure darting about gathering bags of instruments and sterilised containers.

'Ask someone to come in, would ya?' she called to Jo, nodding towards the door.

The pain in his back all but forgotten, he rushed from the room, only to return a moment later, looking gormless and ashen.

'There's nobody around.'

From other rooms the sounds of women screaming and swearing mingled in the cold clinical air.

Millicent tutted and shook her head. 'Well never mind,' she said quickly, flicking her head as a signal for Jo to join her. 'You'll 'ave to help me.'

'*Me?*'

'I want to push!' Susie yelled.

'Not yet, dahlin'. We're not quite ready for you. Just hold on to it for me. Can you do that, dahlin'?'

'I can't hold it. I want to push!'

'Susie, just hang on,' Jo soothed. 'Remember your breathing . . .'

'Fuck off! Just fuck off! Aaahh.'

'That's a good girl. That's it, dahlin',' Millicent cooed as her hands moved urgently over the trolley, pulling at the bags of gleaming instruments.

'Now, come and help me, dahlin'.'

Jo moved obediently to her side and Millicent handed him a bottle of sterilised water.

'Now I want you to take off the lid but don't touch the neck of the bottle wid ya hands, 'cos of the germs. Then ya got to pour the water into this bowl for me, but don't let the bottle touch the bowl. Hokay?'

Jo gave a brief nod and approached the task with the same apprehension one would display at being asked to place a lump of meat into the open jaws of a hungry Rottweiler. When finally he had accepted the bottle into his hands, Jo proceeded with excruciating slowness to unscrew the cap, the burden of responsibility weighing heavily upon his sagging shoulders.

Another contraction threatened to overwhelm Susie. She tried to concentrate on the clock; she tried to focus on the *Madonna and Child* painting they had hung on the wall opposite; but all she could think about was Jo and the bottle and the bowl.

'You're taking off a fucking lid, not doing heart surgery!' she screeched as the wave of pain washed through her, dragging at her insides. 'Oh . . . my . . . God!'

Jo quickly unscrewed the lid and, holding the bottle above the receptacle, gently tilted it so that the water trickled out, dribbling into the middle of Millicent's bowl.

'That's it, dahlin',' she encouraged.

'*Pour* the fucking thing!' Susie screeched. 'Aaahh . . .'

By time the pain subsided, Millicent was standing at the foot of the bed, her trolley laden with the tools of her trade, her plump rubber-covered hands looking absurd as they capped her dark, muscle-bound arms. She stood in readiness.

'Hokay, my dahlin',' she began, laying a hand over Susie's swollen belly, 'when you feel the next contraction, if you want to push, then push.'

Susie nodded, concentrating on the pain gathering strength inside her, like a volcano threatening to erupt, and as it rose to consume her she felt an uncontrollable desire to crap.

'I want to push!' she wailed.

'Hokay, my dahlin', you push for me. That's it, keep your mouth closed and push. That's it. Push. Push. Hokay, hokay. Good girl. Now have a rest.'

Susie's head slumped back on to the pillow, her furrowed brow covered in sweat.

'Hokay, dahlin', you're doing fine. Now, when you feel like it, give me another big push.'

The pain came again all too soon and Susie prepared herself, her arms stiffening, her feet steadying themselves in the stirrups. Jo took her hand and whispered encouragement. 'I'm here, sweetheart.'

'Don't touch me, you bastard. You're never coming near me again!'

He opened his mouth to remonstrate but Millicent looked across and gave a brief shake of the head.

'Oh, my God! Get it out!' Susie yelled. 'Oh, you *bastard*!' And as she clenched her teeth in concentration, her long, manicured nails pierced Jo's skin creating a pattern of four red half-moon shapes across the back of his hand. He yelped and tried to pull it from her grasp but Susie's nails dug deeper.

Each agonising spasm she endured brought with it a fresh rush of hatred for Jo, so that in the end inflicting pain upon any appendage within reach became Susie's *raison d'être*; it was what she clung to. She was way past singing about Miss Polly and her soddin' dolly, focusing on that poxy painting, or listening to some bloody tribe chanting in the rainforest. And as the nails on one hand clawed at his flesh, with the other she clasped a mask to her pain-racked face, the cannister of gas and air to which it was attached cradled in the crook of her arm with the desperation of a drunk to a bottle of vodka.

'Here it comes!' Millicent announced triumphantly.

Suddenly, in Millicent's simple pronouncement, the idea that she would actually give birth to this child became a reality in Susie's mind. She had begun to fear that she would be the first woman in history to prove incapable of doing what was supposed to come naturally. She had allowed herself to drift through fantastic scenarios − the gas mask fixed over her face − whereby medics had been stumped by the child's unwillingness to enter the world and, in the end, had decided there was no alternative but to leave the infant where it was − *for ever*. The baby's fate was to remain stuck in Susie's nether regions, growing bigger by the year, each birthday celebrated by a group of family and friends as they gathered in the shadow of her gaping vagina, their upturned faces smiling as they sang to it, the gentle heat from birthday candles warming the inside of her thighs and singeing her pubic hair . . .

'D'you want to feel the head?' Millicent asked, taking Susie's hand even as she spoke and placing her palm over the lump of soft, sticky flesh trapped in the mouth of the volcano.

Susie flinched, experiencing a mixture of wonder and disgust that a human being should enter the world in such a way. But, for the first time since arriving in the labour ward, her sole concern now was for the safety of her baby. Having touched it, having felt its pulse pumping beneath the spongy tissue, she knew that she could bear the pain, however bad it got.

'Come and have a feel, Daddy,' said Millicent, smiling up at Jo and flicking her head towards Susie's vagina.

Glancing up the bed and receiving no words of discouragement, Jo tentatively placed his hand over the barely visible crown of the baby's head, his face creasing, his mouth splitting in two as his smile spread from ear to ear. He looked up at his wife and, as he reached along the bed for her hand, tears filled his eyes.

In the grip of a fresh contraction, Susie braced herself.

'Hokay, sweetheart.' Millicent laid her hand over Susie's tummy. 'When you want to push, push. But stop when I say so. Hokay? Stop and pant.'

Susie's mouth was pursed in concentration, her lips rolled in on one another like a badly sewn seam. The end was in sight. Now she could bear anything. Glancing up at the Madonna, she screwed up her eyes and pushed.

Two more attempts and beneath Jo's astonished gaze, their baby slithered into the world on a tide of blood and innards. At first glance, he seemed a slimy, blotchy, bald, ratlike creature, but to Susie, staring at him open-mouthed, a thin line of vomit trickling down her chin, he was the most beautiful thing she had ever seen.

'What kind of bleedin' name d'you call that?' Bobby Fuller demanded, cradling his grandson in his arms, his left elbow raised awkwardly so that within seconds his muscles began to ache. Even so, he held it there, his broad, jowly face beaming into the bundle of snow-white hospital blankets, unable to take his eyes off this tiny miracle.

'Well, *we* like it,' retorted Susie, raising her eyebrows at Jo, inviting his support.

'You just need to get used to it,' Jo suggested, with

something less than the wholehearted conviction his wife expected.

'But you can't shorten it, can you?' Doreen complained. Shortening names was the prerogative of one's nearest and dearest — an outward display of love and affection — and it was obvious that Doreen felt she was being deprived.

'No! Exactly! That's why we chose it. I didn't want a name that people'd start chopping about. I mean, we thought of Joseph but then he'd get called Joe, and we thought of Daniel but he'd get called Danny, or Dan . . .'

'Yeah, they're nice names . . .' Doreen offered hopefully.

Susie glanced at her impatiently. 'But we didn't *want* that. We wanted a nice, classy name that people'd have to leave alone.'

'Yeah. But, *Saul* . . .' her father responded, his lip curling in distaste with the strangeness of it as he rocked the baby in his arms, his eyes never leaving the child's tiny, bruised face.

'Saul,' Doreen ventured tentatively. She wrinkled her nose, unconvinced, before trying once again. '*Saul.*' Even Susie winced a little at the sound of it on her mother's lipstick-smudged lips.

''Course, you know what'll happen, don't you?' Susie shook her head. 'It'll get lengthened, won't it?'

'Don't be daft! How they gonna lengthen Saul?'

'They'll just call him Saul-y.'

'Saul-y!' Susie scoffed, grinning across at Jo conspiratorially.

'Yeah. Saul-y. Just like your cousin's kid, ain't it, Bob? She called him Paul. Thought no one'd shorten it. And he got called Paul-y. Mind you, that ain't all he got called. He was a right little sod! Led his mother a bleedin' dog's life.'

'Well,' Susie said dismissively, 'his ain't gonna be shortened *or* lengthened.' And she smiled across at Jo, unaware of the knowing look passing between her mother and father.

They'd named their own daughter after the actress Susan Hayward. Bobby had always had a bit of a thing about her. When they'd had their first child, Doreen had refused to give her the name. In truth, it was jealousy, although it was hard to imagine that now, and she'd opted for Lyndsay instead. You didn't get many kids called that; it was something a bit different. And even when the next one came along she refused; said she wanted to call her Lorraine, and she'd taken a fancy to Gale as a middle name. Bobby had complained that it sounded like a fucking weather forecast — Lorraine Gale — but he appeared to go along with it, right up until they got down to registering the poor mite and the bloke asked for her names. Doreen's lips had barely parted when mouth-and-trousers got there first and before she knew what had happened he'd blurted out 'Susan Gale Fuller'.

Not one for washing her smalls in public, Doreen had kept her mouth shut. Instead she shot him a look that should have poleaxed him on the spot, her face burning scarlet as she'd fought to contain her anger. Tears had seared the backs of her eyes and the bridge of her nose as she'd struggled to control her disappointment.

She had refused to use the name, calling the child Susie instead. Only years later, when passion and jealousy had given way to cosy familiarity, was she able to laugh about it, her anger incomprehensible now that the great tide of longing had passed from her life.

''Ere, let's have a cuddle,' Doreen said, holding out her arms towards the baby. Carefully, awkwardly, her husband passed him across and for a moment watched as she cradled him against her breasts — breasts that had suckled their own children, and not so long ago, it seemed. Susie glimpsed a strangely whimsical look in her father's eyes and wondered if it could be regret at not having been a better parent to her.

Looking across at her mother, she swelled with pride as she watched her coo over her grandson, and felt that, at last, the two women were equals. Finally *she* was a mother; finally *she* had done something worthwhile.

'How's he taken to the feeding?' Doreen said without looking up.

'Yeah, all right, I think.' She forced herself to sound more enthusiastic than she felt. 'But he sucks for ages. Gawd knows if anything's coming out.'

'Well you'd soon know if he was hungry. You used to bawl your head off if you went one minute over your feed time.'

'Yeah, well, it's not like that now,' Susie explained, with an air of superiority. 'Nowadays we feed on demand.'

Doreen laughed loudly, startling the baby with the sudden noise. 'You'll soon get fed up with that when he's keeping you up all night.'

Susie risked a sideways glance at Jo in the chair beside her. His eyes were closed and his chin had dropped down on to his chest.

'He wants to get home and get some sleep,' Bobby remarked, following her gaze. Susie tapped him on the shoulder and Jo jerked awake, his eyes staring unseeing as he struggled to get his bearings.

'I said,' Bobby repeated, laughing, 'you want to go home for some kip. While you can.'

'Huh!' Doreen jeered, leaning forward to return her grandchild to his cot. 'As if you lost a minute's bleedin' sleep with either of ours!' She laid the baby gently on his side, carefully tucking his tiny fist of wrinkled flesh inside the cotton sheet, laying a blanket over the top and pushing it tightly down either side of the thin mattress.

'Ah, bless him!' she murmured, before standing erect,

forcing back her arms to relieve the aching sensation between her shoulder blades. She turned once again on her husband: 'You never once got up in the night. I can remember walking around that bedroom for hours when one or other of 'em had wind or colic listening to you snoring your bleedin' head off.'

She turned to her son-in-law: 'And then I was still expected to have his breakfast on the table — cooked, mind you — before going out meself to do office cleaning. Then I'd get back and I'd 'ave a dozen nappies in soak that had to be—'

'Yeah, yeah, yeah,' Susie interrupted, sighing dismissively. She'd heard the story many times and at this moment did not want to be unfavourably compared with her mother, to have her own achievement cast into the older woman's shadow. This was *her* moment. Now it was *her* turn to be praised, congratulated, indulged. Little did she realise that the first two bring only fleeting satisfaction for such laboured effort and that, for the third, the moment had passed.

A strange catlike mewl rose up from inside the perspex cot, and almost as though she had antennae perched on each nipple, Susie's breasts began to tingle. Doreen was on her feet before Jo could raise his tired body from the chair, her words sounding almost alien as she leaned over the crying baby, his face reddening with the effort.

'Ish my little bubba-wubba ready for his dinny-winny, den?'

Susie placed a pillow on her lap, pulled down her bra flap and assumed position.

Mandy raised the coffee mug to her mouth, rested the rim against her bottom lip and sighed heavily, sending a ripple across the sludge-brown surface.

The two brown envelopes lay side by side on the table. Glimpsed through the transparent address panels, the Mrs in her name struck her suddenly as a total travesty — something she was no longer entitled to but which she had not yet summoned the courage to cast off. She wanted little or nothing now of what married life had brought for the nineteen years she'd been with Pete, but still the thought of admitting — even to herself — that, pushing forty, she was totally on her own was a terrifying prospect.

When Jason had moved in with his girlfriend she'd had the usual maternal misgivings, especially given that at nineteen he was the same age Pete was when they had got hitched. But in truth there was relief too. Jason was so like his father. And though Luke was still at home, he was rarely around, choosing instead to stay with friends most of the time and biding his time until his exams were finished and he was free to do as he pleased.

Steeling herself, Mandy set the coffee down and picked up one of the envelopes, ripping it open and pulling at the contents. She quickly scanned the sheet of paper, with its red FINAL DEMAND heading, defeat dragging at her jawline as her eyes found the boldly printed figure being demanded. *Christ!* The second envelope contained more of the same. With heavy heart Mandy set the two bills aside. She stood up and went over to the sink, pouring the lukewarm coffee away, then stood there, staring into space.

The trouble with getting married young, having your kids young and never having had a proper job was that, when you found yourself on your todd and approaching middle age, it was like being up shit creek without the proverbial. With no qualifications that meant anything — well, did anybody know what a CSE *was* nowadays, let alone care that you had them in religious education and home economics? — and no real work experience to talk of, her job prospects were not exactly brilliant.

It was getting on for two years since they'd split up and,

considering the circumstances, she had to admit that Pete had turned up trumps. In fact he'd been more generous since they had been apart than he'd been when they had lived together, and Mandy sometimes wondered whether it was because he, too, was relieved that, finally, the marriage was officially over. From the start he had covered most of her household expenses, clothing Luke and even keeping her old banger on the road, while he lived at his mum's. Then he had moved into a grotty flat with his brother Barry and continued to cover what he could.

Even so, if it hadn't been for her friends, she'd have probably gone under. It had been hard not having Susie to talk to; she'd always been the one she felt closest to. But Janet, Anna and Karen had been terrific, constantly on the phone making sure she was all right, popping round to keep her company, listening as she poured her heart out and holding her as she cried herself empty. Her family hadn't wanted to know. In her dad's eyes she was in the wrong, was nothing less than a common little tart carrying on like that behind her husband's back. Not to mention being a deceitful bitch by doing it with her best friend's fiancé. The fact that she hadn't known that *her* Jonathan was *Susie's* fiancé, Jo, carried no weight at all in his eyes.

For months afterwards, in the depths of loneliness, endlessly, obsessively, she had wallowed in the memory of their affair. Lying in bed, sitting at the kitchen table, standing in the hallway, her back to the wall, she would close her eyes and imagine she could feel his arms around her; she would breathe deeply, filling her head with the sweet, intoxicating smell of him, and as she ran her fingers lightly up the inside of her thighs she would imagine him there, inside her. But she could never be sure whether the pain she felt was of longing or loss, guilt or envy, and whether she did it for pleasure or punishment.

It had taken this long to get her head back together and to come to terms with the fact that her great romance had been little more than a quick pre-nuptial fling for Jo; just something to steady his nerves. She had fucked up. Big time.

Mandy turned, looking across at the two final demands where they lay on the table. She knew that, eventually, she'd have to shove them in an envelope and send them off to Pete, or give them to Luke to pass on. She had no alternative. But she also knew that he was prepared to take care of her only until Luke left school. Then she was on her own.

The phone began to ring. She went across and out into the hallway.

'Hello?'

'Hi, Mand! It's me!'

'Oh! Hi, Karen. How's it going?'

'Oh, fine.' Her voice sounded strange. Hesitant.

'Where are you phoning from? School?'

'Yeah, I'm on first break. Listen . . .' Mandy could hear Karen's intake of breath as she paused. 'I just wanted you to know that Susie's had the baby.'

Mandy wanted to speak. She wanted to say all the right things. But the words wouldn't come. Nothing. Just a sort of pain in her nose and a tightness in her throat.

'Mandy? You OK?'

Deep breath. Big sniff. 'Yeah. Yeah, I'm fine.' Mandy smiled stupidly into the telephone. 'What she have?'

'Little boy. Seven pounds six ounces. And they're both fine.'

Mandy nodded. Of course she was pleased; of course she wanted them both to be OK. 'She got a name for him yet?'

'Oh, yes. He's got a name all right,' Karen giggled, her pronunciation careful, deliberate: 'Saul!'

'Saul? Saul Ball? She's gotta be having a joke, ain't she?'

'I think not, unfortunately,' Karen giggled.

'Poor little sod!' Mandy could not help smiling.

Karen was the one to break the awkward silence. 'Listen! I'm, er . . . I thought I'd pop up the hospital for a bit this evening. I wondered . . . well, I thought that if you're not doing anything you might want to come along.'

Mandy's body was a tangle of emotions as she fought to find speech, though no words had formed in her head.

'Mand?'

'Um, yeah. It's just that . . . well, the thing is I'm not sure when Luke's coming home. What time you going?'

''Bout seven.'

'Well, if I can make it I'll meet you there. All right?'

'Yeah. 'Course. And I'll even buy you a drink afterwards.'

Mandy replaced the handset, knowing full well that if she was going anywhere near Jo's baby, she'd be visiting the pub *before* she got to the hospital.

Karen's body slumped with relief as she replaced the handset, her shoulders drooping as she visibly relaxed. She hadn't been sure how Mandy would react to the news. On the whole she thought her friend had handled it pretty well, but you could never tell with Mandy.

'You all right?' the secretary asked from behind her desk.

Karen gave a thin smile. 'You wouldn't think it would be so difficult telling people about a birth, would you?'

Before the woman could seize the opportunity to pump her, Karen picked up the handset and punched in the first three digits of Janet's work number. Her finger hovered over the fourth as her brain fought to reassemble the message, to make the words somehow, impossibly, more casual, less important . . . kinder.

Karen dropped the handset into its cradle. She wasn't ready to make this call yet. Maybe she'd talk to Chris about it later, ask her advice. Chris was expert at telling people things they didn't want to hear.

Last night's argument was a familiar one. There were the usual accusations of cowardice and selfishness, and while they no longer stung in the same way, the fact that these confrontations were never resolved meant they would continue to stalk her until the next time; they were always there, waiting.

Although they'd been openly gay among her friends for some time now, Karen still couldn't bring herself to tell her family. How could her mum and dad possibly understand? They'd been so proud when she'd become a teacher. And she knew they wanted grandchildren. But Chris wouldn't have it. It was like she was constantly testing her, forcing her to say which of them she loved the most. And Karen felt the burden of that love weighing down upon her, threatening to squeeze the life from her.

Every time her mum called to say she and her dad thought they'd pop round to see her, Karen made some excuse and paid them a visit instead. Back in the childhood home she allowed herself to fall into the familiar role of vulnerable youngest child, precious only daughter, revered professional, apple of her father's eye of whom so much was always expected, and for that short time she was almost happy to be for them exactly what they wanted. To pretend that she was some other kind of woman. Their kind.

Sometimes she would catch her father's eye and they'd exchange a brief, knowing smile, and at those times the thought of shattering his love for her struck her like a physical blow and she winced, forcing herself to look away.

But there was, she knew, an inevitability about it all. She loved Chris. They lived together. They planned to stay together. Her parents would have to be told sometime. But

Karen wasn't sure what she dreaded most: their pain or their rejection.

Last night they'd gone over the same old ground. Chris was like a Jeckyl-and-Hyde creation: first came the shouting and screaming, the incriminations and rebukes; and then the softly spoken reassurances and encouragements. She'd been there, she'd done it, and she thought she knew. But she *didn't* know, Karen had stormed. How dare she presume to know *her* parents? The rest of the evening had been spent under an enduring, heavy silence.

Karen had brought her tea and toast in bed that morning. She had hovered uncertainly, knowing full well that Chris could see her there, and awaiting acknowledgement like some latterday servant or schoolchild. Finally Chris had looked up, held her gaze for a long, punishing moment before reaching out. And by accepting the tray she had, in the unspoken language of lovers, accepted also Karen's apology.

Karen made another grab for the telephone and got as far as punching in the first five digits of Janet's number before turning round and hurrying towards the classroom and, for once, the welcome distraction of her pupils.

The top three buttons of Janet's uniform shirt were undone even before the front door closed behind her, and by the time she reached the bedroom she had peeled off the shirt, kicked off her shoes and unzipped her sensible knee-length skirt. But only once the garments were neatly folded on the bed, the shoes placed side by side beneath it, and she had pulled on an oversized T-shirt, could she finally relax.

The building society where she worked had been particularly hectic that day, with several members of staff off sick. Mondays were always a pain, constantly busy, with people putting in weekend takings, or drawing out, having been on a bit of a spree. In fact, she suspected that some of the so-called illnesses were psychosomatic, brought on by the need to escape the dreaded Monday. Being one of their older and more experienced employees, she'd found herself lumbered, stuck on the tills all day being polite to people she felt like screaming at. Truth was, she was sick of the place.

Huddled in the corner of the sofa, her knees tucked up inside the T-shirt, Janet felt strangely comforted by the heat from the tea as it penetrated the thick ceramic mug and warmed her hands. A photograph of her and Steve looked down at her from the mantelpiece. It was strange how, at times, it brought her comfort, gave her strength to carry on. As though she could look at the two of them together and remember the day it was taken — at Susie's wedding — after Steve had agreed to go for IVF treatment. They'd had a blazing row, but then, for the first time, they'd talked about it. *Really* talked. She could remember just how happy she had felt: that at last she had hope. But at other times the picture tormented her. She imagined Steve looking down, silently accusing her for not being able to give him the baby she knew he wanted.

The sound of the front door closing made her jump, spilling tea down the front of her T-shirt. She quickly wiped at her eyes.

'Jan?' Steve called from the hallway.

'In here,' she shouted, busying herself with the tea-stained top.

'Hi!' he smiled, looking in from the doorway, his suit jacket hanging over one shoulder, his tie pulled loose. 'What happened to you?'

'What's it look like?' she snapped, slipping past him into the hall, avoiding his eyes. 'I'm gonna run a bath.'

Even as she spoke she wanted to claw back the words, to swallow the anger dripping from each syllable. But as the demon of self-hatred distorted the sounds, she was like a woman possessed. She could feel Steve's misery but was powerless to end it.

Closing the bathroom door behind her, Janet walked across and turned on the taps. She sat on the edge of the bath staring into the water as it gushed into the bath and slowly rose up the sides. Alone, she allowed the tears to flow. Welcomed them almost as her body gave way once more to the pent-up anguish. Steve had once said to her that one of the reasons he was reluctant to go for IVF was because she wouldn't be able to cope with failure; that if they didn't pull it off she'd want to try again, and again. She'd argued, of course. Said it was him and his male ego that wouldn't be able to cope. But he'd been right.

She had been a little disappointed when they had managed to retrieve only four eggs. She'd been hoping for ten; she felt ten eggs would give them a fair shot. But the doctor had told her not to worry. She had a reasonable chance with four. Steve had dutifully gone off and produced his bottle of sperm, handed it over, and they were told to go home and phone in two days' time.

The time in between had seemed interminable. She'd decided to take the time off work; hadn't wanted to talk to anybody; hadn't wanted anyone to ask her about it and almost everything she did came wrapped in superstition: if she didn't answer the phone, then it would be all right; if she didn't think about names, then it would be all right; if she kept busy and pretended that she hadn't even been to the hospital then, hey presto, everything would be fine. She'd told Steve to go to the office.

When finally she phoned, it was to be told that none of the eggs had been fertilised. It was then that everything became unreal. She heard herself thanking the doctor in polite, unemotional tones, speaking rationally, as though this tragedy were happening to someone else, as though, deep inside, her body wasn't screaming.

Fearing the worst, Steve had called eventually. The phone had rung for a long time before Janet answered. She told him the news, though there was no need. He'd said as much, but she made herself tell him anyway, beating herself up with each word she uttered.

Afterwards, she grieved. It felt as though her children had died, and she mourned them. Oh, there were no faces to haunt her and no bodies to bury, but in her mind those four babies had been plucked from her useless, barren body and she had failed them. As hard as she had tried, it had been impossible not to imagine what they might be like; to wonder whether they were boys or girls; and to hope that, at last, a glimmer of light had appeared at the bottom of the black hole into which she and Steve had fallen. And in one brief phone call all her hopes had shattered.

Her mother had told them to give up. She'd said that Janet should be happy that she had Steve; not all women were so lucky. Janet had turned on her, had opened her mouth to speak, but in that moment had seen the pain in her mother's eyes and felt even more acutely the weight of the burden she carried. Others had meant to be kind, but when they had told her to never mind and to try again, like she had failed a driving test, it was impossible to tell them how she felt, even if they had wanted to know. And now, two months later, she was somehow expected to have put it all behind her. As with a drowning woman stretching for a lifeline, her only hope was to cling to the thought that they might be able to try again. That the doctor, like some modern-day God – with the power to save or destroy – might grant them one more chance.

Janet reached across and turned off the taps, then climbed into the warm, inviting water. With the door closed and the filter whirring, she was only vaguely aware of a telephone ringing.

'Hello.'

'Hi, Steve. It's Karen.'

'Oh, hi, Karen. Jan's in the bath.'

Karen's voice sounded suddenly more confident. 'Oh, it doesn't matter . . .'

'Well, d'you want me to get her to call you back?'

'No! No, it's fine. It's just that . . . Well I just thought I'd let her know that Susie's had the baby. Little boy.'

'Oh! Right.' Steve's voice was barely audible.

There followed an awkward moment of silence, although only Karen was aware of it. 'She called earlier, from the hospital, and asked me to do a ring round. A couple of us are going to pop up and see her this evening, so if Jan—'

'No! She can't!' Steve glanced along the hall, conscious that his voice had grown louder. 'It's just that we're, er, going out to dinner. Sorry.'

'No problem!' There was relief in Karen's voice. 'I just thought . . . Well, give her my love, won't you?'

'Yeah. Yeah, 'course I will. 'Bye, Karen.'

As Janet lay in the bubble-filled bath only her head was visible. Beneath the frothy surface her hands moved back and forth over her taut abdomen. She did not hear Steve as he forced himself to sound cheerful for Karen, nor witness the concern on his face as he listened to Susie's news. She did not feel his helplessness as he struggled to know how he could cushion the blow for her, how he could save her from yet more suffering. Nor could she taste the salt from tears that trickled down his face as he, too, felt the hollow pain of their childlessness.

A brief tap came on the door and Janet's hands broke the surface of the water, like those of a child caught playing with herself.

'Jan?'

'What?'

'Let's go out to dinner tonight . . .'

Anna combed her short dark hair, staring at her reflection in the compact mirror. Taking a lipstick from the make-up bag spilling out over her desk, she ran it over her lips with practised ease. In spite of the years she'd worked in women's magazines, and the hundreds of beauty features she'd published, she still chose to ignore the basic rule of always applying colour with a lip brush. Who has time for all that bollocks? She'd once sat next to Princess Margaret at an awards dinner and had watched with fascination and admiration as she'd applied a fresh coat of lipstick, without the aid of a mirror, between each course. That was confidence for you! Anna rolled her lips in on one another, gave a light coating of mascara to her dark lashes, and sighed with dissatisfaction as she stuffed the mirror into the bag.

The last pages of the day had been passed and Anna could sense Rachel's irritation that she, too, had not yet left the office. Rachel was one of those rare women in the magazine world who *wanted* to be editors' PAs, and she took her role very seriously. So much so that she felt she could not leave the office before her boss had, and if this was due to excess of work then that was fine, but she was less tolerant of the senseless hours of hanging around that had become the pattern over the past few months.

Anna observed Rachel's blurred figure through the window wall, and smiled with perverse satisfaction as she watched the other woman's fingers play impatiently over the desktop.

'Raich!' she called. She rarely used the intercom.

Almost immediately she appeared in the doorway. Her eyes were still a sparkling, vivid green as they peered from beneath the thin wisps of her blonde fringe, almost in denial of the dry, lined skin that surrounded them. She smiled hopefully.

'Did you remember to send the flowers?'

If Rachel was irritated by Anna's unnecessary question she did not show it. 'And I told them to make sure they were delivered today, so she should have them by now.'

Anna nodded. 'Is the car here yet?'

'It's been downstairs for twenty minutes.'

Ignoring the accusatory tone, Anna glanced at her watch. It didn't look like he was going to phone now, she had to admit. But maybe she'd wait just another five minutes. Pulling open the bottom drawer, she reached in for her handbag and placed it on the desk. She took out her mobile phone and checked that the battery was OK before replacing it in her bag.

'OK. Tell the driver I'll be there in two minutes. But I've changed my mind. I'm going to the hospital first, so make sure he knows the way. I don't want him taking me on a fucking tour again.'

Anna sat for a few minutes more, staring at the silent telephone, willing it to ring. She glanced at her watch and, with heavy reluctance, stood up from the desk. And even as she left the office – sliding her hand inside her bag to check for her mobile – she would not give up hope that he would yet call.

She had wanted so much for things to work out with Callum. The great love of her life! So that when he'd flown in from New York out of the blue, sweeping her off her feet again, she'd thought that everything was going to be all right. At last.

They'd talked and talked so that, for the first time since it had happened, she felt able to deal with the abortion. This thing that had racked her conscience, her body, her heart for the past two years would, she knew, always be with her, haunting her from some dark dungeon of regret. But at least now she could work through it.

She had listened to him tell her why he'd reacted the way he had; about the sense of loss and of impotence at not being permitted a say over whether or not their baby should be born. The tears had flowed, from them both. And in the end they felt stronger for it, closer, and ready to move forward.

They had been like lovesick teenagers, so that when Callum returned to the States, it had cost Anna a fortune in transatlantic phone calls and faxes. Each day they'd spend ages just chatting, catching up, organising either Anna's next visit to New York or Callum's to London. But each eagerly awaited rendezvous was fraught with the pressures of expectation, of anticipation, so that it was like arriving at a holiday destination only to find that it doesn't measure up to the pictures in the brochure. And afterwards she would plunge into a well of disappointment. And no matter how much she resolved to try harder next time, doubts, insecurities, resentments niggled away, festering in the void of their separation, forming a patchwork cloak of self-preservation that she eagerly wrapped about her.

In the beginning nothing would be allowed to interrupt their conversations, or interfere with their plans. Important calls were put on hold, meetings postponed, clients kept waiting. But in the end these merely served as excuses, for calls that were never made and trips that were cancelled. In the end it wasn't the parting she dreaded, but the coming together.

That it had been true love, Anna had never been in doubt. That it wouldn't work, she had always half suspected.

Her answer had been to immerse herself in her work, to rebuild her career. So that by the time she dropped into bed at the end of each exhausting day, she was too tired to be tormented by the unwanted space about her aching body, embracing sleep and its offer of more gratifying scenarios where happy endings were allowed.

Frank hadn't so much walked into her life as barged his way in. Even during their first meeting — a business lunch for the corporation's magazine executives — she'd picked up on the unmistakable body language, had read the signs of romantic interest. And had chosen to ignore them. She felt the stirrings of sexual interest, certainly, but it was too soon after Callum. And in any case, she just couldn't *do* relationships. So what was the point?

But Frank had been persistent. He'd wooed her and charmed her, and, in the end, seduced her. She hadn't known he was married the first half-dozen times they'd met, and by the time she'd found out, she didn't care.

Anna plunged her hand into the voluminous handbag, pulled out the mobile phone and fiddled with the power button; pressing it off then on again, her shoulders sagging with resignation as she returned it to her bag.

'Do a left at Gower Street, then take the first right,' she ordered curtly, pulling herself forward on to the edge of her seat.

'OK! Drop me here!' Anna had opened the door before the driver had managed to bring the car to a halt. Briefcase in hand, she stepped out on to the pavement and strode off towards the hospital gates.

'I tell you,' Susie said, placing the baby on the bed, 'it ain't as glamorous as it's made out to be! I've got this great bloody sanitary towel they've given me. It's like having a duvet shoved down your knickers. I can't even put me legs together!'

'So what's new?' Anna and Karen looked at one another across the hospital bed and grinned.

'You gotta be kidding!' Susie said seriously, unwrapping the baby from his shawl. 'I don't think I'm ever gonna have sex again!'

'I seem to remember your saying that once before,' teased Karen.

'Yeah, so do I,' Anna joined in. 'Wasn't it after she had it off with Barry Evans that time?'

'Yeah, that's right,' Karen smirked, winking at Anna. 'And by my recollection that resolve lasted what? About a week?'

'If that! In fact I think it was just long enough to get rid of the aftertaste.'

'Yuk! Don't remind me!' And as Susie's nose wrinkled in disgust, the three friends burst out laughing.

Susie reached inside the small cupboard beneath the baby's cot, bringing out a small plastic pot, cotton wool, a tube of cream and a disposable nappy, placing them on the bed beside the baby.

'Do they show you what to do?' Karen asked, looking at the collection of items.

'Well, yeah, sort of. But they're running round like blue-arsed flies most of the time. Specially on this ward, 'cos a lot of 'em 'ave had Caesareans. See her over there.' Susie nodded in the direction of a sleeping woman two beds along. 'She just fell asleep before you two got 'ere, but she ain't stopped bleedin' crying all day long. I felt like giving her a slap. I mean, what's it matter how they got the bloody baby out as long as it's all right? I'm telling you, towards the end of it they could've chopped my fucking legs off and I wouldn't've cared.'

Karen smiled fondly as she shook her head at Susie's pragmatism. But Anna was engrossed in the baby. Lying across the bed, propped up on one arm, she let her finger play over his dimpled fist, the skin transparent and flaky. Then his tiny fingers closed over it, gripping it with almost superhuman strength so that as Anna gently moved her hand from side to side, so his moved also.

Susie and Karen exchanged a brief look.

'You couldn't get us some water, could you, babe?' Susie said, holding out the small plastic bowl to Anna.

'What?'

'Some water. For his bum. Sink's over there.'

Anna followed Susie's gaze, took the bowl and pulled herself up. Walking slowly through the ward, she glanced into every cubicle, more out of interest in the age of each new mother than in the appearance of their offspring.

When Anna returned with the water, Susie was laying an incontinence mat beneath the baby's bottom. With great ceremony she pulled back the sticky tabs on either side of his nappy and peeled down the front, to reveal the tiniest winky, which immediately evoked squeals of delight from Anna and Karen.

'Oh, it's so *sweet*!' Karen cooed.

'Actually,' said Anna, her eyes narrowed in mock concentration, 'I'm trying to think who it reminds me of.'

As she laughed, Susie felt a rush of blood through her vagina and, reaching between her legs, pressed her palm against the crotch of her knickers.

'No wonder you get through so many bleedin' vibrators if that's what you've been used to! It'd be like squatting on a peanut!'

'Su-use!' Karen was aware of other women listening from around the ward.

'Well it's true! I mean to say, I know size don't matter but there's gotta be *something* there, ain't there?'

'Well, no, there hasn't, actually.'

Susie looked to Karen a moment before the penny dropped. 'Well, no. I know there hasn't with you. But with, you know, a man and a woman there has. Ain't there, Anna?'

'Oh, definitely.'

As Karen and Anna caught each other's eyes and grinned, Susie realised she was being teased.

'Cows!'

Leaning forward and taking the baby's hands in hers, she held them to her lips and kissed them gently. 'Anyway, I tell you, if he ends up with half as much down below as his dad he'll have 'em queuing up.'

'Lucky old you!' Anna giggled. 'Anyway, where is Big Boy?'

'Poor sod was knackered. He kept dropping off so I told him he might just as well go home. Which probably means he's gone up the pub.'

'Oh, well, you can't blame him this once,' Karen reasoned. 'I mean, he'd want to tell everybody, wouldn't he? Relive the birth in all its glorious detail.'

'Huh! As though he bleedin' well did anything! Honestly, at one point I thought: If he tells me to breathe one more time I'm gonna twist his balls off with the forceps!'

Susie placed the tiny nappy beneath the baby and fastened it on either side with the sticky tabs. 'The number of these I've wasted,' she said, pushing two fingers inside the nappy to check if it was too tight, pulling back the tabs and repositioning them. 'I'd only changed him four times and I had to send Jo out to get us another packet.'

'You'll get used to it,' Anna reassured her, smiling down at the baby, watching as Susie fastened his oversized vest under the crotch then slipped his sticklike legs into the towelling baby-gro.

'Yeah,' Susie smiled, reaching down and gripping him under the armpits, carefully lifting him on to her shoulder. 'Did you manage to get hold of Mandy, Kar?'

'Yeah. Yeah, I did. Said she'd try and come along if she could.'

'Oh! Right!' There was a hint of surprise in Susie's voice.

'Was she OK?' Anna asked.

'Why shouldn't she be OK?' Susie responded quickly.

'Yeah! She seemed fine.'

'All I meant,' Anna began, 'was that she might feel a little bit, well, *awkward*, in view of what happened . . . you know.'

'It's all water under the bridge, Anna. Mandy got over it a long time ago. Me and her have had it all out and she knows it was nothing more than a fling. So there's no reason why she should feel *awkward*, is there?'

Susie's look challenged Anna to disagree. From the end of the bed she could feel Karen's eyes on her, pleading with her. 'No!' she conceded finally, forcing a reassuring smile. 'I s'pose you're right.'

Alone in the hospital lift, Mandy turned and checked herself in the mirror, relieved there was no sign of redness around her eyes. She'd known it was silly. She had no feelings for Jo now. Every bit of love she'd felt had died the day he'd walked down the aisle with her best mate. Even so, she hadn't been able to stop herself from crying, sitting alone after Karen's phone call. It had just seemed the last straw.

She had made up her mind to visit Susie on the spur of the moment, the bunch of flowers in her hand hastily bought from a mini-market on the way rather than turn up empty-handed.

The lift stopped at the second floor and Mandy stepped out into the brightly lit corridor, making way for groups of chattering visitors on their way out. The unmistakable smell of establishment disinfectant filled her nostrils and from a distance came the sound of crying babies. The lift doors closed behind her, leaving Mandy rooted to the spot, listening. Too clearly she was able to recall how it had been when she'd had the boys; how she'd sat there for hours on end just watching them sleep, waiting for them to wake. She could remember how happy they had been then, she and Pete.

'Excuse me. Can I help you?' Mandy turned gormlessly, as though not understanding the question. 'Are you here to see someone?'

'What? Oh, yeah. A friend. Susie Ball.'

The nurse smiled. 'Ah, yes. Susie.' She moved towards a pair of swing doors and pushed one open, standing with her back propped against it. She looked into the ward, making a tiny flicking gesture with her head as she spoke: 'She's up the end on the left.'

Gingerly, Mandy eased past her. She turned to thank her but the nurse had gone, the door flapping in her wake. Mandy peered along the rows of beds, desperately hoping that Jo would not be there. A peal of laughter rang out, the deep, adult sound of it incongruous among so many tiny, innocent cries. Mandy recognised it immediately.

At that same moment, Anna glanced along the ward and saw Mandy standing there. Still laughing, she waved, before turning back to Susie and Karen.

'Mandy's here!'

'See!' Susie said gleefully, her attention focused on the baby as she tried to encourage him to latch on. 'I told you she didn't 'ave a problem.'

Anna caught Karen's eye and they remained silent.

By the time Mandy stood at the foot of the bed, the baby's mouth was fixed to Susie's nipple like a limpet, and the scene was the idyll of mother and child.

'Ah, he's lovely, Suse.'

Susie looked up and beamed. 'Yeah, he is, ain't he?'

'How was it?'

'Don't ask! They say you forget the pain as soon as you've got the baby, don't they? Well, it's crap! I tell you, it felt like trying to blow a football out of a fucking pea shooter!'

'I wish I'd been there!' Anna laughed.

'Sadistic cow! I tell you, if you had it'd put you off for life.

Jo was as white as this sheet. You should've seen him when the afterbirth came away!'

Karen's lip curled in distaste. 'Yuk! Makes me glad I'm gay.'

Mandy placed the flowers on the table and began to unwrap them. 'Where is Jo?' she said, without looking up.

'He's at home,' Karen said quietly.

There was something in the reassuring tone of her voice that told Mandy she understood, and she acknowledged it with a brief smile, before gathering up the flowers.

'Sorry they're rubbish, Suse. It's all I could get.'

'Don't be daft! They're lovely!' Susie lied. 'There's a vase over there, next to the others.'

Mandy stepped across to where Anna's bouquet had filled three vases, the blooms fresh and exotic. She shoved her own dried and faded chrysanthemums into the stained vase and pushed them to the back.

When the baby's feed was finished and he had finally been winded, Susie wrapped him in his snow-white shawl, lifted him awkwardly and offered him to Mandy.

'D'you wanna hold him for a bit?'

From the look of horror on Mandy's face anyone would have thought she had been asked to go off for a spot of sky diving.

'I've had a bit of a cold,' she said, sniffing for the first time that evening.

'Don't worry. It'll be all right. Just for a minute.' And, aware of Anna and Karen looking on, Susie placed the baby in Mandy's arms.

'It doesn't make you feel broody, does it, Mand?' Anna teased.

'Too bleedin' bad if it does!' Mandy looked up quickly, suddenly aware of how her words could be misconstrued. Suddenly everything was either sensitive or insensitive; there was no normality. 'I mean, I ain't exactly got hordes of willing sperm donors banging on my door, have I?'

'Ditto,' Anna responded dully.

'Ah, poor old biddies,' Susie laughed unsympathetically. 'You'll end up like a couple of bloody bookends at either end of the shelf.'

Anna punched her playfully in the ribs. 'Yes. Thank you for all your support.'

'Well I ain't looking for Mr Right, I can tell you,' Mandy went on. 'I've had enough of relationships to last me a lifetime. What'd be nice is someone to go out with, go to the pictures with . . .'

'Get your leg over with . . .'

Ignoring Karen's remark and her friends' laughter, Mandy continued. 'Nah, it's the company I miss. I don't even get out that much these days.'

'Aaahh!' the girls joined together in mock sympathy.

'Aw, piss off!'

The baby had fallen asleep in Mandy's arms.

'D'you want me to take him?' Susie said, her arms forming a cradle.

'Yeah, you'd better. He's a weight, ain't he?'

Wriggling her shoulders to relieve the dull ache, Mandy looked on as Susie gently laid the baby in his cot.

'Did anyone phone Janet?'

'Yeah. I did,' said Karen.

'Was she all right?'

'I spoke to Steve.'

'What d'he say?'

'Oh, you know Steve. He takes it all in his stride.'

'Yeah. And probably better he tells Jan. I mean, it can't be easy, can it?'

All four women shook their heads, the moment of shared melancholy an all-too familiar one. Each of them had tried to be there for her through the whole IVF thing, but as soon as Susie got pregnant Janet had found it hard to have her around, tormented by her gently swollen body, so that in the end Steve had asked her not to call. He had walked Susie to her car, leaving Janet upstairs in the flat, and had told her about the hours of tears that followed each visit, explained about the night he would now spend holding Janet until she sobbed herself to sleep, her body drained and her heart aching from the injustice of it all. That night Susie had also cried.

'Has anybody seen her lately?' Susie asked quietly.

'I've been round a couple of times since the IVF thing,' Mandy said solemnly. 'But it's difficult to know what to say, ain't it?'

Anna and Karen nodded.

'I gave her a call at work last week — sometimes I think she finds it easier to talk when Steve's not there. But' — Karen shrugged her shoulders — 'she just seemed like she wanted to get off the phone.'

'Mm. I know what you mean,' Anna nodded. 'Then other times she'll want to go over the whole process in the most minute detail. Over and over again.'

An air of gloom had descended and all four women sat there shaking their heads in despair at the thought of their friend's suffering and at their own inability to help her.

'Christ! I'd hate to see you lot at a funeral!'

Jo's face was barely visible behind an enormous bouquet of flowers as he approached the group of women. Around his wrist a length of shiny blue ribbon rose six feet into the air where it was attached to a blue, foil, helium-filled balloon carrying the message IT'S A BOY!

Immediately, Karen, Anna and Susie's mood changed, their faces transformed with broad smiles. Dropping the flowers on to the bed, Jo leaned forward to give Susie a kiss.

'Crikey! You smell like a bleedin' brewery!'

'I had to wet the baby's head, didn't I? Proud father, an' all that.'

Turning round he leaned over the cot, peering in at his son, silently marvelling at this most wonderful creation. Watching him and seeing in his eyes a look of pure joy, Susie glowed with the knowledge that she had given this to him, blinking away the tears that threatened to fill her eyes. Reaching in, he gently ran a finger down the child's cheek.

'Don't you wake him up!'

Grinning at her over his shoulder, Jo scooped the baby out of the cot and into his arms, his eyes never leaving its face, filled with a real sense of wonder at each tiny movement.

'He's gonna spoil him rotten!'

Jo glanced across at Mandy. 'Mand? How you been?'

Not once since their affair, not once since the fiasco of his wedding to Susie when she had discovered who he really was, had Mandy felt that he was sorry for what he had done to her, the way he had deceived her, the pain he had caused her. But with that glance, those few words, things were suddenly better. His eyes now showed remorse and the tiny smile that played on his lips seemed to ask her forgiveness.

'We should leave you two to it,' Karen said suddenly, pushing back her chair and pulling Anna to her feet.

'Er, there's just one little thing I wanna say, Suse.'

All eyes turned in Mandy's direction.

'You gotta be pulling our legs, ain't you? Saul Ball!'

Stepping out into the hospital car park, Anna switched on her mobile phone and checked for voice mail. There were several messages but only one of them interested her right now, and that was the one from Frank.

'Hi, sweetheart. Guess you're busy. But if you fancy a quick drink I'll be in the Pitcher and Piano. Miss you. 'Bye.'

Anna smiled, then, slipping the phone back into her bag, walked quickly over to the car and tapped on the driver's window. At once he lowered the electric window.

'Dean Street,' she said. 'The Pitcher and Piano.'

'Yes, ma'am.'

She slipped into the back, then closed her eyes, enjoying the sheer luxury of it for once. She had offered Karen and Mandy a lift, but they'd decided to go for a quick drink before getting back. So Frank it was — if he was still there.

As the car purred along she thought about Susie and about her evident joy and felt strangely elated for her friend. Strange because she'd expected to feel something different, something much less pure. In that brief moment before she'd pushed through the doors to the ward, she'd felt a twinge of envy, of sheer, unalloyed jealousy, yet in the instant she had first seen Susie with young Saul that had melted away. All she had felt was pleasure at her friend's happiness. And that was nice. Nice because this last year had found her behaving less than nicely.

The thing was, she thought she had grown hard these past twelve months. Selfish and self-obsessed. But tonight . . . well, tonight she had let herself be wrapped up in someone else's happiness; had felt the way she'd used to feel.

Arriving at the bar, she sent her driver home. She would get a cab back. Or stay with Frank, perhaps, in the flat he kept in town.

And if he wasn't there?

But he was. She saw him almost at once, there at the bar where he always sat, and he, looking up from his drink, saw her and smiled.

He had such a nice smile. Pleasant and intelligent. Not like most men's smiles, which were often little more than disguised leers. Frank's smile showed a genuine pleasure in seeing her.

Anna went across and, placing her bag on the bar, turned

and looked at him. 'Sorry,' she said. 'Friend of mine had a baby. I went to see her.'

'One of your girls?'

Anna nodded. She had told him about the girls. Not all of it, of course, but enough to give him the idea. 'Susie,' she said. 'You know, the one who got married.'

'Ah . . .' Frank stared away thoughtfully, then looked back at her, his green eyes smiling at her. 'So? What are you having?'

You, I hope, she thought.

He grinned, reading her mind. 'To drink, I mean.'

She grinned back at him. 'Just a mineral water.'

'Something wrong?'

'No. It's just that I'm not in the mood to drink.'

But she couldn't tell him what she *was* in the mood for, because if she had he'd have run a mile. Besides, she had only really understood it herself at that moment.

I want what Susie has. A baby.

And as he ordered her water — and another Scotch for himself — she studied him, realising that she was looking at him suddenly in an entirely different light. Because if she *was* to have a baby then it would have to be soon, and Frank — who in every other respect was the perfect man — was not, perhaps, the man to father it.

He was handsome, intelligent, and he made her laugh. What was more, he was wonderful in bed. Better even than Callum had been. Even so . . .

You're married, she thought. And what's worse, you have four kids, so no matter how much you might like me — even love me a little — you won't leave your wife for me.

They had never even discussed it, but she knew it for the truth. A man could hate his wife — abhor her even — and yet stay with her, simply because he loved his children. And in Frank's case there was an added complication. He liked his wife. They had been childhood sweethearts. They'd even gone to college together. There was a lot of history.

He turned back, handing her her drink. 'There . . .'

She toasted him back, but there was an uncertainty in her face now.

'What is it?'

She looked down. 'Oh, I don't know. I'm tired, I guess. Overwork. And . . .'

But she couldn't say the rest of it. About the baby and the thoughts it had put into her head.

'You want to go?'

She knew what he meant. Back to his place. And normally she would have gone happily, even if she'd been a bit tired. But not tonight. Tonight she needed to be alone. She hadn't known it until now, but that was what she needed. To straighten herself out.

'Look, I . . . I ought to go home, Frank. I feel . . .' She shrugged. 'I wouldn't be very good company.'

He grinned at her lustfully. 'You think I want you for your company?'

She smiled back, but wearily now. 'Seriously. I . . . need some space.'

Slowly his face changed. 'So why did you bother to come?'

'I don't know. It's just . . .' Again she almost said it. It was seeing Susie's baby. Seeing her so happy. And wanting that for herself. But if she started to explain it to him, then who knew where it would end?

She finished her mineral water, then stood, taking her bag from the bar. 'Tomorrow, OK? I'll meet you after work.'

But when she looked at him there was a sudden hardness in his face. 'Don't bother.'

'What?'

'You heard me.' He finished his Scotch then stood.

'Frank?'

She went to touch him, but he brushed her hand away. 'I'm going.'

'Fuck off then!'

She saw how shocked he was at that. She had never spoken to him like that before, and hadn't meant to now, but his sudden petulance had brought it from her.

He reached down and retrieved his briefcase from where it lay between his chair and the bar, then glared at her. 'You can't piss people about, Anna.'

'Oh, so it's OK for you to call the shots . . .'

'Just leave it. Let's just call it a day, eh?'

Anna turned. 'Frank . . .'

But he was gone.

She sat again, sighing, staring down at the empty seat beside her, noting how the rounded leather cover still held the impression of him.

'Shit!'

Then, angry with herself, she turned from the bar and hurried out, hailing the first taxi that came along, knowing, even as she climbed into the back, that she wouldn't sleep, and wondering — seriously wondering — if she would ever see him again.

'Mand?'

Mandy turned, squinting into the darkness to try to see who it was who had called out to her.

'Debbie? Is that you?'

As the woman stepped out from the doorway into the light from the street lamp, Mandy saw she'd been right. Debbie had been one of her old neighbours, back when she and Pete had lived on the estate. A bit of a gossip, she had more than once put Mandy's nose out of joint, but that was all a long time ago, and as Debbie smiled, so Mandy smiled back at her, genuinely pleased to see a familiar face.

'Hello? How are you?'

'All right. I thought it was you. Been out?'

'Yeah. I went to see Susie — you know, Susie Fuller. She's just 'ad a baby. Lovely little boy.'

'Yeah, I 'eard. So how's things? Got yourself a toyboy yet?'

Mandy laughed. 'Chance'd be a fine thing. Nah . . . Luke's still at home, so . . . it's difficult.'

'Yeah . . .' Debbie smiled, then patted the back of her neat, short-cut hair. 'Still, it must be nice to know Pete's all right. You know, after what happened.'

Mandy frowned. 'What d'you mean?'

'Well . . . you gotta move on, ain't you? Mind, she's a bit young.'

Mandy felt herself go cold. For a moment she hadn't had a clue what the woman was talking about, but now she did. She was talking about Pete and another woman. And a young woman by the sound of it.

'What do you mean?' she asked, unable to stop herself; her curiosity overcoming the urge to walk away.

'Well . . . she can't be much older than your Jason. Mind you, her mum and dad don't seem to mind, so I s'pose you gotta say good luck to 'em, ain't you?'

Mandy opened her mouth, then closed it again. Pete? With a girl of twenty? Impossible.

She almost said it, then stopped herself. If Debbie said it was true, it was true. Or some version of it.

'You didn't know, then?' Debbie said, the first hint of the old malice creeping into her face. 'Oh, I wouldn't have said—'

'No. I . . .' Then, knowing there was nothing more to be said, she smiled tightly, said 'See ya,' then did an about-face and walked away as quickly as she could.

*   *   *

It was well after nine when Karen got back. She hadn't meant to be out quite so late, but then it had been nice to see Mandy again. She'd been meaning to catch up with her for some while now, so it was good to have an excuse to have a chat.

Chris, however, didn't see it that way.

'Where the hell have you been?' she asked, as Karen came into the room.

Karen blinked. 'What?'

'You might have phoned . . .'

'But I did. I left a message with the secretary at your school. You were teaching and—'

'So where *were* you?'

Karen took off her jacket and threw it down on to the back of the chair, then turned back. The sofa bed was made up, she noted, frowning as she took that in.

'Susie had her baby,' she said, distractedly. 'I went to see her at the hospital. Mandy was there, so we went for a quick drink.'

'Oh! *A quick drink.*'

Karen looked down. Chris clearly wasn't listening. 'I hadn't seen her in a while, so I thought . . .' She looked up, beginning to get just slightly annoyed that Chris was doing this to her. 'Look, what's the problem? I left a message. You didn't get it, that's all.'

'You're so bloody thoughtless . . .'

'*Thoughtless?* But I *phoned*. What was I supposed to do? Check up on your secretary to make sure she passed on the message?'

'You could have phoned again.'

Karen huffed, exasperated, yet she knew that this wasn't really about tonight: this was left over from the other night when nothing had really been resolved. But she wasn't in the mood for it right now. She'd had a hard week and she didn't need all this shit. She turned away.

'I'm going to bed.'

'That's right . . . run away as usual.'

'Chris . . . leave it, for Christ's sake!'

'No. Let's have this out now. Let's get this settled once and for all.'

Karen groaned inwardly, yet she couldn't move away.

'If you don't want to commit—'

She turned back, angry now. 'That's nonsense, and you know it!'

'*Do* I? Then what was all that crap with the sofa bed?'

Karen looked aside, stung by the comment, yet she knew there was an element of truth to it. She *had* pretended to her parents last weekend, and she had got Chris to go along with the pretence – even to the extent of going out and buying a new sofa bed to make it seem as if she and Chris slept separately. But it wasn't as easy as Chris made out.

'I need to pick my time,' she began, but Chris wasn't having any of it.

'No. You don't. Either you tell them, and soon, or that's it.'

Karen stared at her lover, as if she hadn't heard her right, but there was a sudden harshness in Chris's face – a stubborn determination to force the issue – that hadn't been there before.

'You can't mean that?'

'Can't I?'

'But—'

'Can't you see what you're doing? It's lies. All of it. Coming out to your friends is one thing, but until you come out to your parents, well . . . you might as well forget about us having a future, because we don't.'

'Chris?' she pleaded. But Chris simply shook her head, then turned and walked from the room.

Karen slumped down into the chair, then sat there, staring

in disbelief across the room. She had been so happy when she'd walked in, so full of things she wanted to share with Chris, but now . . .

Tell them? How could she possibly tell her parents? Even the thought of it brought her out in a cold sweat. Yet if she didn't . . .

Karen sighed. It was heads you lose, tails you lose, and no chance of the penny never coming down.

She stood, then walked over to the door. Their bedroom was just down the hallway. It was such a small distance, yet this once it seemed an eternity away. She hesitated, then walked across and slowly pushed the door open.

Chris was half naked on the other side of the room. Karen's eyes went to her breasts, took in the smooth perfection of her back and shoulders, loving the sight of her; yet even as she did, Chris turned, her eyes glaring at Karen, as if she were an intruder. Between them lay the bed, the edge of the duvet turned back.

'OK,' Karen said quietly. 'I'll tell them.'

Chris straightened, a cold defiance in the way she held herself. 'When?'

Karen swallowed. 'Soon.'

Chris bent down, picking up her nightdress, then pulled it on over her shoulders. She kicked off her briefs, then turned, looking at Karen coolly, as if she didn't quite believe her. 'And how soon is soon?'

'The next week or so.'

'You promise?'

'I promise.'

For a moment they both stood there, a strange awkwardness between them, and then Chris gestured towards the turned-back duvet, reaching across the bed for Karen's hand.

*   *   *

Back indoors, the kitchen lights switched on, the kettle slowly heating up in the corner, Mandy sat at the table and stared at the two brown envelopes she'd left there earlier, stunned by this latest news. Pete? Her Pete and some girl young enough to be his daughter? It was . . .

Mandy shivered, overcome by a sudden, unexpected jealousy. What did she look like, this girl? Was she fat and ugly? Or was she all tits and bleached long hair, with the kind of figure that you saw on the adverts?

And what did they get up to, she and Pete? Was she good in bed?

The very thought of it made her feel old and inadequate, like a discarded car, or a rusty old fridge that had served its use and been dumped on some abandoned lot. It made her feel . . . betrayed.

Her Pete. That's how she still thought of him. *Hers*.

But, of course, he wasn't. He could do what he liked now. See who he liked. Shag who he liked, come to that.

And — strangely enough — she had never thought of that before. She'd thought he would spend the rest of his life a bachelor, living with his brother in that scruffy little flat they'd rented together. Getting old together. Losing their teeth together. Going down the pub together and playing dominoes with all the other geriatrics.

Not seeing girls young enough to be his sodding daughter.

Unaware that she was doing so, Mandy jutted out her chin belligerently, as if the young woman was there in front of her. How dare she? How fucking dare she?

Then reason came flooding back and Mandy slumped, her shoulders sagging as a great feeling of weariness overcame her. That just about capped her bloody day. First the bills, then the news of Susie's baby, and now this. They said bad news came in threes and they were right.

Although the more she thought about Susie and Jo and

the baby the better she felt about it. Sitting there in the hospital she'd realised that she was over all of that. Yeah, and she was actually rather pleased for Susie. Happy that Susie was so happy. And that was good. Even so, she could have done without that bitch Debbie revelling in this latest bit of gossip.

Angry suddenly, Mandy stood up, then went over to the kettle, switching it off. No . . . this called for something a bit stronger than tea.

Yeah, and while she was at it, she'd go through the ads in the local paper. It was time she got off her arse and found herself a job. Time she stopped depending on Pete to bail her out.

Opening the cupboard, she reached up and took down the half-bottle of gin she'd hidden behind the tins, then took the bottle of tonic water from the fridge and poured herself a large one. Then, a new determination flooding her, she sat again, the paper open before her.

She'd show Pete. She'd bleedin' well show him!

Jason and his girlfriend, Gemma, had got themselves a maisonette on the new housing association development near Highbury tube. Gemma's mum had swung it somehow; had a word with someone, and there they were. Mandy hadn't been there often – the truth was she felt awkward whenever she visited, as if she was checking up on Jason – but that morning she decided she had to see him before he went to work. Thus it was that she found herself standing there before their door at half past eight, the strains of Capital Gold drifting up the hallway from the kitchen as she waited in the sunlight.

It was a tousle-haired Jason who answered the door. 'All right, Mum,' he said, grinning. 'What you doin' here?'

Mandy didn't answer and, stepping back to let her

pass, he called after her cheerily, 'Just in time for a cuppa.'

Gemma turned from the cooker as Mandy walked in, a broad beam of a smile on her face. Her long, bleached-blonde hair was tied back in a single ponytail, and her clothes — tight-fitting Levis and a pristine white shirt — made her look like one of those women out of the Persil ads. 'Hiya,' she said cheerfully, grinning and showing Mandy a set of perfect white teeth.

'Hi,' Mandy replied, looking about her at the spotless kitchen, the smell of the fry-up making her feel hungry all over again.

'D'you want some?' Gemma asked, as if she'd read her mind. 'There's plenty 'ere. Jason always says I cook him too much. Spends all morning trying to digest it, don't you Jase?'

Jason, who had sat down on the other side of the table, looked over his paper at his mum and smiled, as if to confirm what Gemma had said.

'Thanks, but—'

A cup of tea appeared by her elbow, as if magicked there. A moment later a little plate of biscuits — Morning Coffee, Mandy's favourites — appeared beside them.

Mandy stared at the tea and biscuits, pleased and yet put out by Gemma's thoughtful efficiency. She was a good girl, much better than Jason deserved, yet something about her put Mandy off. Oh, she was nice enough, and as genuine as they came, but . . .

Mandy looked up, seeing how expertly Gemma loaded Jason's plate from the various pans and dishes: two eggs, the yokes unbroken; four sausages, perfectly cooked, not charred; three slices of bacon, two fried tomatoes, a ladle of beans, two ladles of button mushrooms in butter, and a rack of toast — just like in a hotel. Mandy stared at the breakfast as it was set down before her son, the perfectly arranged food making her acutely aware of her own shortcomings as a wife and mother.

Seeing the delight on Jason's face, she ought to have been happy for him; relieved that he'd found such a gem of a partner. But yet again that imp of jealousy spoiled things for her. And yet it wasn't only that. Gemma acted as though she were a slave to Jason's wishes, and that irritated Mandy. Young women were supposed to be more independent these days, less subservient. There ought to have been progress, generation by generation, but Gemma was a step backwards, as if the tide of progress had come just so far up the beach of sexual equality and then begun to ebb.

'You shouldn't wait on the lazy little sod,' Mandy said, trying to sound light-hearted.

Gemma ruffled his hair affectionately, wrinkling her nose as she looked across at Mandy. 'Oh, I don't mind.'

Mandy took a biscuit and dunked it, angry at herself, knowing how petty she was even to feel what she felt.

'Well?' Jason said, his mouth half full of egg and bacon. 'So what's happening?'

Mandy swallowed the sodden biscuit, then gestured with her head towards the handbag in her lap, where a clutch of white envelopes jutted up.

'I've decided I've sat on me bum long enough. I'm gonna go back to work.'

Jason had been about to dig into his breakfast yet again, but Mandy's words made him pause and stare across at her. 'You what?'

'You 'eard. I'm going back to work.'

Jason sat back, amazed now. 'Where?'

'Well, I don't know where exactly.'

'Oh! So you ain't actually got a job then?'

'No, but . . .'

His laughter disturbed her. It was too much like Pete's. 'You mean you're writing off for jobs?'

'Yeah,' Mandy said, giving him a tentative little smile. 'I went through the paper last night. Secretarial. That kind of thing. I've done a bit of that.'

'Yeah, Mum, but that was twenty years ago. They've got computers now and all that stuff. Besides, there's not that many jobs to go around these days, especially when you ain't got much experience.'

Mandy felt her heart sink to her boots. She'd wanted Jason to be happy for her, encouraging, but *this*. It made her feel like giving up before she'd even begun.

'Rubbish,' Gemma said, putting her hands lightly on Mandy's shoulders. 'Your mum's got *lots* of skills. If you can organise a home, then you can run an office, that's what I say. And what's a computer? Just a glorified bloody TV set with a keyboard attached. Any idiot can use one, given a bit of training. And as for experience . . .'

'All right,' Jason said, raising a hand, clearly defeated by Gemma's arguments. 'But don't go getting upset when they turn you down, Mum. It's tough out there. Not like when you was young.'

And how would you know, you skiving little git? Mandy thought, looking up at Gemma as she did so and smiling, grateful that she'd come to her defence.

Gemma smiled back at her. 'You sure you won't change your mind and have a bit of breakfast after all, Mrs Evans?'

Mandy glanced across at Jason, who, oblivious, had returned to his meal, then looked up at Gemma again.

'Yeah. All right. But no beans for me, OK? And Gemma?'

'Yes, Mrs Evans?'

'Call me Mandy for Gawd's sake.'

In the silent tomb of the hospital waiting room, Janet stared unseeing into the glossy pages of an out-of-date magazine, its spine resting against her leg as she sat with one knee crossed over the other, the brightly coloured pages draped either side of her thigh. Were she even remotely aware of the article's content she might have flipped the page, embarrassed by the irony of the writer's treatise on 'Ways to Keep Your Man Happy in Bed'. It was a long time since she'd made any effort to make Steve happy in bed. She knew that. But making *love* had, like everything else, become a secondary consideration to their clinical efforts to achieve a pregnancy, and in all honesty Janet felt little guilt.

Janet flicked a glance towards the couple sitting in the corner of the room. The woman sniffed loudly and at regular intervals, developing a sort of synchronicity with the loud, dominating tick of the clock. Her husband sat with his arm wrapped tightly about her drooping shoulders, hooking stray strands of hair behind her ear every so often, and then imaginary strands of hair.

Averting her eyes from this intimacy, afraid of it almost, Janet scanned the walls — empty but for the clock. There had been one just like this in her nan's house when she was a kid, she recalled. As she'd lain curled on the settee beneath the eiderdown — her slight head cold barely warranting the day off school or her nan's pampering — she had found the inevitability of that next beat strangely reassuring. It was only now that she wondered why on earth her grandmother had kept it. To be old and listening to the seconds passing was, she knew, tantamount to self-inflicted torture.

Steve reached beneath the edge of the magazine for Janet's fingers and, although she made no move towards him, she allowed him to take them into his palm. She was aware of him staring at her but she looked resolutely ahead, unable to meet his eyes.

The door opened and Janet snatched her fingers away,

knocking the magazine to the floor. The nurse in the doorway directed a tight-lipped, pitying smile towards the couple in the corner, who struggled to their feet, almost as one, and followed her meekly into the corridor. Janet dared not look at Steve. She did not want to see the same flicker of desperation in his face that she herself was feeling at that moment; she could not contemplate that he, too, harboured fears that they were doomed to endure this empty, childless existence for ever.

When the door opened once more and another nurse called out their names, they followed her along the corridor and into the doctor's inner sanctum. They had been here before, and almost immediately Janet focused on the wall of photographs. Babies. Everywhere. The smiling, chubby-cheeked progeny of IVF, displayed like trophies. It felt as if she were a child inside Santa's grotto, her eyes wide with wonder as she surveyed what *could* be hers. *If only she was a good girl.* If only they were able to find some eggs; if only this time they became fertilised; if only the embryos were strong enough. If only.

For now, however, she would be content just to be told they could try again.

Janet waited nervously for Dr Clements to speak, her eyes focused on the shiny crown of his head as he sat with it bowed over the desk. Turning the final page of the medical notes, the doctor removed his glasses and looked up to face them.

'How are you?'

'Oh, well, you know,' Janet said, forcing a smile. 'Disappointed.'

Steve reached across for Janet's hand but she moved to pick at an imaginary piece of fluff on the hem of her skirt, all the while maintaining the same thin smile for the doctor.

'Well, that's only to be expected,' he said, pretending not to have noticed. Replacing his glasses he glanced down at the file. 'But you've decided you want to try again?'

Janet and Steve nodded in mute concurrence.

'There is now, of course, a greater financial consideration
. . .' he began.

'Yes, we realise that,' Janet interrupted, 'but we can
manage. Can't we, Steve?'

Janet's eyes pleaded with Steve not to contradict her.

'Yeah. Yeah, we can manage.'

Dr Clements nodded. 'Shame about losing your GP like that.
He was very sympathetic. Either they are or they're not and,
I'm afraid, you've just struck unlucky with the new chap.
But if he refuses to cover the cost of the drugs I'm afraid we
have no alternative . . .'

'No! It's fine! We understand. Don't we, Steve?' Steve
nodded. 'We want to go ahead, whatever the cost.'

It was only when the words had passed her lips that Janet
realised her mistake. It was the very same phrase as Steve
had beaten her with when they had discussed whether to try
again. Well, it was supposed to be a discussion, but inevitably
it had ended in a blazing row. She'd known, even as she'd
ranted, even as she'd slammed the bedroom door in his face,
that all Steve needed was reassurance. All she had to say
was that she loved him; all she had to do was hold him.
But something had held her back and she hadn't been able
to think about what Steve might need. She'd had enough to
worry about already.

'That's right,' Steve said. Belatedly.

Dr Clements nodded, understanding more than Janet realised. 'OK . . . Well, at least you know what to expect this
time – the sniffing, the injections.'

Janet and Steve made brief eye contact.

Janet laughed. 'Makes me sound like an addict.'

'Yeah, well you are,' Steve said. 'It's just that it ain't the
drugs you're addicted to.'

'Yes, well, we're all addicted to something, I suppose,' the doctor ventured. He turned to Steve. 'Did you manage to help with the injections last time?'

'I tried, but . . .'

'He's a bit queasy,' Janet said, not letting him finish. 'He did it once, then promptly fainted. Left me standing there with the needle sticking out me backside.'

'I *didn't* faint!'

'Well, near as damn it! You sat on the floor for half an hour with your head between your knees.'

The doctor laughed. 'Yes, well, I've always known that whoever spread the rumour about women being the weaker sex must have been a male subversive.'

Janet nodded agreement, in spite of having only an inkling of what he was talking about.

'Well, maybe this time, eh?' Clements said, arching his eyebrows in Steve's direction. 'I'm sure Janet would appreciate it.' His eyes focused on her. 'Am I right?'

'I'll let you know after he's had a stab!' she said, then laughed loudly – naturally – for the first time in weeks.

'So,' Karen began, turning from the blackboard to face the class again. 'What do you think the poet *means* by this poem? What is he trying to *say* to us?'

A dozen hands shot up, Barrett's among them. She ignored him, pointing to Jones instead.

'Is it about Bruce Grobellar, miss?'

There was laughter. Karen let it ride. 'What do you mean, Jones?'

'You know, bribes and all that . . .'

She smiled. 'In a way. But the poet isn't thinking of any specific goalkeeper. He's talking about attitude. About professionalism and its opposite, a simple love of the game.'

'Miss?'

Karen hesitated. 'Yes, Barrett?'

'Why don't women like football, miss?'

She stared at him a moment, as if studying a specimen beneath a microscope. Barrett was the ringleader. The chief troublemaker in 8T. He was surly to the point of obnoxiousness, and his white-blonde hair was shaved close to his scalp. He had dead eyes. Whatever he looked at, there seemed no expression in them. So, too, his voice. All in all he seemed middle-aged, as if he had been taken over, like in some horror movie. Looking at him, Karen felt a ripple of pure loathing pass through her. Even so, she kept her voice even, her emotions in check.

'But some do, Barrett.'

'Yes, miss. But you don't, do you? I mean . . . like football. You like other things, don't you, miss? Plays and books and things.'

'Barrett?'

'Yes, miss?'

'What's your point?'

Barrett sat there a moment, as if he wasn't going to answer, then he looked about him. 'Why did you choose *this*, miss? Why didn't you choose something about women?'

'Women?'

'Yeah . . . *women.*'

There was a silence, then. 'Do you smoke, miss?'

'Pardon?' Then, noting the sniggering and realising she was being set up, Karen quickly changed the subject.

She had chosen the poem — Simon Armitage's 'Goalkeeper with a cigarette' — especially to appeal to the more thuggish elements in the class, to try to get through to them that poetry wasn't just all of that romantic claptrap but could be relevant to their lives. But maybe she'd made a mistake. Maybe they were just impervious to culture. Maybe there was a gene in them that — like a rhino's thick hide — prevented them from seeing beauty in anything artistic. It certainly seemed so some days. Not only that, but sometimes she found herself wishing that something awful would happen to Barrett, so that he wasn't always there, like some dark cancer at the heart of the class, preventing the others from glimpsing what was so clear to her.

And that was why she loved being with Chris so much. Because Chris loved the same things as she loved: a good play, a good book, the wonder of a great piece of music or a good film. Those shared tastes meant so much to her. As much, if she was honest, as the sexual side of things.

At break, Karen stood at the window of the staffroom as the water heated in the urn, staring out across the playground below and thinking of all that had happened last night. Of Susie's baby and talking to Mandy, and afterwards the argument with Chris. Where was the poetry in that? Where the art? It was just life. So maybe — just maybe — the Barretts of this world were right. But she hoped not. She hoped there was some meaning to it all.

She smiled briefly, thinking of the single line in the poem that had caught her eye first time she'd read it.

He is what he is, does whatever suits him . . .

It made her think. Made her wish she could be like that. Brave. Her own person. Not so eaten up by silly fears and uncertainties. But she wasn't, and she knew it. She sighed inwardly. If only Chris understood that about her. But she didn't. Besides, she had promised now. Given her word that she would speak to her parents.

Soon . . .

Karen looked down. The thought of it terrified her. She shuddered and turned from the window, even as the kettle boiled and clicked.

Too late, she thought. I've promised now.

*   *   *

Doreen was looking out of the window as the taxi drew up, and even before Susie had had a chance to hand the baby out to Jo, Bobby was rushing down the front steps to help them.

'Hello, love,' he said, as he reached in to take Susie's overnight bag from inside the cab. 'How's my little mate?'

'He's great,' Jo said proudly, holding the baby so that Bobby could see him better. 'Slept right through last night.'

'Well, from twelve till six,' Susie said, backing out of the cab gingerly, half annoyed that neither of the men had offered to help her, but touched all the same by the delight they were taking in the new arrival. 'Then the little bugger near enough sucked me dry! Forty minutes each side he had!'

'That's my boy!' Jo said, laughing as he beamed down at the well-wrapped bundle in his arms.

Doreen was standing in the doorway now, grinning at the sight of the three of them huddled about the baby. 'Well?' she said. 'Don't stand out there all day. Poor little mite'll catch his death.'

Susie took the baby back, then turned to face her mum.

'Welcome home, love.'

'Ta, Mum. Is the kettle on? I'm dying for a decent cup of tea.'

They went inside, Jo and Bobby hovering behind Susie and making faces over her shoulder at the baby, as if they'd departed their senses.

'D'you mind?' Susie said, as she took her seat at the kitchen table. 'You'll make him cry with your pair of ugly mugs.'

'Go on,' Bobby said. 'He loves it, look at 'im!'

Susie looked, and couldn't help but grin. It really did seem that the baby was smiling back at them.

'He's got wind,' Doreen said, coming across and setting a mug of tea down by Susie's elbow, then stopping to lean forward and coo at the baby. 'Ah, look at 'im. He's gorgeous, ain't he?'

'He takes after my side of the family,' Bobby announced confidently. 'The Fullers always 'ave 'ad good-looking babies.'

'Well, apart from your cousin Harry,' Doreen contradicted.

'You've gotta throw in your tuppence-worth, ain't you?' said Bobby.

Ignoring her dad, Susie turned to Doreen. 'Why? What was wrong with Harry?'

'What was *right* with him? Poor little sod! He had these crossed eyes and these bloody great ears that stood out like jug handles. And as though that weren't enough, 'cos he was the sixth boy his mum'd had after trying for a girl for so long, she went a bit funny and took to tying his hair up in a bow. Poor little bugger didn't know if he was coming or going!'

'Who told you that?' Bobby demanded indignantly.

'Your mum!'

Susie shifted uncomfortably in her seat.

'You all right, love?'

'Yeah. It's just these soddin' things!' Susie pulled at the knee of her trousers in order to release them from the crack of her bum. 'I forgot to pack something to come home in so I asked 'im to bring something in. He only goes and brings me a pair of jeans, don't he?' Susie flashed a look in Jo's direction, shaking her head in despair. 'Look!' she said, lifting the baby to one side and pulling up her top, to reveal an elastic band hooked over the button on her waistband and stretching some six inches across her flabby stomach to be tied through the buttonhole.

'Only a man could expect a woman to fit into a pair of denim jeans a day after giving birth! Dopey sod!'

'Well I didn't know, did I?'

'Here, you couldn't get us a cushion from the sofa, could

you, Mum? Only what with wearing these bloody things and what with me stitches . . .'

'Yeah, 'course, love.' Doreen disappeared out through the door and then her voice could be heard floating in from the living room, gradually getting louder as she made her way back to the kitchen. 'You know what's good for that, don't you? Epsom salts.' She placed the cushion under Susie's bottom as she raised herself off the chair. 'I'll get you some from the chemist's.'

'Nah, it's all right. The hospital said just to use salt.' Doreen raised her eyebrows dismissively. 'They said to put it in me bath a couple of times a day and then dry myself off with a hairdryer . . .'

'A hairdryer!' Bobby appeared to have difficulty visualising it.

'Yeah,' Susie explained. 'Instead of a towel. So as not to disturb the stitches.'

'I don't think I want to know.'

'Nah, you never did!' Doreen sniped, ever eager to criticise his lack of involvement when their own children were born.

Ignoring his wife, Bobby reached inside his jacket, smiling as he pulled out two enormous cigars, holding one out at arm's length. 'Jo?'

'You bleedin' dare,' Susie said, giving Jo a warning glare as he reached across to take it.

'We'd better go in the garden,' Jo said, putting a hand up defensively. 'Don't wanna make him cough, do we?'

'No, you bleedin' don't,' Susie said. Then, softening, she gestured to Jo. 'Go on. But just the one.'

Jo looked to Bobby and winked, then followed him outside into the garden.

Left alone with her mother, Susie relaxed a little.

'That's good he slept through,' Doreen said. 'Gave you a chance to get a bit of rest.'

'Huh! Fat bleedin' chance of that! I thought it'd be handy having the sink nearby, but all night bloody long one or the other of 'em was up and down getting their little bits of cotton wool damp to clean a tiny bit of shit off their soddin' babies' bums. And then there was some girl up the end of the ward who whimpered all night. I tell you, every time I dropped off there was either a bloody woman wailing, a baby screaming or a fucking tap dripping. And there he was. As good as gold.'

Doreen beamed lovingly down at her new grandson. Flicking a glance at Susie as she, too, looked down in wonder at this little miracle of life, Doreen took a deep breath. 'Suse? You thought any more about his name?'

Reluctant to concede defeat but bowing to overwhelming pressure from the girls as well as her family, Susie spoke matter-of-factly, without looking up: 'We've decided to give him Saul as a middle name.' Doreen waited. 'We've settled on Nathan.'

'Nathan?'

'Yeah. There was a kid in a video I watched the other day, and he was called Nathan.'

'What was it, a bleedin' cowboy film? Anyway, I thought you wanted a name that wouldn't get shortened. He'll get called Nat or Nathe.'

'No he won't. Not if I insist on Nathan.'

'That's what you think. But wait till he gets to school.'

'So you prefer Saul then, do you?'

Checkmate! Mustering every ounce of dignity she could muster, Doreen conceded defeat. 'No! Nathan's nice. Nathan! Nathan Ball.'

As if in protest, the tiny baby expelled an impossibly loud fart and proceeded to fill his nappy.

When Doreen and Bobby had gone and Nathan was asleep in his Moses basket, Susie curled up on the sofa, suddenly overcome by a wave of tiredness. She couldn't help smiling with satisfaction as she watched Jo stand over the basket, staring in at the baby. Glancing across, he saw her and laughed quietly, not with embarrassment or self-consciousness, but rather with amazement at his overwhelming feeling of love for the child. He hadn't expected it to be quite like this.

Coming to sit beside Susie, Jo stroked her face. 'Sorry about the jeans.' She gave a small laugh. 'D'you want me to get you something else to put on?'

Susie shook her head. 'I'll have a bath in a minute.'

'I'll have the hairdryer running when you come down,' he joked, and Susie poked him playfully.

'I can't remember the last time I had something hot up my fanny!'

'Tell me about it.'

'Ah, poor baby,' Susie cooed in mock sympathy. 'Still, that's what your right arm's for, ain't it?'

'Yeah, but it's not quite the same,' he said, feeling sorry for himself and nuzzling into the crook of her neck. 'I miss you.'

'Well, you're going to have to miss me for a bit longer,' she laughed, pushing his head away.

There was a tiny mewl from the cot, bringing Susie immediately to her feet, in spite of the elastic band twanging painfully across her stretch marks. But what was one more little discomfort among so many? Her fanny felt like it had gone ten rounds with Mike Tyson, piles dangled from her bum like a bunch of ripe plums, and her nipples were on the unpleasant side of tingling with the after-effects of Nathan's world-record sucking attempt. So a few navel hairs plucked by overstretched rubber! Huh!

Having sat patiently by the Moses basket for five minutes waiting for the baby to wake, Susie decided that he was settled enough for her to risk taking a bath. Once Jo had left her on her own, Susie removed her top, dismayed as she looked at her image in the mirror. Two breast pads peered through the white lace on her considerable bra, and where before there had been cleavage, now there were blue veins, running like some dysfunctional rail track with her areola as King's Cross.

Turning sideways in the mirror, she still looked six months pregnant, what with her sagging stomach tumbling over the top of her knickers. Throughout the pregnancy she had remained resolutely faithful to 'small' knickers that disappeared beneath her swollen belly, rather than succumb to 'big' knickers that covered it but were the kind her mother wore.

Holding on to the front of the sink, she drew on her pelvic muscles to pull in what should've been on the inside but at the moment felt as though it were on the outside. She felt her buttocks clench and her aching vagina pulsate. *Don't forget those pelvic floor exercises, will you, Mrs Ball?* Three more quick squeezes of her cheeks and Susie decided she'd done quite enough. She turned to the mirror to face the full horror of her body. Grabbing a huge handful of flesh in each hand as though assessing how enormous was the task that lay ahead, Susie sighed heavily. This stomach was going to be second priority – after Nathan – she decided. There was no way she was going to even contemplate giving way to her mother's advice to get herself a girdle. That was the beginning of the end.

Removing the lilo-sized sanitary towel from between her legs, Susie stepped out of her knickers and gingerly raised one leg over the bath. With almost precision timing, the moment her big toe dipped beneath the surface of the water, the baby's catlike wail rose up the stairs filling her with momentary panic. Then her breasts started to tingle.

Susie groaned. 'Jo . . . Jo can you . . . ?'

She waited a moment, but Jo clearly wasn't there. Closing her eyes, she sighed, then stepped out of the bath again and slipped a towel about her. Just a quick feed, she promised herself, and then she'd come back.

But Nathan had other ideas . . .

'Christ, Pete! Don't you ever tidy this place up?'

Pete looked about him at the tiny kitchen, as if recognising where he was for the first time, then shrugged. 'Yeah, well . . . that's Bal's job. He's been a bit busy lately.'

'Busy? When in Christ's name was your brother ever busy? Besides, it don't take much to keep things neat and tidy. There's only the two of you!'

Mandy turned full circle, unable to believe what a pigsty the place was. The floor was littered with crumbs and other unmentionables. There were unwashed pots and pans in the sink, and the laundry basket wasn't just overflowing, it was engulfed by a mountain of unwashed clothes.

'Anyway,' Pete said, rather shamefacedly now, 'me mum usually pops round. It's just that she's had a bit of a cold.'

'Yeah, well . . .'

'So?' Pete said, looking at her brightly, more as if she was his sister and not his ex-wife. 'What's up?'

Mandy glanced at the kettle, then gave up on him. Pete was as likely to offer her a cup of tea as get down on his knees and scrub the kitchen floor. She smiled. 'Not a lot. Just thought I'd let you know that I was looking for work. Thought it was about time I started paying me own bills. You know.'

'Yeah?' But it was as if Pete didn't know whether to be pleased about it or not; as though he needed time to come to terms with Mandy taking one more step away from him. Then again, she too had mixed feelings. Looking about her, she felt sad that Pete had been reduced to living like this, and there was part of her that wanted to mother him still, while at the same time another part of her was silently revelling in the fact that he was such a useless bastard without her. He knew now just how much she'd done for him all those years. Yeah. Only now could he appreciate just what a good woman she'd been to him, and what a lazy, good-for-nothing git he'd been. Now that it was too late.

For a moment Mandy positively glowed at the thought of it.

And then she thought of the girlfriend, and the glow vanished, like the sun disappearing behind a cloud.

'Look, Mand, there's something I—'

'I know,' she said quickly. 'I heard.'

'You heard?'

'Yeah.' Then, knowing that she wouldn't get a cuppa unless she did it herself, she added, 'look . . . d'you want a cup of tea?'

Pete glanced at the kettle, then. 'Yeah . . . yeah, if you like . . .'

While he sat, she filled the kettle, then plugged it in again. As she reached up, searching the cupboards for the tea bags, she asked casually, 'So where d'you meet her?'

'Up the market. Just walked into her, didn't I?'

'Yeah?' Mandy found the box where the tea bags were kept. It was almost empty. 'And?'

Pete laughed. 'Nearly knocked her bleedin' teeth out, didn't I? I was carrying some shelving.'

Mandy turned to look at him. 'Shelving?'

'Yeah. Barry was gonna put 'em up in the other room . . . But anyway, I came out between two of the stalls just as she came round the corner, and whallop! The edge of the soddin' shelf hit her on the nose.'

'Yeah?'

'Yeah . . . and, well . . . that was it. I took her for a drink. To say sorry, like.'

Pete looked away, as if embarrassed.

Mandy could imagine the rest, and she didn't like the images that were filling her head. Just as when she'd heard the news last night, she felt an unexpected jealousy flare up in her. Pete and this girl . . . It didn't seem right somehow. Looking across at him now it was like she was seeing him for the first time. Seeing him as another woman might see him.

'So you're seeing a lot of her?'

Pete glanced at Mandy. 'Yeah. We're thinking of gettin' a flat together. 'Cos, well, it's a bit awkward. What with her livin' at home . . .'

'Yeah. I heard she wasn't very old.'

Mandy turned away, busying herself making the tea. But her mind was in turmoil. All of this was happening much too fast for her liking. She'd only just got used to the idea of Pete *having* a girlfriend, and now they were moving in together. Next thing she knew they'd be walking up the aisle and she'd be sitting in a pew at the back with a box of confetti!

'Pete?'

'What?'

She turned, facing him. 'D'you mind if I hang on for a bit?'

'What d'you mean, hang on?'

'It's just that . . . well, I'd like to talk. You know.'

'Talk?'

'About us. About what happened.'

'Mand?'

Mandy looked away. 'Look, if you don't want to . . .'

'Mand . . .'

She glanced back. Pete was smiling now. A warm, understanding smile. 'If you wanna talk, we'll talk. But first of all make the bleedin' tea, eh?'

*   *   *

Signing off from the computer, Janet looked up at Mr Davis and smiled. 'There,' she said, 'done.'

She stood, letting her boss resume his seat.

This happened at least twice a day. He'd be putting the details of some mortgage application or personal loan on to the computer, and suddenly he'd press the wrong key and get in a panic. Not that she minded helping out. After all, it was good that he did it in the first place – not like some of them. The previous manager had refused point blank to have anything to do with keying in his own work, and had always got a junior to do it, the lazy bastard. At least Mr Davis tried, even if, like most of the older generation, he hadn't a clue when it came to the new technology.

'Thanks, Jan,' he said, returning her smile. 'I don't know what I'd do without you. These damn machines.'

'Yeah,' she said, all sympathy. 'They can get a bit confusing at times, can't they?'

Davis grinned at her, grateful for her understanding. But he'd been good to her, too, not making any fuss about all the time off she'd had to have for the IVF treatment. Not that she hadn't made it up outside hours, but . . . well, other bosses might not have been so flexible.

Janet smiled one last time, then backed out of the office. Behind her the tills were busy, a queue of at least twenty people filling the banking hall. She was about to walk through to her own office, when she saw – there, halfway down the queue – a familiar face. A woman her own age with shoulder-length, dyed-black hair.

Janet waved, then, on impulse, went out to greet her old schoolfriend. They embraced.

'Rene! What are you doing here? I thought you'd moved out Romford way.'

'I did. But now I've moved back. Bastard ran off with our neighbour's wife. Took all our savings with him, too. All but this little bit, that is.'

Rene held up her building society book triumphantly.

'Didn't know about this, did he? I was putting a bit aside for a surprise party for our tenth anniversary. Only fucking surprise I got was when he legged it. Fat cow she was, too.'

'I'm sorry.'

'Well, I'm bleedin' not. I'm having a great time without him. New job. Own flat. Lots of fellas. Not that it didn't hurt at first.'

'No . . . Anyway, it's good it's worked out, eh?'

'Yeah . . . talking of which, I'm really pleased for Susie. A little boy, eh? Decent weight an' all, wasn't he, for a first baby? I bet she's over the moon, ain't she?'

'Yeah,' Janet said, brazening it out. 'Look, gotta run. Work to do. But keep in touch, eh? And see you around.'

'Yeah . . . 'bye . . .'

Back in her office, Janet shut the door, then sat, stunned by the news. Susie's baby. She had known all along that it had to be born sometime. Well, it just wasn't possible for the thing to stay in there for ever more. Even so . . .

For a moment longer the numbness had her in its grip. Then, with a little sob, she began to cry, tears trickling one after another down her cheeks.

'Jan?'

Steve stood in the bedroom doorway, looking in, as Janet finished putting on her lipstick, then turned to face him.

'Jan . . . what're you doing?'

'I'm going out,' she answered, matter-of-factly, picking up her handbag and slinging it over her shoulder.

'Out where?'

'I'm gonna see Susie. She's had her baby.'

Steve's mouth opened but no sound came out. Then, getting a grip of himself, he said, 'You think that's a good idea?'

Janet didn't even look at him. She moved past him, stopping only by the hallway mirror to check her hair.

'Won't be late. Dinner's in the fridge.'

But Steve wasn't even thinking about dinner. He was thinking about Susie's baby and the damage this could do to Janet's feelings.

As the door slammed, he closed his eyes, then punched the wall. 'Shit!'

But there was nothing he could do now. Nothing but wait for her to return, and to be there for her, to put the pieces back together again.

Janet sat in the car a long time, the engine switched off, staring across the road at Susie's house. It had all seemed so easy when she'd set out. Like going to the dentist. Something you didn't want to do, but had to face. It might hurt a bit to begin with, but you'd soon get over it.

Only this wasn't like going to the dentist. It wasn't even vaguely like it. Right then, having all her teeth out without anaesthetic would have been preferable to seeing Susie's baby; to seeing Susie herself, happy and fulfilled; a woman – a *real* woman – without any doubts about her femininity. For a moment Janet could even ignore the fact that Susie was someone she loved. For a moment she could wish that it was her friend and not her who had been singled out to endure this barren nightmare.

After crossing the street, Janet climbed the four steps to the front door as though she were scaling Everest; her legs felt like lead weights and her heart pumped loudly in her chest. For a moment her breath caught in her throat and she steadied herself on the railings. Reaching up, she took the brass door knocker in her hand.

From inside the insistent cry of a hungry infant filtered out to where Janet stood motionless, her hand still poised over the knocker, her fingers clasping it more tightly as she listened, transfixed. And even as she did so, she punished herself with the knowledge that it was she who knew what that cry meant; she who had all this love to give; and it was she who was forced to stare down this black hole of infertility towards death.

With tears clouding her eyes and the sound of the baby in her ears, Janet pulled her hand from the knocker and fled down the steps, running across the road and into the silent sanctuary of her car. With her head bowed over the steering wheel, her arms embracing it, she allowed the tears to flow. Noisy, heart-wrenching tears that were as much in anger as self-pity.

She felt trapped. Trapped by her body and by circumstances. Not only that, but everything – every tiny little thing – conspired to taunt her. Everywhere she turned there were mothers and their babies, happy and contented, reminding her of her failure, rubbing salt into the raw wound of her barrenness.

Why me? she asked silently. Why can't I do what practically every other woman does without trying? What did I do wrong to be punished so?

For even though she'd read all of the books on the subject she could lay her hands on, and a dozen articles besides, she still felt it was *her* fault. That somehow she'd been bad and this – this gnawing torment – was her reward.

Ridiculous. Yet it was how she felt, every minute of every day. It was the kind of despair that ate away at hope. Yet hope she did, for without hope she might as well be dead.

She reached out and switched on the engine, revving it a moment. Then, carefully checking in her rear mirror, she began to pull out into the evening traffic.

Tomorrow, she told herself. I'll come tomorrow, when I

feel a little better. But deep down she knew she wouldn't. Not until the hurt went away.

And there was only one way that could happen.

'Hi, Jane, this is Karen. Karen, Jane . . .'

Jane, a big woman with long, flowing, dark hair, embraced Karen warmly, kissing both her cheeks, as if they'd been friends for years.

'It's lovely to meet you at long last. Chris has told me so much about you.'

Karen blushed and glanced at Chris, who gave a facial shrug. Jane worked with Chris, and this was her drinks party. An 'anniversary', Chris had said — though of what she hadn't quite specified.

Karen looked down the long, book-lined hallway of the flat, noting that, while it was crowded, there was not a single man to be seen.

'Go on through,' Jane said, moving aside. 'Drinks are in the kitchen, eats in the living room. Help yourself.'

'Thanks . . .'

Keeping close to Chris, Karen made her way through into the kitchen, feeling shy, tongue-tied almost, nodding greetings to strangers; for, while Chris seemed to know everyone there, she knew a handful at most, and those were merely acquaintances met at dinner parties.

'White or red?' someone asked her. She turned, to find an attractive forty-something woman with long dark hair smiling at her.

'White,' she said, flustered by the power of the woman's gaze.

The woman poured, then handed Karen the glass. 'Here. And I'm Ellen, by the way.'

'Karen,' Karen said, in an absurdly small voice, feeling all of fourteen again; nervous and acutely self-conscious. She wasn't good at this. She'd never been any good.

'I'm with Chris,' she said after a moment, feeling gauche even as she said it. Yet, glancing round, she noticed that Chris was nowhere to be seen.

Ellen smiled. 'And what do you do?'

Ellen's accent placed her firmly. Upper middle class. No rough edges at all. It was yet another thing that put Karen on her guard — not intentionally but instinctively, for she had had to learn the hard way how to 'speak proper' and shed the distinctive accent of her native Islington.

'I'm . . . a teacher . . .'

Ellen smiled, showing perfectly even white teeth. 'It's absolutely astonishing, don't you think?'

'Sorry?' Karen didn't have a clue what the woman was talking about.

'I mean . . . if the parents only knew. It seems that half of the bloody teaching profession seems to be gay.'

Karen looked down. Even the way she said 'bloody' — as if the word had been carefully chosen for effect — distanced her.

'I don't know,' Karen said, because she didn't.

'Not that I am myself,' the woman said, her smile broadening.

For a moment Karen wondered what she meant; whether she wasn't a teacher or a lesbian. Somehow it didn't seem polite to ask.

'Mind you,' she went on, 'it probably raises the standard of culture in our schools. When you think of it, straight society is so busy being neurotic about raising their kids they've barely time to read a book between them!'

Karen smiled politely and sipped at her wine, but inwardly she felt the first tiny seeds of irritation. When she thought of her own friends, she saw how true the comment was. After all, Mandy, Janet and Susie barely read a book a year between them, and the only theatre any of them had been in for the past thirty years was an operating theatre. Even so, to make such a sweeping statement somehow offended her sense of justice. It was claiming too much — making much too much of the simple sexual preference that separated the gay from the straight world.

'What do you do, then?' Karen asked, risking the question.

'I teach,' Ellen answered, surprising Karen, because she'd assumed . . .

'You mean . . . ?'

'I've a husband and three kids,' Ellen said. 'Or did have. Dumped the husband, so there's just the three kids now, though only one's still at home.'

Karen felt a flush come to her cheeks. 'So what do you teach?'

'Maths, when I'm actually in a classroom.'

At that moment Chris returned. Putting her arm about Karen's waist, she smiled at Ellen. 'I see you've met.'

'Yes, we—'

'Ellen's head teacher at my school . . . or has she told you that already?'

'No, I . . .' Karen hesitated; but she found it impossible to say what she'd been thinking. She gave a tiny laugh, then looked away.

'What's funny?' Chris asked, intrigued.

'Oh . . . nothing,' she said, embarrassed now.

'We were talking about teachers,' Ellen said. 'About how many of you lot are gay. Not that I can't see the attraction.'

Chris grinned, then gave Karen a little squeeze. 'Ellen likes to exaggerate. Just because there's three of us, she tends to think that all the rest are closet gays!'

Karen smiled, but now she felt uncomfortable, because as far as the staff at her school were concerned, she was as straight as a die.

If only they knew.

Karen looked down, sighing inwardly. Simply being here at this gathering made her realise that she hadn't yet let go of that aura of 'normality' — that pretence that she was somehow just the same as all her friends. It was almost as if she still fought to preserve that illusion sometimes. Or was it illusion? Looking about her, she knew that she was gay in a different way from most of the women here; that what to them was political was to her a purely personal thing. She loved a woman, yes, and slept with her. But beyond that? That was where she and Chris differed. Chris wanted, or rather *needed*, to redefine herself against society's 'norm'. That was why she was always forcing things; why she was always pushing Karen.

'You're a lesbian,' she would say. 'Start acting like a lesbian.' But how did a lesbian act? Was there a right way and a wrong way to be? And if so, who made the rules?

Besides, why should she exchange one code of behaviour for another? That seemed perverse to her. And then there was the little matter of background . . .

Most of the gay women she'd met came from a different class from her. They had different experiences of life, different assumptions. Like Chris, they couldn't really understand why she clung on to the vestiges of her old life; why she had not cut free of her old, straight friends and adopted a whole new set of acquaintances who were related to her merely by their sexual orientation.

But wasn't that a ghetto? Wasn't that, in its way, every bit as bad as being a 'straight' bigot?

Truth was, she didn't know. She was still very much an outsider, uneasy in both worlds. So maybe Chris was right. Maybe she should take the next logical step and embrace the gay world in its entirety.

Maybe. But something always held her back.

For the next few hours she circulated, meeting this person and that, becoming slowly less self-conscious as the wine began to have its effect. She had even begun to feel comfortable without Chris there next to her, and then it happened.

Karen was talking to a young lesbian couple — neighbours of the host, Jane — about the gay scene that was developing in Stoke Newington, when she heard Chris's voice rise in a crescendo of delight on the far side of the room.

She turned, to see Chris embracing another woman — a slim thirty-something woman with short blonde hair. They were clearly old friends, and their joy at seeing each other was marked.

Karen felt her stomach muscles tense unexpectedly. She saw how they kissed; saw the eye contact, and some instinct told her at once who this was. Sarah. It *had* to be Sarah.

Sarah . . . the great unmentionable. The one regret in Chris's life. The one thorn in Karen's. And here she was.

Karen turned away, then swallowed the remains of her wine. Another woman would have gone across and fronted it out brashly, but that wasn't her style. She hated confrontation. Hated having to smile when all she wanted was to spit.

She was trembling. Karen stared at her hands, astonished. Christ, she was actually trembling! Steeling herself, she glanced across once more. They were still holding each other, Chris's hands on Sarah's upper arms, Sarah's on Chris's hips, their eyes locked as they talked, their mouths smiling. That, even more than the earlier kiss, made Karen shudder with jealousy. If they had caressed each other's breasts it could not have been worse. There was such an awful, casual intimacy between them . . .

Karen stood there a moment longer, then, feeling something snap in her, turned and hurried across the room, vanishing through the door even as Chris turned to look for her.

'Karen . . . ?'

The hallway was packed. She made her way, pushing past the talking knots of people, polite even as she seethed inside.

'Kareñ?'

She heard Chris's raised voice follow her out into the street, but there was no way now she was going back inside. No way she was going to be humiliated in that fashion.

'Karen!'

Karen slammed the door behind her, then ran, wanting to cry now, her evening spoiled. Yet even as she ran she was conscious of Chris running after her, and slowed, letting her catch up; letting her turn her about in the dark yet lamplit street, and hold her.

'Karen . . . what is it?'

'You know bloody well what it is!'

Chris gave a little shudder against her. 'No. No, I don't.'

Karen sniffed, the tiniest bit away from tears now. 'It's Sarah, isn't it?'

Chris took a long breath, then nodded. 'You want to meet her?'

'No, no, I . . .' The truth was she wanted to stab her; to claw her eyes out; to disembowel her for daring to walk into their life. Karen steeled herself. 'I thought you said you hated her,' she accused, with the petulance of a child.

Again there was a long breath before Chris answered. 'That's all in the past. All the bitterness. I realised that as soon as I saw her.'

But Karen could only think of the delight she'd seen in both their eyes.

'Chris . . . ?'

'Yes?'

'Take me home.'

'But, Karen . . .'

'*Please.*'

There was a tiny sigh, then Chris gently lifted her chin and kissed her mouth softly, tenderly. 'All right, my little mouse. I'll take you home.'

As Mandy walked home she felt strangely at peace for the first time in a long while. Talking with Pete had been weird at first, but there'd come a moment when she'd looked up and found him staring at her thoughtfully and had understood, without anything needing to be said, that they had finished with all the hurt and that they could move on from this and be friends again.

That was the trouble with marriage: because it was mixed up with sex and all that, the friendship bit got overlooked. Resentment took its place, and everything went wrong.

Or so it had been between her and Pete. But now she didn't have to resent him any more. Nor have sex, come to that. She could be a friend again. Someone he could talk to, and vice versa. And though Pete didn't really have a lot to say, even at the best of times, when he did she'd be there for him, and that was nice. But it also meant that she didn't have to let go. Not completely.

It was odd, really, because she'd thought that Pete would have blamed her totally for what went wrong, her having been the one who'd screwed around, but to her astonishment she found he blamed himself as much as her. He hadn't tried, he'd said, almost as if he'd been going to New Man evening classes. And she, almost comically, had told him it wasn't his fault, it was his mum's for spoiling him rotten; for making him believe that she, too, was there for his convenience, to be taken for granted. For once, he had laughed and agreed with her. But then, that was easy for him to do, now that he had someone else.

She had tried to get used to the idea of the girlfriend. But the thought of Pete having a relationship with someone else was too much right now. She knew *she* didn't want him, but the thought of him in love with another woman — a younger, *slimmer* woman — was a bitter pill to swallow.

Luke was sitting up when she got back, watching some horror movie on the telly. She went through to the kitchen and put on the kettle, then sat there, staring into space and thinking about her evening. That was how Luke found her.

'You all right, Mum?'

'Yeah, fine. Saw your dad tonight.'

'Oh . . .'

'No. It was OK. We talked.'

'Talked? That must be a first. You sure you weren't talking to some alien inhabiting his body?'

Mandy laughed. 'Go on. Your father's not that bad.'

'No? So what did he say?'

'Oh, this and that. But the gist of it is, we're going be friends from now on. And I'm going to get a job.'

'A job! Great! When did you hear about that?'

Mandy looked down, deflated suddenly. 'I ain't. Not yet, anyway. But I've written off. Hopefully I'll get some interviews.'

Luke came over and bent down, cuddling her. 'Well . . . you'll get one, Mum. I know you will.'

'Yeah. 'Course I will,' she said, with more confidence than she felt and squeezing him tightly for a moment. 'You thought any more about college?'

Luke shrugged. 'Dunno. Don't seem much point. Thought I'd get a job.'

Easier said than done, she almost said. 'Yeah, well . . . we'll talk about that another time, eh? I'm knackered. Thought I'd have a cup of cocoa and get an early night. Don't stay up too late.'

'Nah.' And with a peck on her cheek, he turned and left.

Mandy sighed, then stood and went over to the kettle. It had been a strange day. Oddly eventful. But she'd taken the first step. The rest was out of her hands.

For a moment the prospect of going out into the big wide world again frightened her; then, pushing the thought aside, she reached up and got the cocoa tin down, scooping two heaped spoonfuls into the mug.

Chocolate. Thank God for chocolate.

To Karen there was something special about Saturdays. There always had been. When she was a kid, it meant Saturday-morning pictures instead of school; when she was a student it meant all-night parties instead of studying; and nowadays it meant lazy days with Chris instead of battling to teach a load of pubescent schoolkids.

Most Saturdays they would lie in bed for most of the morning poring over the newspapers, taking it in turns to produce mugs of fresh coffee and plates of wholemeal toast. And sometimes, like this morning, they would make love; slowly, lovingly, without the drain of workday tiredness.

This morning they had caressed each other, each taking time to give the other pleasure, tongues sliding over soft skin, fingers teasing warm, moist flesh.

By the time Karen emerged on to their small sun-soaked patio it was already past lunchtime. The hot sun felt good on her pale skin, exposed except for the areas covered by a scanty red bikini. This tiny space — no bigger than a couple of car ports — was Karen's haven. Banks of terracotta pots lined lush ivy-covered walls, sprouting honeysuckle and clematis and all manner of shrubs and plants.

Karen filled the green plastic watering can and, passing

slowly along one side, across the top and back down the other side of the patio, she sprayed each container, breathing in the sweet scent of their flowers, admiring their beauty.

She often wondered how she had ever managed to live without a garden. There was no better place to relax, to get away from everything. It was her refuge and she treasured it.

Through the patio doors she could hear Chris in the kitchen, glass tinkling as she prepared some cold drinks. Reaching down, Karen removed her paperback from the sun lounger and sank down into its warm floral-covered foam. She kicked off her sandals and drew her legs up on to the bed, aware, even through her sunglasses, of how pale they still were. Sighing, she lay back, her body already tingling from the glare of the sun.

Tommy Barrett was feeling restless and pissed off. It was Saturday morning, but instead of being outside on the five-a-side pitch having a kickabout with his mates, he was cooped up in the small, thirteenth-floor flat looking after his brother and sister. He'd only agreed after his mum had bribed him with the promise of a fiver, but that was when he thought he could take the kids down with him; use them as goalposts or something. But the little shits wouldn't have it. They refused to budge from the flat, and though he was much bigger than they were, he couldn't drag them down there, because he knew from past experience that they'd only grass him up. And he couldn't afford to be a fiver down. He owed it to Pearce at school. And he was a mean fucking bastard!

If he pressed his face to his bedroom window as hard as he could, he could glimpse moving figures as they ran along the far edge of the pitch below. For a moment he watched as two friends scuffled following a hard tackle, and laughed to himself as one kicked the other up the backside before racing out of sight.

Barrett breathed heavily on to the window pane and wrote FUCK with the tip of his fingernail, before turning and making his way along the hall, past where his brother and sister were watching a video in the front room, and into their bedroom. The room was divided in half by two bookcases — one facing his sister's side and the other facing his brother's, in order to provide each with a degree of privacy.

On his sister's shelves was all manner of girly paraphernalia and he spent a minute of two manipulating the Barbies and Kens into various lovemaking positions. His brother's shelves displayed the interests of what he and his mates would disparagingly refer to as a boffin: books, science experiments, magnifying glasses, astronomical charts. At the age of eight his brother could reel off the names of all the constellations and spent hours gazing through his telescope.

Barrett knelt on the bed and placed his eye over the eyepiece, unimpressed by the milky-white light that met his gaze. Tilting it forward, he finally hit the skyline, distant buildings suddenly crowding into view as he swung it from side to side. Closer still, and with a few adjustments to the instrument, he was able to see into windows, and tilting it to its most acute angle, it was even possible to focus on girls in the street below, gazing at their tits with impunity.

Suddenly focusing on a local landmark — the pub on the corner of Drayton Park, near the Arsenal's ground — Barrett twiddled the knob to attain maximum focus. He wanted to look through the window to see if he could see his mum and dad at the bar. They said they were going shopping but they were bound to end up in the pub.

Unsuccessful, he tracked along the backs of the small adjoining terrace, banging his head with the telescope as he jerked it back to recapture the image it had held a split second before: a mass of pale flesh divided by a scrap of flaming red. Hurriedly, he adjusted the lens, reducing the figure so that he focused with trembling excitement on the near-naked body of a woman as she pottered in her garden.

Barrett couldn't believe his luck! As he watched, she emerged through the curtain of leaves, her small, pert breasts peering enticingly from above her red bikini top. As he nudged the telescope up a fraction, his vision was suddenly filled with Karen's face, her eyes screwed up as she peered disconcertingly in his direction before flipping her sunglasses from the top of her head to protect her eyes from the powerful rays of the sun. Tipping the angle with the slightest movement of his hand so that once more he stared into the seductive cleavage of his English teacher, the young boy fumbled at the fly of his jeans with the other, his fingers eagerly reaching inside his pants to encircle his warm, stiff penis.

Chris emerged from the house – a baggy T-shirt over her black bikini bottoms – carrying a small tray laden with two beer bottles, a bowl of pistachios and a tube of suntan cream.

Karen jumped as Chris playfully ran the ice-cold bottle of beer up her abdomen towards her breasts. There was an easy intimacy between them, each enjoying the other's laughter, the other's pleasure; the uncertainties of the night before all but forgotten.

Placing the tray between the two sunbeds, Chris sat on the edge of hers and pulled her T-shirt over her head to reveal her nakedness, her nipples immediately erect in the warm summer breeze.

'Have you put any cream on?' she said.

'Not yet.'

Chris reached for the tube of cream. Squeezing it into the palm of her hand she proceeded to rub it into the skin around Karen's navel, smoothing it up towards her breasts.

'Don't have it all in my belly button, will you?' she giggled.

'Don't worry,' Chris whispered, in spite of their being alone, 'I'll lick it out later.'

'Yuk!'

Chris pulled down Karen's bikini straps and squeezed cream on to first one shoulder and then the other, sliding her hand down over the rise of each breast in turn.

'I don't know why you bother to wear this,' she said, slipping her slim, cool hand inside one of the cups and gently squeezing Karen's nipple between her fingertips so that she quietly groaned.

'Chris!' Karen protested weakly.

'What?' she laughed with ingenuous innocence, while at the same time running her fingertips down into Karen's cleavage and up the gentle rise of her other breast. With the lightest of touches, she ran her nails along the edge of Karen's top before pulling it down to expose her dark-brown bud. And this time Karen intuitively pushed her breast forward, towards the warmth of her lover's inviting lips.

Barrett lay on his brother's bed, excited, exhausted and amazed by what he had witnessed. Never in his wildest dreams could he have hoped that a potentially boring Saturday afternoon could turn out to be so wonderful. He reached into his jeans and laid a comforting hand over his soft, shrivelled prick. Christ, he'd had a good wank! Closing his eyes, he brought to mind the two women in the garden, recalling vividly the way they'd touched and kissed each other's breasts. Shit! It was unbelievable! His fucking teacher and another woman!

Pushing his eye against the eyepiece again, Barrett watched them, prying on them secretly. And in spite of his earlier strenuous efforts, he felt his penis begin to stiffen beneath his touch.

The ringing of the front doorbell drifted out through the open doorway to where the two of them lay like toasting corpses on their sunbeds.

'It's probably just kids again,' Chris said drowsily, making no attempt to move a muscle.

Karen, however, fidgeted beside her, alert to the second ring when it came. Swinging her legs over the side of the sunbed, she reached across for Chris's T-shirt and pulled it over her bikini.

'And if it's Jehovah's Witnesses, for God's sake *don't* let them in!' Chris called after her as Karen made her way into the house.

Maybe it was the different surroundings, or the different clothes she was wearing, maybe it was also a matter of being taken by surprise, but it was a few moments before Karen actually recognised the woman on her doorstep as Chris's ex.

The two women stood there, facing one another.

'Hi! I, um, wondered if Chris was in. I'm an old friend. Sarah.'

The woman held out her hand and, even as Karen's mind raced off in several directions, she automatically took that hand within her own and heard herself say, 'Hi!' with a civility that was as far from what she was feeling as an orbiting moon.

'*Is* she in?' Sarah queried after a few awkward moments of silence. 'Only she said to pop round sometime. So . . .' The woman shrugged, her face creasing into a semi-apologetic smile.

'Yes! I mean, yes, she is in.'

But all Karen could think about was Chris lying semi-naked

in the garden, her tanned skin shimmering slightly in the sunlight, and how she must keep this woman away from her at all costs.

'Well?' Sarah queried, after another pause, and as though struggling to converse with the mentally challenged. 'Can I see her?'

Karen almost ran back into the house, pulling the door to partly, then calling back over her shoulder to Sarah, where she remained on the doorstep. 'Wait there a minute and I'll get her. She's in the garden.'

'I told you what to do,' Chris joked when she heard Karen's footsteps approaching. 'Just tell them you're Jewish and they leave you alone. It saves an awful lot of time.'

As Karen's body towered above her, casting its shadow across Chris's face, she looked up, at first unable to see the blinding rage that distorted Karen's features.

'What the *fuck* d'you think you're doing inviting her here?'

'What?'

'You must think I'm fucking stupid. Don't pretend you didn't know she was coming. What did you do? Phone her up? And look at you!' Karen nodded pointedly towards Chris's bare breasts.

'I don't know what you're talking about.'

'Oh, *really*,' Karen responded sarcastically. 'Sarah! That's what I'm talking about!'

'Sarah? She's here?'

Karen fought to retain the aggression that enabled her to attack. She couldn't afford to let Chris coerce her as that would undermine her anger and force her back on to the defensive. And once that happened she would crumble, as she always did.

'Don't sound so bloody surprised!' she said, but it was with a degree less conviction than before.

Chris's face, however, was a mask of innocence. 'Of course I'm surprised! How *could* I know she was coming round?'

'You tell me.'

Their eyes met and for a moment Chris did not speak. Karen knew — knew unequivocally — that they could not have exchanged addresses at the party. There simply hadn't been time. So they had spoken since. They must have done. How else would Sarah have known where to come?

Averting her eyes finally, Chris swung her legs over the side of the sunbed and slipped her feet inside her sandals. 'I'll get something to put on,' she said, standing up.

'Don't bother on my account!'

Chris and Karen turned as one towards the patio doors, from where Sarah grinned out at them, her look unmistakably mischievous.

Karen blinked, caught momentarily between rage and embarrassment. Embarrassed that they had been eavesdropped upon. Yes, but then how dare the woman just walk into their home? How dare she think she could so casually intrude upon their intimacy?

Sarah looked from one to the other, as if she couldn't understand what the problem was. 'I'm sorry, but I thought—'

'It's OK,' Chris said, reaching up to the washing line for her top, conscious of Karen standing there beside her. 'I'll come through. I—'

'Don't worry,' Karen said, making her way between the two angrily, an unmasked hostility in her voice now. 'I'll make myself scarce. I'm sure you two have *lots* to talk about.'

For once, returning to school on Monday morning filled Karen with a sense of relief. It was like getting back to some state of normality. The only question was whether, in her present condition, she could manage to summon sufficient energy to survive a day in the classroom.

The deep growl of young male voices and excited high-pitched female giggles drifted from the classroom and along the corridor to where Karen was on her way for a double period with 8T. Nearing the door, she took a mouthful of coffee – dark and bitter, the way she liked it – then, sighing deeply, reached for the door handle.

'OK, OK, settle down now!' Karen yelled over the din, walking over to the desk and setting down her bag.

She turned, facing them.

'Right! Today we're going to concentrate on the passage you were supposed to read for homework. So get out your books and turn to page one hundred and ninety-four.'

'Miss! Miss!' several voices shouted at once, hands shooting up to attract Karen's attention. There followed the usual litany of excuses for why the work had not been carried out, followed by a range of appropriate responses from Karen.

'OK! Has everybody got page one nine four?'

From the back of the class came the murmur of voices.

'Barrett! I thought I told you you weren't allowed to sit at the back of my class. Come on. Down here at the front where I can keep an eye on you.'

'It's all right, miss. I'm all right where I am, thanks.'

'Down here . . . now!'

Karen pointed to one of the empty desks in the front row, struggling to keep her cool. She felt awful hating a child, but in this one instance she couldn't help herself: she loathed Barrett. The very sight of him made her tense up inside, like she wanted to slap his face. He was rude, disruptive and ignorant: in all, a real little shit. And what was more, he was proud of it. Sometimes Karen felt relieved that she would never be a parent and run the risk of screwing up a child's life in the way that Barrett's parents had. As Philip Larkin had once written, 'They fuck you up, your mum and dad.' And it was true.

Emerging from his gang of sniggering friends, Barrett swaggered to the front of the class, noisily scraping back his chair before sliding down into it, immediately tilting it back so that it balanced precariously on its two rear legs. Karen decided not to rise to the bait.

'OK! So, who would like to read the first page for us?' Predictably the question was met with the lowering of heads, averting of eyes and a complete absence of raised hands.

'Rachel!' she said, smiling across at a pretty girl in the third row. There was an outburst of loud sniggering around the classroom and Rachel's face reddened in startling contrast to the blonde hair that hung like a curtain on either side of her face.

'Quiet!' Karen commanded, her irritation evident now. Then more softly: 'Rachel?'

Again, there was giggling.

'Oooh, Rachel,' Barrett teased, his voice forced into a high-pitched mockery of Karen's, causing the giggles to grow into full-blown laughter.

Karen could feel her knuckles whiten as she clenched her fist. She would have loved to land it in the middle of the little fucker's face, but of course she couldn't. There were rules, and rightly so. But right then . . .

Glancing at her watch, conscious of the minutes having ticked away, Karen cracked the spine of the book as she opened it at the relevant page. 'Never mind. I'll read it myself.'

It was one of her favourite passages in all of Lawrence, and she knew that, as she read, so her pupils would be trapped by the spell of the words and the magic of the scene, drawn in despite themselves. Even so, two paragraphs in, Karen was aware out of the corner of her eye of Barrett's hand raised in the air. She ignored him, continuing down the page and on. At the end of the final paragraph, she placed the book face down on the desk and moved round to stand in front of it.

'Right! The scene I've just read is apparently a simple descriptive piece about going out on a lake at night in a boat and lighting lanterns. But can anyone tell me what the author really meant by it, and how it links to the greater concerns of the book?'

Karen looked hopefully out across the classroom, conscious of Barrett's hand continuing to wave in the air. All she could see were rows of blank faces.

'Miss?'

Reluctantly, Karen turned to face him, the sarcasm in her voice pronounced. 'Yes, Barrett? You have a thought on this?'

'Well, not exactly, miss,' he said smirking, turning to play to his audience. 'I was just wondering if the book was called *Women in Love* because the two women were in love with each other.'

'Don't be absurd Barrett. It's about women *being* in love. Ursula and Gudrun.'

'That's what I mean, miss.'

Karen sighed, exasperated. 'But they're in love with the men in the book . . . with Birkin and Gerald.'

'So why isn't it called *Men and Women in Love*?'

There were squeals of delight and giggling from all sides of the classroom. Karen steeled herself to answer. The question might be a time-waster, but it wasn't the kind of thing one could send Barrett to the headmaster for.

'Because it *isn't*, OK? In fact, the book was a companion to an earlier novel by Lawrence, which was all about Ursula.'

'And was that called *Woman in Love*, miss?'

There were hoots of laughter this time. Karen lifted her chin angrily. 'Barrett?'

'Yes, miss?'

'Shut up!'

'Miss?' His hand went up again, as if he hadn't heard her. '*What?*'

'I liked the scene where they sunbathed.'

Not thinking at that instant just how strange it was that Barrett had even read a word of the book, Karen frowned, trying to recall the passage, but she couldn't recollect anything offhand.

'I s'pose they didn't have suntan lotion back then, did they, miss?'

Karen stared at Barrett. What was the boy going on about?

'No, Barrett, they didn't.' Sighing heavily she turned back to the class.

'But it's important to use it, ain't it, miss?'

Karen opened her mouth, then closed it again.

'Miss . . . did *you* do much sunbathing last weekend?'

'*What?*' Karen's eyes narrowed suspiciously. 'Barrett, if you've nothing interesting to say, just be quiet. This has no relevance to *Women in Love.*'

'But women *can* be in love, can't they, miss? I mean . . . like, lesboes and all that . . .'

Karen's bark surprised the boy. 'Barrett! Get outside! Go and report to Mr Keen!'

'But, miss . . .'

'*Now!*'

Barrett let his chair slump forward, then slowly stood, slouching his way to the doorway, well aware that there were thirty pairs of eyes watching him with anticipation. Finally, he turned and smiled at her.

'Miss? Red really suits you, you know.'

Karen instinctively looked down at her all-black outfit. Quickly glancing up, she saw Barrett leering at her through the glass panel of the door, but before she could take the first step towards him, he was gone.

*   *   *

— 90 —

As Karen made her way into the staffroom at break, it was with a growing sense that something wasn't quite right. Once or twice she caught one or other of her colleagues looking at her strangely, and the conversation, which seemed to have been so animated when she first entered the room, had almost died.

Coincidence, she told herself, as the talk began to flow again. She was just being oversensitive: the incident with Barrett had upset her, that was all.

Even so, there was a strange atmosphere and she felt distinctly excluded from whatever was going on. It was almost as if everyone was watching her, even if their eyes were averted when she turned to look at them.

She made herself a cup of strong, dark coffee, then went and sat in the corner, pretending to read the women's section of the *Guardian*, but her mind continued to dwell on the incident with Barrett.

Karen shivered, then sipped from her mug.

The door on the far side of the room swung open and two of the male staff stepped inside. Karen glanced at them, noting how they exchanged a look. Or had she imagined it? The older of them, Cliff Charlesworth, was head of geography, and nearing retirement age, while his companion, Frank Hornby, was a good thirty years younger and taught physics; but both were chauvinists of the old tradition, and generally Karen kept well out of their way.

Today, however, it seemed they didn't want to keep out of hers.

'How are we?' Hornby began, setting his mug down on the table and dropping into the seat beside her. Charlesworth stood over them, as if he were studying the poster on the wall beyond.

Maybe it was her general sense of unease, or maybe it was the fact that the two men were little better than irritating schoolboys themselves, but Karen felt unnerved by their sudden interest in her.

'Good weekend?' Charlesworth enquired, his eyes fixing on her now.

Karen forced herself to smile up at him, hating the way he towered above her. 'Yes, thanks.'

'Fantastic weather, wasn't it?' Hornby added, making little effort to conceal his amusement.

'Oh, yes,' Charlesworth chipped in, settling down in a chair opposite. 'Wonderful weather for the garden.'

'I understand you like gardening,' Hornby said, his body half turned towards Karen now, the tone of his voice all different, seductive almost, so that if he had said, 'I understand you like fucking', it would not have sounded out of place.

Karen folded her paper and stood. She didn't know what was going on, but she was on the outside of something and, whatever it was, it was pissing her off good and proper. Pushing between the two men, she marched across the room and out of the door.

And stopped dead in the corridor.

Barrett was standing there, not five yards away, staring at her, a huge smirk on his face. And behind him, grinning like a pack of hyenas, were at least a dozen of his little gang.

Karen stared at them a moment, then, her nerve deserting her, turned abruptly and half walked, half ran, down the corridor towards the secretary's office.

By the time she arrived home that evening, Karen felt seriously depressed. Her nagging suspicion that someone, that *Barrett*, had somehow *seen* her and Chris sunbathing at the weekend had changed into a gnawing certainty as the afternoon had worn on and the sniggering in class had worsened.

It had been awful, truly awful. And standing there, in front of them all, she had felt as naked as if she had stripped off before them.

She put her bag down in the hallway and walked over to the living room doorway. 'Chris?'

No answer.

Sighing, Karen went through to the kitchen and put on the kettle. She'd make a pot of tea and wait for Chris. She'd know what to do.

As she waited for the kettle to boil, she chewed at her thumbnail anxiously. It *was* that little bastard Barrett. She knew it was. But how? How did he know?

The very thought of him ogling her and Chris – of those cold, lizard-like eyes of his watching their most intimate moments – repulsed her. It made her feel unclean, as if Barrett had physically *touched* her. She shivered and reached out for the teapot, rinsing it out with the boiling water before she heaped in the tea.

It hadn't helped that Keen had done nothing, as usual. Barrett had been sent straight back to class without even a reprimand. And how were you supposed to maintain discipline in the classroom when the head teacher was a wimp?

She filled the pot, then sat, feeling restless and nervy. Where was Chris? She was usually home by now.

Ten minutes passed before Karen poured herself a cup of tea. It had gone cold – untouched – when she finally got up and went over to the phone. At first there was no answer, and then one of the secretaries came on the line. No, she said. Chris wasn't there. As far as the woman knew, she had gone home at the usual time.

Worried now, Karen walked over to the window and stood there, staring out past the brick-and-stone stairway at the street below. For a long, long while she stood there, unmoving, then she turned away.

This wasn't like Chris. If Chris was going to be late she'd phone. She always phoned.

In the back of her mind Karen wondered if she had had an accident. If, even now, Chris was lying on a trolley in an operating theatre, or — worse still — on a slab in some hospital mortuary.

It was all morbid nonsense, of course. There was probably some very simple explanation, like her bus had been caught in heavy traffic, or she'd decided to do some shopping on the way home. But it was strange she hadn't phoned. She knew how Karen worried.

Karen poured away the lukewarm tea, then, to keep herself busy, began to clean the kitchen, wiping down surfaces and taking down pots and pans and washing them.

By half six she was convinced that something was wrong and was looking up the number of the local police station when the phone rang.

She almost ran across the room to answer it.

'Chris? Oh, thank God! Where have you been? I've been so worried.'

'I'm sorry. I thought I said.'

Karen frowned, confused now. 'Said? Said what? You didn't say anything.'

She spoke quickly, defying any interruption. 'I'm at Sarah's. At her new flat. She's just moved in today and I promised I'd give her a hand sorting things. Unpacking boxes and that kind of thing.'

'Oh . . .' There was nothing else at that moment she could say. At Sarah's . . .

'Sarah was going to make supper,' Chris went on, 'but the electricity board have let her down, and the supply isn't on, so I said I'd stay the night.'

'Stay?' Karen felt hollow suddenly, empty.

'Yes. It's a bit of a rough area and I didn't like to leave her . . . you know, a woman on her own . . .'

'But Chris . . .'

'. . . and, anyway, I don't have to rush in to work in the morning. I'm not teaching until after lunch, so I thought . . .'

Karen snapped. 'Why didn't you tell me?'

'Tell you? But I thought I did.'

'Oh no you didn't! I'd have bloody remembered if you had!'

There was a moment's silence on the other end, then: 'Is there a problem?'

'*Is there a problem?* Too bloody right there's a problem! Why can't she use candles? I'd've guessed she bought in bulk!'

Chris huffed. 'I can't believe you're behaving like this. Sarah's an old friend, that's all, and I didn't want to let her down.'

'No, but it doesn't matter if you let *me* down, does it? I needed you here, Chris. I needed to talk to you. I've had an awful day and—'

'Look, I can't help that. I've promised Sarah now. And if you don't like it—'

'I can lump it. Right!' Karen drew herself up straight, furious now. 'You're going to sleep with her, aren't you?'

There was a silence – an awful silence after that – and then Chris answered, a contempt in her voice that had not been there a moment before. 'I thought, actually, that I'd sleep on the sofa bed. You know . . . like I do when your parents visit.'

Karen swallowed. The bitterness she felt at that moment – yes, and the anger and jealousy and resentment – threatened to unhinge her. She was trembling badly now. Her voice, however, was tiny, like a child's. 'Chris . . . ?'

'Well, what am I supposed to say?'

'Don't, Chris . . . please. Come home. Please. I need you . . .'

She could hear the long breath that Chris took. Then, more quietly, Chris said. 'I've promised now . . .'

'Well, fuck you!'

Karen slammed down the phone, then burst into tears, her fists pummelling the cushions as her anger overwhelmed her.

Karen lay in bed, alone in the darkened room, curled up on her side. She felt like she was all cried out, but she couldn't stop. All she could think of was them in bed together. It was long after midnight, and she could hear the TV from the other room, but she made no move to get up and switch it off.

She felt dead. Drained of emotion. Yet still she cried.

It was as she lay there, sobbing, that she heard the key go in the front door and the latch click open. There was a moment's silence and then the door clicked shut.

Karen waited, holding her breath, then sensed Chris in the doorway behind her.

'Karen . . .' Chris took a step into the darkness. 'Karen, are you awake?'

Karen let out a tiny sniffle. Chris came closer. Karen felt the mattress shift as Chris placed her weight on the bed beside her.

'Karen, I'm sorry . . . I didn't mean . . .'

Chris placed a hand on Karen's cheek. Karen wanted to flinch away — to show Chris she still had some pride left, in spite of everything — but she couldn't. Like a cat, she let herself be petted, as if that could make everything right again between them, and after a moment she reached up and held that hand, gripping it.

'Karen, I . . .'

'Just hold me,' Karen said, turning suddenly to face her. 'Please, Chris . . . just hold me.'

*   *   *

The clatter of the letterbox woke Mandy from a dead sleep. She stretched and went to turn over, then froze, listening as the clatter came again.

Bills, she thought. More sodding bills. Which reminded her. What with all the talk the other night, she had forgotten to speak to Pete about the latest arrivals.

Later, she thought, rolling on to her back, enjoying the full width of the big double bed. Pete had used to crush her over to one side, but these days she liked to spread out, luxuriating in having so much space.

Lonely? She was never lonely in the mornings. Only last thing at night. It was then that the bed seemed much too big. Morning was always her best time.

Mandy lay there for a moment, then heard footsteps in the hall, padding down to the bathroom. Luke. The lazy sod would be late unless he got a move on.

She sat up, then swung her legs round, feeling for her slippers with her feet. Glancing at the bedside clock, she called out to him.

'Luke? Get a move on. You'll be late!'

'Do us a cup of tea, Mum!'

Mandy shook her head, then got up. She ought to have told him to make one himself, but she rather liked the way he depended on her still.

She pulled on her dressing gown and padded down the stairs. The post was on the mat. Five envelopes. Two brown, three white. She stared at them a second or two, frowning. Now who the hell would be writing to her . . . ?

She felt her heart skip a beat. The applications had been posted Friday. They would have got there Saturday, or Monday at the latest, and if the firms had written back straightaway . . .

Mandy went across and scooped them up, not daring to look at them yet, then turned and hurried through to the kitchen.

Having put the letters down on the table, she filled the kettle and switched it on, then got down two tea bags out of the box and dropped them into the empty teapot. That done, she turned, staring at the letters once again, her mouth dry.

'Go on,' she told herself quietly. 'Open them, you silly cow, there's nothing to be afraid of.'

Luke appeared in the doorway. He frowned at her. 'You wanna watch that, Mum.'

'What?'

'Talking to yourself like that. I'll 'ave you put in a home.'

She swallowed, then stepped across and scooped up the letters again, her nervousness transferring itself to every movement she made.

'Mum? You OK?'

Mandy gave a little nod, then, steeling herself, flicked through the envelopes. As she'd thought, the two brown ones were bills. The others were addressed to her, her name neatly typed.

She sat, then tore the first of them open. Glancing at the company name on the letterhead, she quickly read it through.

'Mum?'

'Shh . . .'

She set the letter down, then tore open the second. A moment later it sat atop the other, the ends of it slowly lifting as it tried to fold itself up once more.

But Mandy was already reading the third of the letters. Setting it down, she looked up, staring at her son.

'Well?'

'I've got an interview,' she said, a look of total bemusement on her face. Then she laughed. 'In fact, I've got three interviews . . .'

A smile began to light Mandy's features, and then her eyes flickered and she looked back at the last of the letters.

'Oh, shit!'

'Mum?'

'It's tomorrow! They want me to go in there tomorrow!'

'Well, that's great, ain't it? I mean, it shows they're keen . . .'

'Yeah, but what am I gonna wear? And what am I gonna say?'

She stopped, staring fiercely into the air as if some great idea had struck her. 'I'll phone Karen. I'll ask her. She'll know.'

'Yeah,' Luke said, smiling now as if the matter had been resolved. 'Now where's that cuppa?'

'Look, Mand, don't panic. Just be yourself, all right? What you don't know you'll pick up quickly enough. All you've got to remember is that none of them knew what they were doing once upon a time. They all had to learn it sometime or other.'

'Yeah,' Mandy answered, grimacing at her end of the phone, 'only I haven't been near a bloody office for nearly twenty years!'

'Look, Mand, secretarial is secretarial. The machines might have changed but the job's much the same. You answer letters, you file things, you make tea. Can't be too much of a challenge, can it? Not when you've been used to running a houseful of men!'

Put that way, it didn't seem so bad, and she had been a pretty good secretary once upon a time.

'Thanks, Kar. You're an angel. How's things with you.'

There was a slight hesitation, then. 'Fine. No, everything's fine. Look, I'd better go. But good luck! OK?'

'OK. 'Bye, darlin'. And thanks . . .'

But the line was already dead. Mandy frowned. Maybe she'd missed something. But whatever it was, Karen hadn't seemed too keen to talk about it.

She pushed the phone away, then got up. A drink, that was what she needed. A nice stiff drink.

But not now, she thought, realising that if she started now she'd be pissed by lunchtime and that would never do. No. Tonight. She'd let herself have one tonight, to help her sleep. Settle her nerves.

Interviews. They couldn't be *so* bad, could they? It was hard to remember. It was like Karen said; all she had to do was relax and be herself. But then she thought of that and sank slowly into her chair again.

Just what was she? An overweight housewife, going on forty, with about as much experience of modern office work as the rawest young recruit to the job market.

It was not exactly true, yet it felt like it. Besides, she'd probably be the oldest one there. There were sure to be others applying for the jobs – younger and more able.

Mandy groaned, beginning to wish she had never written those letters – that she had never opened her mouth to Pete about getting a job. But she'd done it now. She'd committed herself. There was no way back unless she was to admit defeat.

She stood, then went out to the mirror in the hallway, staring at herself a moment, her face creasing with woeful dissatisfaction.

'What do you look like?' she said, eyeing herself critically. 'Who in their right mind is goin' to take you on?'

Yeah, she thought. Then again, what've you got to lose?

With a little shudder, she straightened up, squaring her shoulders, lifting her chin, defying the image of herself she'd projected earlier.

'The only failure is never to have tried,' she said quietly, the old school motto seeming suddenly appropriate. 'So get off your butt and get yourself out there!'

Mandy's lip slowly curled into a smile as she recalled the first proper job she'd ever had — the first interview she'd ever had. She had been sixteen and her mum had made her a dress especially for the interview — a white shirtwaister with little red spots all over it. She hadn't been in the least bit nervous chattering and bluffing her way through it with all the brash confidence of youth.

A lot had happened to her since then, and to her confidence. But it was do or die and Mandy was nothing if not a fighter.

'So, Mrs Evans, you say you've done secretarial work before?'

Mandy sat forward slightly in her chair, nerves making her almost stammer the words.

'Yes . . . b-but it was a long time ago now.'

The woman — the firm's human resources manager — nodded at that, not looking up from the ledger she was making notes in. It didn't help that she was half Mandy's age; nor that after that first long, appraising stare, she had scarcely bothered to look at Mandy again. *Jumped-up bitch!*

'I see. And how long is long?'

A glib retort was on the tip of Mandy's tongue when she bit it.

'Nineteen years,' she said in what was almost a whisper.

'Pardon?'

Mandy concentrated on the stack of box files behind the woman's head and said it again, louder this time. 'Nineteen years. I stayed at home with me kids.'

Once again, the woman wrote something down, making Mandy wish she had worn her glasses after all and not succumbed to vanity.

'And have you been on any courses?'

Mandy blinked. 'Sorry?'

The woman raised her eyes; gave Mandy a cold, hard stare. 'Refresher courses.'

'Ah . . . um . . . no.'

'I see.'

Mandy could feel what little confidence she had managed to muster dissipate as her spirits sank lower by the second. She coughed to break the silence as the woman made another note. Glancing down at her painted toenails peeping from the front of her sandals, she suddenly felt very old and very stupid.

'OK,' the woman said after a moment. 'So let's see what we have. Do you know Word?'

Mandy frowned. 'What word's that, then?'

The woman looked up and smiled patiently. 'Word for Windows.'

Mandy stared at her a moment as if the woman was talking in tongues, then shrugged. 'Sorry! I ain't got a clue what you're talking about.'

There was a sigh, a distinct sigh, and then the woman asked, 'Have you ever *used* a word processor, Mrs Evans?'

There was a split second of indecision as Mandy considered whether she could bluff her way through this one. 'Not exactly,' she conceded finally, 'but I'm a whizz on my son's Game Boy!' She smiled with pathetic resignation.

She watched as the woman wrote a full two lines, then closed the ledger.

'Well, Mrs Evans,' she began, but Mandy interrupted her.

'It's all right! I ain't got it, 'ave I?'

The woman hesitated, then. 'We usually inform applicants by letter.'

'But I ain't, 'ave I?'

Another pause, then. 'No. No, I'm afraid you . . . Look, Mrs Evans. If I were you I'd retrain with new technology.

Get yourself on a course. Get yourself some office skills. Otherwise—'

'I'm wasting my time. That's the bottom line, ain't it?'

The woman looked at Mandy sympathetically a moment, then nodded. 'Look, I'm sorry, but I have to think of the company.'

'Yeah . . . yeah, I understand. Thanks, anyway.'

And Mandy stood, putting out her hand and shaking the woman's, suppressing all the while the humiliation that was burning in her. Useless. She was fucking useless. Too old and too ignorant: she didn't even know what Thingy for Windows was, for Christ's sake! What a sad, pathetic cow!

Outside in the street again, she had to stop and catch her breath. It wasn't so much the rejection — after all, she hadn't expected to crack it first time out — it was someone else actually telling her how little she had to offer.

No, she corrected herself; not little. Nothing! I've got bugger all to offer these people. Not unless they want their shopping done and their beds made.

She crossed the road, entered the park opposite and plonked herself down on a bench, determined at that moment to wallow in the self-pity she felt was her due. The sun beat down and Mandy removed her jacket, enjoying the weather in spite of herself. Gradually the small, neat gardens began to fill with office workers making the most of an hour's respite from the hustle and bustle of big business, the formality of their clothing incongruous as they lay on the grass, or sat on a bench eating their sandwiches. Every so often one or the other would glance at their watch, jump up and be off, and Mandy watched them go with envy. *She* wanted to have somewhere to go; something to do. *She* wanted to be missed if she got back late; wanted to feel a part of something.

It was in a park just like this one that her mother had waited all those years ago while she had gone for her first job interview, wearing the much-laboured-over shirtwaister. And Mandy remembered how proud she had felt, running across into the square afterwards to tell her that she'd been given the job. Her first interview and she'd done it! Who was there to feel proud of her now? The boys wouldn't understand what it meant to her, even if she did manage to pull off a miracle and land herself a job. But her mum would've understood. And for the first time, Mandy was able to understand why.

She picked up her jacket and handbag and made her way purposefully towards the gate, feeling stupid even as she acted out the charade. And for whose benefit? But there was, she felt, something attractive about a person in a hurry. Sighing heavily, she slowed her pace and, pulling from her opened handbag the company brochures from the earlier interview, she dropped them into the rubbish bin and made her way through the gates and out on to the dusty pavement.

Then she remembered what the woman had said about courses. Well, maybe she could get herself on one. Only, she didn't know where to begin.

She didn't know. But, she suddenly realised, she knew a friend who would! Two, in fact! Karen and Anna were bound to be clued up about stuff like that.

The thought of there being *some* hope cheered her a little.

Ah well, she thought, as she waited at the bus stop to go home; it can't get any worse than that. And, from the depths of her memory, she suddenly recalled what Susie had told her once about how she had got a job she wanted by giving the guy who was interviewing her a blow job under his desk, with the promise of another if he hired her.

As the bus drew up, Mandy climbed up on to the platform, smiling to herself at the thought of offering the jumped-up bitch a quick fumble on the office floor.

Nah, she thought. It might have worked for Susie, but

that ain't gonna work for me. If I'm going to get a job, I'm going to have to get myself sorted.

Like Thingy for Windows, for a start.

Mandy sat down, taking a window seat, oblivious of the people all about her.

Anna would be her best bet. She was the one who'd know all the right things to say; how to go about this interview business.

The thought of it perked her up, and as the bus chugged along, Mandy found herself almost excited by the prospect of another interview, the humiliation of the last one pushed to the back of her mind as she began to consider the important matter of what she was going to cook Luke for tea.

'Miss?'

Seated at the front of the class, Karen looked across at the girl in the doorway and smiled.

'Yes, Hayley?'

'Mr Keen says he'd like a word. At break.'

'Ah . . . OK.'

Karen looked down, trying to ignore the faint murmur of whispered voices. She tried to concentrate once more on the passage from Lawrence's novel, but her eyes no longer registered what was in front of them. She was wondering why Keen wanted to see her, and if it had anything to do with that business yesterday.

At break she made her way – slowly, reluctant now – to the headmaster's office. His secretary, Joan, smiled at her as she entered; the kind of smile a doctor might reserve for a patient to whom he was about to give bad news. Karen sat, prepared to wait, but Keen's door swung open almost at once.

'Miss Turner. Please, do come in . . .'

Karen rose from her seat uncertainly, then stepped inside,

letting him close the door behind her. She waited for him to go back round his desk and sit before she took her own seat, then cleared her throat nervously.

'Might I ask what this is about?'

The head glanced at her, then looked back at the slim folder in front of him. There were no more than two or three sheets of A4 paper in it at the most.

'I'm afraid this is all rather . . . embarrassing. Given the choice I'd have preferred to ignore it, if at all possible, but the whole thing has gotten out of hand, so . . .'

He lifted his hands and let them fall, in his best Pontius Pilate impression.

Karen went to open her mouth, but Keen went on.

'You see, there are rumours that you are, um . . .'

'*Rumours?*'

'Yes, er . . . Well, that you're a lesbian.' He met her eyes for the briefest moment. 'Is that true?'

A flash of pure indignation swept through Karen. She leaned forward and held the desk. 'Would it matter if it were?'

'Oh . . . well, it might. You see, I've had the chair of governors and a representative from the Parent-Teacher Association . . .'

And they can shove it up their collective arses! Karen thought, but she sat back, keeping her lips firmly shut.

'Well?' Mr Keen asked after a moment. 'Is it true?'

Karen blushed scarlet. 'I really don't think that that's any of your business.'

'Well, I'm afraid it is. Rumours have been sweeping the school these past two days and things are getting out of hand. If I'm to maintain discipline, then—'

'But it's none of their damn business!'

Mr Keen sat back slightly, then removed his glasses and began to polish them. 'I'm afraid that anything that affects school discipline is *my* business, and if there's any truth behind these rumours . . .'

'Exactly what has been said?'

He hesitated, then, in a smaller voice murmured. 'It's rumoured that you were seen in a state of undress . . . outdoors . . . and with another woman.'

Karen sat back again, mortified. 'I was sunbathing,' she said. 'In my own private garden.'

'Yes, but—'

'And whoever this peeping Tom is – and I've a fair idea – has misconstrued things badly.'

The head teacher looked up at the word 'misconstrued', his face lighting with a smile for the first time. 'Misconstrued . . . ah, good. Do you mind if I note that down?'

'Yes, and add perverted little troublemaker to it, too!' Karen said, standing and turning to go to the door.

'Miss Turner . . .'

Karen stopped, but didn't face him again; didn't dare face him, in case she burst into tears. 'Yes?'

'I think it's best you go home – for today. Give me an opportunity to straighten thing out . . .'

Karen swallowed deeply, then silently nodded.

And then she was out in the corridor again. She stood there a moment, stunned, her whole world turned suddenly upside down. Then, not even stopping to collect the stack of books that awaited her in the staffroom, she turned, heading for the entrance hall, needing to get home.

Mandy's good mood didn't last long. Back in her kitchen, she sat there, nursing her second glass of cheap wine, close to tears suddenly, feeling more inadequate than ever.

She had become used to these mood changes recently, and some days she suspected it might even be the change coming upon her early, but more likely it was just the barometer of her self-confidence swinging wildly out of control.

Mandy sniffed loudly, glad that Luke wasn't there to see her like this. Trouble was, when she was up, she had no one to keep her there, and when she was down she didn't like to admit it, even to herself. She could not bring herself to confess, even silently, that she was lonely. Somehow that was such a terrible and frightening confession, conjuring up images of society's rejects, that it became easier for her to close off her emotions and think in purely practical terms.

Some days she wondered if this was how madness started. She had heard of women having breakdowns, and a good friend of hers had been diagnosed as having manic depression, but was it the same? Was this what having too much time on your hands did to you?

Mandy gulped down the rest of the wine, then reached for the half-empty bottle, and as she did the phone rang.

'Saved by the bell,' she said quietly, then stood and went across.

'Yeah? . . . Oh, Anna, yeah . . . yeah, I went.'

Mandy straightened up slightly. 'Nah . . . no chance. She told me there and then. I wasn't experienced enough.'

She was quiet a moment, listening, then. 'Anna? What's Word for Windows?'

There was laughter on the other end of the phone as Anna conjured up the scene. She quickly explained but it was still all gobbledygook to Mandy.

'Look,' Mandy said. 'You couldn't do us a favour, could you? I mean, give us a crash course, like. You've got a computer at home, ain't you?'

'Sure. Why don't you come round tomorrow night. I'm not doing anything. We'll crack open a bottle and catch up on the gossip at the same time.'

'Great!' Mandy said, cheered by the thought. 'The woman

today said I should get on a course. What d'you reck-on?'

'Trouble is, they cost, Mand.'

Mandy sighed. 'Well . . . that rules that out, then.'

'I can lend you it, if you're short. Till you get on your feet.'

'Thanks, but . . . well, there's the other interviews yet. I'll see how they go first, eh?'

'Yeah. And come round about eight. If I'm going to be any later than that I'll phone you beforehand, OK?'

'Yeah . . . and thanks, Anna.'

'Don't mention it. 'Bye, darling.'

''By-ee.'

Mandy sat again. There. Things weren't so bad. She did have friends. And it was right what she said. Not all the interviews could be as bad as this morning's, surely? Someone had to want her.

She stared at the wine bottle for a time, then picked it up and, securing the cork, slipped it back into the fridge.

Getting rat-arsed was no answer. Not unless the question was, 'Do you want to piss your life away?' But she needed this job. Only now was she beginning to understand just how much she needed it, because if she didn't get it . . .

Mandy teetered on the edge a moment, her mind filled with visions of what life would be like, alone and on the dole, like some poor old pensioner, living out her life, dependent on state handouts.

'Fuck that,' she said quietly, appalled by the idea. 'No bleedin' way . . .'

Even so, the doubts crowded around her like a gang of crazed paparazzi, undermining her, facing her every way she turned.

Confidence. It was all a question of confidence.

Mandy sighed, then stood again, putting on the kettle.

Tomorrow. She'd think about it tomorrow.

'There, my little bubsie-wubsie. Have we had enough, then?'

Jo lowered his newspaper, looking across to where Susie sat with the baby cradled against her, gently tickling his chin with her crooked little finger.

'You'se getting to be a big boy, isn't you?'

Jo smiled. Even he found himself slipping into baby talk now and then. But it wasn't that he was looking at. It was Susie's exposed right breast, bloated from its normal size, the nipple like the nozzle of a grease gun. The sight of it, innocent as it was, made his cock go stiff.

'You don't think I could have a squirt if he's finished, do you?' he quipped, only half jokingly. God, there was nothing he wanted more right then than to close his lips over that swollen berry-brown bud.

Susie rolled her eyes, grinning down at the child. 'That's Nathan's dinsywinsies, isn't it, Nathan? His milky-wilky. And Daddy can't have it. No he can't.'

Jo crossed his legs and groaned inwardly. Don't remind me, he thought. He seemed to have had more wanks these past few weeks than in the whole of his adolescence. And when he had mentioned his problem to Susie, last night, when finally she'd come to bed, she had just laughed, as if it were all a joke.

'You could at least lend a hand,' he'd said, despairingly. But Susie was having none of it. She was too tired, she said; she needed to rest before the baby woke up for his next feed. And so he'd found himself in the bathroom again, trying not to look at himself in the mirror as he got rid of his hard-on.

And so it went on. And most of the time it was bearable, but sometimes, like late at night, he found it hard to adapt. He had been everything to Susie, but now there was this other person in the house. Now Susie didn't look to him first as she once had, but to little Nathan, and though part of him understood

that and loved her for it — for wasn't it *his* son? — another
part of him was darkly envious of this tiny usurper.

'Jo?'

'Yeah?'

'Can you get us a cushion?'

Momentarily, he mused over some erotic use for the cushion.
But, of course, it was for Nathan. The days of placing cushions
under Susie's arse seemed long in the past. Those days of
leisurely lovemaking, of fervent shagging — as if it were an
art — were gone.

Jo sighed and stood.

'And Jo?'

'Yeah?'

'You couldn't get us some of my cream, could you? Only
me nipples are a bit cracked.'

Jo sighed. He could feel another visit to the bathroom
coming on.

'Can I speak to Anna, please? Anna Nichols.'

The receptionist asked her to hold, and while she did,
Mandy looked about her at the kitchen, sighing inwardly.
She'd overslept this morning and, in a hurry to get to her
first interview, had had to leave everything. The dishes were
still piled up in the sink, and Luke's dirty clothes lay in a
heap on top of the washing basket.

Muzak began to play at the other end of the phone line.
Mandy screwed her nose up at it, then reached across the
table, pulling yesterday's *Standard* closer to have a look.

The first interview had been at a clothing factory up
Holloway. She'd got there on time as it happened, but on
arriving was told that the vacancy had already been filled,
so she might just have well not have bothered.

'We did try to phone you,' the girl had said, 'but you must
have left already.'

Just my sodding luck, Mandy thought, wondering how much longer she'd be kept hanging on. Not that the second interview, an hour later, had been any better. That had been at a firm of accountants near the Nag's Head. They'd wanted a filing clerk, but clearly whoever had been dealing with the applications had misread her date of birth, because the office manager — a prematurely bald little git with a cough — had taken one glance at her and tutted. 'Oh, dear, we were looking for someone a little younger. I'm afraid you're far too, er, *mature* for the position.'

She had almost clocked the little bastard. *Mature*? Too *mature*? But she knew what he meant. They were looking for some junior to train up, someone they could pay peanuts, not some housewife whose *kids* were probably too old for the job!

'Oh, come on!' she said impatiently. 'Answer the bloody phone . . .'

The muzak ended abruptly. 'Mand? Is that you?'

'Anna? Are you still on for tonight?'

'Yeah, sure . . . Look, are you OK?'

'Yeah, I'm all right. Two more interviews, two more rejections.'

'Oh, Mand . . .'

'It's OK. I'm gettin' used to it. Must have put on at least three new layers of skin this morning alone!'

'Well, we'll sort you out tonight, OK? Get you a proper CV done.'

'A C-what?'

'A CV. A curriculum vitae. Oh, never mind, Mand, I'll explain tonight. Look, I've gotta run now, there's a bit of a flap on. See you at eight, OK?'

And Anna was gone. Busy as usual. Putting the world to rights.

Mandy placed the receiver back in the cradle, then sat back, blowing out a noisy breath. She had another interview tomorrow and a fifth on Friday. After that she'd have to start again, looking through the papers and writing off.

CVs . . . Word for Bleedin' Windows. And there was she thinking it was all a matter of typing a few letters and filing a few files.

Mandy stood then went over to the sink and ran the hot tap. Still, she thought, as she began to stack the dirty dishes to one side ready to be washed, no use despairing. She'd read of people having to apply for dozens of jobs — even hundreds — before they got a chance. So what were three rejections compared with that?

Suddenly she felt a flicker of admiration for the proverbial ugly bloke in the disco who'd chat up every available girl only to be rejected time and time again. But then, perhaps ugly blokes were born with thick skin; or perhaps after a while it just stopped hurting.

Anna put down the phone and turned, looking across her piled-high desk at Brenda, her fashion editor.

'Sorry . . . now where were we?'

Brenda leaned towards her angrily. 'That bloody man! I asked him to be there at six for the shoot and he wanders in at ten past seven! A whole bloody hour wasted! And we're expected to foot the bill for the models having to sit around on their backsides!'

'Then bill him for it. And if he objects, don't pay him. Use someone else.'

'But he's so *good* . . .'

Anna sat back and laughed.

'What?' Brenda asked, frowning.

'Just that he sounds like a typical man. Keeps you waiting, then tells you that if you don't like it you can shove it.'

'Well, I wouldn't mind, only he will insist on bringing that boyfriend of his. I can't stand the little creep. The way he hovers in the background all the time. And he's so fucking critical.'

'But as you say, he's one of the best.'

'You should hire Callum again . . .'

Anna snorted. 'Over my dead body! Besides, he's not interested in fashion. That's beneath him. Callum's a *serious* photographer these days.'

Brenda looked down. 'I'm sorry . . .'

'Yes, well, that's history. So what did you get? Anything special?'

'There's a couple of shots—'

The phone rang. Anna hesitated, then, smiling apologetically at Brenda, picked it up.

'Rachel? Is it urgent, only . . . Ah . . . I see.' Anna sighed. 'Well, you'd better put her through.'

She cupped her hand over the mouthpiece and looked across at Brenda. 'Give me ten minutes, OK?'

Brenda smiled and quickly left.

Anna waited as the connection was made, wondering what Sheila Bowen could want; she was usually content to deal with Anna's deputy. Sheila was one of her best writers, and her regular column brought in hundreds of letters every week, and Anna was particularly proud of that because she was the first one to recognise Sheila's talent and harness it. She'd taken her out of the becalmed waters of the gardening section and given her a fresh lease of life as her 'Real Life' writer.

There was a click and Sheila's familiar voice came on. 'Anna?'

The tentative way Sheila said her name rang the first warning bells in Anna's head, but she answered brightly anyway.

'Sheila . . . what can I do for you?'

'I . . .' Sheila sighed. 'Look, Anna, this is difficult. I was going to write you a letter, but I thought . . . well, I'm giving you notice.'

'Notice?' Anna felt a ripple of shock go through her.

'I didn't want to leave you in the shit . . . you know, but . . .'

'Hold on . . . what do you mean, *notice*?'

There was a moment's silence, then. 'I'm giving up the column, Anna. I'm going to work for the *Edition*.'

'The *Edition*!' Anna felt like exploding. 'What did that bitch offer you?'

'Anna, I—'

'No! Tell me! What is she paying you?'

She heard Sheila sigh on the other end of the line. 'It isn't just about money, Anna. Barbara is going to give me three pages every issue. Besides—'

'Why in God's name didn't you come and talk to me?'

'I did. Remember? And you weren't listening.'

'So you went to her, is that it?'

'No. I wouldn't have done that. She phoned me, as it happens. She heard I was unhappy . . .'

Anna closed her eyes, furious now. So that bitch had a mole in her office, did she?

'We'll match her offer. In fact, we'll better it.'

Sheila sighed again. 'That's not the issue, Anna. Besides, I've made up my mind now. It's a new challenge, and I need that. I was getting stale.'

'Bollocks you were getting stale!' Anna hesitated, then: 'Look, I'll talk to the management. See if they'll agree to you having more space in the mag. I'm sure I can persuade them.'

'It's kind of you, but . . .' Sheila fell silent.

Anna counted to five in her head, then spoke again, calmly now, trying not to give in to the anger she was feeling; the burning sense of betrayal. 'Look. Just think about it. OK? Don't do anything until you've thought it through. I'll match anything she's offering. You want fresh challenges, we'll find them for you. But don't go. Please.'

'Look, I'm sorry, Anna, but I've made up my mind. I think it would be best for us both.'

'I don't—'

But the line went dead. Clearly Sheila thought she'd said enough.

Anna put the phone down, then sat back, in a state of shock. Her best writer had jumped ship, and just as they were planning the new TV campaign. The management were not going to like that one tiny little bit!

'Shit!'

Then, refocusing her anger, she sat forward, snatching up the phone.

'Rachel? Get me that bitch Barbara Stannard at the *Edition* . . . Yes . . . tell her it's her very good friend Anna Nichols . . .'

The receptionist stared at Anna as she marched past her, then stood, belatedly realising that she was heading directly for the editor's office.

'I'm sorry, but you can't—'

Anna snatched at the door handle, then went through, finding herself standing at one end of a long table littered with photos and page layouts, about which a dozen or more people were seated, clearly discussing the latest issue. Barbara Stannard was at the far end, deep in conversation with her art director.

'You!' Anna yelled at her, bringing an instant silence to the room. 'Yes, you, you bitch! What in fuck's name do you think you're up to, poaching my writers?'

Barbara blinked, momentarily shocked to see Anna there in the flesh, but almost at once an icy composure came over her face.

'Anna . . . how nice to see you, darling.'

Anna smiled acidly. 'I just wanted to tell you to your face what a talentless arsehole I think you are.'

'Ooh, touchy . . . What's the matter? Can't keep your staff?'

There were sniggers from some of the men. She glared at them, then carried on. 'You think you're funny, but you're nothing but a fucking snake, you know that? You call yourself a friend, and then do *that* behind my back.'

Barbara shrugged. 'Business! It's a hard world, darling. If you can't take the pressure . . .'

'Oh, I can take the pressure. Better than you, *darling*, but I do it without shitting on those I call my friends.'

Anna let her gaze travel briefly over the various faces at the table, recognising most of them. The magazine world was a relatively small one and you ended up having worked with most people after a while. So here. There were only two or three of those present she hadn't worked with at some time or other, and some were even friends.

'Still . . . I'm sure I'm saying nothing that hasn't been said a thousand times. I'm pretty sure everyone here knows what a prime bitch you are, or if they don't, they will before too long!'

Barbara gave a pointed look to her deputy editor, a short, camp guy sporting a bow tie and a single earring. Sliding somewhat tentatively from his seat, Gerry Bushier stepped across to where Anna was standing and placed a manicured hand on her elbow, attempting to turn her towards the door.

'Don't lay your fucking hands on me, you sycophantic ponce!' Anna said, shrugging him off. Around the table several mouths curled involuntarily.

'Listen, Anna, I think we all need to cool off,' Barbara suggested, rising from her seat. 'Let's go into my office.'

Anna stared back at her coldly. 'I have absolutely nothing more to say to you. I wouldn't waste my breath.' And with a perfectly executed one-hundred-and-eighty-degree turn, Anna made her dignified exit, a sudden hubbub of talk arising from the room even as the door slammed shut behind her.

The taxi was still waiting. A twenty-pound note had seen to that. As she climbed into the back, Anna felt like giggling, knowing that she'd be the talk of London magazine circles before the day was out.

Well, what the hell! The bitch deserved it. And it would do her own reputation no harm either.

'Where to?' the cabbie asked, turning to look back at her.

She almost said the office, then changed her mind. 'The Clarence,' she said.

'Right you are, love.'

As he pulled out into the traffic, Anna took the mobile from her handbag and tapped out Frank's number. It rang twice before he answered.

'Hello?'

'Frank? Look, it's me, Anna. I . . . I wanted to say sorry for the other night. I was in a funny mood and—'

'It's all right. I shouldn't have left like that.'

'No . . . No, you shouldn't. But I forgive you.' She smiled into the phone. Then, more gently: 'Do you forgive me?'

Frank's warm laughter sent a little ripple up her spine. 'Yes. Yes, I do.'

'And have you missed me?'

'Yes, of course I have.'

'How much?'

'What do you mean, how much?'

'How much have you missed me?'

'Um, it's a little difficult. I'm in a meeting right now.'

Anna giggled, amused by Frank's discomfort. Leaning forward, she closed the glass partition, cutting herself off from the cab driver.

'Are you missing me enough to have an erection? Or do you need me to be there in person. I could run my hands up your thighs and take your cock in my mouth, rolling my tongue over it. Mm. I can taste you . . .'

'Anna . . . I'm at work . . .'

'And I'm sitting in the back of a cab on my way to the Clarence. My nipples are hard just thinking about you. I'm running my fingers up between my legs, over the soft skin above my stocking tops. My panties are wet . . .' Anna softly groaned.

Frank's voice was much quieter than before. 'This isn't fair.'

'The Clarence. And if you're not there in half an hour I'll be gone.'

'Anna, I—'

She switched off the phone, then sat back, smiling to herself.

Men. They were all the same.

Anna watched from the window of the hotel room as Frank stepped from the taxi, then turned to pay the cabbie. As the cab moved away, Frank stood there a moment, looking about him, every bit the guilty man, then, with what seemed from above like a shrug of resignation, he went inside.

She waited, imagining him there in the foyer, searching for her with his eyes. After a moment he would go across and ask at the desk.

Anna smiled. She had done this to him once before, back in the early days of their relationship, and he had laughed then and called her a brazen hussy, like in some Victorian novel, and she had rather liked that.

She moved from the window, surveying the room. The Clarence was what one might have termed basic. There was a double bed, a chair, a low dressing table and a TV in one corner. On the wall over the dressing table was a mirror and facing it a tiny washroom with loo and shower. Unlike many of the bigger tourist hotels, the Clarence catered for more short-term customers. Couples came here in the afternoon to make love, away from their partners and their families, and no questions were asked by the staff. Anna had heard about it first from one of her writers, who had been doing an article on the prevalence of casual sex among professional men and women, and within a month she was doing the same herself.

She stepped across and stood before the mirror, looking at herself. As yet she was fully dressed, not a single button unfastened, for that was half the fun, having Frank undress her. She liked to feel that she was being seduced — that though they were here to make love, that end was far from guaranteed. Only then did it work for her. Only then could she fully let go.

Excitement. She had realised this last year that she was addicted to excitement. She liked taking risks. Liked the thrill of the chase, the touch of a stranger, the sheer bliss of doing the unexpected.

As now.

She had phoned Rachel as soon as she'd got here and told her she would be back at two or thereabouts. Then she had booked the room, knowing that Frank would be unable *not* to come. Whatever difficulties it might put him in — whatever lies he might have to tell — he *would* be here.

And so it had proved.

She stared at herself a moment longer, then turned away. And even as she did, there was a knock on the door.

Anna smiled faintly. 'Who is it?'

As if it could be anyone else . . .

There was a moment's silence, then: 'Anna?'

She walked across and opened the door. Frank stood there with a bouquet of flowers.

'Frank?' She took the flowers from him. 'Where did you get these? You didn't have them when you stepped out of the taxi.'

'I stole them,' he whispered in her ear, then kissed her neck.

'Stole them?'

He pressed against her in the doorway, his lips still warm against her neck. It was delightful.

'Hmm . . .' he said, as if that were an answer. 'God I've missed you.'

She reached down, felt how hard he was beneath the cloth of his trousers and giggled. 'So I see.'

And then his mouth was on hers and they were kissing, the passion of his kiss surprising her. And when she looked at him, his eyes seemed inflamed.

She shivered, wanting him more than she had wanted him for some while.

'You'd better come inside, or I'm going to have you in the corridor.'

He laughed gently. 'It wouldn't be the first time. Remember that magazine conference up in Scarborough?'

Anna giggled. 'I didn't know you properly then. Besides, I was horribly drunk.'

'And wonderful. I thought of you for weeks afterwards.'

She drew him inside and closed the door, then kissed him again, letting her hand caress him through his trousers, even as one of his hands reached up and cupped her breasts, his fingers finding and caressing her swollen nipple.

This was the best of it. Before it began. When everything was still promise. When your whole body tingled, wanting more, like your skin was on fire and your innards ached.

She wanted this part of it to go on and on, but she knew that Frank already wanted more. He wanted to strip her and touch her and feast his eyes on her, and she loved that too, but she liked this best of all. The beginning.

She let him move her slowly to the bed, then gently push her down, beginning to undress her. And all the while he kissed her, his hands caressing her, his eyes making love.

And then, suddenly, he was inside her. She gasped, surprised, even as he laughed and thrust again.

'You're keen . . .'

'And you're fucking wonderful . . .'

She gripped his shoulders and thrust back at him, loving the feel of him inside her, aroused by the fact that both of them were still only half undressed. Somehow the sordidness of it, the sense that this, what they were doing, was illicit, made it all the more exciting. And as the pace of it quickened, so she found herself making little grunting noises — noises that matched Frank's deeper sounds — and that too excited her. And then, as she pushed against him, Frank came with a shuddering intensity that surprised her and pushed her over the edge, so that she too came, her legs and stomach muscles going into spasm, so that she suddenly got the giggles.

And then Frank was laughing, too; lying there beside her in his half-undress, his handsome face smiling at hers as he laughed.

Slowly the two of them fell quiet. Slowly a sense of wonder came into their faces.

Anna leaned across and kissed him gently, tenderly, on the lips. 'I'm glad you came . . . so to speak.'

'I'm glad you let me. Come, that is.'

A flicker of a smile, then: 'Do you want a bath? I'll wash your back for you, if you like.'

'Anna, I . . .' He shook his head. 'Christ! What am I doing

here? I've got two of my colleagues off sick, I'm behind in my work and—'

She put a finger to his lips, then reached down to touch and hold his half-limp penis.

'You're here because you want to be here. Because you like being with me.'

Frank was silent a moment, studying her face. Then he lifted himself up on one elbow. 'Tell me something, Anna. Why did you phone me?'

'Because I've missed you.'

'No. I didn't mean that. Why now?'

She hesitated, then told him the whole story, complete with the argument in Barbara's conference room.

Frank grinned. 'Is that true?'

'Every last word.'

'And then you phoned me?'

She nodded. 'I felt like a fuck. And I thought to myself, Who gives the best shag in London? And you know what?'

'My name sprang to mind?'

Anna smiled. Frank's penis was now stiff and hard where it rested in her hand. 'Come on,' she said. 'Strip off. We can have a quickie in the shower and then I'll let you get back to the office. But you're not going anywhere until I've had you again.'

It was well after eleven and Mandy and Anna had already got through two bottles of wine. As Anna uncorked a third, Mandy wandered through into her kitchen.

'So do you think there's any future in it?'

'Frank, you mean?'

'Yeah . . . I mean, if he's happy at home.'

Anna shrugged, then filled a fresh glass and handed it to Mandy. 'Probably not. But I take each day as it comes these days. And sometimes it works and sometimes it doesn't.'

'And when it doesn't?'

'I work. Or get pissed.'

Mandy raised her glass. 'Thanks.'

They had done Mandy's CV. Or, rather, had *invented* one. Because when it came down to it, Mandy's employment record was more of a handicap than a recommendation. And Anna had also shown her how a word processor worked and what Word For Bleedin' Windows was — or WFBW, as they now called it!

'That's all right,' Anna said, touching Mandy's arm fondly. 'You'd do the same for me.'

'If there was anything I *could* do for you.'

'That's not the point,' Anna said, stopping to knock back half her glass before she refilled it again. 'If you could, you would. And that's what matters.'

Anna had told Mandy all about the incident with Barbara Stannard earlier in the day.

'Friendship!' Mandy echoed, raising her glass in a toast and almost breaking it as she knocked it against Anna's.

They wandered back through and sat down again, Anna on the long sofa and Mandy in the high-backed leather chair. The main lights were off in the room. The only light was from a tiny lamp in the far corner.

'You know what, Mand?' Anna said, a slight slur in her voice now.

'What?'

'You ought to get out more. Make the most of your freedom.'

'You mean cruise around lookin' for a shag?'

Anna giggled. 'Do I?' She considered a moment, then: 'Well, it'd be a start, certainly. But I don't just mean that. It'd do you good — build your confidence — if you joined a few clubs.'

'Darby and bleedin' Joan, you mean?'

'No. Clubs. Somewhere where you can meet people.'

'I used to go to Riley's when I was younger.'

'God . . . is that still going?'

'So I've 'eard.'

Anna giggled. 'I only went there once, and some guy — a total stranger — walked over and, leaning in to me as if he was going to say something, grabbed hold of my tit.'

Mandy shuddered. 'Ee-uk! So what did you do?'

'I kneed him in the balls, what did you think I did?'

'Got engaged?'

Anna laughed. 'These days, well . . . sometimes I wonder about myself. I mean, I didn't use to be like this. Renting hotel rooms. The old me would have died before she'd even walked up to the desk.'

'Yeah, but we've all changed, ain't we?'

'Some more than others.'

'Meaning?'

Anna shrugged. 'I don't know. It's just that some days I wish there was more to it than this.'

'Than what?'

'Than work. And Frank. And—'

'But you've got a great job, and a lover and . . . well, there's your friends, and this flat. I tell you, in my book you're bleedin' lucky.'

'I know, I know . . .' Anna grimaced. 'I can't explain. It's just how I feel sometimes. As if it's all hollow, and that I'm just filling time. As if . . . well, as if something's missing.'

Mandy looked down, quiet suddenly. 'Yeah,' she said finally. 'Yeah, I know what you mean.'

Anna laughed. 'You know, sometimes I even wish I were religious.'

'Religious? You're havin' me on!'

'No. You see these women and they've got God and they're happy. But me . . .'

'Yeah, but . . . I mean.'

The two woman stared at each other a moment, then burst out laughing.

'Another glass of wine, Mand?'

'Yeah . . . slosh it in!'

Mandy woke, groaning, the ringing of the phone seeming to be *inside* her head. She reached out, fumbling blindly for the receiver until the ringing stopped. Putting it to her ear, she mumbled into it.

'Yeah . . .?'

Someone was talking. Saying something. Mandy rolled over, then, her head splitting, tried to sit up.

It was the wrong thing to do. She let her head fall back on to the pillow.

Shit . . . I feel like shit.

'What?'

The voice hesitated, then repeated what it had said. 'Eleven. If that's OK?'

'What, this morning?'

Again, a pause, then. 'Mrs Evans? I am speaking to Mrs Evans, aren't I?'

'Yeah, no, look . . . I'll be there. Where is it?'

'Stapleton's . . .'

'Right. No. Expect me at eleven.'

And with that she fumbled the receiver back on to the cradle.

For a while she lay there, her eyes squeezed shut, the blinding headache she'd woken with threatening to split her skull in two.

'Christ!'

She couldn't even remember how she'd got home from Anna's. Had she walked back or had she got a minicab?

Mandy felt awful. Like death warmed up. God alone knew how Anna could run a magazine after a night like that!

And then it struck her. Eleven. She'd agreed to go in for an interview at eleven!

She opened her eyes a fraction, squinting at the alarm clock. Nine thirty. Thank God! Even so . . .

Bracing herself against the stabbing pains in her head, Mandy eased herself slowly up again, then shuffled back a little, resting the back of her head against the headboard as the throbbing slowly subsided.

'Jesus . . .'

A shower . . . yes, and coffee, and maybe a new head while she was at it.

Mandy winced. Stewart's? Hanson's? Shit! She couldn't remember where the guy had been phoning from.

Stewart's. It had to be Stewart's.

And if it isn't? she pondered.

Mandy groaned, then, swinging her legs round slowly, placed her feet firmly on the floor. It was going to be a sodding miracle if she could even speak coherently, let alone persuade someone to hire her, but she'd agreed to it now.

'You silly cow . . .'

Yeah, and she'd have to walk there now, because if she tried to drive . . .

Mandy attempted to stand, but her head seemed to shift from side to side, as if it were a balloon filled with water, with a great big weight inside that drifted away from her as she moved.

You better pray, Mandy Evans, she thought, placing her right hand firmly against the wall and trying a second time. 'Cos you're gonna need a fucking miracle simply to get there.

Anna glanced up, looking out across the open-plan office, squinting through the dark glasses she was wearing, only to see her worst nightmare heading straight for her.

'Oh, shit!'

She tried to straighten her desk, like some superannuated schoolgirl caught out by the head prefect. But it wasn't her desk that was in a mess, it was her head.

Why, of all mornings, would Samuelson choose *this* one to pay a visit?

Discarding the glasses, she stood, smiling weakly as the big man pushed the door open and strode uninvited into her office.

He never knocked. Never even said hello. In fact, the man had no manners at all.

'Just what d'you think you're playing at?' he began, looming over her desk like a playground bully.

A dozen possibilities crossed her mind, but all she said was 'Pardon?'

'Barging into our competitors' offices and having a slanging match with another editor, like you were two bitches on heat!'

Anna took offence at that. 'Now hold on!'

'I don't care what you *think* you were doing, I'm not having an employee of mine behaving like some demented idiot and showing us up in public!'

'There was nothing public—' Anna began, but Samuelson shouted her down, his eyes wide with anger, spittle on his lips.

'Now just you fucking listen, will you? This is *my* magazine, hear me? Not yours. And you play by my rules or you don't play at all. Is that clear?'

'Yes, perfectly . . .'

'Good. Now you'll sit down and write a letter of apology, a copy to be on my desk by tomorrow morning latest. Understood?'

Anna simply stared at him. Apologise? To that bitch, Barbara?

She swallowed, then said quietly. 'She stole our best columnist.'

'I don't care if she stole your boyfriend and your life savings, I want you to apologise. And *today*.'

And if I don't? But she knew the answer to that one.

After he was gone, Anna sat there, staring into the air. The door had been wide open throughout their exchange, and everyone in the office had overheard. But for once she didn't care. She was thinking about the letter she was going to write; not to that bitch, Barbara, but to that arsehole, Samuelson, telling him where he could stick his job.

But it wasn't an easy shot to call. She knew she wouldn't get a job as good as this anywhere else. Not for a while, anyway. To quit now would be to throw away fifteen months of hard work, and she wondered if she could discard it that readily. It would be better for her to swallow her pride and knuckle under, and Samuelson knew it, and though her pride might be hurt now, it might be easier to live with that than have to face that uphill slog again.

Besides, now was not the best time to make such a decision, not with the kind of headache she had.

Anna groaned, then, standing, she went over to the door, looking across at her PA.

'Rachel . . . bring me a coffee, will you? Black. Then get Barbara Stannard on the phone. I think we need to talk.'

There had been a time — somewhere in the distant past — when Mandy had been able to type. Never very well — she had always had difficulty using all the fingers she ought to — but enough to get her by. These days, however, you might as well have asked her to take charge of the space shuttle, especially as the results of her endeavour came up on a screen, not on a piece of white paper.

'I'm a bit rusty,' Mandy said, looking at the screen — at

the bodged and misspelled words that resembled the slur of some dyslexic drunk.

Mr Johnson leaned over her slightly, looking at what she'd typed, then laughed. 'Surely *Begrudj* has two *j*'s?'

Mandy looked up at him and sighed. 'Don't take the mick. I know I ain't got the job.'

'You know that, do you?'

Mandy indicated the screen. 'Well, look at it! I mean, what soddin' language is that, for Christ's sake?'

Surprisingly Johnson laughed. 'And the CV?'

'Is a load of cobblers. Me and me mate made it up over a few glasses of wine.'

'So you're not hardworking and reliable?'

'Well, yeah . . .'

'Then you're hired.'

'What?' Mandy stared at him, gob-smacked.

'You heard.'

'But what about the computer . . . the typing . . .?'

Johnson smiled. A pleasant, middle-aged kind of smile. 'We can train you up. You're keen, aren't you?'

'You bet!'

'Then you can start Monday. That is . . . if you want the job?'

'If I want it?' Mandy whooped, then hunched into herself, embarrassed. 'I'm sorry, I . . .'

'No, it's OK. We could do with a bit of sunshine in the office.'

Mandy looked down, quiet a moment, then: 'I don't understand. Were all the others *worse* than me or something?'

And in her mind she had a picture of a queue of dysfunctional cast-offs from the employment exchange sitting in some waiting room.

'Not exactly. It's just . . .' Johnson shrugged. 'Well, I'll be blunt with you. It's not an exciting job and the wages aren't great and . . . well, I'm just fed up with training up youngsters only to see them walk out the door after three months. So I thought—'

'You'd get someone old and desperate?'

He grinned. 'And anyway, I'm a slave to gut instinct rather than the CV.'

'Lucky for me, then,' Mandy joked. 'Then I'm yours . . . for the job, that is.'

Johnson hesitated, then stuck out his hand. Mandy took it.

'Monday,' he said. 'Nine o'clock. We'll sort everything out then, OK?'

'OK,' Mandy grinned, then, on impulse, she leaned forward and pecked his cheek. 'Thanks . . . you don't know how much this means to me.'

Back home, Mandy wandered about her kitchen in a daze. The first flush of amazement had turned into stunned disbelief. She'd done it. She'd actually soddin' well done it!

Going over to the phone, she lifted the receiver, then tapped in Anna's work number and waited to be connected.

When Anna's voice finally came on the line, Mandy gabbled, 'I've only gone and bleedin' well done it, ain't I?'

Anna seemed puzzled a moment, then, excitedly: 'Oh! You've got one? A job? Oh, Mand!'

'Yeah! Great, innit? I start Monday.'

She told Anna about the interview; then, sensing that Anna was either busy or distracted, she said 'bye hurriedly and got off the line.

Switching on the kettle, Mandy looked about her and grinned. No more staying indoors for her. No more boring little housewife. She was going out into the world.

'Independent,' she said, smiling at the thought of it. 'I'm finally gonna be independent.'

The front door opened. 'Mum?'

It was Luke.

'Here, love, in the kitchen!'

Luke came through. He was about to say something, but he stopped, staring at her, surprised by the ear-to-ear grin she was wearing.

'Mum? What's up?'

'I got one! I got a job!'

Luke's face lit up. 'Oh, Mum! That's wicked!'

They hugged.

'Yeah, ain't it?' she said. 'You want a cup of tea?'

Then, realising that the moment warranted more than tea, she said, 'Tell you what? Let's 'ave a glass of wine, eh?'

'Mum?'

'One won't hurt you. I'm sure it ain't the first time you've 'ad a drink.'

'Aww . . . all right.'

Mandy went to the fridge and got out the half-empty bottle she'd left there a couple of nights before and quickly poured two glasses.

'There,' she said, handing Luke his, then, clinking her own glass against it: 'To my brilliant career!'

Luke grinned, then toasted her. 'Yeah . . . good luck, Mum. You deserve it.'

'Hi . . . is Karen there?'

'Anna? Hi. Hang on, I'll get her for you.'

As Anna waited, she stared across the room at her reflection in the mirror on the far wall. There she was, Anna Nichols, as others saw her, successful, capable, attractive. She had everything a woman of her age might desire, but sometimes it all felt like nothing. Some days she felt as distant from herself as she was from that image in the glass.

'Anna?'

Karen's voice broke her reverie. 'Oh, hi . . . I wondered if you fancied a drink?'

'What, now?'

'Yes. I thought we might talk.'

'I . . . look, it's difficult.

'Oh . . .'

The dismay in Anna's voice must have registered, because there was a pause, then: 'Look, give me a few minutes, will you? I'll phone you back.'

'OK. 'Bye.'

Anna sat, wishing now that she hadn't phoned. But if she couldn't speak to Karen, who could she speak to? Not Susie, for right now Susie was wrapped up in her baby. And certainly not her mother. No. Her mother would have said what she always said: 'You should have married Callum. You should have made a go of it.'

And maybe she should. Maybe she should have given up everything and gone to live with him in New York. To be his kept thing while he travelled the world, being the glamorous international photographer. But she knew it would never have worked. It would have been at the cost of her self-esteem, and nothing — *nothing* — was worth that.

Anna paused, about to question that in her mind when the phone rang. She took a long breath, then picked it up.

'Karen?'

'Hi, Anna. Sorry about that. Where do you want to meet?'

'The Crown?' Anna glanced at her watch. 'In half an hour?'

'OK. See you there.'

Karen was waiting for her at one of the corner tables. As Anna went across, Karen stood, embracing her.

'Hi . . . what's up?'

Anna shrugged, then sat, setting her handbag down on the table by her. 'Everything,' she said vaguely. Then, as if she had to start somewhere, she added, 'I'm thinking of quitting my job.'

'*Anna?*'

'It's a long story . . .'

Karen smiled sympathetically. 'Then let me get the drinks in.'

Yet as Karen got up to go to the bar, Anna reached out and held her arm. 'Are things all right . . . you know, between you and Chris?'

Karen glanced away. She sighed then. 'Look, let me get the drinks. I think I need to talk as much as you.'

An hour and three drinks later, the two women were still locked in conversation.

'No,' Anna was saying. 'I don't agree. You *know* what you want, even if it's hard sometimes to get it. For you, life's relatively simple. But for me . . . well, most of the time I'm not even sure what it *is* I want. Do I want to be free or do I want to be involved with a man? Do I want a job that's challenging or one that gives me more time? Do I want to stay here in London or do I want to travel the world. Do I want to have a baby or will that be too disruptive?'

'And do you?'

Anna picked up her glass. 'Do I what?'

'Want a baby?'

Anna took a long breath, then nodded.

'And Frank?'

Anna laughed sourly. 'Frank's got four. What would he want with another one? It would only be an embarrassment to him.'

'Then dump Frank.'

'Dump . . . Frank?' It was such an un-Karen-like thing to say that Anna simply stared at her.

'Yes. Dump him and find someone you *can* have babies with. If that's what you want.'

'But Frank's handsome, healthy, intelligent. He makes me laugh. And in bed . . .' She shivered. 'If he were ten years younger . . . and single . . . he'd be perfect.'

'But he isn't.'

'No. He isn't.'

'So look elsewhere.'

Anna drained her glass, then frowned. 'So that's your advice, is it? Dump Frank and have babies?'

Karen grinned. 'It would be less confusing.'

'I'm used to confusion.'

'Yes, but do you want to live with it for ever?'

Anna shrugged. 'Part of me does. Another part of me's shit-scared of it. Like this business with the job. I knew what I should have done, but I didn't. I made my peace. I knuckled under. And sometimes I wonder whether that's what I'm doing in all aspects of my life. You know . . . not making the hard choices.'

'Would it be hard, dumping Frank?'

Anna considered a moment, then nodded. 'He's addictive. Like a good wine. Speaking of which . . .'

She went to stand, but Karen shook her head. 'Look, I ought to get back . . . Chris was . . . well, not pleased, let's say. We've been having a bit of a rough time lately, and . . .'

Anna took her hand across the table. 'It's OK. You go. And thanks. Thanks for being a good listener, as ever.'

After Karen had gone, Anna sat there for a while, cradling her empty glass and thinking about what had been said. Karen was right, of course: the sex aside, Frank really wasn't doing her any good. But it was hard simply to turn her back on him. Harder still when she had no idea who would replace him in her life. Yet until she did . . .

She tapped the empty bowl of the glass with her fingernail, then, standing abruptly, marched across the pub towards the doorway, almost colliding with two young men who were coming in.

'Hey! Careful, sweetheart!'

Briefly his hands were on her upper arms. For the briefest moment she stared into his face and saw that strange, curious smile you sometimes get from a stranger, and felt that anything could have happened. Then he was gone and she was outside, in the half-dark of the lamplit street.

Could she give that up? The adventure of it? The excitement of not knowing what would happen next? Could she just give that up and settle down with someone? Or was *that* what she was addicted to?

Anna looked about her at the empty street; at the blank windows and the rows of painted front doors. There they all were, inside, behind closed doors, playing at happy families, Mum and Dad and the kids, while she was here, outside.

She didn't know who to pity more, them or herself.

Or could she have it all? Her freedom *and* a baby?

She laughed. Preposterous. The very idea of it . . .

Anna looked about her once again, threatened suddenly by the very substantiality of the houses that flanked the road – by the thought that all of this had been built purely for the purpose of having and raising children – then walked hurriedly on, her footsteps echoing after her, as if she were somehow pursuing herself.

The southbound platform of Highbury and Islington station was packed; so much so that it seemed that the only way they could get more people into that long, narrow space was by thrusting them in sideways. Wedged in the middle of that sweating mass of humanity, Mandy recalled a documentary on Japan she'd seen where they did just that.

She groaned inwardly. It was two minutes after nine; she was going to be late. As the train came in — its thunderous roar accompanied by an almost organic movement in the crowd — Mandy clutched her handbag to her chest, trying not to panic.

She'd forgotten this. The only time she ever used the tube was to go up to the West End to shop for special occasions, and then she travelled off-peak. This was like something some sadistic God had devised to test his worshippers.

As the crowd surged towards the train, Mandy was carried along, so that suddenly she found herself just inside the doors, with about nine inches of space between her and the platform. As the doors hissed and began to close, she found herself being ejected, the press of bodies forcing her back on to the platform. In a real panic now, she tried to force her way back on, her voice rising hysterically as she pleaded with no one in particular. 'It's my first day!' she wailed. 'I can't be late!' But no sympathetic crack appeared in the wall of sweating humanity and Mandy could feel the tears of frustration burning the backs of her eyes. Taking a deep breath, she raised her arms in front of her and with brute force, employed them as a battering ram to gain re-entry to the heaving train. Elbowing her way into position, she pushed a short, bald-headed man in front of her into the stomach of a big black youth.

The doors clunked shut. The black youth glared at her, as did the bald man who half turned — as much as he could — and gave her the sourest of expressions.

'Sorry . . .' she began, even as the train jerked and threw her into him again.

Mandy reached up, knocking the back of someone's head with her elbow as she did, and grabbed the overhead rail, her fingers momentarily closing over someone else's, then scrambling along the metal pole to get a better grip.

Shit! she thought, trying not to look at anyone. Why hadn't

she set the soddin' alarm like she'd meant to? Now she was going to look a right prat on her first day, scurrying in after everyone else had arrived!

Yeah, and next time she would walk. Sod this palaver every morning. Besides, the exercise would do her good.

She shifted her feet slightly, treading on someone's toes as she did.

'Sorry . . .'

Again she looked down, a mixture of nerves and excitement making her stomach muscles tense.

She looked up. The black youth was staring at her, nodding his head. For a moment she wondered what he meant, then realised that he was listening to his Walkman. She smiled, and unexpectedly he smiled back.

Yeah, she thought. It's going to be OK.

'Mand?'

Mandy looked up from the machine, then self-consciously removed her glasses and smiled back at the young girl — Cheryl, was it? — who stood there with a mug of steaming hot tea in each hand.

'Yeah?'

'I thought you might like a cup of tea.'

'Oh . . . ta . . .'

Mandy smiled and took the mug, setting it down carefully by the machine. She'd had one of those mornings — mistake after mistake — but Mr Johnson hadn't seemed to mind. 'It'll come,' he'd said patiently, then wandered back to his office, leaving her with young Tracey, who was in charge of the machines.

Right now, Tracey was out to lunch with her boyfriend, so Mandy was on her own. But not, it seemed, for long, as Cheryl settled down in a chair nearby.

'How you finding it?'

'All right,' Mandy said, not finding it hard to say that. After all, everyone had been really nice to her, even when she did the most ridiculous things.

'Don't worry. You'll get the 'ang of it,' Cheryl added, as if she'd read Mandy's mind.

'Yeah,' Mandy said, wishing she could share Cheryl's confidence. It was all right when you were in your twenties, like Cheryl, but when you were coming up to forty . . .

Cheryl hesitated a moment, then. 'Look . . . some of us are going out for a drink after work. It's a regular thing, you know. Anyway, we wondered if you'd like to come along, meet a few of the girls.'

'Me?'

'Yeah . . . or don't you drink?'

Mandy, who had just taken a sip of her tea, almost spat it out again. 'Drink? Me? Not much!' And then she laughed, making Cheryl laugh with her.

'All right,' Mandy said, after a moment, 'count me in. Where d'you go?'

'Oh, only somewhere local. But Fridays sometimes we go clubbin'.'

'Clubbin'?'

'You know. Have a dance and a bit of a laugh. Pull a few fellas if we're lucky . . .' Cheryl grinned.

'Yeah, I can imagine.'

'You should come sometime.'

'Me? Yeah, I can just picture it.'

But the truth was Mandy rather liked the idea. She needed to get out and about a bit, and she liked dancing. Always had done.

Cheryl stood. 'I'll come and see you about five, all right? There'll be five or six of the girls, but don't worry, they're a daft bunch.' Cheryl smiled once more, then. 'OK. See you later.'

''Bye . . .'

Mandy looked back at the screen, noting in passing how she'd added an extra *o* to the word *blocked*, then stared past it into the air, smiling. She was going to be all right. She could feel it in her water.

Part Two

~ *One month later* ~

The late-July sun sparkled off the windscreen as Steve locked up the car, then turned to face Janet. He himself was tense, but, staring at her across the hospital car park, he realised just how isolated she was, how scared.

All he wanted now was for it to be over, one way or the other. He had tried his best to cope with the tension, the mood swings, but Janet was like a time bomb waiting to go off and Steve felt that he, too, was living on the edge. And it wasn't even as though they had been able to comfort one another: at a time when they should have been closer than ever they existed like distant strangers.

'All right?' he said, joining Janet at the top of the hospital steps.

She nodded and turned, making her way inside.

Following the familiar route through the reception area, Janet was struck, as ever, by the sign for the maternity ward, in awe of it almost, and averted her eyes, not daring to allow herself even to think . . .

Walking along the corridor beside Steve, she wanted to reach out for his hand — to have him reassure her — but she couldn't. These past few weeks they had both been walking on eggshells, and in the end it had seemed easier — *safer* — to avoid each another. It had seemed like they were on a course for self-destruction, saying anything — the most stupid things — simply to hurt each other. Janet had no idea why she behaved the way she did. Maybe if Steve had found the right things to say it might have made things easier, or maybe if she had been able to rid herself of the feeling that she might let him down. But it was the uncertainty, the dreadful uncertainty of it all.

Sitting with Dr Clements in his office, Janet and Steve listened in silence while he reminded them of the procedure they would follow for collecting the eggs. Janet recalled every detail of it all too clearly. She had been haunted by the memory of it these past few months in spite of having been sedated throughout.

'Right! Any questions?' he asked finally.

Steve glanced across at Janet but her eyes remained determinedly fixed on the doctor. She shook her head. Steve had accused her once of thinking of Clements as though he were a God, and it was only then that she'd realised that it was probably true. She would have walked on burning coals if Dr Clements had told her to: her life, she felt, was in his hands.

'OK!' he said, smiling encouragement as he levered himself out of his chair. 'I'll get my nurse to show you to your room and you can get yourselves ready.' He glanced at his watch. 'We'll get you to give your sample first, Steve, before we collect Janet's eggs.'

The two of them rose from their chairs as one and followed obediently as the doctor led the way out of the room.

Dressed in blue surgical gowns, their heads covered, they waited. Janet lay on a hospital trolley, her legs pulled up so that her chin rested on her knees, her arms encircling them, hugging them to her.

'I wish they'd get a move on. I can't bear this hanging around,' she whispered, in spite of their being alone.

'Don't s'pose it'll be much longer,' Steve reassured her, though he, too, was feeling the pressure. Most of the time it was Janet who was under scrutiny, who was being examined and monitored, but soon it would be his turn to perform; his only actual participation in the whole process, and he was terrified of fucking it up! Soon he would be given a key and directed along to a room, inside which he would find a selection of dirty videos, porno magazines and a receptacle into which he was expected to come.

Steve's stomach turned at the sound of the door opening and he looked up to see one of the team standing in the open doorway.

The orderly smiled. 'We're ready for you now, Steve.'

'Oh . . . right . . .' Steve answered, moving towards him, avoiding looking at Janet. 'I'd better get on with it!'

And even before the door had closed behind him, Janet could feel the tears tipping over her bottom lashes, the threat of disappointment too much, the longing too great.

Closing the door behind him, Steve slipped the lock. He didn't know if this was the room he had used last time; he guessed they all looked pretty much the same. They had attempted to give it a kind of cosy feel so that men could imagine that they were sitting in their own living room, jerking off over some nubile woman gyrating on the screen. Much the same as any night at home when there was a French subtitled number on the telly, he was feeling horny and the wife was already fast asleep upstairs. But try as they had with the little coffee table, the curtains and the comfy armchair, it still felt like a hospital room and the surroundings did little to relax him.

Squatting in front of the television set, he reached down for the video case. He turned it in his hand and read off the title written in crude capitals along the spine LESBIAN LOVERS. With a mixture of surprise, shame and then relief, Steve felt the first stirrings of interest.

Slipping the cassette into the video machine, he pressed the PLAY button, and with his eyes fixed determinedly on the screen as the opening titles rolled, unzipped his jeans, pulled them down over his buttocks and – with a nervous glance towards the door – sank into the armchair.

It was a Dutch film, with subtitles, as though anybody actually cared what they were saying.

Less than five minutes later – his eyes fixed on the two on-screen 'actresses', who had slowly and sensuously undressed one another so that they now lay end to end, each wearing nothing more than a pair of hold-up stockings – Steve reached across to the coffee table for the small glass receptacle.

It was when the blonde one groaned and made this little movement with her arse that Steve, eternally grateful to her, shot his load into the cup, spilling some down the side.

'Shit . . .'

But it didn't matter. He'd done it! Setting down the container, he wiped himself with the bit of kitchen towel they had provided and hoisted his boxers and trousers up over his bum.

Then, smiling, Steve reached down and ejected the video.

'Nice one, girls.'

'Now you're going to feel a bit of a sharp sting!'

Janet silently winced as Dr Clements inserted the long syringe up her vagina. Beside her, Steve watched its progress on the monitor as the doctor guided it first to one ovary and then the other in an attempt to collect as many eggs as possible. Glancing up at her and seeing how her eyelids were heavy from the effects of the drugs, he was filled with such love for her at that moment that he felt like bursting. Yet that love was also mixed with guilt – guilt that she should have to endure this.

He reached up and squeezed Janet's hand, not daring to look across to where another member of the team sat examining the samples under a microscope. Out of the corner of his eye he was aware of the doctor walking over and looking through the eyepiece; he was conscious of words being exchanged, and then the sound of footsteps – extraordinarily loud – as he approached the trolley.

'Well done!' Dr Clements said, his voice distorted through the blue surgical mask. 'You've got nine!'

'Nine?' Steve could feel a lump rising in his throat. 'Is that good?'

'Not bad. Above average anyway.'

Jumping out of his seat, Steve beamed at Janet, though only his smiling, tear-filled eyes were visible. 'See, Jan! *Nine!* That's bloody brilliant!'

She smiled up at him weakly, pleased almost as much by his pleasure in the news as in the news itself. Even now she couldn't allow herself to get too excited; they still had a long way to go.

'I want to go to sleep,' she said, her fingers closing over Steve's as she closed her eyes.

'OK . . . OK, you sleep,' he said. And as she closed her eyes he lowered his face to hers. 'I love you,' he said softly, but he couldn't be sure that she had heard.

As Susie pushed the pram down Copenhagen Street, heading for Barnard Park, she sang softly to Nathan. He lay there, smiling up at her, one podgy little hand waggling erratically in the sunlight.

In all her life she had never been so happy as in the past few weeks. Nothing she had done, nothing she had experienced, could have prepared her for the depth of feeling she had for her baby boy. If someone had said to her years ago that she could feel this much — after all she'd been through — she would have laughed in their face. But here she was, with not a care in the world, and all of her world encompassed in one tiny, happy smile.

For a week now she had been toying with the idea of coming along to one of the mother-and-toddler sessions at the park, but various things had got in the way. It seemed to take so long just to get out of the door. She could be all ready to leave and the baby would poop his nappy, and then by the time she had changed him, he'd be ready for his next feed. And so it went. Today, however, she had woken determined to go, and as soon as Jo had left for work, she had busied herself, getting Nathan ready: dressing him in his very best for the occasion.

It was a beautiful day. There was a perfect blue sky overhead. Susie looked about her, taking it all in. Once, on days like this, she would have bunked off work and spent the day at the lido, topping up her tan, or in the garden of a pub, getting drunk with some bloke and then staggering back to his place for a fuck. But those days were past. She had changed. She was connected now — to the world and to her mum and dad — in ways she had never imagined she could be. She understood things better now. As she'd said to the girls the other night, she was focused now on what was important in life; her priorities had changed. She had a new perspective: a good, healthy perspective, not the old fucked-up one.

Mandy had laughed at that and told her it would pass as soon as the novelty of having a baby wore off, but Susie didn't think so. Before Jo, she had had nothing. Or nothing worth having, anyway, and even if Jo wasn't a saint, he had given her Nathan. Yes, and he loved them both. And that alone . . . well, it was priceless. There were women who would kill to have that.

Susie lifted her head proudly at the thought, then smiled. The others ought to have kids, she thought, filled suddenly with missionary zeal. Anna needed them. And Janet, too, though Janet was more . . . well, problematical. If only she would relax . . . if only she'd let nature take its course. But Janet was Janet and couldn't relax, and Susie was sad that something as wonderful as Nathan should be the reason that in these past few months they'd grown further and further apart.

But it would be all right in the end. Susie knew it for a certainty. Everything would come good.

She had reached the edge of the park. The mother-and-toddler group was down the hill and along, past the adventure playground and near the football pitches. Turning the pram, she pushed it through the gate. Now that she was this close, she felt a little nervous, but that would pass. Babies were the world's best for making instant friends, breaking down barriers. They were like alcohol in that regard, only without the destructive after-effects.

Susie shuddered at the thought of what she'd done in her past. There would be none of that for Nathan. She'd bring him up right. Yes, and she'd teach him how to treat women properly, and respect them. None of that macho crap she'd had to put up with.

The path branched left. She followed it, seeing the hut a little way ahead. The playgroup was just behind it, facing the soccer pitches.

Glancing across through the wire mesh at the vast expanse of empty tarmac, Susie smiled at the sudden, vivid memories of her youth, hanging round these same pitches with the girls while groups of boys chased a football, seemingly oblivious of their existence until the game was over. Then another game – the mating game – would begin in its most primitive form with members of each sex hurling light-hearted insults at the other, yet where you were always careful to avoid even the most accidental eye contact with the one you actually fancied in case you were found out.

And now she was a mother and approaching middle age! It seemed incredible that it was all so long ago.

Susie wheeled the pram through the gate, then closed it behind her. She could hear the shrieks of children now and the low murmur of adult voices. Pausing a moment, she collected herself, then gave the pram a determined push.

There were about twenty women in all, sitting about in the sunlight in little groups while their toddlers ran about, or slid, or played in the sandpit. Two or three of them, like Susie, had babies in prams, though none, as far as she could see, were as young as Nathan.

There were a few older mums, about her own age, and one or two who were clearly grannies, but mostly they were in their early twenties. More than anything, it made Susie realise just how late she had left things.

As she moved towards them, several of them looked up and smiled at her as one.

'Hello,' one of them — dyed blonde and thin as a rake — said. 'Who's this, then?' And she nodded towards the pram.

'Nathan,' Susie said, smiling down at him, then looking back at the group of women. 'He's six weeks old. A bit young for this really, but . . .'

'Nah! Does you good to get out,' another of them said, getting up and coming round the side of the pram. 'Ah, bless him!'

Susie smiled, enjoying the attention Nathan was getting.

'Big for his age, too,' another of them said, reaching in and gently taking Nathan's hand before beginning to coo at him.

'I'm Susie. Susie Ball.'

'Amanda,' the woman to her left said, smiling back at her. 'And this is . . .'

'. . . Jackie . . .'

'. . . and Rosie.'

'Was it a long labour?' the youngest of them — Rosie? — asked. 'I was nearly thirty hours with my first one.'

'Then you were lucky,' said one of the older women, coming across. 'I was in there two days with my Harry. Had to cut him out in the end. But then that's boys for you, I s'pose.'

Susie laughed, at ease already. 'It weren't so bad, really. Except at the end! Christ! Why doesn't anybody warn you?'

'Because if they did, none of us would go through it, would we!'

They all laughed although each knew that she would endure far worse.

'You forget quick enough, though, don't you?' said Jackie, her emaciated appearance making it difficult to determine her age. 'I mean, look at me! This one's my fourth!'

There was a moment's silence in which there was a good deal of eye contact between the various women, though none with Jackie. Then the older woman smiled at Susie.

'Anyway. Come and sit yourself down, love. He'll be all right there.'

The next hour passed pleasantly. Nathan fell asleep in the sunlight and Susie, for the first time in weeks, found herself almost forgetting him for a time, so wrapped up was she in the conversation.

'Yeah . . .' Rosie was saying, 'said he'd stay with me for ever. But I think he just liked me being pregnant. Found it a real turn-on. Wasn't so keen when I actually had the baby. Some men are like that, apparently. I read it in an article somewhere.'

Susie slowly shook her head. 'You mean he just buggered off? Just like that?'

Rosie nodded. 'And I found out afterwards I wasn't the first, neither. He's got kids dotted all over the place.'

'Dirty bastard.'

'Oh, they're all the bleedin' same,' Geri, the older woman said.

'You can say that again,' Amanda agreed. 'My one stuck around just long enough to give me my second and that was it. He'd had enough. I was holding him back, he said. Restricting his freedom . . .'

'Huh! The old *freedom* bollocks!' Geri said.

The others laughed knowingly.

'Hang on,' Susie said, looking about her. 'You mean none of you lot have got fellas?'

'Oh, I do from time to time,' Rosie said, and winked, 'but yeah, we're all on our own-io.'

'And anyway,' Jackie said, pulling a tissue from her pocket and reaching out with practised ease to grab her passing toddler and wipe the snot from his face without even pausing, 'mine was no bloody help when he *was* there. You know, if I went out I'd have to pay a babysitter even if he was at home. No different to now. Nah! He was only good for one thing!'

'Most of them are!' Rosie added.

'But I tell you what,' Geri said importantly. 'I've never had one that could do it better than I do it myself!' And they all roared with laughter.

But Susie felt a little disconcerted. She'd always imag-ined that she'd had a pretty bum deal in the men stakes, but from what she was hearing here she'd simply been screwed by a fair cross-section of the male population, Gawd bless 'em.

She was about to open her mouth when, from the far side of the playground, a new figure appeared. Susie watched him slowly approach then park his pram beside Nathan's.

'Hi, girls!' he said cheerily.

'Hi, Gus!' Jackie called back in a mildly flirtatious way, then added, 'This is Susie. She's little Nathan's mum.'

Susie exchanged a brief glance with the young father, surprised to see a man here and finding it strangely intrusive.

As she watched, Gus crouched down and began fussing over his child — a pretty little girl of six months or so — then, unfastening the harness, he lifted her out and carried her across to the group, taking a seat beside Geri.

'How's the Monster?' he said, casting an eye over to where Geri's son was charging down a grassy hill dressed as a pirate.

'As you can see,' she said, laughing. Turning towards him, she took the baby from Gus and lifted her into the air.

'Hello, beautiful . . . and how are we today?'

Susie smiled. 'What's her name?'

Gus turned and smiled at her. A kind, perfectly innocent smile. 'Katrina. It was Pat's mum's name. Pat's my wife. Her mum died when she was only eight, so we thought . . .'

Susie nodded. 'That's nice. And you look after her?'

'Three days a week. When Pat's in the office. She's in advertising.'

'How about you?'

'I work from home.' He grinned. 'When this little monkey lets me, that is.' And he took the baby back from Geri and cuddled her close.

Susie, watching this display of fatherly affection, thought of the stories she had just been hearing about men who buggered off at the first hint of trouble, and wondered why blokes like Gus were so different. Was it because their mums had brought them up differently, or was it something in their make-up?

And Jo — her Jo — was he going to be OK? Certainly he loved Nathan, and to see them together was really something.

'Do you find it hard?' Susie asked, wishing Nathan would wake so that she could hold him and play with him.

Gus looked past the child at Susie. 'What? Looking after her?' He shrugged. 'Not really. But maybe that's because I don't have her all the time. I know how hard that must be, like for Amanda here. Bringing up two on your own must be hard work.'

'Gus helps me out,' Amanda added, by way of explaining why she, alone, had been singled out. 'I leave them over at his place now and again. When I need an evening off.'

'Really?' Susie stared at Gus, who was totally entranced by what his young daughter was doing, reappraising him. 'And your wife doesn't mind?'

'Pat? No, she loves kids. We can only have the one, you see.' He shrugged, then buried his face in Katrina's hair, holding her to him as though to remind himself of just how precious a gift she was.

Susie looked down, surprised by his sheer niceness. The blokes she knew simply weren't like that. It was like Gus was a member of a different species altogether. But you could tell from his accent that he hadn't been dragged up on a council estate; that he was educated. And if his wife was in advertising, well . . .

There was a strange little mumbling noise and then Nathan woke and began to yell. Susie jumped up and went over, rocking the pram a little as she reached in and unfastened the strap, lifting him up and cuddling him against her. Instinctively, Nathan turned his face towards her breast.

It was time for his feed, but with Gus about she felt a bit self-conscious. It wasn't easy just to pop out your boob in front of some strange fella. Well, not when it wasn't anything to do with sex. Even after six weeks she hadn't quite acquired the knack of inconspicuous breast-feeding: she aspired to becoming like one of those women — minus the heavy leather sandals and patchwork skirt – that you saw on TV documentaries about New Age travellers, who managed to knit children's balaclavas while effortlessly dangling an infant from their nipple under the cloak of a baggy jumper. Or like those who you tried not to look at in restaurants as they forked a bowlful of spaghetti carbonara into their own mouths while at the same time offering milky refreshment the way Mother Nature intended to some half-concealed baby, defying gravity as she balanced it on her lap without the aid of hidden props.

For Susie, Nathan's meal times resembled a military oper-ation: the breast fully exposed and held up with the left hand, the baby propped up on a pillow in the crook of the right arm and lined up for action, the nipple perfectly positioned in front of the baby's eagerly waiting mouth . . . and then the anguish as he failed to latch on.

Susie looked about her, then, smiling apologetically to the others, took Nathan across and sat just inside the play hut, her back turned on the rest of them as she let him feed.

This, too, no one had told her about. That is, just how satisfying – almost erotic – the experience of feeding was. To have that little mouth sucking on your swollen nipple.

Susie looked down into Nathan's contented face and smiled. 'Come on, then, gorgeous,' she whispered. 'A nice big burp and we can do the other side. Then Mummy can show you off to her new friends.'

Karen set her bag down on the kitchen table, then slumped on to the chair, a feeling of pure despair descending on her.

It was well after six and Chris wasn't there. Nor was there any sign that she *had* been there since they had parted first thing that morning. It was not the first time by any means, but recently Chris had taken to staying out more and more often, and in the past week or so had not even bothered with excuses. When Karen asked where she had been she would simply shrug as though it were none of her business.

But then, Karen *knew* where she had been. Sarah's. Try as she might to conceal it from herself, it was plain now that Chris was having an affair with her ex-lover.

Karen swallowed bitterly. No, there was nothing 'ex' about it. And when was the last time the two of them had made love? Ten days? Twelve? She couldn't even remember.

And maybe that was why she had volunteered to help with the school play. To distract her. To keep her mind from dwelling all the while on what Chris and Sarah were doing, because when she did it was like injecting pure poison into her veins.

Karen shivered. She hadn't known what jealousy was. Nor, truthfully, had she ever thought she would. Before Chris there had been no one to be jealous of, and she had somehow believed — God! how puerile the thought! — that maybe women didn't do that to each other; didn't tear each other apart with jealousy and recrimination, at least, not in the destructive way she had witnessed with most of the heterosexual couples she knew.

But people were people, it seemed, and it didn't matter what their sexual orientation was: the same old problems arose. Love, it seemed, wasn't always enough.

Karen stood, meaning to go across and switch on the kettle, but even in the act of getting up she changed her mind and went through into the living room instead.

There was a full bottle of red wine at the back of the cupboard; a bottle of '95 Domaine de Roueire she'd bought a week ago. She had planned to cook Chris a meal, then run a bath for her and pamper her in front of the fire as in the old days. But Chris had not come home, and the meal she had cooked had ended up in the bin. And when Chris finally *had* come home, she had made up the sofa bed, and in the morning, when Karen had taken in some tea and toast, it was to find that she had already left.

Karen took the bottle back into the kitchen and uncorked it, pouring herself a large glass. Then she sat again, staring at a hole in the wall, trying not to think, not to imagine what Chris was doing. And slowly, very slowly, a tear rolled down her cheek and plopped into her glass.

Karen was curled up in the armchair in the living room, the TV murmuring from across the unlit room, when the front door latch went. She gave a little shiver, then looked at her wristwatch. It was almost eleven.

Chris's footsteps sounded crisply on the wooden planks of the hallway floor. There was the noise of a bag being dropped beside the cloak stand, then silence.

Karen waited, her heart in her throat. To be honest, she was surprised Chris had even bothered to come home this time.

After a moment she sensed rather than heard Chris behind her in the doorway, and turned, looking back at her.

Chris was staring past her at the television, as if its muted images were somehow more important than anything else. In its flickering light, however, Karen could see the indifference in her face, the dullness in her eyes. And when Chris's eyes met hers briefly, there was nothing there for her.

Karen searched for something to say, something meaningful and yet nonconfrontational. 'Hello' might have been good, but to keep it that simple — that neutral — would have been to ignore the bitter hurt she was feeling, the injustice she felt at being shut out time and time again.

Chris hesitated, then made to turn away, as if the moment had passed, yet as she did, Karen finally found her voice.

'So you're home, then . . .'

Chris froze. She was turned away from Karen now. There

was a movement in her cheek muscles, and then she turned back, her face hardening.

'I was working late.'

'Crap . . .'

'I *was* working late. Organising the exam papers for year nine, if you must know.'

Karen unfurled her legs and turned, facing her. 'Until half ten? Rubbish! And anyway, why didn't you phone? You're always telling *me* to phone!'

Chris was silent. Her chest rose and fell, rose and fell, like she was holding in her anger.

Karen swallowed, then said it. 'You've been to Sarah's, haven't you?'

'No . . .'

'You have. I know you have. You're seeing her, aren't you?' Karen paused, then, in a smaller voice: 'You're sleeping with her.'

Chris looked down. She was silent a moment, then gave a great huff of a sigh. 'I'm going to bed. Don't wake me.'

'Oh, don't worry. I won't fucking wake you. I mean, what would be the fucking point?'

There was a flash of anger in Chris's eyes at that, but she kept her voice calm. 'I didn't start this, you know.'

Karen stared at her, incredulous. 'No? So it was me drove you to her, was it?'

'Yes! If you *must* know. At least I don't have to pretend with Sarah! At least I don't have to sleep on the bloody sofa bed!'

The admission of the affair stung Karen. For a moment she was on the verge of tears. Then, anger overcoming the pain she felt, she stood. 'So this is what it's all about, is it? I promised you I'd tell them.'

'Yes . . . a month ago. And have you?'

'I . . .' Karen shuddered violently. 'You're just *so* unfair.

You screw around and try to make out like it's all my fault.'

'Excuses . . . that's all you ever give me. Excuses.'

'Don't you dare turn it on me! They're *not* excuses. You're the one with the excuses! You still love her, don't you?'

Chris stared resolutely ahead.

Karen's voice was shrill and barely under control. 'Admit it, for Christ's sake! You love her, don't you?'

Still Chris refused to meet Karen's wretched gaze.

'This weekend. I'll go down and see them. I promise. But you have to promise not to see her.' Chris looked away. 'Chris . . . you're destroying me . . .'

She saw how Chris looked at her, surprised. There was a hesitation, then. 'You promise?'

Karen nodded, the tears beginning to flow.

Chris stared at her, long and hard – the words hanging in the air between them until, finally, she turned away.

'I'm going to bed.'

Anna slipped out of bed and pulled on her silk kimono, then tiptoed across to the open doorway.

The flat was in darkness, but a full moon shone through the window of the living room. She went across and stood there, looking out along the deserted street. In the pale yellow wash of the streetlamps she could make out Frank's Volvo, parked between a van and one of those newfangled Ka's.

For a time she simply watched, tempted to leave him where he was, asleep in her bed – tempted not to wake him until it was too late, so that he would have to go home and face the music. But she knew she wouldn't. In a while she would go back into the bedroom and rouse him, then sit there as he dressed, watching him, knowing he was returning to her.

That was the mistress's lot: to watch her man leave, knowing that within the hour he would be asleep beside another woman, her only consolation — or perhaps it was her punishment — the warm imprint of his body on her crumpled sheets.

She half turned, staring back across the shadowed hallway at the bedroom door, wondering for a moment if he ever made love to *her* when he went home. But it was something she could never ask; one of those great unspokens that existed between all couples. And if he didn't, what excuses did he make?

It made her wonder if Frank's wife knew, and if she did, what she thought about it.

Anna shivered, then turned away from the window, making her way out into the kitchen. One day she would do it. One day she would leave him there and not wake him, and in the morning he would leave her, to face the consequences. Maybe that was what he wanted; for Anna to force it out into the open. Maybe. But she didn't think so.

Anna opened the fridge door and stared into the brightly lit interior. She was hungry. Sex always made her hungry. Fried-egg sandwiches were best, but right now she couldn't be bothered. A yoghurt then . . . or maybe one of those individual cheesecakes she had treated herself to.

She took one out and, going over to the table, sat and ate it, using her fingers, sucking the rich, creamy mixture from her warm flesh.

Tonight she had cooked for him; had made him a full three-course meal, eaten in candlelight, the wine flowing freely. And afterwards she had spoiled him further, making him come in her mouth, then, after a brief rest, had roused him again and, taking him to bed, had made love to him, slowly.

It had been an *almost* perfect evening.

For now he had to go.

Anna sighed, wondering not for the first time why she did

it. Why did she carry on with Frank when it was clearly going nowhere?

Because of how he made her feel. And, if she was being brutally honest with herself, because she hadn't exactly been mown down in a rush of eligible bachelors wanting to whisk her off her feet.

Anna smiled. For all the flaws in their relationship, there was no doubting that when Frank was with her, it was as if no one but she existed. He made her feel special; made her feel wanted. It was only when he was gone that she began to doubt it all; began to think of it as a game they both played, where the rules had been agreed without ever being discussed.

And then, briefly, she would feel cheapened by the thought of what they were doing.

She looked up. Frank was standing in the kitchen doorway, yawning.

'Hi,' he said. 'What's the time?'

Anna smiled. 'Just gone twelve. I was going to wake you.'

Frank came across and stood behind her, his hands resting on her shoulders, his chest pressed against the back of her head. She could feel his warmth and closed her eyes, nuzzling back against him.

He laughed gently, then tilted her head back, meeting her lips with his own.

'I ought to go.'

She reached behind, tracing the line of his haunches until she came to what she was searching for. As she'd thought, he had a full erection.

'Are you sure?'

'Oh, you're going to kill me with kindness, you know, sweet Anna.'

Anna closed her eyes again. She loved the way he said that. But now she was gently stroking him, tracing the full length of his swollen penis with her fingers, and though he had said he must leave, she could feel that it was the last thing his body wanted.

What will you tell her? she wondered, as her fingers wove their delicate spell. Was it a business dinner this time, or was there a rush job at the office? And would he wash away the smell of her before entering the marital bed?

'Anna, I . . .'

She let go of it, then stood, turning to face him, allowing her robe to fall open so that he could see the naked form of her beneath. Then, confident that she could keep him at least a brief while longer, she reached out and took hold of it again, moving her fingertips gently over its bulbous tip as slowly she drew him back towards the bedroom.

Standing in front of the mirror in the ladies' powder room, Mandy stared hazily at her wristwatch, then grimaced.

Shit! It was nearly half twelve already!

The music was muted here, but the steady boom of the bass was present beneath everything. Hastily applying a new layer of lipstick, Mandy pushed her boobs up inside her wonderbra, then went outside again, to join the fray.

The girls were over by the bar. Grace and Jill had already paired off with some fellas they'd met earlier and were tickling tonsils on the dance floor, but that still left the four of them, and with only an hour to go before chucking-out time they'd have to get a move on or they'd be going home alone.

Mandy looked about her as she crossed the packed floor, eyeing up the totty. Most of them were after much younger flesh, but there were always one or two who'd make an approach.

As she stepped back among the girls, Tracey leaned close.

'I think you've got an admirer, Mand.'

Mandy tried to act casual. 'Yeah?'

'Guy over there in the jean jacket. Couldn't take his eyes off your arse when you walked past.'

Mandy sniffed, then took her mirror from her handbag and, turning slightly, studied the said guy for a moment before closing up the mirror.

He was young — thirty at most — and as blokes went he was nothing special, but when it got to half twelve you learned not to be too fussy. And it helped if you had your Smirnoff glasses on: everyone and everything looked better after eight vodkas.

She smiled at Tracey.

'Well?' Tracey asked. 'You up for it?'

'We'll see.'

Tracey giggled. 'Have another drink. Get you in the mood.'

'I'm always in the mood!'

'Why do you think she spends so much time doin' her washin' when she's at home?' Julie chipped in. 'That spin cycle works a treat, don't it, Mand?'

'Who needs a spin cycle! Standing in my basement when the trains go underneath's enough for me! It don't take much, you know, when you get to my age!'

Leaning closer, Tracey whispered conspiratorially. 'Eh up . . . here he comes.'

Mandy felt her heart begin to beat faster. She'd done this a few times now, and you'd think she'd have got used to it, but it was still a bit of a nerve-racking moment.

'All right girls . . .' Then, turning to Mandy. 'D'you fancy a drink?'

It was bland, but still Mandy felt a thrill pass through her. The chatting up, the chase. In her recent and limited experience it was often more exciting than what came later.

'Yeah, all right . . . a vodka and tonic, thanks, but just a single. I don't want to fall asleep.'

She saw how he did a double-take on that, then smiled at her. 'Name's Pete,' he said.

Great, she thought, letting him take her hand and kiss it. Just my luck!

'Mandy,' she replied, aware of the girls turning away from her now that contact had been established. The ritual had begun. A ritual that she knew would end with the two of them in bed together, and she felt the excitement mount.

She couldn't help herself. It was like something had been switched on in her, reawakening her sexuality, releasing her to enjoy the freedom she had never experienced in her adolescence, allowing her to taste the heady aphrodisiac of transient desire. She wanted to be daring, to experiment in a way she never had when she was younger. To be like Susie had been. And who was to blame her?

She watched him go to the bar, noting a slight stockiness to his build. He had a thick neck and short, almost crew-cut hair. As for his dress sense it was almost nonexistent. He was a jogging-trousers-and-trainers kind of man. The jean jacket was the best of it!

As he returned with the drinks, Mandy smiled. At least the bugger wasn't ugly. He had nice hands and a moderately nice nose. Piggy eyes, though, and a poor complexion, but hell, when you were touching forty you couldn't afford to be too choosy. And there was always the light switch!

'Where you from?' she asked, conscious of his eyes on her cleavage and enjoying the attention.

'King's Cross. I've got a flat.'

'You live alone or what?'

It was up-front, but then she had learned that in this business you didn't piss about with small talk.

'Yeah,' he said, grinning and showing his uneven teeth.

'What's it like? Nice?'

'Yeah,' he said. 'It's rented, but I done a bit of work on

it. Built in some wardrobes, put in a shower and stuff, you know.'

'So,' Mandy grinned, 'you're a bit of a do-it-yourself man, are you?'

'Yeah . . . Yeah! I s'pose I am,' he said, edging a little closer and holding out his hands for her inspection. 'Look at them! They're workman's hands, they are!'

Mandy ran her fingers over his callused palm, then lightly, delicately, up each of his fingers. 'Well, how d'you fancy showin' me some of your handiwork?' she said seductively.

From out of the corner of her eye, she saw the other girls put their hands over their mouths to contain their giggles.

Well, what the hell, Mandy thought. We're both grown-ups. We both know what the score is, don't we?

He stared at her a moment, obviously aroused, then: 'Yeah . . . Great.'

She watched him quickly finish his drink and set the glass down on the bar, then turn back to her, laying his hand proprietorially on her arm.

There, easy, eh? Mandy thought, as she allowed him to pull her closer.

'See you tomorrow, girls!' she called over her shoulder as they began to make their way towards the exit.

And even as she said it, she felt his hand drift down her back and grip her waist. She breathed in.

'You got a car?' she asked, meeting his eyes and grinning.

'You bet I have, darling,' he said, dropping his hand down to cup her buttock. 'And I'm gonna drive you to heaven.'

Mandy reached up over her head with both hands to hold on to the top bar of the iron headboard, at the same time pushing her pelvis up into the air to meet his thrusts, trying hard to ignore the first twinges of cramp that were developing in her right calf.

He had been going at it for over an hour now, and while at first it had been rather pleasant, now it seemed almost a test of endurance. If this was the road to heaven, then she'd settle for somewhere a lot nearer home. Say Canvey Island, or Watford.

She had tried gently stroking his arse and then sucking on his nipples. She had even tried the old trick of wrapping her legs around him, her heel tucked into his crack as she pushed him into her, but all to no avail. He steadfastly refused to come, and only her best efforts had stopped him going limp.

Damn you! she thought. Why do you silly buggers have to drink so much?

But she knew the answer to that one. If they didn't drink so much, they'd not get up the nerve to make the approach in the first place, and Mandy had to admit that a bloke had to have cast-iron balls to chat up a group of hard-nosed bitches like her and her mates.

As her mind drifted away from the physical act, Mandy reminisced on her last four weeks of adventures.

Never in her life would she have imagined what she had done this past month. Before the end of June she had only ever slept with two men. Now, as the end of July rapidly approached, she was almost into double figures!

Fat men, thin men, young men, old men. She'd had them all these past few weeks. Even a bald Greek she'd met in the chip shop in Upper Street! It had got to the stage that when Luke had asked her why she was out so much, she had had to make up a story on the spot about how one of her new workmates was sick, and how she'd volunteered to help out by minding their baby from time to time.

The one thing she hadn't done — yet — was take one of these fellas home. What she did away from home was between her and the bedroom walls, but she didn't want Luke sitting in judgement of her. Not that he would necessarily disapprove, but she wasn't prepared to risk it.

Mandy blinked, coming back to the moment. There was suddenly a bit more urgency in the guy's movements. He was gasping now, like he'd run nine laps and was heading into the last bend. Yes, she thought, smiling to herself, and he was a lot harder suddenly. All she had to do now was push him over the edge.

Keeping from giggling, Mandy began to groan, like she was suddenly in the throes of the most extreme passion. 'Oh, yes . . .' she hissed. 'Oh, yes . . . God, yes!'

Bingo! It was like someone suddenly put an umbrella up inside him. He went all stiff and straight and his face distorted, like he was choking, and he made this distinct gargling noise.

Mandy, caught up in the moment, kept going and, to her surprise, found herself coming, the groans — which had been faked only moments before — suddenly real as she grabbed hold of his fleshy buttocks and pulled him down into her, grinding him against her, like he was some kind of mechanical toy.

Five minutes passed. They lay there side by side, exhausted and silent, the sweat drying on their bodies. There was nothing to say. Nothing now but to wait and maybe do it again later on.

This was the bit she didn't like. The bit she found embarrassing. Because most blokes, once it was over, didn't know what to talk about, and they didn't really like you to talk, either. Didn't want to hear any personal stuff. No. They wanted to sleep. Either that or they wanted to wait half an hour and then have another go — if only to say to their mates that they were at it all night.

She turned slightly, looking down at how her body lay against his. It was so strange, and no matter how often she had done it these past few weeks, she had never quite got used to 'après sex' — of coming to her senses and finding herself lying there naked beside a stranger. If anything was obscene, it was this, because this was oddly more intimate than any of the heaving and grunting. Yes, and that was why she found it harder, because while they were doing it it didn't matter who she was or what she looked like. The bloke she was with didn't give a shit. All he wanted to do was shoot his load. But afterwards . . .

Mandy shivered but lay still. She had had the sudden urge to get up and get dressed and go home, but she knew she would stay.

Because, bad as this was, at least she wasn't alone. At least she could pretend she had someone, even if it was just a fella she hadn't met before that evening and would probably never see again . . .

Mandy went very still, listening, then smiled. He was snoring. It wasn't so different from being married, after all!

Slowly, careful not to wake him, Mandy eased herself up and off the bed, then tiptoed through to the bathroom. Sitting there, having a pee, she thought about the whole strange business of one-nighters. She'd never understood before — never seen the attraction in it — but now she began to see just why people did it. Sure, it could be sordid, but it was also exciting. Exciting to be naked in a stranger's bathroom in the middle of the night, to dry your body on a stranger's towel, to wash your hands with his soap, holding the lather to your nose to breathe in his fragrance. And people needed excitement. They needed it as much as they needed food and drink if they were to feel truly alive!

And though the excitement faded as the miserable reality took hold, still it was there, eternally renewable, like a drug.

Mandy let out a long breath, wondering if that was what

it was. She had read of sex addiction – and who wouldn't want to shag Michael Douglas? – but she'd never considered it a serious problem. Not until now. Now she found herself thinking about it most of the time. Looking forward to the next night out so she could experience these feelings all over again.

And in between times she would fantasise, comparing them. The different things they did. The things they said. Their own personal little tricks.

That was, when they had any. The guy tonight clearly didn't have a clue. His idea of foreplay had been opening the car door for her.

Mandy giggled, then reached for the loo roll. If he didn't wake up, she'd get dressed and make her way home. That was the other advantage of going back to his place. You didn't end up getting lumbered; having to endure sharing the bathroom the next morning, or worse, breakfast!

But if he should wake up?

Mandy smiled to herself, then stood, feeling the slight tingle of anticipation in her groin.

This time *she* would be on top!

Jo staggered up the steps then stopped, swaying from side to side as he searched his pockets for the front-door key. Sod it! Where was the fucking thing?

'Ah . . .'

He took a further step towards the door, then put out his right hand to steady himself against the railings. As he did the key got knocked from his hand and clattered away into the darkness.

'Shit!'

Then, realising he was being much too loud, he put a finger to his lips, shushing himself.

Slowly, like a man with a double hernia, he lowered

himself on to his hands and knees and began to search. Knocking a milk bottle, he just about caught it before it went rattling away, then, more carefully, he groped beyond it.

There!

He lifted the key up in front of his face, grinning with delight, then let out a long belch.

'Fucking good evening . . .' he said quietly. 'Nice lads . . .'

Jo straightened up, resting there on his knees a moment, then, placing the key between his teeth, clawed himself up the railing until he was standing once again.

He took another unsteady step, his forehead banging against the glass panel of the door.

'Shit!' he said through clenched teeth.

Slowly, his left hand searched the smooth wooden flank of the door until he found the lock. Then, keeping his hand there, he reached up with his right hand and took the key from between his teeth and, using his other hand as his guide, slipped it into the lock.

The lock turned, the door slowly creaked open.

'Shh . . .' he said, speaking to no one but himself. 'Mustn't wake the baby . . .'

He was pissed. In fact, he was more than pissed: he was in that state of insobriety the locals called 'rat-arsed'. To get a key *near* a lock, let alone *in* a lock, in his condition was a work of supreme genius. Or luck.

And now his luck gave out as, forgetting where he was, he rested on the door and, losing his balance, fell head first into the hallway.

The clatter as the hall stand went over was enough to wake the dead, yet as he pulled himself up — expecting Susie's angry voice, maybe, from the top of the stairs — all he could hear was the silence of the house.

''S'awright . . .' he said, crawling towards the bottom step. 'S'fine.'

Then, realising he had left the street door open, he stopped.

'Shit!'

He shuffled about, then slowly crawled back down the hallway. For a moment he rested there, enjoying the coolness of the night air after the stuffiness of the hall. For a minute, maybe more, he just knelt there, his head sagging, his eyes closed. Then, with a start, he realised what he was meant to be doing and reached out, at the second attempt grasping the edge of the door and giving it a little shove.

It clicked shut.

Jo yawned. The kind of yawn that can disconnect a jaw.

For a moment he was tempted to forget the stairs and go to sleep right there in the hallway. But he knew what Susie would say about that. Bad enough that he'd look like shit in the morning, but to be lying there like the proverbial bad penny when she came down was not on.

Groaning, Jo slowly turned himself about, then began the long crawl to the foot of the stairs.

Next thing he knew, he was jerking awake, as the sound of a motorbike roaring past outside woke him. His forehead was on the flat smooth surface of the bottom step and his arm was oddly twisted under him.

For a moment he thought he'd lost his arm and gasped. Then he realised that he'd been lying on it and that it had gone to sleep.

What was worse, he felt sick suddenly. He could taste the last few pints. Could sense them in his throat and in his upper chest.

'Shit . . .'

Staggering up, he hauled himself up the stairs, knowing he had to make it to the bathroom before the feeling overcame him, or there would be all hell to pay.

He made it with a second to hand, even managing to lift the seat before he began to puke.

Again time passed. As he jerked awake this time, it was to the smell of his own vomit and the cool feel of the toilet bowl against his forehead. He was lying on his side, a feeling of great peacefulness cradling him.

Yeah. That was better.

Jo reached up, meaning to pull himself up on to his knees again, but the edge of the bowl was slick with his puke. He grimaced, then wiped his hand against his shirt. But his head hurt now. It pounded, like he had builders in and they were knocking down the walls of his skull to add an extension.

Putting his palms flat against the wall, he slowly climbed until he was standing again. He was feeling less unsteady now. God knew how many hours had passed, but now he felt the urge to pee. He turned, facing the bowl, then grimaced at the mess that faced him. Christ! Had he done that? He would have to clear it up. If Susie saw that she'd have a fit! She was very into cleanliness these days.

The light . . . he'd have to turn on the light.

Jo reached out and tugged the light cord.

'Jesus!'

Squeezing his eyes shut, he reached out and jerked the cord a second time, welcoming the sudden return to darkness.

'Jo?'

Oh, fuck! It was Susie. The light must have woken her.

''S'awright,' he called. 'Jus' 'avin' a pee.'

Jo waited. Nothing. Susie must have gone back to sleep. He let out a long breath, then, his left hand keeping his balance against the wall, he moved closer to the pan, unzipping himself as he did.

'Gawww . . . wonderful!' he said, as the blessed relief flooded through him. Sometimes pissing was every bit as good as sex. And a good crap . . .

Jo giggled, then fell quiet, listening again. Was that the baby?

Silence. Only the silence of the house.

He straightened up, then, tucking his shrivelled cock back into his trousers, zipped himself up and turned, his right foot slipping a little on the wet floor.

There was something he meant to do, but he couldn't recall now what it was.

Oh well, he'd remember it in the morning.

Jo smiled, remembering the punchline of a joke someone had told him that evening. He couldn't remember the joke, but it didn't matter. They'd been nice blokes. Good mates.

Outside in the hallway, he stopped, listening. He could hear Susie snoring and, beneath that sound, the baby's snuffling.

Jo walked across and stood there in the bedroom doorway, looking in, taking in the sight. Susie lay on her side, one arm curled about the baby, who was tucked in tightly against her, his tiny face nuzzled in against her breasts.

He smiled, then felt a strange little ripple pass through him. From where he stood he could see the bare curve of Susie's backside, the exposed flesh of the small of her back where her nightdress had rucked up, and for a moment he felt . . . shut out.

It was hard. No one had warned him how hard this part of it would be. To get by day by day without that. It didn't surprise him that some men strayed or went to prostitutes. But Jo was determined not to. He knew it would be all right in the end.

Time. That's all they needed. Just a little time.

Looking past the two sleeping bodies to the empty narrow strip of bed beyond, Jo blew out a long, shuddering breath, then turned away, heading for the spare room.

As Mandy walked into the machine room at work the

next morning, the girls turned as one and gave her a lusty cheer.

'Marks out of ten?' Bella asked, grinning at her from over her VDU.

'Six,' Mandy answered, taking off her jacket and hanging it on the peg.

'*Six?*' Tracey queried.

'Yeah . . . five for effort, one for turning up!'

There were giggles, but just then Mr Johnson stepped into the room from his office. He looked about him and smiled, as if pleased that his girls were happy.

'What's the joke?' he asked innocently.

Teeth bit into lips, stifling laughter.

'Nothing,' Mandy said, going over to her machine and taking the cover off. 'We're just filled with the joy of living, ain't we girls?'

'We know what you were filled with, and his name wasn't joy!' Hayley said under her breath, setting off further giggles.

But Johnson wasn't going to get drawn into this one; he knew what this lot were like and he wasn't up to their banter. He merely smiled and disappeared back into his office.

This was the signal for a whole new eruption of laughter.

'Well?' Mandy said, even as she switched on her computer and waited for all the goobledygook programming stuff to disappear from the screen, 'What have I missed?'

'Nothing by the sound of it,' Bella said. 'Unless you forgot to collect your Air Miles!'

'And I thought *I* was brazen!' Tracey teased.

'Well, I've got a bit of catching up to do, ain't I?' Mandy said.

'At this rate you're gonna hold the fucking world record!' Carol muttered, and they were off again.

'Literally,' Bella said.

'Ha, ha, ha,' Mandy said, typing in the keyword, then sitting back as the word processor set up. 'Where's Grace?'

'Still in bed, I expect,' Tracey answered, and there were snorts of laughter.

'She phoned in sick,' Bella said.

'Sick!' Mandy laughed. 'She's probably up casualty getting his Adam's apple removed from her throat. I tell you, when those two were snogging, it looked like she was trying to clean out his nasal passages from the inside! And what about Jill?'

'I'm here,' Jill said, coming in at that moment with a tray of coffee. 'And before you ask, he was a fireman.'

Mandy turned and stared at her. 'A fireman?'

'Well, I didn't actually ask, but I'd guess that's what he was. He had a bloody long hose! All soft and squidgy till you pressed the button, then all of a sudden it filled up, went hard and whoosh! – the stuff spurted everywhere!'

'Oh, very funny . . . And I suppose Grace got the milk-man?'

'Eh?'

'You know, two pints please and a red top!'

'Oh, Mand, you're disgusting!'

'Apparently, he was a postman,' Bella said in all serious-ness.

'Yeah,' Tracey said, 'with an urgent delivery!'

Mr Johnson re-emerged as the girls fell about once more. 'Mandy? Can you come and take something down for me?'

Mandy nodded to him, then turned and gave them all a look which set everyone off again.

Inside Johnson's office, Mandy closed the door, then sat, taking out her notepad. She couldn't do shorthand, but then he knew that and spoke slowly. And anyway, the bits she didn't quite catch she made up, and he never seemed to mind so long as the gist of it was all right.

'Ready?' he asked, smiling across at her pleasantly.

Mandy yawned. 'Fire away.'

'OK . . . this is to Mr Vierri at Arrizzo & Fellicci.'

Mandy smiled. 'The gangsters.'

'Mandy . . .'

'Sorry . . . it's just that they always sound like something out of *The Godfather*.' She smiled at her boss. 'You sure they ain't a front for something else?'

'Probably,' Johnson said, smiling back at her. 'Now can we get on?'

'Yeah. Sorry.'

And so it went on. In the four weeks she had worked at Stapleton's she had been transformed from a housewife whose confidence matched her credit rating, to someone on whom the whole office seemed to depend. Oh, she was not as competent as some, nor as efficient as others, yet she got things done and smoothed things over — with a telephone manner that not only charmed customers, but got them to place new orders or introduce their friends. Business was booming and Johnson was more than pleased.

As for Mandy, she thrived on it. Pete and Jason might not need her any more — nor Luke, come to that! — but here she was, if not indispensable, then certainly made to feel as if she was.

For now it was enough. For the first time in a long while Mandy considered herself contented. And sometimes more than contented.

As she went back to her desk, ready to type up her boss's letters, she grinned at the thought of what she'd got up to last night. The second time was certainly an improvement on the first . . .

Mandy Evans, she thought. You're a slapper, you know that?

Across the desk from her, Bella looked up and slowly shook her head. 'Aw, blimey, she's off! Look at her!'

But Mandy merely grinned back at her like the Cheshire cat. 'Sod off and leave a sad old lady alone with her memories!'

It was after ten and Nathan had finally settled. He had woken twice in the night and she had fed him, then slept much later than she usually did, giving him his final feed at nine.

In the last few days they had slipped out of their normal routine, but it didn't worry her too much. After all, the health visitor had told her to try to be a bit more flexible. Nathan wasn't a machine, after all, he was a baby, and if he needed feeding then she should go with that and not worry about trying to get him to sleep through the night at his age. It was hard on Jo, of course, but it wouldn't be much longer.

Jo had already gone. As she showered, Susie wondered how his evening had been. He'd gone out with some friends from work and no doubt had a few. But that was OK. He needed to unwind. And it took the pressure off her a bit.

She felt a tiny twinge of guilt about neglecting Jo. He'd been good, and understanding too, and she knew she ought to think of him. But not yet. She wasn't ready for that yet.

As Susie towelled herself dry she caught sight of her reflection in the mirror. The exercises were going well, and she had already lost some of the flab she'd put on during the pregnancy. Not that she'd want anyone to see her sunbathing just yet, but . . . well, she was on her way to getting back her figure.

She turned, sniffing the air. There was a strong smell of disinfectant.

Shrugging, she went back through into the bedroom and began to dress, humming happily to herself as she did, not watching herself in the mirror as she'd used to, but looking all the while at the reflection of her sleeping son.

Maybe she'd go to the playgroup again today, once she'd done the shopping.

Susie smiled, then pulled on her nursing bra, reaching behind her back to fasten it. Yeah, that's what she'd do. And maybe she'd ask some of them back for tea afterwards. After all, it was about time she made the effort.

Jo groaned, then let his head fall into his hands. He was sitting in the upstairs staffroom, waiting for the kettle to boil.

Coffee. Coffee would be his saviour. If only he could take it intravenously he would be OK.

How many did I bloody well have last night? he asked himself, wondering at his own capacity for stupidity. It had been years since he'd been so pissed. In fact, he could name the precise occasion: the West Ham—Liverpool game in seventy-four when he'd drunk a straight eight pints *before* the game.

Yeah, he thought, but I'm twenty-three years older. My body can't take it any more.

But the funny thing was, in spite of the heavy fog clouding his brain that morning, he knew exactly why he had done it. It had come to him even as he had cleaned out the bathroom that morning. And this was the irony. He'd done it to forget: to numb his growing resentment and frustration. If his life was a football match the score would have been Nathan six, Jo nil. Or maybe Nathan twelve, Jo nil.

The door creaked open loudly.

'Jo? Are you OK?'

It was his boss, McKinnon.

'No,' he answered honestly. 'I feel awful. My head feels like it's filled with concrete.'

McKinnon laughed. 'I didn't think you were on top form. What was the occasion? Stag night or something?'

'Or something,' Jo answered, wincing as he raised his head to meet McKinnon's eyes. But McKinnon wasn't judging him, he realised.

'Jo?'

'Yes, boss?'

'Go home.'

Jo took a long breath, then. 'No. I'll be OK in a minute. A gallon or two of coffee—'

'Jo . . .'

'Yeah . . .'

'Is everything all right? . . . You know, at home?'

Jo shook his head. 'No. No, we're fine. He's great, Nathan.'

'Yeah,' McKinnon said. 'Good. But if there's anything . . .'

'Yeah. Great.'

Jo waited until McKinnon was gone, then slowly stood and made himself a coffee. It was no good moping about. No good feeling sorry for himself. He had to get on with things, and learn to be patient, and Susie would come back to him.

She had to. Had to, or he was done for.

He sat again, staring down at his coffee, then shivered. Why had nobody said? Why had nobody warned him how tough it was going to be on him?

'You fancy a quick one, Mand?'

Mandy grinned at the young woman then shook her head. 'D'you carry a spare liver around with you, or what, Tracey?'

'Can't stand the pace, eh?'

'Too bloody right. I'll see you lot tomorrow.'

Mandy crossed the road, then glanced back at the building, looking up at the windows, making sure that no one was watching her, then, rolling her eyes, amazed that she was actually doing this, she hurried down past the side of the station and along past the taxi rank.

He was waiting there in the usual place. Seeing his bottle-green cab, she felt a small flutter of excitement in her stomach.

Jimmy wasn't much to look at, but he was a decent bloke. Nicer than most of the guys she met, anyway.

As she tapped on the window, he looked up from his paper and smiled at her, like she was just any fare.

'Where to?' he asked as she climbed into the back.

'Chalk Farm,' she answered, playing the game that had grown between them. 'What d'you reckon?'

'What do I reckon?' he said, and started up the engine. 'Let me see, what do I reckon?'

Mandy giggled. She liked Jimmy. She liked the way he was always up for a lark.

'I mean,' he went on, pulling out into the early-evening traffic. 'Chalk Farm's a bit too . . . well, chalky.'

'Green Park?'

'Too green.'

'Wimbledon?'

He laughed. 'Too fucking far.'

'So it's under the arches again then?'

Jimmy glanced round and smiled at her. 'If that's all right with you, missus.' And with that he slewed the cab round and stopped it in front of a pair of the big brown-painted doors.

Mandy watched him get out and unlock the doors, then waited, her heart begin to beat faster, as he slowly manoeuvred the cab inside. She waited as he closed the doors and switched on the lights, then shamelessly slipped off her knickers and lay back waiting for him.

She didn't have to wait long.

'Fuckin' 'ell, Mand. I've 'ad a stiffy all day thinkin' of you,' Jimmy said, as he climbed into the back with her and began unbuckling himself. 'I had this fuckin' woman in the back earlier and she kept crossin' an' uncrossin' 'er legs and I was—'

He grunted as he slipped it into Mandy.

'Oh, shit, that's lovely . . .'

And it was. Jimmy was no fancy man, and he was quick, but he was big for such a short bloke and his sheer urgency was exciting. Mandy gritted her teeth as he thrust into her and tried not to cry out, but it was hard.

Two minutes later and he was done.

'Where you want droppin'?' he asked as he zipped himself up again.

'Tesco's. I gotta get something for Luke's dinner.'

'All right.'

She watched Jimmy get out, then resume his seat in the front and wondered just how this had come about. After all, it wasn't as if she'd been drunk or anything.

'Jimmy?'

'Yeah?'

'How's your wife's chest?'

He grinned back at her, just a taxi driver once again. 'She's all right, Mand. Doctor said it was just a bit of 'eartburn.'

'Oh, good.' And Mandy bent forward, picking up her knickers and placing them in her handbag. 'I was a bit worried about her.'

Anna shut the door behind her, then turned, closing her eyes as she slumped against the wall.

Tired? She was exhausted. In the past few weeks she had worked harder than she'd ever worked before. But now it was done.

OK, bring on the TV advertising, she thought, smiling to herself, pleased that she had proved that bastard Samuelson wrong and shoved his criticisms back down his throat. She was the best bloody women's magazine editor in London, and he knew it.

Yes, she thought, but will it be enough? That arsehole doesn't like me. I know that now.

Anna looked down. There were several letters on the mat,

including a large envelope that bulged like it was five months pregnant.

She bent down and gathered them up, then carried them through into the kitchen and threw them down on to the table. There was a half-empty bottle of wine in the fridge and she poured herself a glass before sitting down.

There was a phone bill and a postcard from her friend Maggie, who was off holidaying in Alaska of all places. There was a reminder card from her dentist and then there was the big envelope.

Anna balanced it on the palm of one hand, as if trying to guess what it was by its weight, then turned it over, looking at the typed address label.

She slid her nail under the gummed flap and slit it open, then held it up, letting the contents tumble out on to the tabletop.

Letters! A dozen or more letters!

And then it clicked, and her heart went all fluttery. These were the answers to her personal ad. She had been so busy that she'd almost forgotten about it.

A week or so ago, angry with Frank about something or other, she had filled out one of those ads and posted it off together with her cheque. She had regretted it almost as soon as she'd done it, especially as she had made things up with Frank that very evening, and told herself she would bin any replies. Assuming that anyone *did* reply, that was.

Anna downed the wine and poured herself another. Then, realising she hadn't done it yet, and wanting to postpone the whole business of actually opening the letters, she walked through and rewound the answerphone, turning up the volume and then pressing the PLAY button as soon as it clicked.

'Anna . . . it's Mummy . . .'

She hesitated, then stood there listening as her mother went on about the tests she'd been having. It was all rather vague, which was typical of her mother, who was rather coy about such things, but she sounded upset. The message ended with a request for Anna to phone her — when she'd time.

'Tomorrow, Mum,' Anna said quietly, then began to walk back to the kitchen.

The next message was from Frank.

'Hi, darling. You still OK for Friday? There's a possibility I might even be able to stay over. Only a maybe, though. Lots of love.'

Anna stopped and turned. Had she heard that right?

There were several other messages, including one from her dentist to say that she had missed her appointment and could she phone to make another?

Anna picked up the reminder card, then swore. She'd forgotten it was yesterday. Then, smiling, she drew the pile of letters towards her.

Men . . . all these men, desperate to meet her. And, cynically, she placed the emphasis on *desperate*. For a moment she thought of Frank and wondered what he'd make of her doing this. Then again, it was none of Frank's business. He had his wife and family and, nice as he was to her, he wasn't going to give that up to come and live with her. And so what she did when they were apart was her business.

Anna flicked through the envelopes, studying the way they were addressed, sorting them into two piles — those that were handwritten and those that were typed — then set the typed ones aside.

She had read an article way back about how handwriting reflected one's personality; how one could gauge what a person was like — how flamboyant, or confident, or how tight-arsed — from the way they formed their letters. Looking at these she felt a slight dismay. Most of them looked as if they had been written by drunken spiders, or by men so sad they were having a wank even as they wrote on the envelope.

Only one caught her eye as being elegant. She set it aside, then, one by one, began working her way through the others.

The first was from some prat called Paul. 'Hi, Anna,' he began. 'I'm twenty-eight with distinctive looks, single and a commodities broker in the City. I own my own flat, drive an MG and like to party.'

'Oh, *do* you?' Anna said, picturing in her mind some smug, besuited type, full of his own self-importance.

'I like good wines, good restaurants and travel,' it went on, 'and enjoy sports and going to the theatre.'

'OK,' she said, sitting back, 'so why hasn't some female City-type swallowed you up and carried you home to Mummy? 'Cos you're a fucking liar with a face like an old tea bag and a winky the size of a Rothman's!'

Anna set the letter aside, then opened another one. This was from a 'home-loving guy' named Geoff. He was – apparently – a middle-aged divorcee and described himself as 'kind-hearted and cuddly'.

'Fat and stupid, and closer to sixty than forty if I'm any judge.'

And broke, no doubt.

'You love home because you're too bloody poor to go out!'

Yes, and desperate, too.

Then again, what was she, to have written the ad in the first place?

Anna sat back, thoughtful a moment. Placing the ad had been a joke, a moment's madness. Or had it?

She worked her way slowly through the pile, noting how they seemed to fall into three distinct types – the Sad, the Desperate and the Too-Bloody-Cocky-By-Half.

The Sad were simply that. Immensely sad. It permeated everything they wrote, everything they said in their letters. She could imagine a convention of them, all wearing woollies that their mothers had knitted, every single one of them long abandoned by wives who, late in the day, had realised just what they had married and had run off with the nearest accountant, in search of excitement.

The Desperate were a different matter. They were not so much sad as sleazy failures who saw this dating lark as a chance to get as much sex as they could without having to pay for it. There was nothing wrong with that, only these guys were so cheesy only a starving mouse would fancy them, and she was no mouse.

The Cocky ones seemed, on the surface, to have everything going for them, only why then were they advertising in the first place? No. They could be defined as the Successful Sad. Unlike the Sad, they were young and – in the world's terms – prosperous. But these were the kinds of guys who thought a meaningful relationship was being on first-name terms with their prostitute's maid.

So what was left?

Anna gazed across at the remaining envelope – the elegantly addressed envelope she had left until last – then, with a sigh of despair, reached over and began to tear it open.

As she did, a photograph fell out.

Anna put the letter down, and picked up the photo, flipping it over.

'OK,' she said quietly, 'so why is a good-looking guy like you advertising in the personal columns? Why haven't you got a dozen women knocking on your door at night?'

Setting the photo aside, she began to read the letter, stopping halfway down to glance up at the address and phone number.

It was almost tempting . . .

Michael. His name was Michael.

Anna smiled, then, reaching into her handbag, got out her mobile phone and began to tap out the number.

* * *

Sunday came, a perfect day, blue skies and a warm, light breeze. As she walked down the street in which she'd been born and knocked on the door of the house in which she had grown up, Karen ought to have felt at peace, yet there was a tightness in her stomach, a fear in her eyes, that no amount of sunlight could relieve.

Her mother answered the door, a great beam of a smile coming to her face as she saw who it was.

'Karen! What a lovely surprise! Come in, love, the kettle's on . . .'

Her dad was at his seat in the kitchen, the newspaper spread out before him, a mug of tea at his elbow. The ruins of his breakfast lay on a white china plate beside the drainer. He glanced up at Karen as she stepped into the room and smiled.

'Hello, love. Didn't expect to see you. How is everything?'

'All right, ta,' she answered, but there was a hesitancy in her voice.

She sat just across from him, watching him read the *News of the World* as her mum pottered about just behind her.

'How's school?' her mum asked.

'It's fine . . . I'm helping with the school play this year.'

'Yeah? And how's Susie? How's her baby?'

Karen turned, looking back at her mum. 'She's great. He's a lovely little thing. You wouldn't know Susie. She's really into the whole thing.'

'Ahh . . . lovely. You've heard Jill's pregnant again?'

'No! Really?' Karen's heart sank. Jill was her sister-in-law. She already had four — three boys and a baby girl. But that wasn't the point. Karen's mum always raised the matter of Jill and her fecundity — 'she only has to sneeze and she's pregnant' — so that she could introduce the touchy subject of when Karen was going to settle down and start a family.

Bad timing, Mum, Karen thought, taking the mug of tea she was offered.

Her mum sat down to her left, between Karen and her dad.

'So to what do we owe the honour?' her dad said, without looking up. 'You're not short are you, love? 'Cos you've only got to say and—'

'No . . . no, I'm fine. I . . .'

She couldn't delay this. The longer she waited the harder it would be. It was now or never.

'I . . . I've something to tell you.'

Karen saw how her mother's eyes lit at that and hated herself for having to disappoint her. She knew her mum wanted grandchildren from her only daughter. She had suffered too many years of crudely unsubtle hints *not* to know. But she was never going to have a baby, because she was never going to have a man.

'Go on,' her father said, looking across at her, neglecting his paper for a moment. 'Don't tell me. You've finally managed to find yourself a fella?'

That was typical of him. That semi-mocking tone.

Oh, she knew that he loved her in his own way.

Which was what made this now so hard.

'It's about me,' she said. 'About who I am.'

'What d'you mean? About who you are?' he said, frowning.

Her mum just stared. She clearly didn't follow what was meant either.

'Yeah . . . about why I *haven't* got a fella.'

'Oh, so it's not wedding bells then? I tell you, it's 'cause you don't try,' her dad said, turning the page of his paper. 'You don't make the best of yourself. You should tart yourself up a bit more. You're not bad . . .'

'Dad!'

He scowled at her. 'I beg your pardon.'

'Dad, please, listen to me. This is hard enough as it is.'

Her mother seemed to be shrinking into herself moment by moment, but still she said nothing.

'I've got something that I need to say. Something I've been wanting to . . .' She looked up into their bewildered faces and in that split second could not help but feel pity for them. She took a deep breath. 'I'm a lesbian.'

There. She'd said it. She hadn't *imagined* saying it, she had actually *said* it.

She glanced from one to the other, seeing the stunned look on each of their faces.

Her dad opened his mouth then shut it again.

'Do you understand?' she said, as if it hadn't been clear enough. 'I'm . . . well, I'm living with another woman. With Chris. We . . .'

Her courage failed her. The look in her mum's face was awful, and her dad . . . well, her dad looked like he'd been poleaxed. Only it wasn't funny. His eyes looked distant suddenly, empty.

And then, without a word, he stood and left the room. Karen closed her eyes, wishing now that she hadn't come, that she'd left them in blissful ignorance, but it was too late.

The front door slammed. A moment later she heard the car start up. Karen went to get up, but her mum stopped her.

'Leave him,' she said, her tone cold, like something had died in her.

'Mum?'

But her mother merely shook her head then stood, going over to the sink to begin the washing up.

The tide was out, the Thames estuary a flat expanse of mud beneath the late-morning sun. There was the distant shimmer of water but it was far out, halfway towards the Kent coast.

To the right of the almost deserted car park, on the side wall of a single-storey cottage, the fading painted face of a young woman beamed down, like a slowly vanishing ghost, advertising some product from years before.

To the left a stack of lobster baskets were piled drunkenly against the heavily rusted doors of a long-abandoned garage. A rectangular sign — CASTROL — was riveted to the brickwork next to it, its green paint blistered and flaking, a filigree of orange forming a crescent up its right-hand side. Nearby, where the petrol pumps had once been, were now a series of white stumplike bases, like upturned bidets embedded in the cracked and weed-strewn concrete.

Despite the heat, it was a forlorn place, stranded as it was between the great sprawl of London and the faded glories of Southend. A non-place. Yet it was here, years ago, that they had come in the holidays. Here, when the place was not quite so dead as now, that they had spent some of their best times.

The polished red Allegro looked out of place in that setting. It looked almost as if some underage joyrider had stolen it and dumped it here at the very heart of nowhere, but that wasn't so, for an ageing man — a big man, with neat-cut dark hair and a manual worker's build — sat in the driver's seat, his broad shoulders slumped forward over the wheel.

It was quiet. The seabirds were far out in the central channel, the traffic on the Southend road a good three miles distant. Quiet. So quiet that one might have thought the world had ended.

Yet there was a sound. It came from inside the car. From the man slumped over the wheel.

Looking closer, you could see how his shoulders rose and fell in a strange jerky fashion; how, from time to time, he seemed to lift himself slightly before yet another shudder overcame him.

Looking closer you could see the desolation in his face.

In his car, forty miles from home, Karen's father sat and cried.

Recovered now from the effects of the sedatory drug, Janet sat beside Steve, waiting for Dr Clements's news. Replacing the telephone, he looked up at them and smiled.

'Well, good news! Six have fertilised and four are doing better than the others. Those are at six-cell stage so they're the ones we'll select from.'

'Is four good?' Janet asked uncertainly.

'It's more or less what we'd hope for. Now . . . unless you have any more questions, we'll see you in a couple of days. Oh . . . and maybe I should remind you that there should be no intercourse for a fortnight.'

Janet's laugh was natural. 'I don't s'pose we'd remember how to do it, anyway!'

Steve smiled, more at the sound of her laughter than at what she was saying, and as they walked down the long corridor towards the main entrance, he placed his arm around her shoulders, pulling her close. And this time she did not shrug him off.

'There you go, son, get that down you.'

Bobby Fuller set the pint down in front of Jo, then sat facing him, a broad smile on his face.

'So what's up, then?'

Jo sighed, then blew out a breath. 'Oh, I don't know. Nothing I s'pose. It's just Susie . . . she's changed.'

Bobby looked at Jo as if he was completely dumb. 'Of course she's bleedin' changed. That's what women do. You marry them, they change. You give them a baby, they change. It's only us men who stay the same.' He lifted his pint. 'For ever young, that's what we are.'

'Yeah, right, but . . . well, is it, like . . . *permanent*?'

Jo had to wait while Bobby sank half his pint, then extravagantly wiped his mouth with the back of his hand. 'Lovely drop of ale, that!' he said. Then, as if he'd only just heard what Jo had said, he nodded. 'Honeymoon's over, Jo, me old mate. Real life's started.'

'So where does that leave me?'

'Where it left all of us. Floating around like a spare part. You've gotta take care of yourself now, boy.'

'So what are you suggesting?' Jo's brow furrowed as he struggled to decipher his father-in-law's advice.

'Well, once you accept that for the time being you're gonna take second place to the little 'un . . .'

Jo groaned. He supped at his own pint in a desultory fashion, like it had suddenly lost all its savour.

'Once you accept that,' Bobby went on, 'there are some consolations.'

'Yeah?' Jo looked up hopefully.

'Yeah. You can get away with bleedin' murder, for one thing. You see, deep down they *know* they're neglecting you but they can't help it — hormones or something, they reckon. Anyway, that makes 'em feel guilty. 'Cos, like, before the baby came along you were probably at it like rabbits . . .' Bobby Fuller put up a hand. 'No details, please, this *is* my daughter we're talkin' about . . . but it's true, ain't it? One moment it's the Kama-bleedin'-Sutra, the next . . . wham! Nuffin'. You're a bleedin' monk!'

Jo looked down, a sad, almost sheepish expression on his face.

'All I'm sayin',' Bobby went on, getting to his feet, 'is that you get used to it.' He grinned, then lifted his empty glass. ''Nother pint, my son?'

Jo smiled tightly, then made to stand. 'I'll get these.'

'No you won't. You keep your money in your pocket. This is my shout.'

He watched Bobby a moment as he stood at the bar flirting with the barmaid and smiled to himself. He liked Susie's dad a lot, but he didn't want to *become* him. Neither, for that matter, did he particularly want Susie to become like her mum. But fate had other ideas. As he was beginning to find out, life seemed to follow this predetermined pattern. You fell for a woman, you married her, things changed. You got bored, you strayed and you got caught. And as for babies . . . Christ! How was it that you could love your child so much and yet . . . ?

He looked up again. Bobby was sitting there smiling at him, two fresh pints resting on the table between them.

'Now, strictly between us, I'll tell you a little story about something that happened to me some years ago, when Doreen had just had our Lyndsay . . .'

Back at work, Jo found his eyes glazing over as he read through the file of the latest properties. He really shouldn't have had that third pint. He'd never been any good at lunchtime drinking and he'd not really fully recovered from that session the other night. Not only that, but Saturday afternoons were particularly busy.

'Jonathan?' He looked up at his colleague. 'Can you deal with this lady for me, please? She's looking for a one-bedroom flat. Up to one hundred and fifty thousand.'

Jo closed the file and slipped it into the drawer, then looked up again, even as the woman slid into the chair opposite with a rustle of silk stockings.

'Hello,' she said, smiling at him with both eyes and mouth. 'I wonder if you can help me.'

Karen was sitting quietly in the corner of the staffroom, her head down, lost in her thoughts, when the headmaster's secretary, Joan, approached her.

'Miss Turner?'

Karen looked up. 'Sorry?'

'Miss Turner . . . I'm sorry to disturb you, but the head would like to see you in his office.'

'Oh . . . right . . .'

Karen waited for the woman to leave, then got up, wondering what it was this time. Since that earlier business with Barrett things had remained on a fairly even keel. Whether Mr Keen had had a word with Barrett − or his parents − she didn't know, but the boy had been marginally more tolerable of late. Or as tolerable as a natural-born troublemaker could be.

She picked up her briefcase and, tipping the dregs of her coffee into the corner sink, made her way out and down the corridor.

'Go straight through,' Joan said from behind her desk as Karen entered. 'He's expecting you.'

Karen went inside and pulled the door shut behind her.

'Ah . . . Miss Turner.' The head indicated the chair facing him. She went across. 'How's the play coming on?'

Karen straightened the briefcase on her lap. 'Very well, thank you. It should be quite something. The sixth-formers are—'

'Good . . . good . . .' He hesitated, then, his face screwing up into a kind of pained frown, leaned towards her. 'Look, I'm sorry about this . . . I mean, I thought we had cleared up this matter, but I've been approached once more by the chair of governors. She, er . . . well, she claims to have conclusive proof that you are . . . ahem . . . cohabiting with another woman.'

'I live with another woman. You know that.'

'She says that . . . well, that her former allegation has been substantiated by a third party.'

'I beg your pardon?' Karen felt a flush rise up her neck

and over her face, condemning her. She fought to retain her self-control.

'I'm sorry, Headmaster, but I fail to see what business it is of the governors what my sexual orientation is. And even if there *were* any substance to these allegations — which there isn't — unless the governors have a complaint about my teaching abilities, how I conduct my personal life is entirely up to me.'

Keen scrutinised her across the desk, then nodded apologetically. 'I'm sorry, Karen, but you know how these things can get out of hand. And the chair was most insistent that I should speak with you . . .'

'I understand,' Karen said, barely concealing the insincerity of her smile.

The distant sound of children's voices filtering up from the playground filled the awkward silence.

'So,' he said, somewhat sheepishly, 'I can reassure the governors, then?'

'I think I've made my position very clear,' she said, wanting at that moment to lean across the desk and slap him for being so spineless. 'If they want to pursue the matter I think I should inform my NUT rep . . .'

'Oh, I'm sure there won't be any need to get the union involved in this,' he said irritably, as though it were she who were being unreasonable.

She nodded, believing they had reached an understanding. 'Will that be all?'

'Yes. Yes, thank you.'

Karen turned and marched from the room, not looking back; but outside in the corridor, her anger turned to despair, and she stood there for a minute or more, trembling at the thought that her most personal behaviour was the subject of so much public debate.

And then the anger returned. How dare they? Did *she* ask

questions about what *they* got up to in the privacy of their own homes? Did *she* pry and snoop and ask whether they did it this way or that? Whether they tied one another up, or used whips or . . . ?

No. Nor should they ask *her*. It was the ultimate imperti-nence!

Karen straightened up. As she did, the bell for the next lesson sounded. She had to go. She was teaching English to 8T — and Barrett.

'Barrett, bring whatever that is you're showing Cutler to me now!'

'But miss . . .'

'You heard me. Out front, *now*!'

Barrett shrugged, then slowly, with about as surly a manner as he could possibly adopt, he began to slouch towards the front of the class, his hands pushed deep into his blazer pockets. He stopped, no more than a foot or so in front of Karen's desk, and smiled at her. It was an ugly, insolent smile.

'Well? Hand it over.'

Barrett lifted out his right hand, then let a crumpled ball of paper fall on to Karen's desk.

'Miss . . .' And with that he turned.

'Stay where you are, Barrett.'

Karen picked up the ball of glossy paper. Cutler had been sniggering, and as she carefully peeled back the layers of paper, a wave of subdued giggling rippled through the class.

Karen glanced up. Barrett was watching her like a hawk, the smile transfixed on his face. More than ever he looked as if he wore the mask of a demon in a Japanese Noh play.

She shivered. If she had been wise she would have trusted her instinct and dropped the thing in the bin and forgotten all about it, but she couldn't. Her curiosity was roused.

Slowly she uncrumpled the paper, and as she did she saw the unmistakable flesh tones of a page from a pornographic magazine.

Karen swallowed, chilled by the image that met her eyes. There, in the most graphic image possible, was half a photograph of two naked women in the act of making love. On this section of the picture, one woman had her head between the other's legs and a speech bubble had been drawn on with 'Oohh, Chris. Stick it in' scribbled inside.

Karen could feel the blood pumping through her head. Her heart raced in her chest. She glanced up, and saw Barrett smirk at his classmates. Walking round to the other side of the desk, she propped herself on the edge, now almost touching the boy. She held out her hand.

'What, miss?'

'Empty the other pocket.'

'I ain't got nothing in there, miss.'

'Empty it, Barrett.'

'But I ain't—'

At that moment something snapped inside her and Karen lurched forward, grabbing at the boy's pocket, inadvertently pushing him so that he stumbled backwards.

'Fuck off!' he yelled, a look of surprise on his face.

'Get up, Barrett.' Karen's mind was racing now, the importance of the paper forgotten. She could be in real shit for this. She made a move towards the boy.

'Fuck off, you fucking lezzie!' he spat, sliding away from her and towards the classroom door. Then all of a sudden he was on his feet.

'Come back here, Barrett!'

But the door was already open and as Barrett slammed it shut behind him, the wall shook and, in no doubt as to the seriousness of the incident they had witnessed, the rest of the class stared at their teacher in silence.

*　　*　　*

'You understand that I had to inform the police.' The headmaster shrugged. 'It's the law.'

Karen sat there in the head's office, looking down, unable to meet his gaze.

'He claims you pushed him over.'

Karen flashed a look of contempt. 'He fell! I reached across to take something from his pocket and he fell!'

'Well, the police will get to the bottom of it.'

'What happens now?' This was a nightmare. She felt like a common criminal.

'They'll make their enquiries and decide how to proceed. It could be a warning. It could be criminal prosecution . . .'

'Prosecution? That's ridiculous! I didn't *do* anything.'

Keen smiled weakly, apologetically. 'I'm sure it won't come to that. Meanwhile, though, I have no alternative but to suspend you, I'm afraid.'

'But that makes it look like I'm the guilty one in all this.'

'That's the law, Karen. It's out of my hands.'

She shook her head in disbelief. 'And what about Barrett?'

'What about him?'

'What punishment is meted out to him?'

'That's not the issue here, unfortunately.'

'Well, it ought to be the damn issue! The verbal abuse, the insolence, the malice. Perhaps if he had been dealt with effectively . . .'

The headmaster straightened in his seat.

'The suspension is effective immediately. I shall keep you informed, of course.'

Dismissed, Karen meekly stood from her seat and turned towards the door.

'Oh, and Karen.' She glanced back. 'On this occasion I think the union rep would be a sensible precaution.'

Yet even as she moved towards the door she could feel

the tears searing the back of her eyes and willed them
not to fall.

Anna had arranged to meet him at the Café des Amis in Covent
Garden. She had told him to be there at eight, though she
herself arrived some fifteen minutes earlier.

She had chosen the restaurant with care. While it was a
popular place for lunch — a 'buzzy' French diner with its
own distinct feel — in the evening it was not often frequented
by people from the magazine world, and that was important.
She didn't want anything getting back to Frank, however
innocent this might turn out to be.

Likewise, she had taken care over her clothes. Not wanting
to seem too grand or businesslike, she had shunned the suit
she'd first selected from her wardrobe, opting instead for jeans
and a little lycra body — white, with a black belt and a black
suit jacket.

As she went inside, she glanced around, trying to seem
casual as a girl came across and asked if she could help.

'I'm early,' she said. 'Table for two in the name of
Nichols.'

'*Oui, mademoiselle*,' the girl said. 'Your table's just here.
Would you like a drink while you wait?'

'No, I'll . . . visit the powder room . . .'

'Of course . . .'

Anna went downstairs and into the ladies', reapplying her
lipstick — a slightly bolder shade of red than she usually wore
— and checking out her hair.

Then, feeling a slight nervousness, she took out his letter
again and read it through, then studied the photograph one
last time.

If he even looked vaguely like that photo then he would
do.

For a night, at least.

Anna studied herself in the mirror a moment, trying to see just how she had changed. She knew she had, but it couldn't be discerned — not with the naked eye, anyway. Yet here she was, meeting a stranger, an unopened packet of condoms in her handbag and filled with a determined ambition to use them that evening.

'You old tart,' she whispered to herself, yet there wasn't quite the jokiness behind the words for once. She had a strange feeling about this. Strange because this was intended as nothing more than a one-nighter. And because she was the one doing the cheating this time — albeit on the cheat, Frank — that felt strange, too. Very strange. It was not, after all, as if she had vowed to be faithful to him, but she knew that if he found out he would be hurt.

And that wasn't what all this was about.

She turned her face, studying each profile in turn, then, satisfied that she looked the part, she picked up her bag, ready now for that drink, to steady the nerves.

Anna went back upstairs and was beginning to cross the room when someone called to her from her left. She stopped and turned, slightly flustered, then saw who it was.

Oh, fuck!

She went over to the table and greeted him as he stood, kissing him on each cheek. 'Mark . . . how lovely to see you, darling! How's things?'

'Wonderful . . . how about you? You look terrific.'

Mark Hadley was in his early thirties and short and stocky, yet he had the kind of close-shaven good looks that ensured popularity with women, added to which he was powerful, having recently been appointed editor of the new men's magazine, *GOdown*. Anna had worked with him some years ago, when he'd been a fresh-faced hack just up from the sticks. She had been kind to him, but also tough, and whenever they met he made sure to remind her of it.

'Darling,' he said, turning to the woman seated to his right. 'This is Anna Nichols. You recall me telling you about her? Anna edits one of the women's mags in our group.'

Anna leaned across Mark to shake hands with the woman, not certain whether this was his girlfriend, his wife or someone else's wife. Word was he slept with any good-looking woman who came through the door of his office, and in a slow week resorted to members of the canine club. She'd heard he'd even slept with Samuelson's eldest daughter, and she was an ugly bitch if ever there was one!

'Look, I . . .' She glanced behind her, hoping that Michael wouldn't choose that moment to make his entrance. Mark Hadley had a mouth on him.

'Sure,' Mark said, understanding. 'but give me a bell sometime, OK? We should go for a drink.'

Anna smiled. Yes, and the rest of it, she thought. But Mark Hadley wasn't ever going to get inside *her* knickers, no matter how desperate she might be, because he'd sure as hell find an opportunity to use it against her someday. 'Love to,' she said, then, nodding to the rest of the company about the table, she made her farewells, smiled and backed away . . .

Straight into a tall, attractive guy wearing jeans and a black suit jacket.

'I'm sorry, I . . .'

Anna stopped dead. '*Michael?*'

His smile was disarming. He was every bit as good-looking as in the photograph. 'Anna?' Then, gesturing just beyond her to the stairs. 'I was just . . . you know . . .'

'Oh, sure. I . . .' Anna swallowed, then began again. 'Can I get you a drink?'

'A single malt?'

She smiled, then, gesturing towards the vacant table the girl had shown her earlier: 'We're just over there.'

'Right. See you in a moment.'

She watched him go, then walked over to her table, conscious that Mark Hadley had witnessed everything.

Shit! she thought. Shit! Now Frank was bound to find out. But maybe that was a good thing. Maybe it would bring things out into the open.

Anna looked up as the young waitress came across again. She smiled and took the menu from the girl.

'Two single malts, please.'

'*Oui, mademoiselle.*'

She set the menu down and placed her handbag on the floor, then sat up straight, feeling a little shiver run down her spine. It hadn't been an auspicious beginning to the evening, but he looked nice — yes, and smelled nice, too. Things like that were important, in the beginning at any rate.

She could still remember the smell of a boy she'd been in love with when she was fifteen, in spite of never really having had a conversation with him. They had danced together — twice — and although she could never bring to mind what he had looked like, she could still close her eyes and smell him, remembering the way he had held her on that dance floor, the way they had kissed and the sweet sickly fragrance of adolescent aftershave which had seemed so sophisticated back then.

Anna smiled. She liked men who smelled nice. Most either didn't bother or tried to mount a full-scale pheremonal assault on your senses. But the smell of Michael had been . . . well, *discreet*. Pleasant without being intrusive.

She wondered if that was a key to the man.

Then, out of the blue, the thought of him down there in the toilets standing at the trough with his penis in his hand came to mind and she found herself grinning, because he, like her, would be wondering how this evening would come to end, and he would surely be hoping that it would be her hand that would be holding that warm slip of flesh come the early hours.

She was still smiling as Michael came back, just ahead of the waitress.

'Hello again,' he said, standing aside as the girl set down the two tumblers. 'Michael.'

'Anna,' she said, letting him take her hand.

He relinquished it and sat, but the feel of that handshake stayed with her. Smiling, he leaned towards her. 'You seemed amused.'

'Just something I was thinking about.'

'You must have a vivid imagination.'

'I suppose so. Did I put that in my ad? I can't remember.' And immediately she felt embarrassed for mentioning it.

Michael smiled as he reached for his glass and raised it towards her. Anna picked up her own and clinked it against his.

'To vivid imaginations!'

She didn't know why she said it, but it seemed like the die had been cast, and in for a penny, in for a pound.

'To mutual understanding!' he toasted back, surprising her. From her experience the last thing most men wanted was to *understand* a woman.

She stared at him a moment, then, 'Sorry, but . . . well, it's just that you don't seem the kind of guy to . . .'

'To what?'

'To, um, well, to go in for this sort of thing.'

Michael shrugged. 'I don't.'

'What do you mean?'

'I saw your ad. And was intrigued. I . . .' He sat back slightly, smiling and shaking his head again. 'It is strange, actually, because I don't even buy that paper usually. A customer must have left it in the car, and I was just flicking through and . . . well, there you were!'

Again Anna felt a strange little ripple of excitement pass through her. She loved the way he talked, the easy, relaxed way he smiled. He was a man very much at ease with himself. She couldn't quite place his accent but he clearly wasn't your usual car salesman.

'To be frank, Anna, you'd normally find me taking the piss out of those kind of ads. You know the sort of thing – Urban Tarzan seeks Jane to climb his vine?'

She giggled. 'Yes, I know exactly what you mean. Half the creeps in London have written to me! I got some truly horrendous replies!'

'So I was the best of a bad bunch?'

Anna smiled. The way he had looked at her just then had made little goosebumps race up her arms.

'So why *are* you here?' she asked. 'What was it that intrigued *you*?'

'Three words.'

'Which were?'

'Tired of pretending.'

'Oh, God!' she said, covering her face with her hands. 'Did I write that?'

She had forgotten that she'd put that in, but it was true. And now that she thought about it, it was exactly *that* which most rankled with her about her relationship with Frank. The pretence.

He laughed. 'Well, it grabbed me.'

Anna looked up and met his eyes. 'So who have you been pretending to?'

'Oh, there's no one else involved.' Michael thought a moment, then: 'In my experience, the biggest problem in any relationship is self-deception. And I guess what we're all looking for is someone we can be ourselves with all the time. That is, if we've any inkling who precisely we are.'

Again she stared at him. They had been sitting here only ten minutes and already she was speaking to him more intimately than she'd spoken to anyone for . . . well, for as long as she could remember, actually.

'Do you always talk like this?' she asked, her eyes narrowing.

He laughed. 'Christ! No!'

She looked at him, not sure she'd heard that right, then roared with laughter.

Anna raised her glass and grinned mischievously. 'Well, here's to whoever was kind enough to leave that paper in your car!'

'You know what?' Anna said, as the waiter brought across yet another bottle of the excellent Bordeaux, 'I was sure you were going to come out with some story about your wife having died, or . . . or having had to nurse a sick mother, or . . .'

Michael was grinning now. He reached across and, turning her hand over, laced his fingers into hers.

'I've never been married,' he said, staring down at where their hands were linked. 'And my mother is in excellent health!'

Anna, watching him, feeling how gently he held her hand, experienced that old familiar sensation. Right then he could have picked her up and carried her downstairs and had her, there against the wall in the ladies' rest room. Her heart beat more quickly at the thought. But she was also conscious that there was more to this than sex. She knew, with a sudden certainty, that she could really fall for this man. She felt . . . so at ease with him. As if she'd known him years, not a single evening.

'You want something else to eat?' she asked.

'I'd like to eat you.'

Anna smiled, then looked up at him again. 'With relish?'

'Or chocolate sauce or—'

She shivered. 'Don't.'

He shrugged, the smile remaining on his lips. Nothing seemed to faze him.

'Michael?'

'Yes?'

'Was there . . . well, was there someone special? I mean, there must have been someone.'

'Yeah. Sure.'

Anna felt a small stab of jealousy. She had meant to steer clear of all this, but she couldn't help herself. She wanted to know who this man was, and so this — this most difficult part of it — seemed unavoidable.

'And?'

He hesitated, then: 'I don't believe in dwelling on the past.'

She liked that.

'And you?' he asked.

'There was one guy, but he let me down.'

'Ah . . .'

His thumb was gently caressing the backs of her fingers now. The simple feel of it was so nice, so erotic. She looked up and saw that he was watching her intently.

'What?'

'Just you,' he said. 'You're not what I expected.'

And you? she asked herself. Were you what I expected?

No. Michael had been a complete surprise.

'So,' he said.

'So.' She leaned forward a little, her elbows resting on the table. 'What now?'

A smile slowly came to his face. 'How about a brandy?'

'Karen! Ka-ren . . . open the bloody door!'

Karen, who, at the first sound of the hammering on her front door, had grabbed the phone to call the police, now put the handset back in the cradle and hurried to open the door.

'Jack?'

Jack pushed past her, then turned, his face suffused with anger.

'Just what the fucking hell d'you think you're playing at?'

Karen stared at him, unable almost to recognise her younger brother, his face was so distorted. 'What are you talking about?' she said, stunned by the ferocity of his accusation.

'What am I talking about? I'm talking about you and this latest little *fantasy*.'

Vaguely she realised that he was talking about what had happened at the weekend. Her mother would have phoned him. She shook her head, her voice defensive.

'It's not a fantasy, and in any case my sexuality has got bugger all to do with you!'

'Oh, hasn't it? So you think it shouldn't make any difference to me that my sister's a bloody dyke!'

She clenched her teeth, containing her pain and her anger. 'Don't you understand? I'm no different to how I always was. It's just that I want it out in the open. It's how I am.'

'Feminist bollocks!'

'Jack . . .'

'She was crying all last night. You know that? And Dad . . . Dad's devastated.'

Karen looked down. 'They'll get over it. I know it must've come as a shock . . .'

'A *shock*!' He laughed derisively, shaking his head. 'You just couldn't keep it to yourself, could you? You couldn't just let them believe . . .'

'Why the fuck should I?' She tried to calm herself, putting out her hands as if to ward him off. 'I'm not allowed to let them know anything about me, my friends, my life. Things that actually matter. Because it makes you lot feel uncomfortable. What about *me*?'

'I'm not talking about you. I'm talking about them!'

'But it's *my* life, Jack, not *theirs*.'

'Oh, that's easy to say. How d'you think they feel knowing they raised you to become a fucking lesbian! That's really something for them to be proud of. Something they can boast about to the neighbours.'

'Ah, now we're getting to the point . . .'

'They gave you everything and you piss all over them with this shit!'

Karen froze. Then, a slight tremor in her voice, she answered him. 'It's *not* shit, Jack. It's what I am.'

'A fucking queer! Great!'

Karen stared at her brother, seeing him anew. She had always thought him better than this.

'Get out.'

'What?'

'You heard me. Get the fuck out of my flat! I don't have to put up with this kind of crap from the likes of you!'

She saw how his nostrils flared at that and for one absurd moment thought he was going to hit her. But Jack merely glared at her, then, pushing past, slammed the door behind him.

Karen slumped against the wall. For all she had been through these past few weeks, her troubles with Chris, and the whole business with Barrett at school, nothing – *nothing* – was as awful as that look Jack had just given her. It had seared her. Had told her, clearer than any words, that she was no longer welcome in that place she had always thought sacrosanct. The door to her own family was barred to her.

And as that realisation struck her, so she cried out, even as a key turned in the latch and Chris stepped inside.

Chris stared, shocked by the sight of her, slumped there, tears streaming down her face.

'Karen?'

Karen let her head fall, her shoulders shuddering as she began to sob, all self-control suddenly gone.

Chris watched her a moment, then, pushing the door shut, came across and held her.

'What is it? What in God's name has happened?'

Chris picked up the phone and dialled, waiting as it rang at the other end.

'Hello?'

'Sarah?' Chris kept her voice low. Karen was sleeping now, and she didn't want to wake her. Didn't want her to know what was going on. Not just now.

'Where are you? I've been expecting you for ages.'

'Look . . . something's cropped up. I can't make it tonight.'

'Chris? You haven't changed your mind?'

'No, but . . . it's difficult.'

'Karen?'

'Yes, but . . . Look . . . she had a fight with her brother. She's . . . in a bit of a state.'

'Chris . . . I need you.'

Chris smiled, but it was strained. 'I know. And I'll see you. Tomorrow.' And with that she put down the phone.

For a long time she simply sat there, staring into the air, and then she sighed — a deep, heavy sigh that seemed to reach right down into the bone.

Tomorrow. She would sort it all out tomorrow.

Anna had tried to argue with him, but Michael had been insistent about paying the bill. Now, as they stood outside the restaurant, she turned to face him, knowing that the moment had come.

'Look, I . . .' she began, but he placed a finger to her lips.

'Anna . . . whatever happens next is up to you. Whether we go home alone or spend the night together . . . that's your decision. But let me say this. Whatever happens, I want to see you again.' He smiled. 'Your treat next time, OK?'

'OK . . .'

But she had hardly been able to say the word, her mouth was so dry, her heart was beating so fast. Then, running her tongue over her lips, she gave a tight little smile.

'Your place or mine?'

His grin made her go weak at the knees. 'Your decision.'

Anna swallowed. God, the way he looked at her! 'Yours,' she said softly, and felt him put his arms about her and place his mouth to hers. As he kissed her, out there in the alleyway, all thought of who might see was momentarily forgotten.

It was all Anna could do to stop herself from having him in the taxi. As it was, by the time they got back to his place, they were hardly strangers any more. They had kissed, a lingering, passionate kiss, almost all the way home, and Anna was wet from sheer desire for him. She had felt his hands on her breasts and had gently stroked his chest beneath his denim shirt. Now she wanted him, naked and glorious in bed beside her, and as he undid the lock and pushed the door open, so she felt something give in her and, as he closed the door and turned to face her again, she reached forward and unzipped him, taking the swollen length of it into her hand, then, kneeling down in front of him, placed the hot tip of it into her mouth.

'Anna . . .'

For a moment his hands were on her shoulders, drawing her on to him. He groaned and slowly his hips pushed and then pushed again towards her. But then, even as she had begun, he drew back, and gently lifted her back on to her feet.

'Not here,' he said, carefully drawing up the zip with one hand. 'Upstairs.'

She took his hand. Like innocents they climbed the stairs, watching each other and smiling, and the mere touch of his fingers against hers was enough to inflame her.

His bedroom was huge, the bed king-size. An *en suite* bathroom could be glimpsed off to the right. Deep-pile carpet covered the spacious floor.

Michael stopped just inside the door. Pulling her to him he ran his hands up inside her jacket, each muscle tensing beneath his opened palms. Taking his time to kiss the exposed flesh of her neck, he allowed his fingers to move with painful slowness over each button of her jacket before slipping it to the floor, lowering his head to kiss the tip of each breast through the lycra body, teasing each nipple with his teeth. Then that, too, was gone as he pulled it down off her shoulders to reveal her nakedness. Her breasts ached for his touch and as he took one dark bud into his mouth, a gentle moan escaped from Anna's lips.

And then she was helping him pull his shirt up and over his shoulders and tugging off his jeans, anxious now. And as he eased her trousers over her hips, peeling off the lycra body like a skin, his fingers whispered over her pubis and a breath caught in her throat, until finally they both stood naked, facing each other.

Anna trembled. He took her hand, then, turning her, like a king taking his queen to bed, he slowly walked her across the room.

Never, in all her life, had there been a moment like that, when she stood there, facing Michael at the end of that huge bed. Never had she felt so special, so *desired* by a man. She could see how much he wanted her, and yet he waited, prolonging the moment, his eyes feasting on her, linked to her by that warm handclasp.

'So here we are,' he said, his voice soft in the darkness.

Anna shuddered. If she waited a moment longer she would go mad, and as if he sensed that, Michael drew her to him slowly and kissed her once again, her naked body pressed to his, the long, hard length of him lying against her abdomen, so hot she ached to have it inside her.

Taking his weight on his right knee, he knelt on the edge of the mattress, then lowered her slowly on to the bed, all the while kissing her and caressing her with his fingers, his touch so gentle and yet so erotic that when finally he spread her legs and entered her, she came at once, crying out as it swept through her. And still he moved against her, the hardness of his cock as it slid back and forth inside her giving her the most intense sustained orgasm. For an eternity it seemed to go on, his body moving in perfect coordination until, with a quickening of his pace, he too shuddered and came. And as he did, she held him to her, smoothing his shoulders and his back, her hands tracing the warm, hard shape of his body from his buttocks to his neck, while she covered his neck with tiny, wet kisses, only half conscious in the throes of passion that the condoms remained unopened in her handbag.

Anna stepped from her shower and wrapped a towel about her, then stood before the steamed-up mirror, smiling at her misted image.

The night had been wonderful, and if she hadn't had to work she would have stayed for breakfast and maybe made a day of it with him, but Michael understood that, just as he seemed to understand everything else about her. *Everything* . . .

She shivered at the thought of how he had made her feel. And it wasn't just the sex, though that had been sensational: it was the way he looked at her, the way he listened attentively to everything she said; that casual, easy manner of his.

Anna turned from the mirror and walked through to her bedroom, pulling clothes from drawers as she began to dress. And as she did, the phone rang and her answer machine clicked on. As she pulled on her bra and fastened it, she heard a voice drift through to her. It was Frank.

'Hi . . . I phoned you last night. Wondered where you were. Phone me when you've a moment. I could be free tomorrow evening. 'Bye.'

She felt a momentary twinge of guilt, but strangely no more than that. Frank was Frank. Michael . . .

Well, right now she couldn't stop thinking of Michael. Of how he'd looked in the morning light, lying there beside her, of the smell of him and of how it had felt to have his hands caressing her body. She shivered at the thought of it.

From his physique, Michael clearly worked out, and guys who worked out were usually vain beyond belief; yet there seemed nothing vain about Michael, just a calm self-assuredness.

She smiled. She had told him he had aquiline features . . . Michael had liked her saying that. Then again, Michael had seemed to like everything about her. She recalled now what he had said about strong, intelligent women and what a turn-off they were for most guys. But he wasn't threatened by that, it seemed. He had encouraged her to talk – to give her views on things. In that, too, he was unusual. Most men had to have their say, no matter how dumb or uninformed their opinions.

'Watch yourself,' she said, glancing across at her dressing mirror. 'Michael isn't perfect.'

No. But he came pretty damn close. At least, on an evening's acquaintance.

And Frank?

As she pulled on her leather trousers and zipped them up, Anna found herself wondering how difficult it would be to have *two* lovers on the go. Or was that tempting fate?

She smiled. Yes, but first see if he phones you, like he promised.

Susie stood on the chair, reaching up to get at the smear at the very top of the window, then turned, smiling across the room at Nathan where he lay, gurgling in the baby-bouncer.

'There you are, peachy-weach. All done!'

It was just after nine and they weren't due to come until half ten, but she wanted to be ready. She wanted everything to be nice. After all, she'd never held a coffee morning before.

She clambered down, then, snapping the cap on the Windowlene, took it quickly through to the kitchen and slipped it into the cupboard under the sink. As she did, Nathan began a hesitant but fretful little cry.

''S'awright, darling,' she said, hurrying back into the room, then crouching before him, a big reassuring smile on her face. 'Mummy's here.'

Good as gold, Nathan immediately cheered up and began gurgling once again, his podgy little hands fumbling with the big, brightly coloured wooden beads that lined the handbar of the bouncer.

'You'se a clever bab, isn't you?' Susie said, adopting her special talk-to-baby voice. 'You'se gonna be a good boy today.'

For a moment she simply stared at him, smiling, her right hand gently stroking the soft skin of his cheek and neck. Then, with a little shiver, she stood and looked about her.

Now what?

She'd hidden away Nathan's best toys, not wanting to risk their getting broken by some of the rowdier kids. And she had been out and got some special juice from the health-food shop: no sugar, no additives, and no taste as far as she could tell. But apparently it was what you were supposed to give the children these days, and some of the mums were a bit fussy; a bit *organic*.

In fact one of the women at the toddler group had boasted that her two-year-old had never eaten anything with sugar in it, and so Susie had been delighted to catch him in the playgroup hut, his mouth so stuffed with biscuits he'd pinched from the tin that he wasn't even able to grind them down. Trying not to laugh, she had made him spit them into her hand just so that he didn't choke, but had given a few back and told him to go into the Wendy house and eat them slowly. Poor little sod! But the incident had done wonders for her confidence.

She had also bought a coffee percolator yesterday and had made Jo test it out for her last night. Not that she liked coffee particularly — she preferred a nice cup of tea — but who'd ever heard of a *tea* morning?

That stray thought of Jo made her feel guilty once again. It was six weeks now since she'd given birth and it was probably about time to resume normal service in the sex department. But last night she'd been tired — more tired than Jo had probably realised — and though she understood his frustration, she didn't want to do it like that. Not simply to gratify him. And besides, the baby had been fretful. If Nathan had woken halfway through she'd have had to see to him, and then had to put up with Jo all horny and miserable beside them.

No. It was best to wait a little longer. To make sure that they both felt right about it when it happened. Anyway, she wanted to get her six-week check-up out of the way to make sure everything had gone back into the right place. Guiltily, Susie clenched her buttocks together and did ten pelvic thrusts.

Even so, she knew he had been angry. It wasn't the first

time he'd slept in the spare room, but it had felt different this time. Like he wanted her to know that he was blaming her for something.

She looked across at Nathan once again and smiled. 'It's your silly dad,' she said. 'He's fed up pulling his plonkie-wonkie in the bathroom.'

Nathan grinned and gurgled, understanding nothing, and Susie, noting that it was almost ten past now, began to fuss about the room, plumping up cushions and checking that she'd not overlooked anything with her duster and her can of Pledge.

Anna's assistant, Rachel, met her outside the lift as she emerged on to the sixth floor, taking her aside and talking to her in an urgent whisper.

'Samuelson was here! He wanted to know where you were!'

Anna glanced at her watch. 'But I'm never in before ten. He knows that.'

'I know. But he was furious. Said he wanted to see you in the penthouse just as soon as you arrived.'

Anna felt her stomach tighten. 'What about? Did he say?'

Rachel shrugged, but it was clear she was holding something back.

'Rachel?'

Rachel seemed close to tears. 'I'm not sure, but I think he might be going to replace you, Anna. The last few days . . .'

Anna stared at her, thinking back over what had been happening. 'What? What have I missed?'

'There've been rumours.'

'What kind of rumours?'

But just then the cookery editor came through the doors. Seeing Anna and Rachel there, she gave an apologetic smile then turned and went back the way she'd come.

That confirmed it. She was out. The bastard had gone behind her back. All that remained was for him to tell her to her face.

She turned angrily and jabbed at the button to call the lift, then looked back at Rachel.

'OK, Raich . . . you'd better get back. And thanks.'

Rachel gave what was almost a curtsy, the same apologetic smile on her face as on the cookery editor's, then disappeared inside the suite of offices.

Left alone, Anna felt a little shudder of rage ripple through her. How dare that fat prick treat her like this! Especially after all the hard work she'd put in!

The doors hissed open. Thankfully the lift was empty. She stepped inside, a cool clear anger burning inside her now.

Well, if the old bastard was going to give her the push, she wasn't going to go quietly.

As the lift climbed, she thought of all the casual insults she had had to put up with from her proprietor, of all the shit he'd shovelled her way, and felt almost a kind of glee at being liberated in this manner.

What made a pompous arsehole like him think he could treat people the way he did just because he had money? How was it that a pig like him wasn't regularly on the end of a good poke in the guts?

As the lift hissed open again, she calmed herself. There was a security camera in the corridor here and special locks on the reinforced doors.

She waited, wondering if he was watching her even then, or whether it was one of his minions. And then the door to her right clicked open.

A middle-aged man in full servant's regalia stood there.

'Miss Nichols,' he said, 'please step this way.'

Like a medieval king, she thought, and wondered if that was how he perceived himself.

Mind you, from her reading of Renaissance history, that was precisely what the early kings were: fat merchants who had built up their power base until they eventually ran the great cities. Only this was meant to be modern times, and there weren't supposed to be any kings any more. At least, none with any power.

Anna followed the man, noting the casual yet outrageous wealth displayed in the rooms she passed through. There were paintings on the walls worth millions and elaborate nick-nacks on marble-topped tables which, she was sure, were worth quite staggering sums.

Samuelson himself was sitting in his office at the very back of the penthouse, behind a desk the size of a white-water raft, the huge wall of window behind him giving a view of the river and — not a mile away — the Houses of Parliament. He looked up as Anna came into the room and scowled.

'How good of you to grace us with your presence!'

She walked across and stood the other side of the desk to him. 'Yes, well here I am. Now what was it you wanted?'

There was a flicker of surprise in his deep-set eyes. His jowls made a strange little jerky movement, then he sneered.

'I don't like your attitude, d'you know that? So what I *want* is for you to clear your desk and get out of my magazine. An hour should do it.'

But Anna wasn't going anywhere. 'Is that it, or do I get a rational explanation?'

Samuelson smiled sardonically. 'You get nothing.'

'Oh, I think my solicitor might have something to say about that. And be warned. I'm not cheap!' He looked up at her, a look of enjoyment almost in his eyes. 'And who's going to replace me?'

'That's none of your business.'

'No? Well, maybe not. But I'd like to know.'

Samuelson had looked down at a file on his desk, as if

he'd done with her, but now he looked up again. 'Well, if you must know, I've given the job to Jackie Kingsley.'

Anna laughed, but the news was a shock to her. Jackie was her deputy editor and, she had thought, a friend.

'When was this?' she asked quietly, subdued momentarily by the news.

'Last night. I tried to get you, but you'd gone,' the criticism in his tone only too evident.

A flash of anger went through her at that. 'I left this place at *seven thirty*! Or did you expect me to sleep here?' Her voice was dripping with sarcasm. But Samuelson's head was bowed over a pile of correspondence.

'Can I just say one last thing before I go?'

Samuelson glanced up at her contemptuously. 'You won't make me change my mind. You're out. And you're staying out.'

'And you,' she said, 'are a fat pompous old bastard.'

Surprisingly, he laughed. 'Yes. But *you* . . . are out.'

There wasn't much, when it came to it. What she hadn't already packed into her briefcase fitted into two large carrier bags.

Standing there, looking about her office, Anna felt a sudden surge of regret that she wouldn't see this through. She had built this magazine and it was on the verge of real success, but now she wouldn't get the credit for that.

Jackie, she noted, had disappeared without trace. Unable to face me, she thought, and partly – only partly – understood. This was a tough business, and much of the old Thatcherite attitude – that awful dog-eat-dog ethic – remained unalloyed. But, to her at least, a friend was a friend, and she'd hoped that those she worked with considered her as much a friend as a boss.

But who knew what they really thought? When you were

in a position of power it was impossible to judge. People who had been your bosom buddy one minute wouldn't take your call the next. It was sad but a fact of life.

Anna sighed, then, knowing there was one last thing to do before she left, she picked up the phone and called Frank.

'Hello?' he answered, after only a single ring.

'Frank? It's Anna, I—'

'Oh . . .' There was a distinct sulkiness about his voice. 'Look, I'm really, really busy . . .'

'I know, and I'm sorry I was out the other evening, but . . . well, I really need to see you.'

She heard him sigh, then. 'OK. How about tomorrow night?'

'No. Today. This lunchtime.'

'I can't,' he said bluntly. 'I've got a business meeting.'

She hesitated, then. 'Please, Frank. I really need to speak to you. I've just been sacked, and—'

'*Sacked*?' She heard the shock in his voice. There was a moment's pause, then: 'Look, all right. I'll cancel. Where do you want to meet?'

'Mon Plaisir?'

She had almost – *almost* – suggested the Café des Amis.

'OK,' he said. 'Twelve thirty?'

'Thanks . . .'

'Are you OK?'

Anna smiled, warmed by the concern that was in his voice. 'Yeah. Well, as OK as can be expected when you've just been kicked in the teeth!'

She heard him sigh. 'I'm so sorry . . .'

'Yeah. Me, too. Look . . . I'd better go. Not my phone any more. See you at half twelve.'

'See you.'

Anna sat there a moment, then looked up. Jackie was standing in the doorway.

'Anna, I—'

'It's OK,' Anna said, feeling that it was anything but, but at least glad that Jackie had had the guts to see her before she left. 'Just don't let that fat fucker trample all over you, OK?'

Jackie smiled awkwardly. 'I'll try.' She stood there, not knowing whether to stay or go. 'Look, Anna. If you need a bit more time . . .'

Anna laughed, walking round to the other side of the desk. 'No! I'm outta here! It's all yours!'

'Another cup of tea, Annie?'

Annie — who had one of those perfectly rounded faces, surrounded by dark, Shirley Temple curls — looked up and smiled. 'No, thanks, Susie. My bladder's not what it used to be!'

'Geri?'

Geri looked up from where she sat on the sofa between Gus and Rosie and grinned. 'All right. Then I gotta go. Scott'll need his lunch.'

'Scott?'

'Henry's dad. He's been stayin'.'

'Ah . . .' Susie nodded. It never ceased to amaze her how one moment these women were bad-mouthing their absent blokes and the next cooking them meals and not only putting them up, but giving them rumpy-pumpy on the side! She went out into the kitchen and put on the kettle once again, then paused by the sink, looking out across the garden.

'Oh, shit!'

Throwing open the back door, Susie bellowed at the crew-cut four-year-old who was systematically plucking the petals from the roses her dad had planted the weekend after Nathan had arrived.

'Henry! Don't *do* that!'

The other children — two boys much younger than Henry,

and a girl almost his age — stopped playing and stared at Susie in surprise, but Henry merely turned to her and scowled.

'Fuck off!'

Susie blinked. She was about to answer him when Geri stepped past her.

'*Henry!* Get in here, you little bugger! How dare you talk to Susie like that? Say sorry.'

But Henry wasn't saying anything. He skulked back indoors, getting a clip around the ear as he walked past his mother.

Geri looked to Susie and smiled. 'Sorry. It's 'cos his dad's home. Little sod always plays up when Scott's about. Thinks he can get away with murder!'

Susie nodded, her own smile weary. Her dad was going to go mad when he saw those roses! She'd have to get Jo to replace them.

With a sigh she turned away and, picking up the teapot, tipped away the old tea bags and washed it out. Talk about a strain. Babies were easy compared with these little horrors. If they weren't destroying your garden, they were drawing on your walls or pulling each other's hair. Not to mention the language!

She wasn't one to mind her Ps and Qs, but hearing one of the smaller boys call the girl a 'fucking bastard' was, she felt, way beyond the pale, especially as he managed it with perfect pronunciation, which was pretty impressive considering he was barely two and couldn't even manage his own name properly.

But then, they had to have got it from somewhere. And if their parents behaved that way then, of course, they would too. It was how kids learned anything, and it always seemed to be the things you *didn't* want them to pick up that they managed most easily. Susie made a mental note to mind her mouth in future.

As far as she could see, few of the women made any attempt to discipline their kids. Their bad behaviour was either ignored or explained away with a litany of excuses: 'He's tired', when they threw their dinner in your face; 'I'm sure he's going to be artistic', when they crayoned over your non-washable vinyl; or, best of all, 'he's just trying to be friendly', when they punched another kid in the head. Just occasionally they would be deemed to have overstepped the mark, and then the full wrath of parental retribution fell on them.

Among this particular group, Gus was the exception, and the more Susie saw of him, the more she liked him. She liked the way, earlier, when one of the kids had fallen and cut himself after trying to climb the tree at the end of the garden, Gus had taken charge, picking up the boy and soothing him; sitting him on the drainer and talking to him as he cleaned the cut and applied the plaster, joking with the kid until he, too, was laughing, then finally putting him down and patting his head, praising his bravery.

Susie smiled at the recollection. That was how Steve would be if ever he and Janet managed to have a kid. And Jo, too, maybe.

The kettle boiled, then clicked off. She picked it up and poured the scalding water into the pot. Beside it stood the percolator. The jug of coffee she had made remained practically untouched. Gus alone had had a cup, early on. Susie reached across now and switched it off.

It was early days yet. Nathan, lovely as he was, was barely more active than a big amoeba compared with some of these kids, and apart from sitting with him and talking, there wasn't much that Jo could actively do with him. But in her mind she pictured the two of them playing football in the garden, or going swimming together, or . . . oh, a hundred different things, and she wondered what the hell she had been doing with her life before she'd had Nathan.

Treading water, she thought, slipping the lid on to the pot, then reaching up to get down another packet of biscuits.

From the living room came the sound of a child wailing.

'Oh, for Christ's sake, Chloë!' Annie yelled in a voice that was totally at odds with her sweet-as-pie looks. 'I told you to ask for the potty!'

They had all gone home. All, that was, except Gus. He had been settling Katrina, giving her her feed, then rocking her gently in his arms until she slept. Now he was putting her down in her buggy while Susie stacked the dishwasher.

It felt strange, being alone in the house with a man other than Jo, and in the old days she might have felt the urge to flirt, but this wasn't like that. She felt comfortable with Gus. He didn't threaten her, nor were there any sexual undertones to their relationship. Their point of contact was their kids and if this was the New Man, then she approved thoroughly.

'At last!' he said, coming into the kitchen and smiling across at her. 'She just wouldn't give in.'

'Another cup of coffee?'

'No, thanks. I'd better get going. Get some shopping done while she's asleep. We've got friends round tonight — colleagues of Pat's — and I need to get some bits and pieces. Some onions and—'

'I've got onions,' Susie said, eager to help out.

'No, I can't . . .'

'Don't be silly,' she said, going over to the vegetable basket and taking out two large onions. 'There . . . anything else?'

She realised what she'd said just as soon as she'd said it, and felt a little awkward, but Gus seemed not to notice.

'You wouldn't have a couple of bottles of Chardonnay?'

'What?' Then, realising he was teasing, she grinned. 'I only drink champagne!'

His smile didn't falter. 'Thanks for these. Look, I'll see you tomorrow. And thanks. I enjoyed this morning a lot.'

'Me, too,' Susie said, though the truth was, she'd found it all a monumental strain.

Once he had gone, Susie walked through into the living room. Nathan was asleep in the travel cot in the corner. She went across and leaned over, watching him for a moment, adoring the sight of him, so vulnerable and yet so sturdy. Her little boy.

Then, knowing she had to do something about those roses before her dad came round and saw them, she went over to the phone and picked up the receiver, tapping out Jo's number.

Jo put down the phone and groaned.

'Soddin' garden,' he murmured under his breath.

'What's up?' his colleague Andy asked him.

Jo grimaced. 'She only wants me to get some rose bushes on my way home. I mean! Where am I going to find rose bushes at six o'clock at night?'

'Try Yellow Pages. Get some delivered.'

Jo grinned. 'Brilliant! Thanks, mate!'

But even as he thumbed through, he felt his irritation grow. Why couldn't Susie do this? She had bugger all else to do, after all, apart from sit at home and play with the sodding baby!

And as he dialled the first of the numbers in the list, he found all of his grievances bubbling up. Rose bushes! Bloody *rose bushes*! So what if her dad got upset! And, anyway, what was she doing holding bleeding coffee mornings? Filling his house with strangers and their brats!

'Hello . . . yeah, right . . . erm . . . I want to get hold of a couple of rose bushes . . .'

* * *

Frank set down his wineglass and sat back. 'Christ! I bet that pissed him off!'

Anna nodded. 'And d'you know what he did? He laughed. The arrogant bastard just sat there and laughed!'

'Well, he mustn't be allowed to get away with it.' Anna glanced at him over the rim of her wineglass. 'I mean, it sounds like a pretty straightforward case of unfair dismissal.' Frank reached into his jacket pocket, opened his wallet and took out a card. 'Here. Go and see this woman.'

Anna took the card and studied it. 'Is she any good?'

'The best. She knows industrial law inside out, and she's not afraid to take on a fat cat like Samuelson.'

'I don't know. I mean, Samuelson's lackey's already seen me. They're offering me three months' salary.'

'Well, sure, but that's not really that brilliant when you think about it. What did you tell him?'

'I said I'd get back to him. I thought I'd probably manage to get them up a bit from that.'

Frank looked doubtful. 'You've also got to consider the possible damage this will do to your reputation, and to your prospects of getting another equivalent job. Don't forget what it was like last time.'

Anna nodded vaguely. She didn't want to think about that, and hadn't even begun to worry about *another* job. She was just about coming to terms with having lost this one!

She looked at the business card again. 'Is she expensive? This Virginia Sweetman.'

'Very. But worth every penny. She'll screw Samuelson until he howls.'

'Hmm . . . And how do you know her?'

'Ginny?' Frank grinned. 'We had a fling. Oh, years ago, when she was a fresh-faced barrister. That burned itself out pretty quickly, but we've been friends ever since.'

'I see.' And, surprisingly, Anna felt the slightest twinge of jealousy. But it was just as well to know. She didn't like going into situations without all the facts.

'Frank?'

'Mm?'

'I'm sorry about last night. I had to go and see my mother. She's not been well recently and . . . well, it was late and I decided to stay over.'

'It's fine. I missed you, that's all.' He smiled and, reaching out, took her hand. Anna shivered, a strange sense of dread descending on her as she found herself comparing it to Michael's touch. 'Maybe we can meet up tomorrow night? Sheila's taking the kids to the theatre, so I could stay late.'

'Maybe . . .' Then, knowing how churlish that sounded. 'Yes . . . yes, why not?'

As Karen set the mug of coffee down on the table in front of Stuart Milne, he looked up, smiling his thanks. He was young and keen and had proved an effective union rep since his election the previous autumn. These days it needed someone with energy, someone prepared to battle their way through all the bureaucracy and inflexible legislation.

Karen slid wearily into the chair facing him, cradling her own mug to her chest.

'So,' he began, like a judge pronouncing sentence, 'basically what they're saying is, now that they've interviewed the kids, they're prepared to accept your explanation that Barrett slipped. However . . .'

'I knew there'd be a *however*.'

'*However!* The fact of the matter is, you *did* lay your hands on him and . . .' He stopped and shrugged. 'Well, Karen, you know the score as well as I do.'

Karen nodded solemnly. 'So what are the police actually saying?'

'Well,' he said, his tone a little brighter, 'they're not going to proceed with a criminal prosecution . . .'

Karen slowly shook her head at the absurdity of the notion.

'But they *will* have to give you an official warning. I know,' he said, raising his eyebrows sympathetically, 'and the police realise how bloody ridiculous the whole business is, but it's the law.'

'I know. I know,' she said, forcing a smile. 'And thanks, Stuart. You've been a star.'

He smiled again, pleased to have his efforts appreciated.

'So what now?' Karen asked.

'Well, it goes on your record, of course. Three warnings and . . . well, it's not likely to affect you really. And as far as the suspension goes, you can start back on Monday.'

Karen sighed heavily. 'And what about the other problem?'

'Well,' he said, leaning back in his chair, 'the school has absolutely no grounds for complaint even if you were to confess to being gay . . .' Karen shot him a look. 'Sorry. It makes you sound like a witch, but you know what I mean. Even if it were true.'

He had never actually asked her. Not outright. Well it wasn't PC, for a start. They had agreed to proceed with the union line that if Karen had kept her sexual orientation a private matter and had not flaunted or promoted it, then there was certainly no question of *misconduct* to answer to. She had categorically refused to deny that she was a lesbian on the grounds that it was nobody's business one way or the other. But, still, she had been conscious of Stuart looking about him as he sat in her flat and knew that he must be casting about for clues, if only to satisfy his own curiosity.

'It's just that the chair of governors . . .'

'*Bitch!*'

Stuart smiled, but carried on. 'Well, the woman seems to have got the bit between her teeth. And she's certainly been busy. I hear on the grapevine that the head has had calls from several other governors as well as someone from the Education Department.'

'No chance he told them to go to hell, I s'pose?'

'Not his style, unfortunately.' Stuart leaned forward again in his chair, gathering his papers, which were spread over the table. 'Listen, Karen! This is not something for you to worry about.'

Her laugh was loud and false. 'No?'

'No! The good news is there's no assault charge. This other crap'll blow over by the time you get back next week. I've got a meeting with Keen tomorrow and the chair of governors is going to be there.' He grinned. 'I'm sure I'll manage to persuade her that this is not the most productive use of her time.'

Stuart took a mouthful of his coffee, then, pushing back his chair, he stood up and made his way round the table towards the door, talking over his shoulder to Karen as he went. 'You know where I am if you want to talk. You should receive a letter from the head in the next day or two.' At the door he turned to face her. 'OK?'

'And what's happened to Barrett, eh?'

But Stuart merely shrugged. He could not provide any kind of answer that Karen wanted to hear. As he'd said earlier, he'd seen the same kind of injustice on scores of occasions.

'Something's gone wrong somewhere,' Karen said quietly, unable to prevent her voice from cracking.

Stuart reached up and squeezed her arm. ''Bye,' he said, opening the door.

Karen simply nodded. She could not trust herself to speak.

Signing her name across the bottom of the letter, Karen quickly read it through. She folded it in half, pushed it into an envelope and sealed it before turning it over and printing the headmaster's name.

For the first time that week, she felt at peace with herself. There was something peculiarly satisfying — if, ultimately, self-defeating — in penning your resignation.

Karen stood, placing the envelope on the shelf over the fireplace, then went over and stood by the window looking out. She didn't know what she would do. Teaching was all she was good at. And even if it was poorly paid and the kids were often awful and some of the teachers just as bad, it was the only thing she'd ever wanted to do.

And now she was going to say goodbye to it. Just like that.

Karen sighed, then, knowing she would need to keep herself occupied if she was going to get through this in one piece, she turned and went over to the phone and tapped out Mandy's work number.

'Hi, Mand . . . yeah, I got your message. I'd love to come. Yeah . . . count me in.'

Anna stopped just inside the door and bent down. There was a tiny envelope on the polished floor — one of those small, gift-card envelopes, with just her first name written on it

She picked it up and looked at it, then walked through to the bedroom and, slumping down on to the end of the bed, kicked off her shoes.

'What a day . . .'

Then, some part of her knowing already who the note was from, she slit it open with her thumbnail and took out the card.

It was a drawing of an orchid, the exotic bloom gaping like a woman's private parts. She smiled, then opened it.

'Dearest Anna,' it read, 'thank you for a wonderful evening

and an even more wonderful morning. Can I see you again? Friday, maybe? Love, Michael.'

The words sent a little shiver down her spine. Even so, she felt confused now, and wishing suddenly that she hadn't seen Frank. No matter how often she reminded herself that each time he left her, he went home to his wife, she couldn't stop herself from feeling guilty about Michael, and wondered if this was something peculiar to her sex. Certainly it didn't seem to bother Frank.

Anna lay back, her hands beneath her neck. God, she could have done with Michael right then. Just the thought of him aroused her . . .

Friday . . . could she possibly wait until Friday?

She rolled over, then stood, going out and across to the telephone. The answering machine was on. There had been six messages.

Anna frowned, then, sitting by the machine, pressed REWIND. As it stopped whirring and clicked on, she pressed PLAY.

The first message was from her mother. She'd not been feeling well and—

'Why don't you ever phone me at work, Mum?' Anna said, as if speaking to her. But she knew why. Her mother didn't like to 'intrude'.

The second message was Mandy phoning from work, trying to organise a night out with the girls. The next three messages were all blanks. Someone had obviously phoned and, finding the answering machine on, had hung up. The last message was from Frank.

She smiled. It was an old message; curt and irritable, and she wondered if he had guessed she'd been out with some other man. Why else that undertone of undirected anger?

Switching the machine off, she dialled Michael's home number, then waited. Nothing. He wasn't there. Ah well . . .

Anna stood, meaning to go and make herself something to eat; then, changing her mind, she sat again, tapping out her mother's number. She might as well do it now and get it over with. If she phoned later it could take up the best part of her evening.

The phone rang and rang. She was about to put it down when someone answered.

'Hello? Who is that?'

'Auntie? Auntie Charlotte?'

'Oh, Anna. Hello. How are you?'

'Fine, thanks. Is Mum there?'

There was the smallest hesitation. 'I'm afraid she's not very well, dear. We had to have the doctor in.'

'The doctor?' Anna felt a fresh surge of guilt. 'Is she OK?'

'Well, we're not sure,' the older woman answered, as if she and the doctor had been consulting on the matter. 'He's coming back in an hour or so to see how she is. But she's looking very poorly.'

'Well, what does he think's wrong?'

But Aunt Charlotte wasn't listening. 'I tried to phone you,' she said, 'but that blooming machine was on.'

Well, that was that mystery cleared up.

'I've been tied up with work,' Anna said. 'Things are a bit difficult at the moment.'

'You should be here. Your mother needs you.'

'Yes, Auntie, but—'

'You'd never forgive yourself, you know. If anything was to happen.'

Anna closed her eyes. Her mother was as tough as a rhino, and her Aunt Charlotte knew it.

'Look, it's probably just a bug. Tell Mum I'll pop round at the weekend.'

She heard her aunt draw in her breath. 'Anna . . . I don't want to tell you your business . . .'

'Then don't!' And she slammed down the phone. '*Shit* . . .'

Picking it up again, Anna redialled, waiting as it rang and rang. It was a full minute before her aunt came on again.

'Yes?'

'I'm sorry, Auntie. I've had a bad day. I got the——'

'That's no excuse. Your mother should come first, and if I thought it was just a bug I wouldn't have wasted her phone bill trying to get hold of you.'

'I'm sorry. But I need to make some calls first, OK?'

'That's more like it.'

Anna closed her eyes. Why was it that your mother's sisters felt they had the right to order you about? Or was it just something about getting older, as though wrinkles gave you carte blanche to be as rude as you liked.

'I'll come over as soon as I can. OK? 'Bye.'

And she put the phone down again, before her Aunt had the chance to resume the 'duty' lecture.

'Oh, fuck . . .'

Doris was right. She ought to be there. But first she needed to sort out a few things, like arranging a meeting with this Ginny Sweetman of Frank's to sort out a payoff. And then?

Then she'd go and pay Michael a visit at work, and see if she could persuade him to take an hour off.

Mandy heard the unfamiliar expletive that had issued from Bob Johnson's lips after he'd put the phone down, and went across, poking her head round his door.

'Anything wrong?'

Johnson smiled painfully. 'I've got an urgent package to go. I promised Hescott's I'd bike it round, but I can't get hold of a single bloody courier. Half of London's moving bloody packages about today!'

Hescott's, Mandy knew, was just off Essex Road. She could

jump in a cab but if not, a bus would only take twenty minutes.

'Give it to me,' she said. 'I'll take it.'

'But you've work to do, Mand.'

'It's all right. I'll stay on an extra hour tonight. I was only going for a drink with the girls. I can catch them up.'

Johnson grinned broadly. 'You'd be doing me a big favour. Thanks, Mandy.'

She smiled back at him. 'You're welcome.'

Mandy stepped off the bus near Islington Green and walked down past the antiques shops. Though she liked the atmosphere of the office, this too was pleasant — was like a little adventure, breaking up her day. It had been no hardship at all playing the helpful volunteer.

Mandy paused at one of the stalls a minute, looking at some of the baubles that were on sale. That was another good thing about being at work. She could treat herself now from time to time. Nothing big — she was only just getting used to paying the bills for herself, after all — but the odd little thing to brighten up her place.

She had plans. Plans that included redecorating the kitchen and her bedroom, and buying a new carpet for the hallway. It would be nice, too, if she could save enough to go away on holiday next year. Ibiza, maybe. Or the Canaries. Pete hadn't been a great one for going abroad, other than for the occasional international when the England football team was playing in Europe.

Cutting down one of the tiny side streets, she began to hum to herself, her head filled with plans and hopes and dreams. Yet almost at once she saw the car, recognising it immediately. She stopped dead.

Jo! That was Jo's car parked there in front of the house with the FOR SALE board outside!

Instinctively she moved aside, placing herself behind some tall railings, out of sight. Even as she stood there she wasn't sure why, exactly, she was doing it, but as memories of their ill-fated affair came flooding back, Mandy knew that the reminder of her own humiliation helped ease the guilt she felt over the way they had deceived Susie. And then, suddenly, the door opened and Jo appeared at the top of the steps. A moment later a woman joined him there. Smiling, she took his hand and shook it, but watching her, Mandy knew that look; remembered it. And immediately she guessed what they'd been up to.

'You bastard!' she said beneath her breath, feeling a mixture of pain and jealousy and sheer indignant anger. 'How could you do it to them?'

Mandy watched them go to their cars and drive away, and for a second the memory of what she'd had with him was so fresh and so painful that her knees went and she had to grab hold of the railings with her left hand to keep herself from falling. Then, as that awful first wave of emotion passed from her, the anger came to the fore again.

Susie . . . she'd have to tell her. She had a right to know.

Then she suddenly thought that maybe Susie wouldn't thank her for it; in fact, she might think it was spite.

No . . . maybe it wasn't such a good idea after all.

Mandy opened her mouth as if about to say something to herself. Then she realised that she was still holding the package.

She walked on, deciding to sleep on it. Deciding not to do anything rash.

But one thing was for sure. Even if she didn't tell Susie, she wasn't going to let that cheating bastard get away with it. Not this time!

*   *   *

Janet sat beside the young black nurse, her broad smile hidden by the blue surgical mask she wore. Over her shoulder, Steve watched as the nurse adjusted the monitor, bringing more clearly into view a magnified image of the embryos they would be inserting into Janet's uterus later that morning.

'You can see if you look here,' she was saying, pointing at a shape on the screen. 'These ones have already divided into six cells.'

Steve shook his head in wonder. It was hard to believe that one, or maybe more, of these could end up being their own living child.

'They're a bit like balls of chewing gum, ain't they?'

Both Janet and the nurse looked up at him without saying a word.

'The shape of 'em, I mean.'

The nurse smiled kindly. 'I've heard cauliflowers, honeycombs, leather footballs, but never chewing gum. Chewing gum's original.'

Janet shook her head, turning back to the screen. 'It's great so many of 'em have done so well.'

'Strong sperm, you see!' Steve said, puffing out his chest.

'Oh, of course. Mr Universe.'

'Well, at least it means that some can be frozen. You've discussed that with the doctor?'

Janet nodded, feeling a momentary twinge of sadness. Even in this primitive form she thought of them as her babies, and for those that had not been fertilised she grieved. If she tried to explain it, she felt it sounded stupid; that she sounded hysterical comparing her loss to that of someone suffering the bereavement of a child they had known and nurtured. But they at least were able to focus their grief, to see a face and to remember: she had only the sense of loss and the emptiness of failure. There was no hierarchy for grief.

'There you are,' the nurse said, handing Steve a floppy

black-and-white print of the embryos they had observed on the screen. 'Something for your wallet.'

He shook his head and smiled, in awe. Janet glanced up at him, moved by his obvious delight. She wanted this child so badly that the need itself consumed her like a cancer, eating away at her bit by bit so that sometimes she felt there was nothing left except the shell. It wasn't like that for Steve. He could cope. And sometimes she hated him for it.

The nurse looked down at her watch as she made her way across to the door. Half turning, she smiled kindly at the two of them. 'Just make yourself comfortable,' she said to Janet, motioning towards the trolley with a brief nod of her head. 'The team'll be in in a minute.'

Janet felt the muscles in her abdomen tense. Relax, relax, she told herself. But of course it was impossible.

Her legs were bent at the knees, the soles of her feet placed firmly on the surface of the trolley. She stared at the ceiling and focused on a speck of dirt. The noises from various pieces of medical machinery filled the room, seeming much louder than before.

At the foot of the bed, Dr Clements slipped a long metal needle on to a slide and drew the embryos into it.

'Now, I'm going to replace the embryos,' he said. 'There shouldn't be any discomfort.'

Janet winced as the tube moved up her vagina.

'That's it!' the doctor announced seconds later, the muscles in his face relaxing as he sat upright, discarding the needle on a tray.

Janet's body, too, seemed to slump with relief.

'I hope you put some superglue on 'em, Doc.'

Pulling down his mask, the doctor smiled at Steve. 'Let's hope we don't need it, eh?'

Steve and Janet exchanged a look and he reached down to squeeze her hand.

'Now,' the doctor said. 'I want you to lie quietly for about half an hour and then you can go home. Make an appointment at the desk before you go, for two weeks' time.'

'And what do I have to do in the meantime?'

He smiled at her sympathetically. He knew from past experience that the next fortnight was going to be the hardest time of all and would seem like an eternity. 'We've done all any of us can do now. Just go away and think positively. Tell yourself you're pregnant. When you come back in we'll do a test and . . .'

Patting Steve on the back, he turned to go, his services needed elsewhere.

'Thanks, Doctor,' Janet called after him. 'Thanks for everything.'

He returned her smile hoping, as he always did, that the patient would still be smiling in two weeks' time.

'Thanks for seeing me at such short notice.'

'That's all right,' Ginny Sweetman said, leaning forward across her desk. 'Frank said you might contact me. I'm pleased to be of help.'

Anna smiled, instantly liking the woman, recognising at once what Frank might have seen in her. She was slim with short dark hair — not unlike Anna's own — and had pleasant but strong features.

'So,' Ginny continued, 'let's begin with basics. How long were you editor of *This Woman*?'

'Eleven months.'

'And what was the circulation of the magazine when you took it over?'

Anna smiled. She *did* know her job. 'Just over seventy thousand.'

'And when you left?'

'One hundred and thirty, and climbing.'

'And how does that compare to, say, *Cosmopolitan*?'

'About the same.'

'So you could argue that you put the magazine on the map.'

Anna grinned. 'You could argue that. Or you could say that I turned a dying venture into a red-hot success.'

'Good . . . And they were offering, what? Three months' salary?'

'Uhuh.'

Ginny finished making her note, then looked up. 'Frank tells me you had a stand-up row with an editor of another magazine.'

'So?'

'So it might affect things. Samuelson might claim you were a loose cannon. That he had to fire you before you completely lost it.'

'I had a genuine grievance. The bitch stole one of my best writers. So I went to speak to her about it. To have it out with her. I'd say that was a perfectly healthy thing to do.'

'So would I,' Ginny said, and her eyes held Anna's for a moment. 'It's precisely what I would have done. So just what was Samuelson paying you?'

Anna named the figure, and liked the way that Ginnie just wrote it down without comment. Some days it seemed quite obscene to her what she earned, especially in the light of what her friends took home from work. But that was how it was.

'And have you a copy of your contract of employment?'

Anna opened her briefcase and took out the folder she had brought with her. In it was everything she thought might be relevant to her case.

She handed it over.

'Good,' Ginny said, looking through the documents. 'I'd say we had a good case.'

'How good's good?'

Ginny looked across at her and grinned. 'I'd say good enough to nail his bollocks to the floor!'

Anna paid off the cab driver, then turned, facing the huge window of glass, behind which could be seen an array of some of the most expensive cars in the world — Rolls-Royces and Bentleys.

You weren't kidding, she thought, walking towards the glass door to the right of the window. This is impressive.

Michael had played down his place of work. 'A car salesroom is just a car salesroom. Ours is just a little bit more swanky.'

Swanky wasn't the word for this, however. Joe Public might stand outside and gawp, but to walk in and ask to test-drive one of these beauties you'd have to have a full credit check that didn't send the red lights flashing before they'd let you get anywhere near the driver's seat.

Anna stepped inside and looked about her. Even the air — pure and sweet, like someone had filtered out all the car oil and sprayed essence of peppermint into the air-conditioning — was different. And before she had gone even two or three paces, a young man, clean-shaven and impeccably dressed, his hair cut in a fashionable but unshowy manner, approached her.

'Can I assist you, madam?'

Anna smiled at him. 'I've not come to buy, if that's what you mean.'

The young man raised an eyebrow. 'Madam?'

'Michael Cook,' she said. 'I believe he works here.'

Yet even as she said it, she heard his laughter from the other side of the sales floor, and glimpsed him, holding open the door of a Cornishe as he talked to someone inside the car.

'Shall I—' the young man began, but Anna interrupted him.

'It's OK. I'll wait until he's finished with his customer.'

The young man smiled. 'Would you like a coffee while you wait?'

'That would be nice. Black, no sugar. Thanks.'

He turned away, leaving her alone.

Anna looked about her, wondering idly what one of these cars would cost. Nothing was priced. That would have been far too vulgar. If you shopped there, they assumed you could pay for the goods, whatever they might cost.

Stepping across, she studied the cream leather interior of a Bentley sports, feeling a strange mixture of desire and aversion for all this. Part of her rebelled against the kind of person that could afford to buy this kind of luxury car — it was almost an obscenity when there were families struggling to get by — yet she could not deny the beauty of the machine, nor a dormant longing within her to own such a vehicle.

Anna turned back, looking across to where Michael was, and now saw who he was talking to.

The woman was in her thirties. She was tanned — that kind of year-round tan that only the idle rich can afford — and her clothes were expensive and stylish, their designer labels worn on the inside. Not only that, but she was attractive. Incredibly attractive, in fact, and with a bone structure to die for. And as she talked to Michael, Anna could see how he responded to her, his body language accommodating hers.

Had he touched her knee as he reached across her? Anna thought he had.

She felt herself go cold. Michael was flirting with the woman. And this time when he laughed, she felt a tiny shiver of anger race up her spine that made the fine hairs at the base of her neck stand on end.

Suddenly she knew that it had been a mistake to come

here. No matter how hard she willed herself to be rational, told herself that it was all harmless fun, her heart thumped in her chest and the blood rose up, filling her head so that it felt as though it might explode.

And when, slowly, she began to walk towards him – while Michael, unaware of her, continued to joke and flirt in that casual way of his that she had liked so much the other evening – it was as though she were someone else; as though she were no longer in control of her own body.

The woman noticed her first, the smile on her face fading into a quizzical look. And then Michael, following her gaze, turned and saw Anna there.

'Anna?'

'Enjoying yourself?' she said, glancing down at the woman's long, smooth legs as they stretched towards the driving pedals.

Michael looked stunned. 'Pardon?'

'You really had me fooled, you know. Mr Charm. Mr Sincerity.'

'Anna, I don't know what you mean.'

'I think you know *exactly* what I mean!' And Anna gestured towards the woman, who was by now looking quite uncomfortable.

'Anna!' He turned to the woman. 'I'm really sorry. Would you excuse me a moment?'

Michael stepped across and, lowering his voice, leaned towards Anna. 'What are you doing here? And what is this? I'm dealing with a customer.'

'Yes,' she sneered. 'I can see that!'

'Anna!' For the first time a note of real irritation entered his voice. 'This is my job.'

'Oh, I see. So you get to screw all the female customers as a perk, right?'

'Anna! Grow up!' he took her arm, meaning to lead her away, but she shrugged him off.

'*Me* grow up! It's men like you who need to grow up.
Another notch on the bedpost. Another conquest to brag about
up the pub, eh? God, what an idiot I've been! I really thought
you were different, you know that? But you're just like all the
rest of them, aren't you?' She laughed bitterly. 'Oh, you were
right, Michael. For all the frills, you're just another cheap car
salesman!'

He glowered at her. 'Said enough?'

Anna swallowed, then nodded.

'Good. Now leave. Before I have you thrown out.'

Anna shivered, her voice small now. 'You wouldn't dare.'

'Wouldn't I?' And suddenly she saw a toughness in him she
hadn't suspected. 'Listen. I liked you, Anna, and I wanted to
see you again. But I'm not putting up with this kind of crap.
I was being nice to a customer. That's my job. And it goes
no further than that. ' He shook his head, then looked down.
'You'd better go.'

She wanted to speak. She opened her mouth to speak . . .

'Just go.'

Anna turned, her face burning with embarrassment, then
walked back the way she'd come, not daring to look back.
And as she stood outside on the pavement, only half aware
of the empty cabs rushing past her in the tree-lined square,
she realised suddenly what she had done and the first tears
fell, smearing her make-up as they trickled down her cheeks
and on to her neck.

Karen paused before the door, then knocked.

'Come in . . .'

Mr Keen's secretary, Joan, looked up as Karen entered.
'Oh . . . Karen, I didn't think . . . Look, take a seat. He's
got someone in with him right now, but—'

'Thanks.'

Karen sat on one of the three low chairs to the left of the

office, feeling more like a pupil who was about to be chastised than a grown-up teacher. The letter of resignation was in her bag and she was determined to give it to him now, before her nerve failed her. She had come straight here, not able to face the ordeal of the staffroom.

'Coffee?'

'What?' Karen looked across. Joan was one of those women who seem to have been in their positions for ever. She never aged and she was never sick. She had been mid-fifties, it seemed, for a good decade or two.

'Coffee? There's a fresh pot . . .'

Karen smiled, meaning to say no, then changed her mind. 'OK. White please, and no sugar.'

She looked away, trying to still the sudden beating of her heart, as the older woman pottered about on the far side of the room, making the coffee.

'There,' Joan said, after a moment, leaning over Karen as she handed her the cup. Then, unexpectedly, she sat down alongside her.

'Look, tell me if it's none of my business, but I just wanted to say that I think you've had a rough time of it, and that if it means anything, you have my sympathy. Who you are or what you do in your own time is none of their damn business and I think that ghastly woman has a nerve poking her nose in.'

Joan drew in a breath, real indignation burning in her momentarily. Then, with a self-deprecating laugh, she said, 'There. I've got it off my chest.'

'Thanks,' Karen said, genuinely touched by the other woman's concern; for the first time in a long while feeling that she might not be alone.

'Just hold on in there,' Joan said, squeezing her arm briefly. 'And don't let that arsehole browbeat you. Stand up for yourself.'

Karen almost laughed. She had always thought that Joan idolised the head. But now she knew. She smiled. 'I will. Stand up for myself, that is.'

'Good.' Joan stood again, then went back to her desk. 'Oh, and by the way, you'll be glad to know that Barrett was suspended the other day.'

'Suspended?' Karen almost spilled her coffee.

'Seems he took a swing at Mr Cousins in the gym. Put the poor man in hospital.'

Karen's mouth fell open. '*Really?*'

Joan grinned. 'Nothing serious. Bruised pride more than anything. But Mr Keen acted swiftly . . . for once.'

Karen shook her head. She was surprised that Stuart Milne hadn't been on with the news. She went to speak, to ask Joan a question, but just then the door to Keen's office opened and he stepped out, followed by an elderly-looking woman.

The woman was smiling and nodding, but when she saw Karen the smile drained from her face. Tersely she said goodbye to Keen and left.

He turned to Karen, a little shaken to see her there. 'I didn't expect—'

'I'm not suspended, am I?'

'No, it's just . . .' Keen swallowed, then. 'Come in.'

Karen moved past him and walked across, taking her seat; turning to watch him as he came round his desk.

'There have been developments,' he began, clearing his throat.

'Barrett's been suspended, I hear.'

'Yes, I, er . . .'

'That was the chair of governors, wasn't it?'

Keen almost squirmed in his seat.

Karen nodded. 'I thought so.' She took a breath, then: 'I understand my union representative has already been in touch.'

'He has.'

'Then there'll be no problem about me resuming my duties?'

'No, but . . .' Keen hesitated. 'Look, Karen. I'm prepared to back you up when it comes to the governors, but as for your future conduct, well, you have a warning on your record. Any further lapses of behaviour . . .'

She stood. 'I understand. Well . . . I'd like to get on, now . . . if that's all right with you?'

Keen nodded slowly. 'Karen . . .?'

'Yes?'

'I don't care what you are, but . . . well, discretion's the name of the game.'

Karen smiled, wishing for a moment that he could know the contempt she held him in.

'Yes, headmaster.'

Outside in the corridor, she stopped, silently whooping for joy, the letter in her bag forgotten. Then, realising that she was late for her first lesson, she turned and hurried towards the staffroom. It was time to put it all behind her.

It was the last period of the morning, and Karen, sitting there at the front of the class as they read aloud the duel scene from *Hamlet*, found herself staring out of the window, smiling.

She was back in control of her life. Oh, there were still problems with Chris, but she felt she had the strength now to face them and resolve them. After all, the worst of it was behind her now. She had told her parents.

No. There would be no more pretending. They would accept her on her own terms or not at all. Chris had been right. You couldn't live life on your knees. You had to be open about what you were. Yes, and she had worried far too much about what other people had thought, and where had it got her? Close to losing the best friend she had ever had.

It was only six days now from the end of term. The school holidays loomed. Well, she would do something positive with them this time. Maybe book a holiday with Chris. Go to the Greek Isles or something.

'Karen?'

She turned to see Joan standing in the doorway. The various readers had fallen silent.

There was something odd about her expression.

'Can I have a quiet word?'

Karen frowned, then turned back to her class. 'All right. Just read silently for a while, class. I won't be a moment.'

She went out, into the corridor. 'Yes?' she asked, wondering what was going on. 'Has he changed his mind or something?'

But Joan reached past her and closed the classroom door. 'I'm sorry, Karen, but we've had a phone call. It's your father . . . it seems he's had a heart attack.'

Part Three

— Two weeks later —

'Bloody hell!' Mandy said, coming back from the dance floor to rejoin her workmates, who were sitting about one of the tables at the side. 'Don't they ever play any slow ones?'

'It's called Jungle,' Tracey said, leaning across and yelling at her as the music started up again. Lights began to pulse frenetically.

'*Jungle?*' Mandy said, yelling back at her. 'Well, give me disco any day of the week! Anyone want another drink?'

There were nods from all round. Jill reached out and touched her arm. 'I'll come and give you a hand.'

She knew what they all wanted. Like herself, they were creatures of habit. Two vodkas, one white-wine spritza, a Becks Ice, a gin and tonic and an orange juice.

The orange juice was for Tracey. But then, Tracey took other things to get her high, and Mandy knew better than to ask. After all, as long as no one got hurt, who was she to judge?

Jill led the way through the packed room until the two of them stood at the bar. Mandy ordered, then turned, glancing along, eyeing up the talent. She had barely checked out more than a handful — most of them eyeing the younger, more slender female specimens that crowded the dance floor — when she did a double-take, her mouth falling open.

'Mand?'

'What?'

'You look like you've seen a ghost.'

'Do I?' Mandy forced herself to meet Jill's eyes, then, leaning closer, keeping her voice low: 'I just recognised someone, that's all. Over there!' Mandy nodded in Jo's direction.

'What, the one with his hands all over the Pamela Anderson lookalike?' she asked, glancing over her shoulder.

Mandy swallowed. 'Yeah. That's the one.'

It was two weeks now since she had seen Jo come out of that house off Essex Road, but she'd seen the woman clearly enough to know that she was the same bint as was now sitting at the bar with him.

She moved back a little, so that Jill stood between her and Jo's line of vision, and as the barman brought their drinks, so she paid him as quickly as possible, moving away before Jo looked up and saw her watching him.

Returning to the table, she and Jill handed out the drinks, then took their own seats.

'Well?' Jill asked, raising her voice so that everyone was included. 'Who is he, then?'

'Who's who?' Tracey asked, casting her eyes over the guys propping up the bar.

'Just someone I used to know,' Mandy said, sounding calmer than she felt.

'Well, I wouldn't mind getting to *know* him,' Jill said. 'He's bleedin' gorgeous. And I do love a mature man.'

'Where d'you know him from, then?' Jackie, the new receptionist, asked. 'An old flame, is he?'

'No,' Mandy said, picking up her vodka. 'He's me best mate's husband, actually.'

'What? That's not her over there though, is it?'

Mandy shook her head solemnly, looking across at the two

of them as they laughed, their heads close, mouths almost touching.

'Dirty little bugger! Mind you, she looks a right old slapper.'

Yes, Mandy thought, but Jo knows exactly what he's doing! She took a large swig of her vodka and grimaced.

'So she don't know about her, then. Your mate?' Jill asked.

Mandy shook her head. 'She's just 'ad a baby, too. Eight weeks back. Lovely little thing. And here *he* is . . .'

'So what you gonna do? You gonna tell her, or what?' Jackie asked, her eyes wide with excitement at the notion that Mandy's best friend's husband was misbehaving right before their eyes.

'I wouldn't if I was you,' Jill said. 'A friend of mine did that. Her mate's husband turned up at her flat and made a pass at her so she grassed on him. And what did she get for her pains? A good hiding and a load of verbal from her so-called friend. As for the husband, well the wife couldn't do enough for him after that.' She shook her head. 'Amazing, ain't it?'

Mandy stared down into the remains of her sixth vodka. Maybe, she thought, but I can't let him get away with it. Susie may not thank me for it now, but in the long run . . .

The incident had soured her mood. Before she'd seen them, she'd been up for it. Game to end up in some other stranger's bed, 'playing with the old man's train set' as Tracey called it. Now she just felt miserable and depressed.

Grace nudged her. 'Why don't you just go over and slap the bastard?'

Mandy smiled weakly. It was what part of her felt like doing — because deep down she felt it wasn't only Susie he was betraying, it was her.

She finished her vodka, then picked up her bag. 'Look . . . I think I'll get an early night.'

'Ma-and?' Jill said, disappointed now. 'Don't go! I thought we might have a foursome . . . with those two over there.' She nodded towards a couple of middle-aged men standing at the edge of the dance floor, visibly salivating over the sight of so much gyrating female flesh as their sensible shoes tapped the wood, out of time with the music.

'Per-lease!' Mandy said, her face creasing with distaste as she rose to her feet. Jill grinned and Mandy gave her a playful punch. 'You find a couple of willing blokes who haven't been given free bus passes, you bring 'em round. You know where I live.'

'Will do, Mand!'

'See you, Mand!'

'Take care, Mand!'

'See you tomorrow . . .'

Mandy smiled and gave a little wave to each of them in turn, then quickly wove her way through the crowd, stopping briefly behind a huge pillar to make a call on her mobile. Then, making sure she kept over to the left, well out of Jo's eyeline, she finally emerged into the street, relieved to taste the cool night air. Oblivious to two couples arguing animatedly just a couple of feet away, Mandy leaned against the brick wall allowing herself, finally, to absorb the full shock of seeing Jo with that woman again.

What *was* he up to? Had things gone wrong that quickly between him and Susie? He had seemed fine at the hospital — elated, *besotted* with little Nathan. But changing dirty nappies looked to be the last thing on his mind right now. The only underwear *he'd* be removing in the next few hours would be flimsy and silken!

Well, she wasn't having any of it! If Susie chose to tell her to fuck off and mind her own business, so be it, but she couldn't just carry on as though nothing had happened.

She took a long, calming breath, then, hearing the distinctive sound of a taxi, pushed away unsteadily from the wall, and, waving an arm vigorously at the approaching vehicle, flagged it down.

'You took your time,' she said as she climbed in the back.

'That's all I need. A stroppy customer!'

Mandy smiled, meeting the driver's eyes briefly in his mirror.

'So! Where to, then, love?' he grinned. 'The arches suit you?'

'Here!' Doreen said, holding out her arms towards Susie. 'Let me hold him while you go upstairs and run his bath.'

Handing Nathan over, Susie made her way along the hall and up the stairs. As she climbed, the sound of her mother's singing filtered up to her, the familiar words of the old music hall songs imprinted in Susie's memory from childhood. Turning on the taps and placing her hand beneath the running water, she listened to the wildly inappropriate lyrics − about drunks mopping whisky off the floor − and smiled to herself.

As the water splashed into the bath, Susie walked through to her old room, where the travel cot had been erected and placed beside the bed. Lyndsay had given it to her mum years ago, so that when her kids stayed over there was an extra bed. Now, when Susie spent the occasional night there, it was where Nathan at least started off the evening, invariably waking the next morning snuggled beside Susie, his head resting in the crook of her aching arm.

Susie pulled a nappy, vest and babygro from the overnight bag and laid them out on the bed before making her way across the landing towards the bathroom.

'Mum!' she yelled down the stairs. 'His bath's ready!'

She walked into the bathroom and turned off the hot tap, tested that the water was just right, then squirted in some bath liquid and draped the towel over the radiator. She listened as her mother's heavy footsteps sounded on the stairs, then looked up as she appeared in the doorway.

Doreen propped herself up against the frame, Nathan resting on her hip.

'I tell you what, Suse! He ain't half getting heavy!'

Susie grinned as she stepped across and took the baby from her, lifting him high into the air, making him giggle. Sitting on the edge of the bath, Nathan balanced on her lap, she peeled off his clothes and dropped his soiled nappy into a perfumed plastic bag. Then, leaning over, she carefully lowered him into the warm bubbly water, one arm across the back of his neck, her hand hooked under his armpit.

The baby squealed and gurgled with delight as Susie gently splashed water over his tiny body, his innocent pleasure filling her with joy.

Doreen looked on, watching the two of them together. She had almost given up on Susie, fearing she might remain on her own for ever. It was something that had concerned her, particularly in her darkest moments, when she'd worried about dying and leaving her youngest child behind with nobody to look out for her. No matter how old your kids got, nor how sophisticated *they* thought they were, they were still just kids. But then Susie met Jo. And now she had Nathan. Doreen had to admit that it was a relief.

'How's Jo?'

'Oh, all right,' Susie answered, massaging bubbles into the baby's shoulders.

'So where's he gone tonight?'

Doreen stepped over to the airing cupboard and took out a fresh flannel.

'Just up the pub with his mates, I think.'

'Your father went for a drink with him the other day. Did he say?'

Susie glanced up, reaching out for the flannel Doreen held out to her.

'Yeah. He did mention something.'

The truth was she couldn't remember whether he had or not: half the time she wasn't listening to what he said and the rest of the time it just didn't seem to stay with her.

'Your dad enjoyed it.'

'Well he would, wouldn't he. They were in a pub.'

'Now don't be unfair!' But Doreen smiled in spite of herself. 'Actually he said Jo seemed a bit . . .'

Kneeling beside the bath now, Susie looked up at her. 'A bit what?'

Doreen shrugged. 'Oh, I dunno. It was probably just your father . . .'

'No. Go on. Seemed a bit what? Drunk? Ill? Hungry? *What?*'

'Well,' Doreen started, partly regretting having brought it up, 'all he said was that Jo was feeling a bit . . . neglected.'

Susie laughed loudly, relieved. Standing up, she scooped Nathan out of the bath. 'Give us the towel, will you?'

Doreen handed over the warmed fluffy towel and Susie wrapped it round the infant, cuddling him to her as she sat on the lid of the toilet seat.

'Well, your dad seemed to think it was serious.'

'Serious? 'Cos Jo's feeling *neglected*? Do me a favour, Mother. He's just feeling bloody sorry for himself. What's he think *I* feel like? Knackered, that's what!'

'I know, love. But you know what men are like. They're just big kids themselves. They ain't got no idea what it's like, running round trying to do everything. They can only think of one thing at a time and . . .'

'Yeah! And at the moment the one thing Jo seems to think about *all* the time is our bloody sex life!'

Doreen was feeling like the devil's advocate but Bobby had told her that it was her place to have a word with her daughter; get her to come to her senses and find a bit of time for her husband. He had said no more than that, but Doreen knew from bitter experience what could happen if a man thought he wasn't wanted any more . . . even if Bobby didn't know she knew.

'I know it's hard, with the baby waking for his feeds an' all that . . .'

'Yeah! See, he don't think of that! *I'm* the one up three times in the night. *Five* times the other night! No wonder all I wanna do is go to sleep!'

Doreen nodded sympathetically. 'What about if I had Nathan for you one night?'

'What?'

'Well, I could have him round here. You and Jo could go out for a meal or something. Relax a bit. You could pick him up in the morning.'

'Ain't you forgetting something?' Doreen stared at her. 'Well, unless you think you're gonna be able to strap me boobs on you, you ain't gonna be able to feed him, are you?'

'I thought you had one of them pump things. You could express the milk then I could give it to him in his bottle.'

'Nah! He wouldn't like it,' she said, squeezing Nathan to her, safe in the knowledge that he was too young to contradict. 'And, anyway. It'd kill you, up and down all night.'

'Granted! If I had to do it all the time. But not just for one night. And anyway, you're forgetting. I have got four other grandkids. I've done all this before, you know.'

'I know you have,' Susie said, getting to her feet. 'But he's too young yet. Thanks all the same, though, Mum.'

Doreen nodded, feeling a little hurt. 'Well, if you change your mind . . .'

Susie smiled. Walking past her on her way to the bedroom, she called over her shoulder, 'Don't worry. Jo'll be all right.' But even as she said it, she knew that it was herself she was trying to reassure.

It was a cold, unseasonable morning. Rain had fallen in the night and the streets were dark and wet, the sky overcast, as Karen stepped down from the bus and turned into the narrow side street, heading for her parents' house.

It was two weeks now since she had stood at the side of her father's hospital bed, shocked by his appearance even as she tried to comfort her mother, who sat there, bewildered, holding her husband's pale, limp hand, unable to understand what all the drips and wires were doing connected up to this man who, until a day or so before, had been as robust as a prize bull.

Karen had felt guilty, of course. No matter how many times Chris had told her she was not to blame — that this kind of thing just happened, especially to men of her father's age — she kept wondering if her news had brought this on; whether the shock of it had triggered some deeper, physical malaise.

Her brother, naturally, had blamed her totally, and had told her bluntly on the phone that she was not to visit her father again. Afraid of doing any more damage, she had complied, but now he was well enough to be allowed home, and she felt she *had* to see him, if only to make her peace.

Even so, walking those last few yards up the path to the doorway, she felt a genuine fear engulf her. She stopped, breathless suddenly, for the first time in her life afraid — *afraid!* — of knocking at her own door.

It was absurd. This was her family, the people who were supposed to love her no matter what, and what had she done to them? Nothing! And yet she felt the hostility even before she took those last few steps and reached out to grasp the familiar stainless-steel knocker.

There was movement in the shadows of the hallway beyond the frosted glass, and then the door swung open.

'Oh . . .'

Her mother frowned, then stepped back. No smile. No cheery greeting, just 'Oh . . .' and that distant frown.

Her brother's voice sounded from the kitchen. 'Mum? Who is it?'

Her mother looked down, then looked up again, meeting her eyes coldly. 'He won't see you, you know.'

'What?'

'Your dad. He won't see you.'

Karen's heart was going like a steamhammer in her chest. 'But he must. He can't send me away.'

Her brother called again. 'Mum?'

'Look, love, just leave it for now. Please. Don't make a fuss. When he's a bit better . . .'

'But, Mum . . .' she was almost in tears now, 'I *have* to see him. I have to talk to him.'

'Oh, it's you is it?' her brother said, coming alongside her mother, a scornful sneer on his face. 'I'm surprised you've the nerve to show your face!'

Karen ignored him, looking to her mother. 'Mum . . . please . . .'

'I can't, Karen . . .' Her mother sighed. 'Your dad's already said.'

'Yeah, too bleedin' right he's said,' her brother chipped in. 'Now bugger off back to your *friends*!'

'Jack!' her mother said. But nothing more. Nothing to suggest she felt any different from her son.

Karen stood there a moment longer, then, with a shudder that went right through her, she turned and slowly walked back to the gate, conscious of the two of them watching her go. It felt like she was in a nightmare, such that even the simple act of walking seemed unreal, and it was only when she was back at the bus stop, her back against the glass of the shelter, that she began to feel normal again.

'Are you all right, dear?'

Karen turned. An elderly woman sat next to her, looking up into her face, concerned. 'Pardon?'

'I said, are you feeling OK. You look a bit distressed, my love.'

'Distressed?' Karen gave a half-smile, almost laughing at the understatement. Distressed. She felt like she had just died and come back as a ghost. 'No,' she said, keeping the bitterness and the anguish she was feeling from her voice. 'No, no, I'm fine, thanks.'

Anna closed the door behind her, then carried the bags through into the living room, setting them down on the sofa. Sighing, she went across and poured herself a large gin and tonic, then walked over to the answerphone.

No messages. She had been out six hours and no one – not a single soul – had rung.

She took a long refreshing mouthful of her drink, then settled down on the sofa next to her purchases. She had been up to Knightsbridge, indulging in a little comfort shopping in an attempt to raise her spirits: a skirt and little knitted top from Nicole Farhi, a sexy Versace dress, a trouser suit from Armani and some Emma Hope shoes.

All in all it had set her back just over thirteen hundred pounds. She could afford it now that they had settled with Samuelson, but even she recognised that it was a symptom, like the drinking, of a deep-rooted unease at the way her life was heading.

Frank, for instance. Only yesterday he had phoned to say

that he couldn't meet her tonight. His wife, it seemed, had become suspicious, and so he thought it best if they cooled things for a while. Although surprised, she had accepted it without a fuss. But later, musing over it, she had suspected that it might be more to do with her recent depression over the loss of her job and Frank's fears that she might become too demanding, too dependent on him.

And maybe he was right. She *had* been drinking a lot more than usual, and only last week a minor disagreement between them had got out of hand and ended in a full-blown public row. It wasn't their first, but it had been severe enough to leave them both in a state of shock.

And then there was her mother. For years now Anna had suspected that many of her mother's so-called ailments were little more than attention-seeking devices, to make her feel guilty enough to pay a visit. But, seeing her the other weekend, she had realised that the woman really was unwell, and for the first time had contemplated that there might be something seriously wrong with her.

Michael, too, had been a problem. She had thought it all done with after that row at his workplace, and had never expected to hear from him again, but he had left several messages on her answerphone, asking her to call him.

She hadn't, of course. She felt too embarrassed by the thought of what she'd said and done to even contemplate phoning. Even so, it was yet one more thing nagging at her.

Anna took the shoes out and tried them on, walking up and down the polished boards. Then, sighing again, she slipped them off and took out the dress.

It was beautiful — probably the nicest dress she had ever bought herself — but what good was a beautiful dress unless you had someone to wear it for?

The temptation to phone Michael — to swallow her pride and beg him to see her tonight — was enormous, but she knew she wouldn't. Anna reached across and picked up her glass again, draining it, then stood, meaning to go out to the kitchen and pour herself another, yet as she did the phone rang.

She turned, staring at it as it continued to ring. As her message ended and the answerphone clicked, she listened.

'Hello, Anna? This is Piers Crowley from MPA. It's two fifteen on Friday and I'm phoning to see whether you could come in and see us Monday morning at nine. If that's difficult let me know . . .'

At the first mention of Piers's name, Anna had hurried across. She picked up the phone.

'Piers? Hi! I've just walked in the door . . .'

'Hi, Anna. I'm glad I caught you. Look, I can't speak now, but can you make it on Monday?'

'Well, yes, but what's it all about?'

'As I said, I can't really discuss it on the phone. But I think you'll be interested.'

'Nine? At your offices?'

'Right. You know where we are.'

She smiled. 'I most certainly do.'

'Then I'll see you there. 'Bye.'

The phone clicked and then burred. Anna replaced the receiver, then looked back across the room thoughtfully. MPA were Samuelson's main rivals in the magazine publishing world, and if they wanted to talk . . .

Then again, she recalled the last time she had been in their building, that day she had chewed out Barbara Stannard.

For a moment the thought that they were going to offer her a job as that bitch Barbara's assistant flitted through her mind. It was the kind of hideous thing some people did; they got a kick out of tormenting you when you were down. But she didn't think so. Piers Crowley had always struck her as a decent bloke, so maybe, just maybe, they were going to offer her a job.

'OK,' she said, beginning to organise herself. 'First you're going to put on a pot of coffee. Then you're going to run yourself a deep, bubbly bath.'

Yes. It was time she stopped moping about and feeling sorry for herself. Time she got back on her feet and back into the fray.

Anna smiled, then walked across to the sofa and pulled the Armani suit from its bag.

Mandy closed the tiny circular door of the washing machine, set the controls, then jabbed the button. At once the thing began to hum.

That was that. Her chores done for the day. Or almost all of them. There was just one more thing.

She glanced up at the clock on the wall. It was almost a quarter to three. Jo would still be out at work, so if she went round now . . .

Her mouth went dry at the thought of what she was about to do. Even so, she knew that she would go through with it.

Picking up the phone, she dialled Susie's number, then waited as it rang and rang. For a moment she felt relieved that Susie wasn't there, but then she answered, sounding breathless.

'Hi!'

'Suse?'

'Oh, hi, Mand? How are ya?'

'Fine. Listen, Suse! You in for a bit? Only I thought I'd pop round.'

'Yeah . . . Great! I've got Michelle from next door here but we're just havin' a cup of tea. It'll be nice to see you.' Mandy hesitated. 'Anyway,' Susie laughed. 'It'd be good to catch up on all the gossip.'

'You sure?'

'Yeah, 'course.'

'OK. I'll see you in a mo.'

She put the phone down, then stood there, chewing on a thumbnail, nervous suddenly. She'd wanted to catch Susie on her own. But there was no going back now. She'd just have to wait until this Michelle had gone home.

Mandy gathered up her jacket and her coat, then went out, locking the door behind her. It wasn't often that she had the sense that she was doing something important — something memorable — but as she walked along in the afternoon sunlight, she seemed suddenly aware of everything about her. If things didn't go well, this might be it between her and Susie. But that was a risk she would have to take. *She* knew she was acting in Susie's best interest. There was no other way. Well, there was, but confronting Jo was not an option: too much had gone on between them; too little resolved, by them at any rate.

It was that — the thought that Susie had forgiven her once already — that Mandy held on to now. She knew that their friendship could survive this, but even so she crossed her fingers.

It took her just over ten minutes to get round to Susie's, and as she walked up the stone steps she thought of Jo — of him sitting at work even now, unaware that his world was about to be blasted apart — and felt a small twinge of guilt. But that wasn't going to stop her. She wasn't the one who was screwing around this time, it was him. And if he couldn't behave himself, then he deserved everything he got. Susie had been an angel, and this was how he'd repaid her.

Mandy rang the bell, hearing a child's shriek from inside. A moment later Susie opened the door.

'Hi, Mand! Come on in!' And she reached out, kissing Mandy's cheek cheerfully. 'It's chaos, but . . .'

Mandy moved past her, then stopped, there in the hallway, just outside the living room, turning to face Susie.

'Suse . . .'

But at that moment the child's shrieks rose up again and a little boy of three or four rushed out past Mandy, heading for the stairs.

'Jamie . . .' Susie called to him. 'Slow down or you'll have an accident!'

She looked back at Mandy. 'He's Michelle's little boy. You know, from next door. Here . . . come in and I'll introduce you.'

'Suse, I . . .'

'I'll make a fresh pot in a minute,' Susie said, moving past her, seeming not to have heard the strange tone in Mandy's voice. 'Anyway . . . come in . . .'

Mandy sighed, then turned and followed Susie through.

'Christ!'

Music was playing, low in the background. Classical music with violins. But it wasn't that which made Mandy exclaim out loud. There, sitting on Susie's sofa, a tea plate on her knee, busy gorging herself on a large cream bun, was the blonde woman Mandy had last seen propping up a bar with Jo.

Susie looked to Mandy, then grinned. 'Yeah, well, Gus lent me it . . . Apparently it's good for little 'uns. Very soothing.'

'What?' Mandy looked to her, gobsmacked.

'The music. It's some bloke called Vivaldi.' Susie shrugged. 'Mind you, I think I prefer Sting meself . . .' Then, smiling. 'Anyway, Mand, this is Michelle. Michelle's been my saviour. When I first had Nathan she was round all the time, helping out, weren't you?' Michelle smiled, enjoying being described thus. 'Anyway . . . Michelle, this is my best friend, Mandy.'

As in a dream, Mandy found herself putting out her hand, the absurd but vivid thought that that same hand had probably been holding Jo's prick only hours before, making her draw it back just as quickly as she decently could.

'Hi! Nice to meet you, Mandy,' Michelle said, smiling openly, clearly not recognising her from the other evening. Jamie ran back into the room, slamming into Mandy's legs. Michelle pulled him away, turning him in the direction of the open patio doors. 'You got kids, Mandy?'

'Two,' Mandy said, her mind reeling, wondering how she was going to broach the subject now. 'But they're grown up.'

'Mand?'

Mandy looked to Susie. 'What?'

'You gonna sit down, or what? Here . . . and give us that jacket. I'll hang it up for you.'

'Oh . . . right . . .'

She handed Susie her jacket, then sat in the armchair across from the woman. As Susie left the room, Mandy found herself looking down at her feet, suddenly embarrassed. The urge to say something – to let this cheating cow know that she knew – was overpowering, but she held her tongue. And then Susie was back in the room and the moment had passed.

'Well,' Susie said, standing there, holding out a plate of doughnuts. 'Anyone for something fat and sticky?'

Mandy stayed an hour, then hurried home. It was half four now, but Jo would still be there at his desk. That was, if he wasn't out shagging some other woman on some unsuspecting client's floor.

She had no need to look up his number: it was still imprinted in her mental address book. Suddenly, he was on the line.

'Hello, Jonathan Ball speaking . . .'

Mandy swallowed. 'Hello, this is Mandy . . . Mandy Evans . . .'

'Mand,' he said, a tone of genuine delight lighting his voice, 'how are you?'

'I'm fine, thanks. That's not why I'm phoning. I want a word.'

'Yeah . . . sure . . . fire away.'

'No. I mean I want to see you. Tonight. In the Crown.'

There was a pause, then: 'I don't think that's a good idea, Mand.'

'Don't flatter yourself. I want to talk.'

'Talk? Talk about what?'

'About you . . . and your ever so friendly neighbour.'

'Neighbour?'

'Yes. The blonde one with the big tits.'

'Oh, shit!'

'Yeah . . . So you be there. Eight o'clock. OK?'

He seemed totally subdued now. 'Yeah . . . right . . .'

She put the phone down, trembling now with indignation. For a moment she leaned against the table, waiting for it to pass, then she straightened and, going over to the washing machine, switched it off.

He'd better be there. Because if he wasn't . . .

Mandy stopped, staring out through the window, pained suddenly by the thought of that woman sitting there in Susie's living room, drinking her tea and eating her cakes, and all the while . . .

The bitch!

Yeah, well, she'd have her, and no mistake. But first, Jo!

''Bye, then, Jan. And take care. I've got me fingers crossed for you, all right?'

As Mandy's voice broke off at the other end of the phone, Janet smiled for the first time that day. She'd not been the cheeriest of souls lately, but that was understandable. Waiting to discover whether all the hope, the emotion and the money you'd invested in pursuit of a baby had paid off was *not* a fun time.

She replaced the receiver, then looked about her at the spotless living room.

At the hospital they had told her to go away and act as though she were pregnant. But how could she do that? How could she allow herself to indulge in what was still, after all, only a fantasy? How could she wander through the baby department and think about what she might buy and in what colour; imagine how she might decorate the baby's bedroom; or consider the possibility of a family holiday? To do any one of these would be to risk even greater disappointment.

For now she had simply to endure, to hang on in there in limbo, harbouring the faintest glimmer of hope that just maybe . . . *maybe* she might be *pregnant*.

Janet closed her eyes. Even to say it sometimes made her feel uneasy, like she was tempting fate. And fate, she felt, had not been kind to her up till now.

Of course, every time she felt a twinge – or imagined she had – she worried. Every time she convinced herself she felt nauseous, she silently celebrated. But all she could do was wait.

Steve picked up the remote control from on top of the television and sat down beside her on the sofa, pointing his arm towards the screen and surfing the channels. Sighing, he pushed the control button, plunging it into grey nothingness, and slid the remote behind a cushion.

'What about if I go up Blockbusters? Pick up a video? I could get us some Chinese as well, while I'm out.'

Janet wrinkled her nose. 'I'm not hungry.'

She *wanted* to feel sick; it was good for morale.

'Well, what about a video, then?' Janet shrugged. 'I could try and get that new one with Michelle Pfeiffer.'

Janet gave a hollow laugh. 'You'll have to put bromide in your tea again if you're gonna ogle her all night!'

Steve's lip curled, pleased that she at least realised how much he missed making love to her, being close to her.

Even now, when they were so near, when they should have been there for one another, Janet knew that it was only their shared pain that bound them. That and their desperate need. And soon, God willing — yes, she had even started praying! — that would be over and she could allow herself to *feel* again. But for now it was hard enough just getting through.

Steve pulled the remote from behind the cushion and activated the television, staring vacantly at the game show, turning down the volume to make it more interesting.

'What did Mandy have to say?' he said, his eyes still fixed on the screen.

'Oh, you know. Wanted to know how it was going.'

'What d'you say?'

'Well, I told her, didn't I! So far, so good.'

'Any of the others phoned?'

'Yeah.'

'Susie?'

'No. But I'm gonna give her a ring.'

Surprised, Steve glanced at Janet, but she averted her eyes. 'Good!' he said, trying to suppress his delight; this was real progress.

When they got to the point where the embryos had been replaced, he'd imagined they had survived the worst. But he had soon discovered that the further along the course you travelled, the higher the stakes . . . and the greater the pressure to succeed. He hoped to God that after all this they managed to pull it off, because he wasn't sure he could go through it all again.

The phone rang and in spite of being on the table beside Janet, Steve automatically reached across and answered it.

There were some people — like her mother — that Janet found it hard to take, and Steve had perfected the art of plausible excuse-making to those with whom she did not want to speak. While others were often treated to the minute detail of their treatment, those closest to her were the ones she chose to shut out, as though she were punishing them in some way for her predicament; as though she felt that in some way they were to blame.

'Hello.'

'All right, Steve. It's Paul.'

Steve smiled. 'All right, mate?' He shook his head at Janet.

'How's it going, then?'

'Yeah. Not too bad. How 'bout you?'

'Yeah. Great! Listen, I wondered if you fancied meeting up for a pint.'

'Yeah. Great! When?'

'Tonight! Meg's working late so . . .'

'Tonight?' Steve could feel Janet's eyes on him. 'Hang on, a minute.'

Covering the mouthpiece, Steve looked up but Janet's eyes were now focused on the rolling credits for the game show. 'It's Paul. Wants to know if I wanna meet up for a drink.'

Janet shrugged, refusing to meet his gaze. 'Up to you,' she said coldly. 'Do what you want.' Reaching along the sofa she found the remote control and pointed it towards the television, flipping the channel.

Steve stared at her a moment. He desperately wanted to understand her, to hold her . . . to *slap* her. Removing his hand from the mouthpiece, he forced himself to sound cheerful.

'Paul? Sorry 'bout that, mate. Listen! Another time, eh? It's just a bit difficult tonight . . .'

For a few minutes more they talked about the Arsenal squad

for the forthcoming season and discussed who should be in and who out of the England team, before agreeing to get together before too long; maybe one Saturday after a home game.

But even then, there was no mention of his *problem*. Paul didn't ask him how *he* was; how *he* was coping. Just superficial chat about twenty-two blokes chasing a ball. A momentary bitterness enveloped him. A feeling of isolation bordering on loneliness.

Replacing the receiver, Steve looked at Janet, seeing how her eyes were focused resolutely on the newsreader.

'You should 'ave gone,' she said tonelessly. 'If you wanted to.'

'Yeah,' he said, getting up, a feeling of weariness overcoming him. 'S'pose so . . .' Then, forcing himself not to mope, not to take it out on her, he turned back and gave her a smile.

'D'you fancy a cup of tea?'

Chris pushed the door shut behind her and walked through, setting her shopping down just inside the living room door.

'Hi . . .'

Karen was sitting on the far side of the room, her back to her. When she didn't answer, Chris went across.

'Karen?'

She made to place her hands on Karen's shoulders, but she shrugged her off, then turned angrily. She had been crying.

'It's all your fault!'

Chris stepped back a pace. 'Sorry?'

'For pushing me. For goading me into telling them. Now my dad's had a heart attack and won't even speak to me. He doesn't even want to see me. And my brother—'

'Your brother's an arsehole.'

Karen's eyes flared angrily at that, but she at least didn't contest it.

'Look, I'm sorry . . .' Chris began, but Karen shook her head.

'*Sorry*? What fucking good is sorry?'

Chris bridled at that. 'Look . . . you can't go blaming me for their prejudices! I'm not the one rejecting you!'

'Aren't you?' Karen shook her head in disbelief. 'So what's been happening these past few months? Why do you keep on seeing her if everything's so bloody rosy between us, eh? Tell me that! What do you call that if not rejection?'

Chris looked away, then: 'Maybe you're right.'

'Yes, maybe I *am* right. And maybe I've just been naïve, and trusting and . . . well, just plain fucking *stupid*!'

Chris met her eyes briefly, a smouldering anger there. 'You're a big girl now.'

'Yes, aren't I?' Karen laughed bitterly. 'Oh, I've grown up one hell of a lot these last few weeks. I've had my eyes opened about any number of things.'

Chris was silent for a while, and then she shrugged. 'I think I'd better go.'

'Yes. I think you'd better go.'

Chris's chest rose and fell, then, with a little nod to herself, she turned and left.

Karen stood there a moment, unable to believe that it had ended quite like that. She wanted to rush out and catch Chris up and throw herself on her knees before her to apologise, but something held her back. Not pride, and certainly not hatred — she didn't hate Chris — but some self-preserving quality. After all she had been through, after all the hurt and suffering, she needed to find herself again. *Herself*. Not that person who had been immersed in Chris, but her real self.

But the sudden realisation that she was on her own now — that Chris would exist in another life, elsewhere, with another partner — took Karen to the edge. With a shudder, she slumped down on to the sofa once again, succumbing to the overwhelming sense of loss that welled up in her suddenly, the tears flowing freely now.

It was over.

Jo looked up sheepishly as Mandy walked across and settled herself on the stool next to him.

'What you having?' he asked her.

'Double vodka.'

The young Aussie barman nodded and turned away.

Mandy stared at Jo a moment, then shook her head. 'Don't you ever bleedin' learn?'

Jo gazed down into his pint uneasily, then shrugged. He seemed about to say something when the barman returned.

'Double vodka,' he said, setting Mandy's glass down in front of her. Jo paid, giving the young man a thin smile.

'And another thing,' Mandy said, leaning closer. 'I'd have thought you'd learned your lesson about shagging so close to home.'

Jo squirmed. 'Keep your voice down. I don't want everyone to know.'

'Well, you didn't seem to care who saw the pair of you the other night up the Venue.'

Jo's head jerked up at that, shocked. 'How'd you know about that?'

She stared a hole through him until he lowered his eyes again. 'Haven't you got any sense at all?'

Looking at the way he sat there, hunched in on himself, his chin resting on his chest, Mandy couldn't help but feel a tiny twinge of pity for him, the poor, pathetic bastard. She forced herself to sound tougher than she felt. 'Have you got any idea what this would do to Susie? She took you back after . . .' Mandy faltered. 'She took you back and you piss all over her. And what about Nathan?'

Jo slowly shook his head, raising his eyes to look at

Mandy. 'She's changed though, Mand. Everything's different now . . .'

He didn't specify, but Mandy could guess easily enough what the problem was.

'Of course it's different! She's just had a bleedin' baby, for Christ's sake.' Seeing several drinkers turn round and look at her, Mandy lowered her voice. 'So! You married a sex siren and you're lumbered with the Earth Mother, is that about it?'

Jo couldn't help but smile.

Mandy's voice was markedly softer when she next spoke. 'Look, Jo, you're no different to everyone else. Of course you'd prefer your wife to wear a little satin negligée rather than a Mickey Mouse nightshirt, but the fact is there ain't nothing sexy about breast pads and leaky tits no matter what you dress 'em up in. At least women don't think so. I know I didn't.'

The moment she made the reference to her own body she regretted it; embarrassed by the intimacy of it. But Jo was oblivious.

'It's not just the sex, Mand. It's everything. She's got no time for me. All I get is Nathan, Nathan, Nathan . . .'

'You selfish bastard! You sit there . . .'

But Jo's hand was on her arm, his other hand clasped to his head in despair. 'You know I didn't mean that the way it sounded. I love that baby. It's just . . .'

He looked so wretched, Mandy almost felt moved to wrap her arms about him and comfort him.

'D'you want another drink?' she said.

Mandy ordered herself a large vodka and another pint for Jo and they waited in silence for the barman to bring them across. Casting her eyes around the pub, Mandy noted with mixed feelings the change in decor: fresh, Art Deco, trendy. Like the fancy overpriced menu, she guessed it was intended to appeal to a different breed of clientele from the locals who had frequented it in her youth.

'So, how'd this *Michelle* thing get started, then?'

'*She* did all the running,' he said defensively. 'At first she just kept popping round when Susie was out. You know, being a bit flirty and that. Then she turned up at the shop. Made out like she was looking for a property and asked me to show her a few places. It was on a plate, wasn't it?'

Mandy sat back a little, stung by the reminder. The barman brought their drinks and she took a sip before looking back at Jo.

'So she dished it up and you just *had* to have a little nibble?' Jo lowered his eyes. 'You gotta start thinking about what you're doing to other people, Jo.'

Yet as she watched him, peering into the depths of his glass as though searching for some kind of answer, she remembered why she had fallen for him. The intoxicating mixture of vulnerability and charm. She sighed. 'I really loved you, you know.'

Jo did not look up and she was grateful.

'And when it all came out. You know, when you and Susie got married. Well, that really hurt and it took me a long, long time to get over it . . .'

Jo opened his mouth to speak but Mandy held up her hand.

'Susie loves you. She must do to have put up with . . . well, with everything that happened. But if she finds out you've let her down again, it'll break her heart. And I wouldn't wish that on anyone.'

Jo looked at her, pained now. Then, unexpectedly, he reached out and covered Mandy's hand. 'I'm sorry, Mand. I didn't mean to hurt you. I didn't mean to hurt anyone . . .'

'But you did.'

'I was weak.'

'Bollocks!' She drew her hand away. 'It won't wash, all

this *weak* crap. And if you ain't strong enough to pass over a bit of bleached-blonde nookie, then your wife and kid are probably better off without you.'

Jo sighed; so deep and heartfelt a sigh that Mandy felt her heart go out to him.

'I do love her, Mand. More than anything.'

'Then act like it, for God's sake! Be a man, not a bleedin' snake! And the first thing you can do is give this Michelle the elbow.'

'But what if she tells Susie?'

Mandy raised her chin challengingly. 'Is that what you're afraid of? That she'll talk?'

Jo took a sip of his beer, then nodded.

'Will you promise me you won't see her again?'

'I promise. I swear to God I won't see her.'

'Then leave her to me.' Mandy smiled tightly. 'You know what? I think I feel a little home visit coming on.'

Luke looked up from the sofa as Mandy came into the room. She was a lot later than she'd expected.

'Hello, love,' she said, putting her handbag down and glancing at the TV. 'You had something to eat?'

'Nah.'

'Fancy a fry-up?'

Luke grinned. 'Sounds great!'

'Two eggs or three?'

'Two's fine, Mum.'

She smiled and went through, busying herself in the kitchen. After a while Luke joined her there, taking a seat at the table.

'Mum?'

She peered at the bacon under the grill. 'Yes, love?'

'Me and me mates 'ave been talking . . .'

'Yeah?' Mandy reached out and twisted the control knob

for the front left burner on the hob, then took an egg from the box and broke it into the pan.

'And . . . well, we thought we might get a flat together.'

Mandy was just about to crack the second egg against the edge of the frying pan, but hearing what Luke had said, she hesitated and the egg broke in her hand, bits of shell dropping into the sizzling oil.

'What?'

'It's just that Kenny says I can work on the stall for him part-time. And he reckons he knows a couple of other blokes up the market who are looking for someone. So the rent'd be no problem.'

'Oh . . .' Mandy dropped the main bit of the egg shell in the box, then began to gingerly pick the tiny fragments from the pan. But her mind was only half on the job. She felt as though she had been smacked with a heavy object.

'It won't be for a coupla weeks anyway,' Luke went on. 'Joe and Danny are gonna sort the rent out with the landlord. Joe's dad's gonna be the guarantor or something, and . . .'

But Mandy wasn't really listening. She was just thinking that she'd be on her own in an empty flat with no one to come home to, and the thought of it was . . . well, *unbearable*.

'But you can't go and work up the *market*! I mean, I thought we talked about college. You don't want to throw your life away, darling. Believe me, I know.'

'Mum!' he said, laughing. 'Don't get so heavy. I got loads of time to worry about college and gettin' a proper job. Anyway, there's nothing wrong with the market.'

'Huh! You say that now the sun's shining. You wait till you gotta stand out there with your arse freezing off in the middle of winter. And there'll be no football, you know! You'll have to work Saturdays!'

'I know! I know! I ain't completely stupid!'

'No, I know you're not, love,' she said, her tone softer now, cajoling. 'But I don't want you to rush into things just 'cos your mates——'

'I can make up my own mind, you know, Mum.'

'Yes, I know you can, love,' she said, turning back to the stove, the smell of burning bacon in her nostrils. 'It's just that . . . Yeah, I know you can.'

In a daze, she dished up Luke's meal on to a plate, then set it down in front of him.

'Smashin'! Thanks, Mum!' he said. Cutting into the egg so that the yolk flooded the plate, he grinned up at Mandy. "Course, you know I'll be coming home for me dinner!'

She smiled down at him, watching with delight as he wolfed it down, but at the same time saddened by the thought that soon she would have no one to cook for. No matter what Luke said. She watched him clear the plate, then belch, and smiled to herself. But it was a muted smile.

Luke pushed away his plate and stood up from the table. Stepping across to Mandy, he kissed her cheek. 'That was great! I think I'm gonna go up now, Mum. I'm knackered.'

'Go on, then,' she said tenderly and reached out to touch his cheek. Then he was gone and Mandy was alone in the kitchen.

She sat down heavily on the chair, looking about her and wondering suddenly where it had all gone. All those years of nurturing, and now . . .

Without realising it, she found she was crying. And not just crying but sobbing, her shoulders heaving up and down as she thought of all those lost years. Years that would never come again. And as she cried she realised that she was afraid — afraid of the well of loneliness that was opening up before her. She'd thought of herself as being on her own, but there had always been Luke. Her connection with the past. Living proof that all those years with Pete had not been wasted; his presence a daily reminder that she had achieved *something* worthwhile. That there was a purpose.

On a sudden wave of panic she realised that the split with Pete had initiated merely the first stage in the reinvention of Mandy Evans, and that with some trepidation she was about to enter the next.

Mandy shuddered and wiped her hand across her face, then stood, busying herself, clearing up after her son.

Jo turned in the doorway, looking up at the clear night sky, his eyes going to the moon. It was not often he was even aware of what was overhead, but tonight . . .

He smiled, then turned and stepped inside, pulling the door shut quietly behind him. After Mandy had gone, he'd ordered another pint, brooding over what had been said between them. She was a gem. He only really understood that now.

And she was right, too. He ought to be thankful for what he had. There weren't many like Susie. And it was only natural that she should be all wrapped up in the baby.

Taking off his shoes, he tiptoed up the stairs, closing the bathroom door behind him before he peed, careful to aim at the rim of the bowl so he wouldn't wake them. Then, slipping off all but his boxers, he tiptoed through into the bedroom.

Susie was asleep on her side in the middle of the bed, little Nathan tucked into the crook of her left arm.

For a moment he simply looked, filled with an overwhelming love for them both. Then, careful not to disturb Susie, he slipped into the narrow space beside her, putting his arm round her shoulder, the fingers of his right hand resting on Nathan's tiny back. And as he did, Susie made a tiny little noise and snuggled back against him.

The warmth of her inflamed him, made him want to have her there and then from behind. But, mindful of what Mandy had said to him, he simply lay there, his eyes closed, keeping as still as he could, holding the woman he loved and listening to the peaceful pattern of her breathing, until he, too, slept.

Anna sat in the plush outer office at the top of the MPA building, her legs crossed, the Armani suit she had bought only two days back providing the ultimate in power dressing. From time to time the receptionist would look up from her desk on the far side of the luxuriously carpeted room and glance across at her, but Anna feigned a casual disinterest.

Truth was, her heart was going like an express train and now that she was here it was more fear than excitement she felt. Not that she needed to fear anything – her CV and her own personal qualities were enough to carry her into almost any job in the industry – it was just that Samuelson had dealt her self-confidence a severe blow when he had fired her. It had made her question whether she really was as good as she thought she was.

The oak-panelled door to her right swung open and Piers Crowley stepped out, smiling across at her.

'Anna . . . Glad you could make it. Come on in.'

Anna got up and, as calmly and casually as she could, walked across, entering the room.

There were five people there, not including Piers. An elderly but distinguished-looking man sat behind the desk by the window. To his left sat a dark-haired, youngish woman wearing a pair of very stylish glasses. Two middle-aged, besuited men sat on a long black leather sofa to her left, half-filled cups of coffee on the coffee table in front of them, while another woman – a good ten years Anna's senior – stood beside the coffee-maker in the right-hand corner of the room.

'Would you like some coffee, Anna?'

'Please . . . black, no sugar.'

Piers closed the door then came and stood beside her. 'I think you know everyone here.'

Anna smiled. 'Hi . . .'

There were smiles and murmured greetings. It was only nine, but they had clearly already been in session for some while. Various papers were scattered over the big polished desk, as well as on the two large rectangular coffee tables that rested between the sofas in the centre of the office.

Piers gestured towards the other sofa. 'If you'd take a seat, Anna, we'll get straight to business.' He smiled. 'We've a proposition to put to you, and I *think* you're going to like it . . .'

Half an hour later, Anna sat back, her head in a spin. The job sounded wonderful — astonishing, even — but there were still questions to be asked.

'OK,' she said. 'I've heard you, and I like the broad sketch of things, but what you're proposing is basically a male-orientated magazine . . .'

'So why not a male editor?' It was the older woman, Sonya Kavitz, who spoke. 'Simple. Because everyone else has one. We want this to be different. Ballsy but not self-indulgent. And though we intend to compete with the other male glossies, we also want to go into new territory.' She smiled. 'Remember the way *Cosmopolitan* became a crossover magazine in the late seventies and eighties? How men suddenly began to read it? Well, we want to achieve the same kind of thing, but from the other direction.'

Anna nodded. 'Something that doesn't put up walls about itself that say "Men Only".'

'To coin a phrase . . .'

There was laughter at that. Relaxed laughter. Anna knew, then, that she only had to say yes. Even so . . .

'Do you have a title for it yet?'

One of the middle-aged men — Rob Storey, who had worked with Anna years before on *Nineteen* — chirped up. 'We thought of something like *Truce*. Something to suggest an end to the sex wars. Or, at least, a temporary surcease.'

'Why not *DMZ*?'

'*DMZ*?' Piers stared at Anna quizzically, not recognising the reference immediately.

'De-Militarised Zone. You know, like they had in Vietnam.'

'Right!' Piers looked to the others. There were smiles and nods. The elderly man behind the desk shrugged.

'I like it,' Piers said after a moment. 'Sounds a bit like *GQ*. Good . . .'

'So,' Sonya said, interrupting Piers. 'What do you think, Anna? We'll give you the resources.'

Anna tilted her head a little to one side. 'I like the idea. But what kind of package are you offering?'

The elderly man behind the desk had been quiet through-out. Now he spoke up. 'A very attractive one. We're aware of what Samuelson paid you, and I think I can safely say . . .' He gave a short, knowing laugh. 'Well . . . One hundred thousand basic, with all the usual benefits. BUPA et cetera. Added to which, we're prepared to cover whatever legal costs you might incur when he tries to recoup your settlement.'

Anna blinked. She counted to ten in her head, trying to calm herself and persuade herself she wasn't dreaming, then smiled at him.

'OK, Mr Groeger, you've got yourself an editor.'

There were cheers and whoops. Piers reached across and shook her hand, while Sonya, seated next to Anna on the sofa, merely smiled and said, 'Welcome aboard, Anna. Let's hope this is the beginning of a long acquaintance.'

Anna stayed for another coffee and to discuss when she might start, then went, leaving them to continue their meeting. She had been quite calm about it all, but now, descending in the lift, she felt a huge wave of euphoria sweep over her and, on whim, got out her mobile. She wanted to go out and celebrate. To paint the town a dozen shades of red.

'Mand? It's me,' she said, as Mandy finally came to the phone. 'You know you were on about us getting together?'

'Yeah.'

'Well, how about tonight?'

'Tonight?'

'Yeah, I fancy getting pissed. You doing anything?'

Mandy laughed. 'No, I'm not, as it happens.'

'Well, the Moët's on me. I just got a new job!'

'Great!' Mandy was at once enthusiastic for her, forgetting her own troubles. 'It's a good one, I take it?'

'Couldn't be better, Mand. But look . . . I'll see if I can round up the others. We could meet in the Slug and Lettuce, then maybe go on for a meal. My treat.'

'You sure?'

'The amount they're going to pay me?' She grinned. 'I think I can stretch to it.'

'Lucky old you!'

The lift slowed and stopped. The doors hissed open. 'Look, I'll phone you again later, Mand. Lots of love. 'Bye.'

Anna switched the phone off and stepped out, looking about her as she crossed the massive vestibule, no longer the stranger she'd been on entering. This was her place now, and she was one of their most important editors. The thought of it gave her an added spring to her step. She walked over to the main desk and, unclipping the plastic pass from her lapel, she handed it to the receptionist and gave the girl a beaming smile.

'Thanks. And see you soon . . .'

Steve sat at his desk at work, staring out of the window. He had a view of the company's car park and, just beyond it, several of the other buildings on the industrial estate, but just then he didn't take any of it in. He was thinking. Or, rather, he was trying not to think.

Tomorrow was the day they'd have their pregnancy test and, try as he might, he couldn't concentrate on anything else.

'Steve?'

Steve looked up and blinked, like he was coming round from a coma. 'Polly? What?'

'You. You were miles away.'

Polly was twenty-two and PA to Marchant in Shipping. Long red hair and a good figure. She sat on the chair next to him, leaning towards him.

'So what's up?'

'You don't wanna know,' Steve said, looking to the screen of his VDU and noting that he hadn't finished the letter he'd begun half an hour back.

'Try me,' she said. 'I'm a good listener.'

Steve looked back at her and smiled sadly. 'Jan's got the pregnancy test tomorrow.'

'It'll be fine.'

Steve smiled. He knew that it made people feel better to say that. 'Yeah, well, maybe . . . but it's hard to get me head round much else right now.'

Polly nodded towards the basket of unanswered letters beside the word processor. 'You want me to do those for you?'

Steve looked to the basket, then back at Polly. 'You sure? I mean, would you mind?'

'I wouldn't offer if I did. Anyway, I've got a bit of free time. Old Marchy's off in Sweden, so I've been catching up on my filing.'

Steve smiled. 'I'd really appreciate it. I've been gettin' a bit behind . . .'

She leaned a little closer. 'I *could* stay on, if you like. Give you a hand.'

'No . . . No, it's all right.'

Steve sighed.

'You sure you're OK?'

'Yeah . . . yeah, it'll all be over tomorrow.'

One way or another . . .

Polly stood, slowly smoothing her dress down her body. She let her hand rest briefly on his shoulder as she passed. 'Look . . . if you ever need a friendly ear . . .' She smiled. 'A spritzer buys you an hour of my time . . .'

Steve smiled back at her. 'Thanks, Poll. I'll bear it in mind. I'm a sucker for a cheap date.'

But when she was gone, Steve simply sat and stared, everything forgotten except for the ordeal that lay ahead.

'To success!' Mandy said, sitting up straight on her chair and raising her fluted champagne glass high.

'To success!' the other three echoed, raising their glasses.

'Well done, you,' Karen said, laying her hand on Anna's arm. 'It sounds wonderful.'

Anna grinned. 'I know. I still can't believe it. I really thought they were going to offer me something dreadful, like *TV Guide* or . . . well, a gardening mag or something. But a new *men's* magazine . . .'

'You should do a piece on New Men and babies,' Susie said, pouring some orange juice into her champagne glass.

'Why? How many New Men do you know?' Mandy asked, smirking. 'They're more like Stone Age man round where I live.'

'I do know *one*, actually,' Susie said, defensively. 'Goes to our mother-and-toddler group.'

'I know the sort,' Mandy said. 'Beard and glasses. Pasta for every meal and gets out of bed to fart.'

Susie laughed. 'Well, I wouldn't know about the last bit.

And anyway, you're wrong. He's clean-shaven – well, a bit stubbly – and wears contact lenses.'

'Mm. Sounds a bit of all right. And I like pasta,' Mandy teased.

'He's very married,' Susie said, nudging Mandy playfully.

'Aren't they all?' Anna sneered.

Mandy avoided Susie's eye.

'Well . . .' Anna said, before this got too serious, 'when we have the launch party you're *all* invited.'

'Ooh, good! So when's that, then?' Mandy asked.

'Oh, not for a while yet.'

'But I thought you started . . .'

'Yeah, Mand,' Karen said. 'But it's not like the magazine exists. Anna's got to start it up from scratch. She has to hire writers and editors, organise schedules . . . It's a lot of work.'

'You bet!' Anna said and, draining her glass, reached out to pour another round. 'Mind you . . . the rewards are pretty damn good.'

'So how much exactly *are* they paying you?' Mandy asked. 'If you don't mind me being nosey.'

'*Mandee!*' Karen was sensitive to things like that.

Anna laughed. 'No, it's all right. A hundred thousand.'

'*A hundred* . . . ? Fuck me!'

'Plus expenses, and the usual benefits,' Anna added, making Mandy shake her head in disbelief.

Susie, too, was pretty incredulous: it was more than three times what Jo earned. 'I remember a time when we worked in that baker's together, when our *benefits* was as many cream cakes as we could eat and a company overall!'

Mandy was still bemused by the very idea of someone being paid so much money. And it wasn't even manual work.

'So what do you have to do for that much dosh?' she asked. 'Offer anal sex to the owner's dog?'

'Mand!' Anna gave her a disgusted look, then smiled again. 'I hope not, anyway . . . I hear he's got a St. Bernard!'

'Ouch!' Susie feigned a pained expression and the table erupted with laughter.

''Ere, talking of sex with animals, I've got one for your magazine, Anna,' Mandy said enthusiastically. 'You should do a survey of them dating clubs. Interview a few of the blokes about what they're looking for . . .'

'I should think it's bloody obvious what they're looking for,' Susie interrupted.

'Yes, we know *that*. But I mean, what attracts them to a woman, and how do they make contact. All that. I mean, it's a bit of a cattle market, ain't it?'

'Why? You ain't been to one, 'ave you?' Susie said, wrinkling her nose.

'Well, not exactly. Mind you, it's a good story. Thing was, I was s'posed to go to one with a mate of mine but she chickened out. Anyway, I'd got all dolled up so I thought, Sod it. What've I got to lose? So. She tells me where the meeting is — some little place off Oxford Street — and off I go . . .'

'Do you have to pay to go along?' Karen asked.

'Well, yeah. She'd paid already and I was gonna pay when I got there, so I thought I'd just make out I was her, like. Anyway, I finally found this gaff and asked some bloke who was coming out if I was in the right place for the group meeting. He says yeah, so in I go. Well, there's a small bar down there and people standing round talking. Lots of blokes, so I reckoned I stood a good chance of pulling . . .'

'Mand, you sound like some adolescent oik!' Anna giggled.

'I know. Shameless! Anyway, I get meself a drink and I think, well, there's no point standing round staring into space. We all know the score. Everyone's here to get off with someone. So I goes over to a group of blokes and starts chattin' 'em up. You know, getting a bit flirty. And I thought they were looking at me a bit odd, like. So I went over and tried me luck with a few more. Same thing happened.'

By now Susie, Anna and Karen were smiling in antici- pation.

'Well . . . I was getting just a bit pissed off by this time so I went over to get another drink. Next thing I know, some tight-arsed little git — horn-rimmed specs and nasal hair — lays his hand on my arm and tells me to leave . . .'

'Why?' Susie was indignant on her friend's behalf.

'Well, to cut a long story short, we had words, and when he said my sort wasn't welcome I turned round and was about to wallop him when someone caught hold of me arm and they threw me out. It was only when I was outside, fuming and wondering where the nearest police station was, that I saw this sign. Really fucking small it was . . .'

Anna leaned towards her. 'What did it say?'

'It was only the AGM of the Skoda Owners' Club, wasn't it! They thought I was a fucking prostitute! The place I wanted was next door!'

Susie couldn't talk for laughing, and Anna made herself a mental note to look into these dating clubs. There was certainly mileage in the idea.

'So did you go in? To the right place?' Karen was fascinated. This was all so alien to her.

'Nah. I was too mortified, weren't I? Mind you. It was lucky I didn't pull. I mean. A fucking Skoda!'

'By the way,' Susie said, as the laughter faded. 'Did you manage to get hold of Janet in the end?'

'No . . .' Anna turned to Susie. 'No, I phoned her a few times . . .'

Susie sat back, a morose expression on her face. 'I haven't spoken to her since I had Nathan. I don't think either of us know what to say.'

'You should ring her,' Mandy said, reaching out to take the bottle now that Anna had done with it. 'But I'd leave it a day or two.'

'When does she get the results, then?'

'Tomorrow. She has to go to the hospital for a blood test.'

Susie slowly shook her head, feeling guilty once again for the ease with which she had conceived Nathan.

'Yeah. I spoke to her yesterday about it. She seemed quite cheerful, though you never really know with Janet, do you? And I mean, it must be hard.'

'Very,' Karen added solemnly. 'After all, she's been trying for so long now. And there's the added pressure of her age.'

'Yeah, well she deserves some good luck,' Susie said, pushing her glass away. 'Look, Anna, I've gotta go. I've left Nathan with me mum and—'

'Jo not babysitting, then?' Mandy asked.

'Nah. Had to go out. Business meeting or something.'

'What about that Michelle next door? Don't she baby-sit for you?'

'Used to. But she's turned a bit funny. Haven't seen so much of her these past few days.'

'Anyway,' Anna said, rising out of her seat. 'It was lovely to see you, Suse. Take care, eh? And give that gorgeous little boy a big kiss from his Auntie Anna.'

''Ere are, Suse. You know who to choose for his God-mother,' Mandy said, nodding towards Anna. 'At least he'll get decent birthday presents!'

Susie grinned. Then, looking round the table. 'See you, Kar. See you, Mand. Take care.'

She leaned across, kissing Anna on the cheek, then got up and quickly left.

Anna smiled, then looked across at Mandy, noting how her gaze had followed Susie out of the door. She frowned. 'What's up?'

'What?' Mandy looked back at her, then smiled again. 'No . . . no, I was just thinking, that's all. How much Susie's changed. I mean, back in the old days she'd have had this New Man of hers for dinner.'

'What's to say she hasn't?'

'No . . .' Mandy shook her head. 'I don't think she's that keen at the moment.' Then, abruptly, she turned to Karen, giving her a big beam of a smile. 'So how's Chris?'

Karen looked down. 'You might well ask. I haven't seen her lately.'

Mandy's mouth opened, then closed. She glanced at Anna, who smiled tightly.

'What d'you mean? It's over?'

Karen shrugged.

'Ah . . . I'm sorry. I liked her. Still . . . life goes on an' all that, eh?'

'Yeah . . .' Karen looked up and gave a brave smile. 'You seem to have landed on your feet.'

'Yeah. I'm getting there.'

'*Getting there!* Sounds to me like you've arrived, you old tart!' Anna exclaimed affectionately. Turning to Karen, she went on. 'Has she told you about all these blokes she's been seeing?'

Karen shook her head, smiling.

'She's been picking up toy boys at the clubs . . .'

'Mand! You haven't!'

Mandy beamed with pride.

'And,' Anna continued with relish, 'she's been humping a taxi driver!'

Karen spat her drink into her glass, mopping her wet hand on her jeans.

Mandy's tone was suddenly more serious. 'That's finished now, though.'

'Since when?' Anna was still smiling.

'Since he put his fares up,' Mandy blurted out, collapsing in a fit of giggles. Recovering finally, she wiped her sleeve across her nose and gave a heavy sigh. 'Actually, we have decided to knock it on the head. I'll miss him, though.' She looked up at her friends, her eyes doleful. 'I'll have to start getting the fucking bus again!'

Anna roared. 'Well, you sound like you're enjoying yourself, Mand.'

'Yeah . . . well, you should make more of an effort. Get out a bit more. I mean, it's not as if you have to answer to anyone, is it?'

'No, but . . .'

'Well, there you are, then. In fact, if you fancy coming out one night with me and the girls from work . . .'

Anna smiled politely. She couldn't imagine anything worse.

'And you, Karen. You should get out and meet some new people. There are clubs, ain't there? You know, for gay people. And there's the small ads. You know, "Me Jane, You Jane!"'

Karen swallowed, then looked down. 'Yeah, but . . . not just yet.'

Mandy and Anna exchanged looks, and as Anna reached across to squeeze Karen's hand she looked up, her lips curling into a thin smile.

'Let's get another bottle,' Anna announced.

She made to stand up, yet as she did her mobile phone started to ring. She took it from her handbag, unfolded it, clicked it on and held it to her ear.

'Hello?'

'Anna? It's Frank. Just heard the news . . .'

'News? What news is that?'

'About your job. I bumped into Piers earlier. I think it's wonderful, darling. Just the challenge you need . . .'

'Frank?'

'Yes, darling.'

'Just fuck off.'

Anna switched off the phone, folded it up and dropped it into her bag. 'Now where were we? Ah yes . . . another bottle of that lovely bubbly . . .'

Karen closed the door behind her, then reached out and switched on the light, smiling to herself. She had stayed much longer than she'd planned, going on with Anna and Mandy for a bite to eat, and had drunk probably more than was good for her. In fact, she felt decidedly woozy.

It had been great to see the girls again, and both Anna's obvious delight in her new job and Mandy's in her new life had served to raise her own darkened spirits. But now she was home, and slowly, very slowly, the reality of her own situation began to sink in.

There was no work tomorrow — school did not start again for another three weeks — so it would have been easy for her to spend the day in bed, doing nothing. But Karen found it hard to do nothing. And besides, it was no fun doing nothing when you were on your own. She had to fill her time — to keep busy — so that she didn't succumb to that debilitating feeling of lethargy that would descend every time she thought of Chris.

Don't even think about it, she told herself. But it was like telling herself not to breathe.

Conscious that she had already had far, far too much, Karen walked through to the kitchen and, switching on every light, went to the fridge and took out a bottle of wine. Uncorking it, she poured herself a glass, then sat there at the kitchen table, wondering just where she went from here.

Mandy was right, of course. Time did heal. And in time she would doubtlessly find someone else and she would be happy again. But that was somewhere far in the future. In between times she had to get through each day and each long lonely night. Had to suffer the torment of knowing that the woman she loved was lying in another woman's arms.

Karen lifted her chin, stretching the muscles of her neck, moving her head from side to side to try to ease the stress, but the stress wouldn't go away. It was like she had been overwound, and the next little twist of the key would make her snap and break.

The wine had helped . . . a little . . . but not enough, it seemed. And it had only served to make her more melancholic. More . . . emotional.

'Damn you!' she said, speaking to no one in particular. Why wasn't there a switch you could flick to turn off your feelings? Some little button at the back of your head you could press and . . . presto!

Karen shivered. She didn't want to cry. She felt all cried out. But as she started 'coming down' after the evening out, her spirits sank lower than they'd been all week.

She sipped at the wine, then pushed the glass aside. That was no answer, even if she was tempted to drink the whole damn bottle. And she knew she wouldn't sleep. Not now.

Standing, she went through into the living room and, searching among Chris's drawers, found her address book. For a moment she hesitated, the small, green-covered book held in both hands, then she sat down on the sofa and began to leaf through.

She didn't know Sarah's surname. It had never cropped up in conversation and she had never really felt like asking, but she knew, as soon as she saw the crossed-out address and the new one scribbled underneath, that this was it.

For a moment Karen simply stared at it. She knew the place. Knew the road and the houses in it. One of her schoolfriends had lived there. But now that she knew

Sarah lived there, the place was transformed in her mind, becoming . . . *sinister*.

It was strange, but she could not think of Sarah as just another woman like herself, with the same wants and needs and desires. The very manner in which she had come into her life and taken Chris from her set her apart; and it made her think of Sarah as someone evil and manipulative. Someone who would do anything, say anything, to get what she wanted.

Sarah had hurt her. Not Chris. *Sarah*. And it was Sarah she wanted to punish.

Reaching across, she picked the phone up from the coffee table and dialled the number from memory.

'Ladycabs? I know it's late but . . . yeah . . .'

She gave her address, then the address to which she wanted to be taken. It was only a mile or so, but it was late, and a woman alone didn't walk the streets this time of night.

Then she sat back, waiting, wondering what she would say when she got there.

It had to be now. Any other time and she wouldn't have drunk enough — wouldn't have the courage — to do this. Even so . . .

The car came quickly. Karen slipped her jacket on, picked up her shoulder bag and went down. Sliding into the back seat, she gave the address again, then sat back as the car drove through the familiar streets.

She was there before she knew it. It was a simple two-storey terraced house with a sloping roof. There was a light on over the porch, illuminating the door number, which was etched into the glass panel. Upstairs was dark, but there was a light on downstairs, though the curtains were drawn.

'That'll be three fifty,' the woman driver said, switching on the light and turning to her. But Karen was barely listening. She was staring at the muted light from the downstairs window, wondering what Chris was doing at that moment, and knowing that she didn't have the courage to get out of the car, let alone knock on that door and confront the pair of them.

The woman driver was still staring at her. 'Are you all right, love?'

Karen turned and looked at her, a sigh shuddering through her. 'Yes . . . look, I'm sorry. Just take me home again. I . . . I made a mistake.'

The woman made no comment, just turned and, switching off her light, put the car back into gear and pulled away again, while in the back of the car, Karen turned, looking back at that diminishing glow, feeling as though her heart had been torn from her.

Anna poured herself a coffee, then sat down, drawing the pile of Sunday papers towards her. Frank had left three messages on the answerphone. The first two had been before he'd tried her on the mobile, the last of them after she had told him to fuck off.

She smiled. Oh, he might be abject and apologetic now, but it was too bloody late. His wife could have him, for all she cared. No, Mandy was right. It was time she moved on. Time she found herself a new man. But this time it wasn't going to be somebody in the same business. She'd already made that mistake: twice.

Taking the *Style* supplement from the *Sunday Times*, she flicked through until she came to the 'Encounters' section. There were clubs here she could join with names like 'Avenues' and 'Duet', and there were endless personal adverts from 'Shy Guy' seeking 'Broad-Minded Lady' to 'Wild Woman' seeking 'Brave Man'. It was to these last that she was drawn, reading down through the columns and circling any that looked vaguely interesting.

She hadn't told the girls about the ad she'd placed, nor about Michael. She'd felt a little ashamed — a little sad — to be advertising for a partner. It was almost like an admission of failure — that she needed help to do this most basic of things.

But then again, if it worked, it worked. So Michael had proved to be a shit. Did that mean that every other Romeo was going to piss on his Juliet?

Anna hoped not. Oh, it might take a while before she found the right man, but she had time. She wasn't forty yet, after all.

Not yet.

Besides, what was it Mandy had said? Oh yes . . . that she ought to open herself up to a bit of fun — to taking things less seriously. Only then — when she wasn't actively looking — would she find what she wanted.

Anna blew out a breath. Oh God, let's hope it's true, she thought. Let's hope it wasn't just some romantic bullshit Mandy read in a magazine article!

Then, taking a sip of the strong, bitter coffee, she got down to it again, surfing the columns for a sensitive Scorpio.

As Steve pulled up at the traffic lights, Janet glanced at the dashboard to check the time. Their appointment wasn't for another twenty minutes but they were nearly there already.

Her hands were clasped together in her lap, and as she sat there, so she nervously played with her ring, turning it round and round on her finger. Steve had bought it for her after they had made the decision to go for IVF treatment, as a sort of good-luck token. He'd joked that when the baby arrived he'd buy her one with a *real* diamond in it.

'All right?' Steve reached across and squeezed her hands.

Janet nodded, grateful for once for the intimacy.

The lights turned to green and Steve reached for the gearstick, pushing it gently into first.

She hadn't been able to sleep last night. As Steve had lain beside her, snoring gently, she had stared through the open window at the night sky, developing scenarios in her head for how the next day might end. She had worked out that if she were pregnant the baby would be due in April, which would mean that she could start her maternity leave at Easter and be at home with it – or them – right through the summer. The hospital had given them the option of replacing up to three embryos and they had opted for two. A flicker of guilt passed through her every time she thought about the baby they'd rejected.

And as hard as she fought to repress it, she could not deny herself a passing thought of how she would break the news to everyone; compiling a telephone list hierarchy in her head.

She had been to the bathroom several times during the night; each time with a sense of dread. And each time she followed the same ritual: standing with her back to the toilet, her eyes shut tight, she had pulled down her knickers and sat on the pan. Only then had she opened her eyes and looked into the crotch of her white cotton pants, the relief complete when there was no sign of blood.

It seemed that they had failed so often, it was inevitable that they should do so again.

And this morning, before they left, she had checked again. So far, so good . . .

Emerging from the bathroom, she had picked up her bag from the hallway and turned, heading for the front door. Steve had almost thrust the telephone receiver into her face, smiling apologetically as he spoke.

'It's your mum. She just wants a quick word.'

Janet had shaken her head, but Steve had been insistent, almost placing the handset to her ear.

'Hello?'

'Jan? Is that you, love?'

Janet sighed impatiently. 'Yes, Mum. Of *course* it's me!'

'I rang last night but Steve said you were asleep. I just wanted to wish you luck, love. That's all.'

'Thanks, Mum. Look, I'd—'

'And just remember what I said. As long as you and Steve have got one another . . .'

Janet interrupted curtly, making no attempt to hide her irritation. 'Yeah. OK, Mum. I gotta go. Phone you later.' And with that she slammed down the phone.

Why did she always have to say that?

'Lot of people here today,' Steve observed as they drew into the hospital car park, passing alongside the IVF unit, its windows decorated with crudely drawn Mr Men: Mr Happy. Mr Sad . . .

Slowly Steve made his way up and down the narrow lanes between the rows of parked cars, on the lookout for a space. 'There's one!' he shouted jubilantly, after their third circuit. Picking up speed, he swung the car round and manoeuvred into the gap.

'OK?' he said gently, his arms encircling the steering wheel.

Janet did not answer. She was staring resolutely ahead.

'You wait here a minute and I'll get the parking ticket from the machine.' He reached across and squeezed her hands before stepping out on to the tarmac. After glancing at her briefly through the windscreen, Steve made his way through the maze of vehicles towards the ticket dispenser.

But inside the car Janet could feel the warm blood between her legs and, silently, she was screaming.

The seconds passed. Steve returned, whistling as he peeled the back away from the ticket and placed it on the windscreen. Only then did he look across at her.

'Jan? *Jan?*'

For two days Karen had moped about the flat, not even bothering to get dressed, slowly working her way through the contents of the fridge rather than go out of her own front door. Then, realising that it couldn't go on, and, desperate for some chocolate, she had showered and gone shopping.

Safe enough, one would have thought, but then she saw them, getting into a car together just outside Sainsbury's. They didn't see her. Karen made sure they didn't see her. But it was enough to send her scuttling home, bleeding inside, the wounds reopened.

Which was why, now, she was dialling Sarah's number, her heart pounding in her chest as it rang and rang.

A click, and than, 'Hello?'

'Hello, is . . . is Chris there?'

It was her, of course. Sarah. With that sweet, deceptive voice of hers.

'I'm sorry . . . who is that?'

Karen swallowed. 'It's Karen, I . . . I need to speak to her.'

There was a pause. 'Hold on a moment.'

She held on, wondering what the murmured conversation in the background was about, straining to hear, but there were no raised voices, no tense mutterings. There was a long, long pause, then she heard footsteps.

'Hello?' There was a sigh, then: 'What is it you want, Karen?'

'Chris . . . look, we need to talk.'

A silence, then. 'I don't think so.'

'*Please*, Chris.'

'Karen! There's no point. You're only making this worse.'

'For who?' Karen snapped, then immediately consumed by regret, she apologised urgently. 'Sorry! Sorry, I didn't mean—'

'It's over, Karen,' Chris said, matter-of-factly. Then, in a quieter, kinder voice. 'It's over.'

At the other end of the line, Karen was crying, the hot tears rolling down her cheeks one after another, dripping down on to her hand as it gripped the handset to her ear.

'But I miss you so much.'

Her voice, pathetically small, was distorted as Karen fought to retain control over her pain-racked body.

There was a moment's silence from the other end of the line, and then it went dead.

Karen heard the key go in the lock and rolled over, staring at the alarm clock. It was twelve minutes past ten. Blinking against the sunlight, she struggled up, resting her back against the headboard, then sat there, listening as Chris walked about the flat.

There had been heartache in the night and she had cried herself to sleep, her skin tight where tears had dried on her face and neck. But now she felt nothing. Getting up, she quickly dressed, then went out.

Chris was in the living room, her back to Karen. She was busy taking things from drawers and packing them into two large holdalls that rested on the floor beside her.

Karen watched, saying nothing, and for a while Chris seemed not to notice her there. Then she glanced round.

'Sarah's downstairs,' she said. 'I'll take what I need and come back for the rest.'

It was said so matter-of-factly that one might have thought there had been nothing between them — not even friendship. But Karen was beyond being hurt. She watched silently, knowing that there was nothing more to be said.

It didn't take long. One moment she was there and the next . . . gone. Gone for ever, Karen realised, and she sat, staring at the blank space on the wall, where Chris's picture of the caged songbird had been. It might almost have been symbolic but for the fact that neither of them had been able to sing a note.

Karen took a long breath. She ought to do some shopping. Yes, and there was a stack of preparatory work to be done, as well. For instance, she really ought to reread *Sons And Lovers* again, seeing as it was one of the set books next year.

Ought to ... but a kind of weariness kept her pinned where she was, staring into the air. Did it matter? Did any of it matter?

The phone rang. A jolting sound that seemed to wake her from the torpor into which she was drifting.

She stood and walked across, her voice lethargic as she answered.

'Hello?'

'Is that you, Karen?'

She didn't recognise the voice. 'Yes ... Sorry, who is that?'

'Hello, love. It's Daisy. From next door to your mum and dad.'

Karen felt a chill stab through her. Everything was suddenly very, *very* sharp. 'Daisy! Is something wrong?'

'Your mum asked me to phone you, love ...' There was a pause, then: 'I'm sorry, dear, but they've taken your father into hospital again. It looks like he's had another heart attack.'

She kept herself calm. 'Do you know which hospital?'

'The Essex ... Your mum went with him in the ambulance. He didn't look too good.'

'Thanks ... I ...' Karen sighed. 'Thanks very much for phoning. I ... um ... thanks.'

She put the phone down and closed her eyes.

Oh, God! Oh Jesus!

Then, knowing she could not sit at home and wait for news

– knowing that her mother wouldn't have asked Daisy to phone her unless she meant her to be there – she put on her coat and went out.

She would have walked straight past them without noticing, had Chris not leaned out of the car to call to her as she stepped out into the road, forcing them to swerve in order to miss her. She had turned, her eyes staring vacantly, unseeing.

'Karen? Karen . . . are you all right?'

She turned. The two women were sitting there in the car, Chris in the driver's seat, Sarah beside her.

She did not move. It was as though her feet were embedded in the tarmac. She stared at them through the windscreen, her knees almost touching the bumper. Eventually Chris stepped out of the car, but even then she would not move away from the driver's door.

'Look, Karen, you've just got to accept—'

'My dad's had another heart attack.'

'Oh, shit . . .' Chris glanced at Sarah. 'Where is he?'

'The Essex.'

Chris glanced at Sarah again, and this time Sarah nodded. 'Look, get in. We'll drive you there.'

In a daze, Karen climbed in the back, squeezing in beside the two holdalls.

'I'm sorry,' Sarah said, looking back at her, as Chris pulled out into the traffic. 'About your dad.'

Karen looked to her and gave the slightest nod.

'It won't take us long,' Chris said consolingly. 'We should be there in twenty minutes.'

But Karen merely sighed, and stared out through the window, watching the passing shops and houses, conscious – suddenly, overpoweringly conscious – of just how little control she had over her life.

Falling. She felt that she was falling.

And when she finally hit the ground?

Her father looked pale and wasted, close to death. Nurses moved urgently about him, silently checking this machine or that, their faces closed, their eyes giving nothing away. And all the while her mother looked on with such meagre hope in her eyes that that alone made Karen's heart break.

Had *she* done this?

She could not stay in the room long. It was like torture, seeing him like that and being able to do nothing. She wanted to talk to him, to apologise, but she knew that anything she said was superfluous now, or at worst would only add to her mother's burden. All her mother wanted right now was to be reassured that everything would be all right. But Karen couldn't do that. She couldn't *feel* it. Looking at her father, she saw a corpse, not the vigorous man he had been − the one man she'd strangely loved. No . . . no one could look like that and still be alive.

She sat on a chair in the corridor, hunched into herself, her hands over her mouth, and after a moment she sensed rather than saw someone sit beside her and place an arm about her shoulders.

'I'm *so* sorry . . .'

She glanced up, meeting Chris's eyes, then burst into tears.

'Oh, God . . .'

Chris held her for a while. Comforted her. And for a moment it was all right. Then she heard raised voices and, looking up, saw her brother, Jack, not twenty yards away, arguing with a nurse at the entrance to the ward.

'But he's my *father*!'

'I know that, Mr Turner, but you *must* calm down. You're not helping anyone . . .'

Karen got up and started walking towards him, but seeing

her, Jack flew into a rage. Pushing past the nurse, he walked
at Karen, his arm raised, his finger pointing.

'You're the last person he'd want to see!'

'Jack . . .'

'Well, who d'you think's responsible, eh? He was all right
till you landed your little bombshell! You might just as well
have put a fucking gun to his head!'

'Now hold on . . .' It was Chris who spoke up, stepping
up beside Karen, her face dark with anger. 'You don't
seriously—'

But Jack's own anger was a blazing fire. Her words merely
placed another log on that inferno. 'And you, you bitch! You
can just fuck off out of here! You're the one who put her up
to it . . . you fucking dyke!'

Karen brought her arm back and slapped him hard.

She could feel the stinging on her palm, could see the
bright red weal on Jack's face, but she could not piece things
together. She saw him raise his hand, his face distorted with
the most violent rage. His eyes seemed strange and dark. And
then, inexplicably, he was weeping. Down in a hunch and
weeping.

Karen stared at her brother, bewildered now.

Beside her, Chris gave a shudder, then, touching her arm,
the faintest touch, said, 'I'd better go.'

Karen nodded, hardly aware of her.

'Jack . . . Jack, I'm sorry . . . I didn't mean . . .'

But Jack turned away, pushing through the door into the
death room. And as it closed, so Karen's whole life seemed to
snap shut on her, like a trap.

Chris was waiting for her when she got back to the flat. It
was late, the sun's rays a roseate glow in the living room.

'Hi,' Chris said gently, getting up from the sofa. 'How is
he?'

Karen sighed. 'Not good. They've put him on a life-support machine. He . . .' She swallowed. 'He looks so dreadful.'

Chris came across and held her. 'Your mum's stayed on, I take it?'

Karen gave a little nod. 'And my brother . . .'

'That little sod.'

Karen moved her head back a fraction, meeting Chris's eyes. 'He's not so bad. This whole business . . .'

Chris let out an exasperated breath, then smiled gently. 'You need some rest.'

'I'd rather talk.'

Chris considered that a moment, then shrugged. 'OK.'

They sat, either end of the sofa, facing each other.

'Do *you* blame me?' Chris asked, after a moment's awkwardness. 'I mean, you said . . .'

'I was angry. I . . .' Karen shrugged. 'I don't know . . . I mean, how can I blame *you* for what I am.'

'He does though, doesn't he?'

Karen hesitated, then nodded. Then, because she needed to know, she asked. 'Where is she now?'

Chris had looked down, now her head came up again. 'Sarah? She's at the flat. She knows I'm here. I told her you might need me.'

Karen smiled faintly. 'She understands that?'

'Yes.'

Karen sighed, wondering if she, in Sarah's position, would have been quite so liberal. Probably not. Not that it mattered. Sarah had won. Sarah had got Chris.

'What happened?' she asked.

'What do you mean?'

'Between us.'

'Ah . . .' Chris let her head fall back a little, staring up at the ceiling as she considered. 'I guess I'd just forgotten.'

'Forgotten?'

'How much I loved Sarah.'

'Ah . . .' It made sense, but it was curious how much pain those simple words caused Karen. As much pain as she had felt staring at her father earlier. Confused, she tried to put the two things together in her head and make sense of them; but they made no sense. These were just things that had happened. No one was really to blame. Those were the facts. The trouble was, she didn't *feel* like that. She felt she was to blame for everything, and when she had slapped Jack earlier she had felt that it was *she* who deserved the punishment.

'I still love you,' she said, looking at Chris again.

'And I love you . . .'

'But not enough . . .'

That cost her. Cost her all she had left, and after she had said it, the tears began to drip down her cheeks again. And seeing that, Chris moved across and gently kissed the tears from her face and slowly, tenderly, began to make love to her for the last time.

'Steve? Are you all right?'

Steve looked up and, unable to help himself, sighed. His coffee had gone cold, and for the last half-hour he had simply stared into the air.

Polly sat down, facing him, then reached across to take the untouched coffee from his hand.

'Here. Let me make you a fresh cup.'

Steve shook his head. 'No . . . it's OK. I . . . thanks, anyway.'

'You should go home. You look awful.'

'Nah . . .' Again he sighed. Home was the last place he wanted to be right now.

Polly set the coffee down. 'You wanna talk about it?'

'I dunno, I . . . She came on . . . in the bleedin' car park of the clinic.'

'Oh . . .' For a moment Polly seemed totally at a loss. 'It must be hard on you . . . emotionally.'

'Yeah, and the worst of it is I can't comfort her. She won't let me. It's like . . .'

Steve stopped, his eyes pained. Polly reached across and, taking his hands, gave them a gentle squeeze.

'You'll be all right.'

Steve looked up at her, grateful. 'I wish I could be sure. But sometimes . . .'

He didn't go on.

Looking down at where he held her hands, Steve smiled, and gave them the smallest squeeze back before relinquishing them. 'Thanks. I'll be OK.'

'Yeah . . .' Polly smiled sympathetically. 'Look . . . I'll be in Stones . . . you know, the wine bar, after work tonight. If you want to talk some more, or just have a shoulder to cry on, well . . . you'll know where I am.'

'Thanks.'

The rest of the day passed slowly, and when five o'clock came round Steve sat on at his desk, unable to face going home.

He could see Janet in his mind, there, at home. Could see those red-rimmed eyes and that way she had of turning in on herself, of isolating herself from everyone and everything about her, and realised that he couldn't face her. Not yet. Not without a few drinks inside him, anyway.

For a time he sat there, wondering whether he should take up Polly's offer. After all, what was the harm? And he needed to talk to *someone*. He'd go stark staring mad if he didn't.

Stones was on the way to the tube station. He could look in for an hour, maybe. Then again . . .

Locking his briefcase in the top left-hand drawer, Steve pulled on his jacket and left. Outside Stones he stopped, gazing through the etched glass window towards the bar.

There she was, her drink on the bar in front of her. He had only to go in.

Steve walked on, along the crowded pavement and down into the tube station.

Home. It might be unbearable right now, but it was where he ought to be. With Janet. Even if she didn't want him there.

Hearing the door, Janet looked up, then stood and walked over to the doorway, pushing it shut.

She heard his footsteps in the flat; knew he was looking for her.

'Jan?'

If there had been a lock on the door she would have turned it. She didn't want him here. Didn't want anyone. She wanted only to lie there, as she'd been lying there these past few hours, absorbed by the grief she felt at the loss of her babies.

Not eggs. She couldn't see them as eggs. They were babies. Defenceless little babies that her body had rejected.

'Jan?' Steve's voice was closer; was just outside the door. 'Jan, you in there?'

She could hear the weariness in her voice as she answered him. Could hear the desolation. 'Leave me, Steve.'

'But Jan . . .'

'*Leave* me.'

She sensed his hesitation, then heard his footsteps, quicker now. There was a moment's silence, and then the front door slammed.

Janet stood there a moment, listening, hoping he would come back. Then, when the silence drew on, her face slowly cracked and the tears began to fall.

It had been a bad day.

Dragging the pram into the hallway, Susie kicked the door

shut behind her, then turned to confront the howling baby whose incessant screams had accompanied her all the way back from the supermarket.

She knew what he wanted. He was hungry. He was also dirty. But if she stopped to change and feed him now she'd never get the shopping put away before Jo came home.

Trying to ignore those flailing podgy fists, that puckered red face, Susie began to lift the heavy shopping bags from the handle of the pram, but as she did one of the plastic bags snagged on the edge of the pram and its contents – including a punnet of strawberries and a bottle of brown sauce – spilled out all over the hallway.

'Oh, shit! Shit! Shit! *Shi-it!*'

Nathan stopped a moment, a shocked expression on his face as Susie's voice increased in pitch, then he began to wail with even greater energy.

It hadn't helped that he'd so noisily filled his nappy at the checkout. Nor was it just the noise. Even the women in the next queue had turned and made faces as the pungent odour wafted across.

For a moment Susie stood there, her arms at her sides, surveying the wreckage. The bottle of brown sauce had cracked and its contents were slowly seeping out over the carpet. If she didn't see to that . . .

She hurried out into the kitchen, grabbing a handful of kitchen towel from the roll, then hurried back. Kneeling, she began to clear up the sticky brown mess, only to discover that she had knelt on a couple of rogue strawberries, squashing them into the woollen pile.

'Oh . . . *fuck* it!'

For a moment she knelt there, close to tears, the baby's howling like a baton beating her head, her breasts full and aching.

Getting to her feet, she turned, then, unstrapping Nathan,

lifted him from the pram. For a moment he seemed to calm down, his mouth puckering expectantly; then, when he found no nipple clamped to his mouth, he let out an almighty wail.

'Just *wait*, will you? I'm not soddin' Superwoman!'

Carrying him through to the bathroom, she took down the changing mat and laid him on it, then began to undo his clothes, her patience close to being shredded as he howled and howled and howled.

The mess in his nappy was worse than she'd thought. It had oozed out of the sides and into his dungarees, squelching up his vest as far as his armpits, so that everything seemed glued together by the sticky yellow-brown goo. And the smell!

A bath. She ought to run a bath . . .

Reaching past him, she made to run the hot tap, yet even as she did, Nathan rolled on to his side and put his hand — splat! — into the middle of the mess.

'Oh, Nathan . . .'

Grabbing his hand so that he didn't put it straight into his mouth, she reached up to her left and pulled the blue box of baby-wipes from the top of the trolley, beginning to clear up the mess.

She had mopped up the worst of it when the phone began to ring.

Sod it! She would have to let it ring.

Yeah, but what if it was Jo, or something important?

Lifting Nathan under one arm, his rear end pointing away from her, she hurried out into the hallway and picked up the receiver.

'What?'

'Susie? Are you OK?'

Susie closed her eyes. Her sister! That's all she needed!

'Lyndse, what is it? I'm a bit busy?'

'What's up?'

'Nothing. I'm fine. Really.'

'Yeah, you sound it. You sure you don't want me to come round and give you a hand?'

'No, no I . . .' Susie took a long breath, then, realising that her sister only meant well, smiled falsely down the phone. 'Yeah . . . no, that would be good. Really helpful. I've had a shitty bloody day.'

Lyndsay laughed cheerfully. 'I'll be round. Give me a quarter of an hour.'

Susie put the phone down. Nathan, beneath her arm, was still howling away. She lifted him slightly, then cradled him, smiling for the first time in hours.

'All right . . . let's give you what you want. Auntie Lyndsay will clear up all the crap.'

I mean, why not? she thought. She's so keen to help. To *bond* with me.

Susie carried Nathan through, then sat on the sofa, undoing the top three buttons of her top, then slipping out her breast and offering it to him. He latched on to it like a drowning man grabbing at a lifebelt, the urgency with which he sucked almost comical.

She'd known men who fucked like that.

As he sucked she felt relief flood her. Thank God he'd stopped howling. That sound . . . it was like nothing she'd ever imagined. Nor was it anything to do with how loud or constant it was, it was just something about it. You couldn't possibly ignore it. Or you could, but if you did — as she had had to — it slowly drove you mad.

Gus had said something about it being specially designed that way. He'd muttered something about evolution and all that, and how all of these basic instincts were . . . what was the word? Oh yeah . . . *encoded* in you.

She liked that idea. It made her feel a lot easier with herself. The need for sex, the desire to have a crap, the pleasure of breastfeeding, the sound of an infant's cry: all of these things were encoded in you, and it was no use fighting against them. They were all nature's way of reminding you that you were only human.

'There,' she said, as Nathan surfaced briefly. 'That's what you needed, wasn't it?'

She lifted him up on to her shoulder and patted his back and, after a moment, Nathan rewarded her with a resounding burp.

'There's a good boy!'

Gently she brought him down off her shoulder and turned him about. She'd give him the other side first, then bath him, and then . . .

She heard the key go in the door.

'What the . . . ?'

Susie looked down, embarrassed, as Jo came into the room. 'What the hell's been going on? It's like World War bloody Three out there!'

Susie bristled at the undeniable criticism in his voice. 'I had an accident . . .'

'An accident . . . and look at the state of him!'

Susie looked down at Nathan's yellow-stained torso.

'He had an accident.'

'Oh, so you *both* had accidents.' Jo shook his head despairingly. 'I've had a shitty bloody day. It'd be nice to come home to a bit of order.'

Susie stared at him a moment. She could not trust herself to speak and so carried the baby through to the kitchen. Pulling a length of kitchen towel from the dispenser she wiped at the poo stain on her jeans.

Jo followed after her, watching her from the doorway. 'D'you want me to take him while you sort this hall-way out?'

Susie could feel the frustration ballooning up inside her

chest so that she found it difficult to breath normally. She continued to rub at her jeans, treating his comment with the contempt it deserved.

'Fine! I'll do it,' he said finally, his voice dripping with sarcasm. He walked across to the sink and ran the dishcloth under the hot water. Hooking the baby on to her hip, Susie flicked the kettle on before reaching up to take a Pyrex bowl from the shelf.

'It's no joke, you know. Working hard all day then coming home to *this*.' Jo turned off the tap and squeezed out the excess water. 'It'd be nice to be able to relax a bit. Just the two of us occasionally. I mean, you're either busy with the baby or you're too tired.'

Susie unscrewed the lid of the sterilising unit and plunged her hand inside, bringing out a bottle, a teat and a lid, and laying them on the work surface. She'd give him some boiled water once he'd had his bath.

Nathan was starting to get restless again, nuzzling against Susie's breast.

'In a minute, darling,' she soothed, lightly kissing the top of his head.

Jo turned, resting his back against the sink, the damp cloth balanced in his open palm.

'I mean, what I can't understand is, what's the big deal? How difficult can it be to look after one little baby? You shove milk in one end and wipe crap off the other. End of story.'

Susie stared at the kettle, watching the steam pour from the spout.

'I know it takes a bit of getting used to, but he's eight weeks old now for Christ's sake . . .'

Susie had put out her hand to pick up the kettle to fill Nathan's bottle. But, as if in a dream, she scooped up the glass bowl and, swinging her body round, threw it with as much force as she could muster.

She watched with detached fascination as it flew across the kitchen, curious as to where it would land . . . or, rather, whether it would actually hit its intended target.

The bowl glanced against Jo's shoulder as he swerved out of its path, a look of shock on his face. Amazingly, it did not break. Bouncing off his shoulder, it had hit the washing-up rack before dropping to the floor, a hairline crack now visible right through the centre of it.

They both stared at it as it spun on the tiles, neither of them able to look elsewhere — certainly not at each other.

For once the baby's cries brought welcome relief from the awful, deafening silence.

'I'm gonna give Nathan a bath,' Susie said, her voice barely audible as she walked towards the door.

In the bathroom she sat on the edge of the bath, Nathan's eager mouth clamped over her nipple. Hearing Jo's footsteps above the sound of the running water, she quickly wiped away the tears streaking her face. Without looking up she could sense him in the doorway.

'I'm sorry,' he said weakly.

Her eyes remained fixed on Nathan as her fingers played over his soft downy hair.

'I love you, Susie.' She gave a brief snort of derision. 'It's just . . .' His voice had cracked and, try as she might, Susie could not help looking up into his face, surprised by his agonised expression. 'It's just that . . . I *miss* you.'

Now she could not take her eyes away.

'I just miss you so much. It's just that . . . it feels like I've lost you, I s'pose. In my head I know you've got to look after Nathan and that he's got to take priority. I love him, too, you know. But . . . well, I feel so . . . shut out. And it's so lonely.'

The tears were rolling down Susie's cheeks now and plopping on to the baby's head. And as he came closer, kneeling on the floor in front of them, it was clear that Jo too had been crying.

Lifting Susie's chin, he leaned closer and placed his lips over hers, each tasting the other's salty tears.

It was amid this tangle of tears, snot, shit and milk that they found themselves when the doorbell rang.

'Oh, shit . . .' Susie said, smiling at Jo and stroking his cheek tenderly. 'That'll be Lyndsay . . .'

The flat was dark and silent as Steve stepped through into the hallway, closing the door quietly behind him. It had rained, but he had hardly seemed to notice, even though he was soaked through.

He crouched, unlacing his shoes before he slipped them off, then shrugged his jacket from his shoulders and let it fall on to the hallway floor. His tie was already loose. Pulling at the knot, he tugged it off and let that fall also, then, feeling a little unsteady, put a hand against the wall.

He had gone back to the bar where Polly had been, but she had already left. Maybe she had returned to the office and, finding him gone, had decided to go home. Or maybe she just hadn't waited that long.

One thing he was sure of. If she had been there, he would have gone home with her and slept with her. It had been a certainty in his mind as he stood there on the tube, heading back. And he knew she would have let him. He had picked up the signals; knew that she fancied him, and that all her recent kindness was to a single end. But he was glad now that she hadn't been there. Glad because he knew deep down that it wasn't what he wanted; *she* wasn't what he wanted. And though he had drunk too much, he had at least betrayed Janet only in his mind; had been unfaithful only in his imagination.

He unbuckled his trousers and allowed them to fall, then

reached down and peeled off his socks. They too were wet, and he smiled as he thought of himself, walking all the way home in the rain. It had, at least, served to sober him up.

Wearing only his shirt and pants now, he padded through to the bathroom and, closing the door behind him, switched on the light. Taking the towel, he mopped at his slickly wet hair, then, throwing the towel into the bath, began to unbutton his shirt.

He had a good body, and he had kept it trim over the years. Janet had often commented upon it in the past, but these days she didn't seem to notice. He might as well have been a thing of glass and stainless steel — a syringe for the purpose of inserting sperm.

Steve sighed and, leaning on the edge of the sink, looked at himself up close. His eyes were a little bleary, but otherwise he looked fine. He could at least still look himself in the eyes without flinching — not like some of the blokes he knew.

It was hard, yes, but it was harder yet for Janet. He reminded himself of that now, thinking of her sleeping in the next room, a tenderness for her filling him. So why did she make it so difficult for him? Didn't she know how he felt about her?

He stepped across, turning off the light before he opened the door, not wanting to wake her. But as he slipped in beside her, Janet turned over and, laying an arm across him, cuddled in to him. Her voice was the faintest murmur.

'Hi!'

The simple feel of her against him aroused him. The warmth of her flesh was something else. But he was determined not to succumb to it. Not to irritate her in any way. Even so, he felt his penis grow hard.

Janet moved slightly, burrowing into him, her thinly covered breasts brushing against his chest, making him part his lips with the pleasure of it. And then slowly, incredibly, her hand moved down until it covered the swollen length of his penis.

He swallowed, unable to move or say a word, as slowly Janet delved beneath the soft cotton and held it, her fingers slowly stroking him, making him gasp, before she raised her head and, moving above him in the darkness, kissed him.

'Make love to me, Steve.'

He held her and kissed her, and slowly, very tenderly, they began to make love in the shadows, her passion surprising him until, with a cry, he came, her own cries coming only seconds afterwards, the two of them clinging to each other.

And after, in the long darkness of the night, she lay there against him, sleeping peacefully, as she had not slept in a long time, no longer the stranger she had been to him these past five months.

Part Four

~ Three months later ~

It was already growing dark when Janet pushed through the double doors of her local health centre and went up to the reception desk. The wind outside was biting cold, but in here it was warm, and she found herself relaxing slightly as the woman told her to take a seat until the nurse called her.

The waiting room was more than half full, mainly with victims of the latest strain of flu that was doing the rounds. One glance about her at the coughing hordes persuaded Janet that she would be better off in the tiny adjoining room. She would hear the nurse call her easily enough from there.

Her urine sample was safe inside her handbag, the cap tightly screwed on and the small glass receptacle doubly safeguarded by being inside one of those tiny padded jiffy bags Steve brought home from work.

Thinking of Steve made her feel tense again. She hadn't told him she was coming here, and last night, goaded on by God knew what, she had gone on at him about starting a new course of IVF treatment. He had told her bluntly that they couldn't afford it – not yet, anyway; not so soon after their last failure – but, obsessed by the thought of her frozen embryos, she had been unable to stop herself, and they had rowed.

The hospital had told them to wait a couple of months, but now she had to feel she was doing something.

Janet closed her eyes, her heartbeat quickening once again. It was far too early to let herself hope. She had failed so often now that it was hard to imagine something actually going right for once, but the truth was she had missed two periods. At first she had told herself that it was something to do with the treatment and that her body was taking its time getting back to normal. She had been too scared to pick up the phone to the hospital and ask. Scared because, deep down, she didn't want their assurances.

But lately she had been unable to sleep. Lately she had lived on her nerves until – after that awful row last night – she had forced herself to call the health centre and book herself in for a pregnancy test.

'Janet Crossley?'

She looked up, startled, then hurried over to where the nurse was standing, returning the woman's pleasant smile with her own tense grimace, before following her through to an inner room.

'Have you brought a sample, dear?' the nurse asked, as she sat, flicking through Janet's notes. She waited while Janet fumbled in her bag and almost – almost – dropped it on the floor, she was so nervous.

While the test was carried out, the nurse chatted, but she might just as well have been talking in a foreign language as far as Janet was concerned. She said 'yes' and 'no' to order, as if she was carrying on a genuine conversation, but all the time she was watching the woman's hands, watching as she squeezed drops of urine on to the circular slide, hoping, *praying*, that at last she had succeeded: it was almost impossible to imagine.

She waited, each second an agony of suspense, and then, with a little sound of surprise, the nurse turned to her. 'Do you feel any different?'

Janet's heart skipped a beat. She shook her head.

'Well, you should,' the nurse said, smiling. 'You're pregnant.'

'*Pregnant* . . .' Janet spoke the word as if it were both strange and at the same time sacred. She swallowed, then, feeling her mouth go dry, asked quietly, 'Are you sure?'

The nurse's smile broadened. She nodded emphatically. 'Positive.'

Outside, walking back home along the shadowed streets, Janet felt a huge beam of a smile fill her face, transforming it. She had known, of course. Part of her had known all along, ever since she had missed her first period, but only now did she allow that knowledge to fill her. Only now did she dare remove the straitjacket of fear that had constrained her all these weeks and kept her from blurting it out.

Now she couldn't wait to get home. For Steve to come back from work and for her to tell him. To watch his face light up with happiness.

Oh, it had been so hard. So horribly, miserably hard. But it had all been worth it. The joy she now felt – the happiness – was beyond description. No . . . no one could imagine how she felt. *This* was a special pregnancy.

Back indoors, she went over to the phone and picked it up, then set it down again. She was tempted to phone him and tell him straight away, but that would spoil it. She wanted to see his face. She wanted to see that incandescent light of joy kindled in his eyes. More than that, she wanted to hold him. Steve deserved that, after all he'd put up with.

Laughing, light-headed, Janet turned full circle in her kitchen, then whooped.

It was going to be all right. Everything was going to be . . . wonderful!

Steve sat at his desk, one of the Stockholm contract files

open in front of him, the computer screen shining its blue light out across the surface. He was supposed to be doing a summary on them for McGovern, but he was barely aware of either. In his mind he was running through the argument with Janet for the hundredth time and wondering what on earth he might have said to incite things.

Unreasonable wasn't the word for it. *Impossible*, more like. But there was only so much shit a person could be expected to take – no matter what the circumstances.

'Steve?'

He looked up, surprised to see Polly there. He'd thought he was alone in the offices.

'Polly! I . . .'

'It's gone seven,' she said. 'What're you still doing here?'

He laughed sourly. 'Working . . . or s'posed to be.'

'Shouldn't you be going home?'

'Eventually.'

She looked at him a moment. 'You fancy a drink?'

Steve had been looking away, staring glumly at the screen with its blocks of figures. Now he looked back at her, his eyes taking in the shape of her. Then, leaning forward, he punched the off button on the computer, not even bothering to close the file before he did so.

'Why not?'

Mandy stood at the sink, humming the theme to *EastEnders* as she washed up the single plate, knife, fork and mug she had used for her dinner.

It was not like the old days, when she'd have had a draining board full of crockery, and it wasn't that she really missed it, but . . .

Some days she'd have welcomed a bit of company.

Pulling the tea towel down from the peg, she dried off her hands, then began to wipe the plate, when the doorbell rang.

Mandy half turned, almost as if she hadn't heard things right. She wasn't expecting anyone, and it was well after eight.

Putting the plate down on the work surface, she walked through, switching on the hall light before staring through the glass panel of the door.

'Mand?'

Mandy gave a little laugh, then pulled the door open. 'Alex! What are *you* doing here?'

Alex was thirty-five and balding, but not a bad-looking guy. Mandy had first met him twenty years ago, when he'd played in the same Sunday football team as Pete. Recently they'd met up again, at a club. Like her, he was recently divorced.

'I was just passing, and I thought . . .'

'You thought *what*?' But the glint in Mandy's eyes gave her away. She was pleased to see him and he knew it.

Alex smiled, suddenly as smooth as Valentino. 'I thought I'd come and see my favourite girl.'

'Oh, yeah?' Mandy said, stepping back to let him come inside. 'What you mean is, you was wondering what lonely old cow was bound to be at home that you could call round on.'

'The trouble with you, Mandy,' he said, moving past her into the hallway, 'is that you ain't able to accept a compliment.'

'Oh, really?' she said, grinning.

'Yeah. Really. I mean, well, the body doesn't lie, does it?'

Mandy frowned, not quite understanding his meaning.

Alex took hold of her hand. 'Feel that!' he said, laying her palm over his crotch.

His penis was stiff beneath his jeans and as she felt it she pulled her hand away, giggling like a teenager.

'It's all right, Mand,' he said, unzipping his fly. 'It won't bite.' And with that he unfurled her fingers and pushed them beneath the stiff denim.

Mandy grinned. 'You dirty little bastard,' she said, reaching up with her other hand to turn off the light.

Janet sat at the kitchen table, the phone in front of her. It was now 8.47 according to the neat white circular clock on the wall over the fridge, and she was beginning to get worried. Steve was working late quite often recently, but usually he phoned, and rarely was he *this* late.

What if he'd had an accident . . . ?

Janet told herself not to be silly. He had just forgotten to phone her, that was all. Even so . . .

She picked up the receiver and tapped out his work number.

It rang and rang.

Finally, she put the phone down.

'Where are you?' she said, frightened suddenly. 'Where the bloody hell are you?'

Steve reached over to the bar and set down his empty glass, then looked about him at the crowded room. Everywhere he looked, people were deep in conversation: relaxed, animated, laughing. It was coming up to nine and he knew he really ought to be getting back, but the mere thought of going home – back to Janet and her cold hostility – made him want to sit there and order another beer.

He looked down at his shoes, pondering the alternatives. Polly had been a sympathetic listener, and it had been good to be able to talk to someone for once, but at the same time he felt guilty discussing Janet with another woman, but at least it had been someone who didn't know her: somehow that had made it easier.

A moment ago he had watched her as she'd made her way towards the ladies', and had been struck by what a pert little arse she had.

Steve smiled at the memory. She was a nice girl. Not quite his type, but . . .

Suddenly he felt a hand on his shoulder and turned to find her standing there. 'Are you ready?'

'Ready?'

Polly smiled. 'We can get a taxi back.'

'Back where?'

'To my place, silly.'

Steve looked away for a moment or two, unsure of his ground suddenly.

'Look! Polly . . .'

'Don't tell me it hasn't crossed your mind.'

He looked up at her. Her smile was so warm and inviting. He willed himself to think of his argument with Janet the night before, forcing her image from his mind almost at once.

'All right,' he said quietly.

Polly looked at him a moment, a half-formed smile on her lips, then stepped closer and, laying her hands gently on his cheeks, placed her mouth to his, kissing him for the first time.

It was a long, passionate kiss, and as they broke from it, Steve stared at her, surprised.

'Come on,' she said, taking his hand and pulling him up from the bar stool. 'Before I change my mind.'

Mandy lay back, her eyes closed, enjoying the simple feel of Alex's firm, naked body next to hers in the bed. In the end they had done it twice, the second time with her on top.

'Are you sure?' she'd asked. 'It could kill you, you know.'

But he'd simply laughed and reached up for her breasts, burying his face in her deep, dark cleavage.

Now she was relaxed and, dare she say it, even happy. She would not allow herself to wonder how she would feel later on, once Alex had gone. For now he was here and she loved the warmth of his body beside her. Opening her eyes, she smiled, noting how the hairs on his chest glistened in the light from the portable TV on the dressing table. The sound was turned right down.

'Alex?'

'Yeah?'

'Where does she think you are?'

'She' was Alex's latest girlfriend, a young woman called Shelley from the Packington Estate.

'Darts,' he said, his eyes never leaving the screen. It was one of the European games, and Arsenal were clearly losing.

'*Shit!*' he hissed, as the ball whizzed past the goal.

But Mandy wasn't interested in the football. Turning over slightly, she snuggled into him, laying her arm across his chest.

'You can stay over if you want,' she said hopefully.

'Nah . . . I'd best get back. See the end of the football first, though.'

Mandy sighed inwardly. Men were a sad, immensely selfish race, interested in only three things: food, football and fucking. With a wry grin, she decided she might as well exploit at least one of those weaknesses to her own benefit.

She let her hand stray down, until it covered his flaccid penis where it lay between his hot, moist thighs like a tiny chick.

'Go on!' he said. But he was talking to Ian Wright, not to her.

Mandy giggled. 'Blow your whistle for you, ref?'

Alex glanced at her. 'What's that, Mand?'

She smiled up at him. 'Nothing. Just playing with Lazarus.'

'You'll be lucky,' he said. 'Twice is me limit.'

'What! A stud like you!'

He draped his arm over her shoulder and, reaching down, covered her breast with his hand, squeezing the soft flesh.

'Don't take the piss,' he said, good-naturedly.

'Oh, I'm not.' She giggled. 'It's just that I thought you youngsters were supposed to have a bit of energy!'

'Yeah, well, it's the darts. It takes it out of you, you know what I mean!'

Mandy smiled. His penis had grown noticeably in the past few moments. It was more like an uncooked sausage now. She ran one finger down its length and felt Alex give a little shiver.

'It's like Aladdin's lamp, ain't it?'

'If you say so.'

'Yeah,' she said, feeling it go stiff. 'Bloody magic. If I had one of these I'd be playing with it all the time.'

Alex laughed. 'Save me doin' it meself, I s'pose.'

Mandy looked up at his face, suddenly interested. 'Do you?'

'What, wank? Yeah . . . sometimes. All blokes do. We're more highly sexed, ain't we?'

'It's a bit messy though, ain't it?'

'Nah.' Then, 'Look, Mand, d'you think you could wait till the game's finished?'

Mandy's hand slowed, then stopped. Moving it away, she hauled herself up into a sitting position. 'Right! Might as well make a cup of tea, then.'

She was about to get up when the phone rang. She reached across and picked it up, glancing at the digital readout on the alarm clock. It was 9.04.

'Hello.'

'Hi, Mum! It's Jason.'

'Oh! Hello, love,' she said, conscious suddenly of her nakedness. She pulled the duvet up over her breasts. 'How are you?'

'Great. Look, Mum . . . I've got some news.'

'News? You're all right, ain't you?'

'Yeah, yeah. Fine. Listen! Are you sitting down?'

Mandy glanced at Alex. 'Go on.'

'It's about me and Gemma. We're . . . well, we're gonna have a baby.'

Mandy blinked. 'What?'

'Yeah. It's cool, ain't it? You're gonna be a grandmother.'

She talked for a while, then put the phone down, but it was like she was in shock. A baby . . . her Jason was going to have a baby. It wasn't possible. She could remember as clearly as if it was only days ago when he had been *her* baby, bathing him, seeing him lying on his back in the tiny blue plastic bath and giggling, his little arms and legs jerking erratically as she splashed the water over him. It seemed like only days ago . . .

'Who was that?' Alex asked, glancing at her as she got up and took her dressing gown down from the peg on the back of the door and pulled it on.

'Jason,' she said distractedly. Then, 'You want a cuppa?'

'Smashing.'

Mandy walked through, then stood beside the kettle, dazed by the news, unable to think almost. She blew out a long breath, feeling suddenly very old. Oh, she wasn't forty yet, and these days forty was nothing, so they said, but *this* . . . A granny? The thought of it horrified her. Grannies were old and grey and . . . *sensible*. She didn't want to be sensible. She'd had a fucking lifetime of being sensible . . .

She closed her eyes. It seemed that no matter how fast she ran along the track of life, time was always there, just a couple of steps ahead of her. Walking across, she picked up her make-up bag from beside the phone and took out the tiny circular mirror, studying her face in it, looking for . . . what? Reassurance?

Christ! The big Four-O was bad enough, but *this*!

Mandy groaned. Ten minutes back she had been happy, but now it was like someone had come along and hit her with a sledgehammer. Young? Of course she wasn't young, in spite of how she felt inside. But this! Her new status would place her firmly — *irrevocably* — among the crinkly-wrinklies!

Nanny Mandy . . .

It sounded ridiculous. Absurd.

'Mand?'

Alex's voice calling from her bedroom jerked her back to reality.

'Yeah?' she called, walking over to the door.

'The football's finished.'

Steve stood there, watching her as she hailed the cab, then stepped in after her. Her lips were pressed to his almost from the moment he slumped down beside her on the long back seat, her warm tongue probing his mouth.

At some point, he realised, she had sprayed herself with perfume, and its heady scent, combined with her warmth, was intoxicating. He brought his hand up around to her shoulder, but she took it and gently lowered it to her breast.

'It's OK . . .' she whispered.

And when he was slow to take the hint, she unbuttoned her blouse for him, to expose her pert but wonderfully shaped breasts, the nipples stiff in the half-light.

As his fingers traced the shape of one, he found himself aroused and lowered his head towards it, brushing his tongue against its tip.

Her hot mouth whispered in his ear, her wet tongue traced its shell-like shape. 'Oh, yes . . . that's it . . . oh, God, I want you, Steve . . .'

To be wanted. The very thought of it inflamed his senses. As she reached down to brush against the soft cloth at his groin, he groaned. This was wrong, he knew, but he could not help himself, and when she lifted herself up and, raising her skirt, sat astride him, he could do nothing but succumb.

That next kiss was heavenly. With the warmth of her groin pressing against his own, the soft flesh of her breasts beneath his fingertips, he could not help but push up against her, as if to enter her. And her laughter — soft, whispered laughter — was like temptation itself.

His penis was painfully hard now.

Her hand rested on his chest a moment, then slowly travelled down.

'No . . .' he said, his eyes meeting hers. 'Not here.'

She smiled, then put her face to his again, wriggling against him now excitedly.

Steve reached up, tracing the shape of her neck, her head, then slowly let his hands travel down until they rested once more upon her breasts. She moaned and the sound of her pleasure sent a shiver through him.

'Epping Avenue,' the taxi driver announced, as if nothing unusual were going on in the back of his cab. 'You want this end or the other?'

Polly moved back slightly, quickly, expertly buttoning up her blouse before swinging her body round. 'This'll do,' she said, laying her hand gently but deliberately over Steve's swollen penis as she resumed her seat beside him.

The cab slowed and stopped. 'Three eighty,' the driver said, switching on his light then turning with a smile. He had, of course, seen everything.

As Polly threw open the door and jumped down, her hand inside her bag, rummaging for her door keys, Steve took his wallet from his pocket and removed a fiver. Looking up, he watched her for a moment as, key in hand, she turned towards the house. It was the briefest moment, then, reaching across, he pulled the door closed.

'Drive on.'

The driver shrugged, then did as he was told.

Polly was halfway up the path when she heard the taxi pull away. She giggled and turned, thinking to find Steve there behind her, but there was no sign of him.

'Steve . . . Steve?'

In the cab, Steve sat back, the stiffness of his penis a torment. But at the last moment he had been unable to go through with it. Something – some tiny trace of conscience – had prevented it.

Oh, he had wanted to fuck her, and if she had but kept hold of his hand and pulled him from the cab, that's how it would have ended. But she had let go, and the spell had broken . . . and now he was here, heading away from her.

'Where to?' the cabbie asked as they got to the top of the road.

'Percy Street.'

There was a moment's silence, then the driver chuckled to himself. 'Not your girlfriend, then?'

Steve smiled wryly. 'Girlfriend? No.'

'Well, she was up for it all right!' His laugh was deep and dirty. 'I tell you, mate. I admire you.'

Steve looked away, embarrassed now.

'Mind you, you two was nothing! I've seen 'em get up to all sorts in the back there. Specially when they've 'ad a drink inside 'em. And I reckon the girls are worse than the blokes!'

'Yeah, well . . .'

The cab driver glanced at Steve in his rear-view mirror. 'So. I guess you must have someone pretty hot to go home to, eh?'

'Why d'you say that?'

'Well, no bloke with all his bits between his legs is gonna give a bird like that the elbow unless he's got something better lined up!'

'Nah . . .' Steve said, as if in agreement. But Steve was feeling very sober suddenly, and though he knew he had done the right thing, part of him was angry. Angry with himself that he hadn't been able to go through with it. After all . . . who could blame him?

Fuck it! he thought, close to tears suddenly. Why can't you be like that for me, Jan? Why can't you want me that much?

Steve closed his eyes and let his head slump back against the juddering seat back, falling over to one side as the cab turned left into Percy Street.

Janet sat there at the table in her kitchen, the silent phone in front of her. Behind her, the flat was dark, the TV off. Only the ticking of the wall clock broke the deathly silence. The air was cold. It was as if it had frozen all about her.

Her day of joy was ruined now. All of her plans, all of those happy scenes she had imagined, were beyond achievement now. He had not come. And still the minutes ticked away. The awful, endless minutes.

A noise from the road below caught her attention: a taxi cab, coming up the narrow close. It stopped, the distinctive sound of its engine as it idled, accompanied by the clunk of a door shutting behind the emerging passenger.

She waited, listening for laughter maybe or some other sound, but there was nothing. And then the cab drew away, turning and exiting the close.

There was the sound of approaching footsteps, and then the front door opened.

Janet didn't need to turn. She was facing the doorway as he came along the hall. She saw him pause, a sheepish expression on his face. His head ducked down. 'I'm sorry, Jan, I—'

'Where've you been?'

Steve took a shivering breath, then shrugged. 'Out.'

Janet stood and walked over to him, smelling the perfume on him even before she got close. Her eyes went to his, accusing him, and for once he did not look away.

'You've been with someone, haven't you?'

The anger in her voice masked the trembling that had overcome her.

Steve swallowed, then gave a single nod.

A tear ran slowly down Janet's face.

'I went to the doctor's today,' she said, her voice almost breaking.

The news meant nothing to him, except maybe to prepare him for renewed arguments over IVF. But even the thought of that brought Steve momentary relief.

'Had to have a test.'

'Test?' This time his eyes registered puzzlement. 'What kind of test?'

'And I've been sitting here all this time, waiting to tell you. Only you didn't come home. You didn't soddin' well come home.'

'Janet! What *kind* of test?'

'I'm pregnant! I had a pregnancy test and I'm pregnant!'

Slowly it dawned on him. Surprise warred with guilt in his face, but the pleasure that should have been there was muted. All this while she had been waiting for him. Waiting to share with him this unbelievable news. News they had waited so long to hear. A look of pain crossed Steve's face.

'Are you sure?'

'Yeah,' she said, a real hardness coming to her face. 'I'm having your baby, Steve. I'm sorry that wasn't worth coming home for.'

Karen turned, watching Lucy prepare a salad for herself, then answered Mandy at the other end of the phone.

'Look, it's understandable. I mean. I'd feel the same if I

was about to become a granny. It's a shock, that's all. No one's suddenly going to expect you to sit at home knitting little bonnets or whatever.'

'Yeah,' Mandy said on the other end of the phone. 'I s'pose you're right. And I do love 'em when they're tiny. But . . . well, it's all a bit sudden, you know? I mean . . . I thought it'd be a few years yet . . .'

'I know, but, well, there it is. So you might as well try and look on the positive side. It's something for you to be proud of, Mand. I bet Jason and Gemma are, aren't they?'

'Yeah . . . yeah, they are. But it's gonna make it a bit awkward with Janet, ain't it?'

Karen hadn't thought of that. She turned, watching Lucy go through into the shadowed living room, then smiled down the phone. 'Anyway, listen! You take care of yourself, eh? And remember. You're as young as you feel.'

'Well, after last night's marathon, about ninety-four at the moment!' Mandy laughed coarsely down the phone.

Karen smiled to herself. 'I don't think I want to know.'

'No! I don't think you do! Mind you, Kar. It could put you back on the right track.'

'I'm perfectly happy with the track I'm on, thank you very much.'

'Yeah. Yeah, 'course you are. Listen! Don't s'pose you fancy meeting up for a drink tomorrow night?'

'I don't want to be corrupted.'

'Too late, darling!'

Karen laughed. 'No, actually. I can't, I'm afraid, Mand. I promised my mum I'd pop round.'

'Things any better?'

'No. Not a lot.'

'Ah well, never mind . . . there's always Anna's do to look forward to, ain't there?'

'Yeah . . . Look, I'd better dash, Mand.'

'OK . . . I'll see you next Friday, then. Take care.'

'I will. Byee . . .'

Karen put the phone down, then stood there for a moment, reluctant to go into the living room. Mandy's phone call had not come a moment too soon, just as a full-blown row was about to erupt between her and Lucy. But it had only postponed things. The problem still had to be faced.

She had known Lucy now for almost six weeks. They had met at a drinks party at a mutual friend's and had arranged to go to the theatre a week later. One thing had led to another, and Karen had found herself staying the night at Lucy's.

It had been, perhaps, the strangest night of her life so far. Strange because far from being confident in her new sexuality, this business of taking on a new partner had thrown her into a state of real confusion. It had been easy to be with Chris. Things had just happened naturally between them, and though she'd been afraid at first, Chris had seen her through that. This now, with Lucy, was quite different.

Lucy, though smaller physically than Karen, was by far the more dominant of the two. Not only that, but she conformed far more to the lesbian stereotype than either Karen or Chris had, with her short red hair and her almost masculine clothes. And when it came to sex, it was Lucy who called all the shots. And that had frightened Karen. Even now it frightened her.

Yet strangely she had become dependent on Lucy, even after this short period. Lucy made her laugh. More than that, Lucy made her think. But now Lucy was beginning to push for more than she could give, and the parallels with Chris and how that had ended were beginning to rear up in Karen's mind.

Steeling herself against the coming fight, she walked through, standing behind the sofa where Lucy sat, cross-legged, gazing at the TV, the sound barely audible.

'Mandy, I take it?' Lucy said, between mouthfuls.

'Her son's having a baby.'

'Physically impossible, I'd say.'

'You know what I mean.'

Karen waited, as Lucy shovelled down another mouthful of the salad. Then Lucy turned, glancing up at her. 'So are you coming?'

'I've already—'

'Look. I want you to come. They're my friends. I want you to meet them.'

'And *I* want to meet *them*, but I promised my mother.'

Lucy turned away, making a noise of exasperation. 'I don't know why you keep going. The old bastard never speaks to you.'

'That's not the point. My mum wants me there. Besides, he can't keep this up for ever.'

'No?' Lucy was quiet a moment, then. 'OK . . . your loss! But if I have to go alone. I'll be staying over.'

Karen looked down. That was what she feared. 'You do what you want.'

'I always do.'

It was said provocatively; knowing how Karen felt. Karen knew that. But knowing it didn't help one tiny little bit. It was as if she were subject to some madness, and that madness's name was jealousy. Try as she might, she could not stop herself feeling hopelessly insecure about the women she went out with. It had happened with Chris, now it was happening with Lucy. It was horrible, and she did not know how to cope with it.

'I'm going to bed,' she said, unable to keep the note of irritation from her voice. But Lucy just sat there, smiling at the TV screen, and as she turned away, Karen knew that she had lost even more of what little ground remained hers in this relationship.

Susie drew back the curtains, letting the morning's light

flood into the room, then went across and lifted Nathan from his cot.

'Good morning, handsome. Who was a good boy and slept right through, then?'

Nathan gurgled and smiled. In the bed beyond, Jo poked his head up from the tangle of the blankets and grimaced.

'What's the time?'

But Susie didn't answer him. She spoke to Nathan instead in her tiny baby voice. 'Poor Daddy's got a sore head because he drank too much happy juice. He's a naughty boy and it serves him right.'

'Oh, Suse . . . give us a break, will you?'

'It's Mister Grumpy, and he's late for work.'

'Late?' Jo sat up and threw off the cover. 'Why didn't you tell me?'

'I just did.'

'But . . .'

'You should have set the alarm . . . either that or drunk a bit less. Christ . . . how many did you have?'

'Eight . . .'

'*Eight!*' Susie looked back at Nathan. 'Good job we get the family allowance today, eh, sweetpie?'

But Jo was at the wardrobe now, pulling down a tie, then taking a fresh suit from the hanger. 'That's all I bloody need,' he moaned as he pulled on his trousers. 'We've got some important clients coming in today from Hong Kong.'

But Susie merely grinned at Nathan and said, 'Velly good . . .'

Nathan bawled. He screwed up his face and howled.

Jo looked across and grimaced again. 'Can't you feed him or something? He's doin' me bleedin' head in.'

Susie sat, then took out her left breast, placing the heavy, milky nipple into Nathan's mouth. At once he fastened on and began to suck furiously.

Susie stared at Nathan a long while, barely conscious of Jo getting ready in the room, recalling instead how she had tiptoed across to the cot in the night and, by the light of the moon, had watched as he sucked at an imaginary nipple, his little mouth puckering, his tiny fingers twitching. He was so beautiful. So perfect.

She felt a hand on her shoulder and looked up as Jo pecked her cheek. 'Gotta rush. See you tonight. I'll try to be early, OK?'

'OK . . .'

Susie heard the front door go, then stretched her neck, enjoying the sensation of Nathan at her breast. She smiled, wondering if Jo even remembered making love to her last night. He had been very drunk. Even so, it had been nice for once to have the bed to themselves, and towards the end she had even found herself enjoying it.

She grinned. 'He's a very naughty Daddy . . .'

Nathan looked up at her, surprised to hear her voice, and the nipple popped like a rubber bung from his mouth. She lifted Nathan up on to her shoulder and winded him, then cradled him against her once again.

'Other side?'

Nathan stared back at her, his tiny mouth sucking, keen for more milk.

Expertly she turned him, experiencing relief as he began to empty her right breast. That was the only trouble with his sleeping through. Her breasts would ache by the morning and the bed would be wet from the leaking milk.

Still, she was coping much better these days. She no longer woke in that state of sheer panic she had experienced in those first few weeks. In fact, though she said it herself, she was doing all right. Even Lyndsay said so, and Lyndsay gave nothing away.

The phone in the hallway began to ring.

'Hang on, gorgeous. Let Mummy just answer the phone.'

Pulling Nathan away from her nipple, she put him on her shoulder and carried him down, patting his back with one hand while she picked up the phone with the other.

'Hello?'

'Susie?'

'*Jan?* Is that you?'

'Yeah, look . . . can I come round?'

'Sure, babes, but—'

'I'll be about half an hour. 'Bye.'

Susie put the phone down, frowning. She hadn't heard from Janet since Nathan had been born. In fact, Janet hadn't even *seen* Nathan yet.

Nathan lifted himself the smallest little bit and gave an almighty burp.

'There's a good boy,' she said automatically, smoothing his back, but her mind for once wasn't on her son; she was wondering what Janet could possibly want to talk to her about.

As Anna walked back into her office, the four who were waiting there looked up, anxious to gauge her reaction.

'Well?' her art director, Des Arnot, asked, watching Anna take her seat behind the desk and, pushing the dummy magazine aside, begin to sort through the stack of showcards she had brought back with her. 'What did he think?'

'He thought your work was bloody marvellous, Desmond, my boy. His words, I think, went something like . . . the best-designed magazine in the group . . .'

Des beamed, but the other three were frowning. Anna's very sobriety worried them.

'Yeah, but what about the content?' Jacqui Pierce, her associate editor, asked. 'Did he find it too wacky?'

Anna stopped and looked up at her. '*Wacky?* Why should

he find it *wacky*? No. He loved it. Said it showed real imagination. And a good range, too.'

'So what *didn't* he like?' Jake Moseley, her features editor, asked. 'He can't have liked everything.'

'No, he didn't,' Anna said, turning to place three of the boards against the wall behind her. 'He thought our advertising budget was way out.'

'Shit!' That was Rose Field. Rose was in charge of budgeting the magazine.

Anna looked across at her and smiled. 'I'd agree. Only he doubled the budget. Says he wants to launch with a real splash.'

'Then . . .' Jacqui began.

Anna looked about her at the team she'd put together. A team she was really proud of. 'That's right. He's given us the green light. We launch in two months. It's tight but, hell, we can do it!'

There were whoops and cries of 'Well done!' and Anna even allowed herself a little smile. But her mood was muted. She had heard only that morning that her mother had cancer.

'So can I get the ad team started?' That was Rose again.

'Yep,' Anna said. Then, more businesslike, 'Jacqui, will you do me a great favour?'

'Sure. What is it?'

'I'm supposed to be going to a do this Saturday evening and I wondered if you could stand in for me. I know it's short notice but . . . well, I need to go and see my mother.'

Jacqui smiled. 'Sure. It'll be a good excuse to wear my little black number.' Then, more quietly: 'How is she?'

Anna took a long breath. 'Not good.'

'Ah . . .'

There were exchanged looks, then Des stood. 'Right . . . I'd better get those two shoots sorted out . . .'

'Yeah,' Jake said. 'Things to do, eh?'

'Me, too,' Rose added, getting up hastily.

In less than a minute Anna was alone in her office. She sat there for a time, her hands steepled in front of her, and then she sighed. For years now she had thought of her mother as something of a fraud; her mysterious ailments as the product of a hypochondriac mind. Even when she'd gone and had the tests Anna had not been unduly concerned. Her mother had seemed tired, sure, but that was to be expected in a woman of seventy-three. The news, therefore, had come as something of a shock: a reminder from reality that there were more important things than magazines.

Six months was what they had given her, but the doctor had told Anna that she might just as easily go in six days, such was the nature of the disease.

'Shit!'

Anna stood, then walked over to the window. She was eighteen storeys up and from where she stood she could see halfway across London. If she'd had a map she could probably have worked out where her mother lay right then, in that upstairs bedroom where she had given birth to Anna and where her father had died in his sleep. And now it was her turn.

The thought of it blotted out all of the happiness she ought to have been feeling. It made a nothing of her achievement.

'Trust you, Mum.'

But she didn't blame her. If anything she felt guilty. Guilty because she had not understood how real the pain had been; how real the suffering. She'd thought her a fussy old woman, and this was how reality repaid her.

'Shit!'

Yes, and there was one other thing about all this that scared her. Something which she had thought about for the first time this morning. With her mother gone, she would be alone, an only child and the next in line: there, out front, *exposed* to death; no one shielding that chill wind from her with their physical presence.

A single woman.

No, she thought, exposing the real fear she had. It isn't just that I'm single, it's the fact that I'm childless.

It was *that* which had kept going through her mind all the time she was doing the presentation this morning. For the last three months she had been able to forget about it – to kid herself that her work was enough – but she was fooling no one, least of all herself. She still wanted a baby. And never more so than now when her mother was dying.

Anna closed her eyes, trying to still her racing thoughts, then turned, making her way through to the ladies' room.

She pushed through the door, into the marbled interior . . .

And stopped dead, her mouth falling open.

A baby lay on the laminate worktop beside the right-hand sink. A changing mat lay beneath it and one of those plastic carry bags with nappies in it rested on the floor nearby, but of the mother there was no sign.

Anna stepped forward, looking about her, then saw the half-open cubicle, the feet emerging beneath a door, and understood.

She walked across and stood there, looking down at the child. It could not have been more than three or four weeks old, with a tiny blur of down on its skull, but it was awake and its blue eyes stared straight up at her.

Beautiful. It was breathtakingly beautiful.

There was a noise behind her, a low grunt of noise that made Anna smile and almost laugh. Not a quick pee, then!

Anna's heart was beating fast suddenly. She daren't . . . But why not? She wasn't going to do the child any harm?

Quickly, yet with exaggerated care, she picked the baby up, surprised that it remained silent, its big eyes wide, watching her. Quietly she cooed to it and rocked it back and forth, like she'd seen Susie do to Nathan. And as she did, she felt a strange contraction in her womb.

Anna shivered, then turned. The mother had finished and was standing there. Without a word — a faint flush colouring her youthful features — she came across and took the baby from Anna, replacing it on the mat.

Anna made to speak, but found she had nothing to say. Your baby's beautiful? Yes, but she knew that. She was its mother, after all.

She could have asked the young woman what she was doing there in *her* magazine's toilets, but then equally, the woman could have asked her why she was holding *her* baby.

In the end she simply smiled and, backing away, her purpose for going there forgotten, she quickly left. But the feeling of the baby in her arms and the sight of its big blue eyes staring up at her remained, searing her, making her take her coat and hurry to the lifts, anxious to get away.

Susie carried the tea things through on a tray, then sat, facing Janet, giving her an encouraging smile.

'It's really lovely to see you, Jan.'

'Yeah,' But Janet's smile was tentative. 'How's the baby?'

'He's sleeping now, but . . . well, he's fine.'

'Good. Good, I'm . . . glad. Really, Suse.'

Susie looked down. This was awkward. How awkward she hadn't guessed until now. Normally she would have been keen to show Nathan off, but this once she was glad that he was asleep in his cot upstairs. She glanced back up. 'And what about you?' she asked, reaching across to pour the tea.

Again Janet's smile was hesitant. 'I'm fine. In fact . . . I'm pregnant.'

Susie's head sprang up. 'Jan!' Then, seeing Janet nod, she put the teapot down and, with a big beam of a smile, went round and gave her a hug. 'Oh my God! Jan! That's wonderful! I'm so *pleased* for you.'

'Yeah,' Janet said, smiling despite herself.

'When did you find out?'

'Yesterday.'

'Brilliant! And how far along?'

'Not sure. They're sending me for a scan . . .'

'Do the others know yet?'

Janet shook her head. 'Not yet.'

'So how's the expectant father? Delirious, I bet.'

Janet's head went down. Her face closed over like a steel door had fallen.

'You have told him, ain't you?'

Janet looked up, meeting Susie's eyes; then, unexpectedly she burst into tears. Surprised and confused, Susie clung on to her, letting her sob against her, rocking her to and fro as Janet's pain drained away from her. Then, when Janet had calmed down a little, she asked, 'What is it? Is it Steve?'

Janet swallowed, then reached into her bag for a tissue and made a show of blowing her nose and dabbing at her mascara.

'Jan?'

'Bastard's been playing away.'

'What!' The look of shock on Susie's face was almost comic. Steve? Playing away? The thought of it was . . . well, ridiculous. 'Are you sure?'

A little shudder ran through Janet, then she nodded. She sniffed loudly. 'He came in late. He never phoned or nothing. Just said he'd been out. So I asked him.'

Susie closed her eyes and groaned inwardly. 'And?'

'He said he'd been with her. This girl from work.'

Susie looked at Janet again. 'What d'you mean, been with her?'

Janet looked away, a flicker of pain crossing her face. '*Been*

- 344 -

with her. What else could it mean?' She gave another huge sniff, then went on. 'We'd had a big row, you see. I was so wound up, what with wanting to talk about the IVF, and knowing that I hadn't come on . . .'

'Did he know you hadn't?'

Janet shook her head miserably. 'So I thought I'd better go for a test. But I didn't tell him.'

'Oh, Jan . . .'

'I know, but I didn't want to disappoint him again, and I wasn't sure, and . . .' Her face cracked and Janet dissolved into tears again.

Susie held her a while, her mind in turmoil at the thought of Steve — the only really loyal bloke she knew — being unfaithful. Shit! It was like finding out that Tony Blair liked dressing up in Janet Reager underwear!

As Janet grew still again, Susie said, 'I can't believe it, Jan. Are you positive?'

Janet's eyes flared. 'He said so, didn't he?'

'Well, I don't know. Did he? I mean, he said he went with her. Went *out* with her, or slept with her?'

Janet stared at her, confused now.

'I mean, if he just had a drink . . .' Susie made a sympathetic face. 'Look, I know it's crap timing, either way. I mean, I'd cut Jo's balls off if I found out he was taking another woman out, but . . . it might have been a one-off. He might have just gone for a quick drink with her and they got talking and . . .'

'Yeah, it's the "and" I don't like.'

The remark was so much like the old Janet she knew and loved that Susie laughed. Then, all sympathy again, she said, 'You've got to ask him.'

'Ask him?'

'If he slept with her.'

Janet looked horrified. 'I can't.'

'Why not?'

She looked down. 'He knows what I think. He didn't deny it.'

'Janet! I can vouch for the fact that most of the time it's *impossible* to guess what you're thinking. Just admit that you won't ask him 'cos you're too fucking proud!' Janet looked up at that. 'Steve loves you, you know that.'

Janet gave a shuddering sigh, then nodded. 'Yeah. I know.'

'Then give him a chance.'

'And what if he did?'

'Then I'll lend you my knife sharpener!'

Janet looked up at Susie and smiled weakly. Then, the pain resuming its hold on her expression, she reached out and held her again.

'I'm glad I came, Suse. I've missed you.'

Still in shock from Jason's news, Mandy had phoned in sick. But being at home was just as bad as being at work and, setting the long-neglected ironing to one side, she pulled on her coat and went out.

Sainsbury's wasn't as crowded as when she usually went. Even so, she hurried down the aisles, filling her basket with the pitifully few items she needed these days, praying that she wouldn't bump into anyone she knew. She couldn't bear the thought of people knowing about Jason, and the jokes she knew she would have to endure.

Mandy stood at the checkout, glancing nervously about her. She knew that she ought to have been pleased at the news, for Jason and Gemma, if for nothing else. But she couldn't. This was about her as much as it was about them. She was just getting herself on an even keel, had achieved a bit of balance in her life – a bit of normality after splitting up with Pete – but now she felt she had gone back to Square One.

She had been somebody's daughter, somebody's wife, somebody's mum, and now she was about to become somebody's nan.

She paid for her things then left, hurrying along Liverpool Road, eager to get home again. Yet as she went to cross the little zebra crossing at the top of Cloudesley Place, a guy in a white van rolled his window down and called out to her.

'Mand?'

Mandy glanced across. 'Pete?'

'Get in . . . I'll give you a lift.'

She went over and climbed into the passenger's seat, cramming her shopping into the space between her legs, then pulled the door closed.

'This new?' she asked, as he pulled away.

'Nah, it's Barry's. I'm borrowing it for the day.' He glanced at her. 'Well? I s'pose he's phoned you.'

'Who?'

'Don't play silly beggars. You know who. Jason . . .'

'Ah . . .'

'What d'you mean, ah . . .'

Mandy looked down. She didn't really want to talk about what she'd been going through since she'd heard, but Pete seemed oblivious.

'I think it's ace. Gemma'll be a great mum. And it'll do Jason a lot of good too. Time he had a bit of responsibility.'

Mandy was silent. So silent that Pete glanced at her and frowned.

'You all right?'

She shrugged.

'They'll be fine. Don't worry.'

'I know. I know.'

'Well, what's the matter, then?'

Mandy gave a tiny sniff and shook her head.

'You wanna talk about it?'

She shrugged.

Pete glanced in his mirror, then slowed and pulled in to the side of the road. 'C'mon. What's up?'

'I dunno. I . . .' Mandy sighed.

'Look,' Pete said, a kindness in his eyes. 'D'you fancy a quick cup of tea? I've gotta pop home and pick something up.'

'Nah . . . I ought to get back.'

But Pete was insistent. 'Don't be daft. You got the look of someone who shouldn't be left alone with a sharp instrument.'

Mandy gave him a little smile. 'It's not *that* bad.'

Pete grinned. 'So. A quick cuppa?'

'All right. But you laugh, I'll kill you.'

Pete didn't laugh. But then, he didn't really understand, either.

'I don't see it, Mand,' he said, getting up to put the kettle on again. 'You're as young as you think you are. I mean, blimey, you ain't even forty yet!'

'Yeah, well, that's easy for a man to say. When men get older and greyer they just become *distinguished* . . . you know, *experienced*. Women, on the other hand, become pathetic and tarty. I don't want to be seen as someone whose life's nearly over when inside I feel like I ain't even had a life yet. Not a life of my own, anyway.'

Pete glanced up at her, then quickly looked away, busying himself.

'Christ Almighty, Mand! Anyone'd think you was already drawing your pension! You got your job, ain't you? And from what I've heard you're not exactly begging for company!'

Mandy looked down, wondering what exactly Pete *had* heard. Yes, and how flattering or otherwise it had been. She was about to speak again, when the front door opened.

'Hi!'

Mandy looked up, shocked. She hadn't expected this; hadn't prepared herself. Her face creased into a fixed grin as Pete's girlfriend came into the room, a bag of shopping in each hand. Mandy noticed that she'd been to Marks and Spencer's.

The girl looked to Mandy, then to Pete, then back to Mandy. 'You must be Mandy.'

She was small and slim and pretty; yes, and every bit as young as Mandy had heard she was, and looking at her, Mandy felt a flash of resentment streak through her.

Putting down the shopping, she turned to Mandy. 'Wait for him to introduce us, I'll wait all day. I'm Emmy.'

'Hi . . .'

'I recognise you from the photos.'

'Oh,' Mandy said, nodding. 'He ain't cut 'em in half then?'

Emmy laughed but Mandy just felt embarrassed, and dowdy and . . .

'Pete's made you a cuppa, then. Good! Pour me one too, would you, baby? I'm gasping.'

Before Pete had a chance to avoid Mandy's eye, she silently mouthed the word *baby*, a smirk splitting her features.

Pete moved across to the kettle and as she walked past him, Emmy laid a hand proprietorially on his backside, stretching up to kiss the back of his neck. He remained staring at the wall cupboard and Mandy looked away, alarmed by the sudden stab of jealousy searing through her guts.

Reaching down for her shopping bags, Mandy was half out of her seat.

'I'd better be going.'

'Nah! Finish your tea!' Emmy said.

Obediently, Mandy dropped back into the chair and reached across for the mug of lukewarm liquid.

Emmy sat, smiling pleasantly across at her. 'Great news, eh? I mean, about Jason. I bet you're proud as punch.'

'Yeah,' Mandy said, bluffing it out. 'Yeah, I am.'

'She's worried,' Pete said, even as he poured the tea.

'Worried?' Emmy turned and glanced at Pete, then looked back at Mandy. 'What about?'

'About being called Granny,' Pete answered for her, bringing two fresh mugs of tea across.

'But I think it's great,' Emmy said, staring at Mandy as if she couldn't believe she had a problem with it. 'I mean, look at me! I'll be a sort of step-granny and I'm only twenty-nine.'

Mandy resisted the temptation to smack her in the mouth and nodded agreeably.

'That ain't it,' Pete said, sitting down on a chair between the two of them and looking from one to the other. 'She thinks everyone'll suddenly think she's an old bag.'

''Course they won't,' Emmy said consolingly.

That's easy to say, Mandy thought, when you can fit both cheeks of your arse on to one chair.

Mandy looked down. 'It ain't funny. It's like . . . well . . .' And she shrugged again. How could she describe it to these two. Or to anybody.

Emmy leaned across and put her manicured hand on Mandy's. 'You'll be OK once you get used to the idea.' She giggled. 'We'll have to take turns to baby-sit.'

'Yeah,' Mandy said. And somehow the thought of it made her feel like throwing up.

Janet closed the door behind her and hung up her jacket, then stopped, listening. She had heard something. Someone was in the flat.

Her mouth suddenly dry, she tiptoed through.

'Steve?'

Steve was bending down, taking something from one of the

drawers of the dresser. An open case was on the bed beside him. Hearing Janet, he froze, then slowly straightened up.

Janet stared at the half-filled case. 'What are you doing?'

Steve didn't turn. He glanced at Janet's image in the mirror, then averted his eyes. 'I'm going to stay with Paul for a bit. He's got a spare room, so . . .'

His voice trailed off. He stood there, defeated, abandoned.

Janet stared, mortified by the sight of him packing. She swallowed, then in the tiniest voice asked the question that was haunting her.

'Did you sleep with her?'

Steve sighed, then shook his head.

Janet took a long, shivering breath. 'Steve?'

'Yeah?'

'I don't want you to go.'

He hesitated, then turned, looking at her for the first time. Janet's eyes were moist, fearful.

Again he sighed. 'I love you so much.'

She nodded.

Slowly, he stepped across to her and, as if she were made of the finest porcelain, gently took her in his arms. And as he did so, Janet burst into tears.

'I never meant to hurt you, Jan.'

She didn't have to answer. The way she clung to him told him all he needed to know.

'It was just that I had no one to talk to. And it all got too much for me, and . . .' He caught his breath. 'I didn't mean to ruin everything.'

Janet wiped at her eyes one at a time, then raised her head, looking at him. 'I know.'

'And then last night, all I could think of was the baby, and—'

She put a finger to his lips, then gently kissed him on the brow and nose and mouth. 'Even when things were really bad. You know, both times when we failed. Even then, deep down, I knew we would be all right. And we are.' She took hold of his hand and placed it over her taut belly. 'It's gonna be all right.'

Karen put the stack of exercise books down on the coffee table, then walked out into the kitchen and, opening the fridge, took out the half-bottle of Chardonnay she had left there the evening before.

It had been one of those days — a day when she had not so much felt herself a teacher as a ringmaster, cracking her whip at cage after cage of wild and restless animals.

Part of it could be blamed on hormones and the ravages of puberty, but she could still recall her own schooldays, and while she and the girls hadn't been model pupils — far from it! — they most certainly hadn't been anything like *this* lot!

She sounded like a old fogey when she said it, but it was true — discipline was breaking down. Once upon a time, the teachers had beaten the pupils. Now it was the other way about, and heaven help the teacher who fought back!

Karen poured herself a large glass of the chilled wine, then walked back through, noticing the note for the first time. Setting her glass down on the mantelpiece, she took it and slit it open, reading it almost at a glance.

'Gone out. Don't wait up. Lucy.'

She tucked it behind the clock, then picked up her glass again, sighing to herself as she walked over to the sofa.

Karen sat, then took a long sip of her drink. She really ought to get her marking done and out of the way, but there was one other thing she had been putting off.

She had decided to write a letter. A letter to her father, explaining herself.

All day she had toyed with phrases in her head, trying to find the right words to make him understand — to make him see her clearly, yes, but also to ask him to love her in the same way she'd thought he'd loved her before all this.

And as she'd struggled to find the words, so she had seen just how complex it all was. Complex and yet simple. She had always been gay. Even when she hadn't known it, her instincts had always been the same. For a long time she had convinced herself that it was purely the *kind* of men she met, and that at some nebulous future date Mr Right would appear and all would be well. But that had been naïve. She recognised now that the crushes she had had — powerful, sometimes overwhelming crushes that she had tried to deny, even to herself — had always been on other girls. She had told herself that it was only a form of hero worship, and that she'd grow out of it. But she never had.

During their teens, while Susie and the others had had pictures of David Cassidy or Donny Osmond or Rod Stewart on their walls, she had had pictures of Suzie Quatro, *Marie* Osmond, and Debbie Harry on hers! She could laugh about it now, but it was evident even then, and she blushed to think of it.

But the deception — a case of self-deception as much as anything — had left its scars. It had led to the habit of concealment and self-denial and to the awful *pretence* of normality which — when she had finally cast it off — had caused so much damage.

It wasn't easy to say all this in a letter. To say it and not blame her father for his role in things; for if she was honest, it was a fear of him — of his scorn and ridicule — that had made her maintain the deception.

She didn't *want* to blame him. She wanted to be reconciled with him. To be understood and accepted by him for what she was.

But it took courage to be honest in the way she wanted to be honest, and at times she wondered if Chris had not been right to call her mouselike. She was, by nature, timid, and it was her timidity as much as anything that had led her to embrace all those deceptions about herself. And though the lies had been exposed, the timidity remained. She was still afraid. Afraid he would dismiss her letter as she laid herself bare before him.

And if he did?

It did not bear thinking about. She was his daughter; his child. It would be the ultimate rejection.

Even so, she would write her letter. Because to write it down would be to free herself finally of the fear and the pretence.

Karen reached out and, taking the notepad from the top of her bag, opened it to the first clean page.

Picking up a pen, she hesitated a moment, then began.

Dad,

I know all of this is hard for you to understand, but please try. I do love you. Always have done. And I need you to love me. It's important to me. So please, think back over my life and remember the child you raised and loved, read these words and try to understand what I'm saying. Because I need you to understand, more than I've ever needed anything in my life . . .

Karen paid off the cab driver, then turned to face her parents' house. As she did, someone hurried down the pathway of the house next door.

'Karen!'

'Daisy . . . ?'

Moving past her, Daisy yelled at the cab driver, who was just about to pull away. 'Hey! You! Hang on a minute!'

The cab moved two or three feet and stopped, the engine idling.

'I'm sorry, love,' Daisy said, taking Karen's arm and leaning in, so that her face was only inches from Karen's, 'but your dad's been taken ill again. They've rushed him to the hospital. I tried to phone you . . .'

Karen felt a moment's giddiness. Her stomach tightened. 'When did they go?'

'About ten minutes back.'

'Thanks, I . . .'

'Go on, love. Hurry now.'

Karen turned, then climbed back into the taxi.

'Which hospital is it, love?' the driver said, glancing back at her sympathetically.

'The Essex.'

'Hang on, then. I'll get you there in no time.'

It was too late. He had died in the ambulance of a massive coronary. Her mother sat in the room beside his bed, just staring at him, as if she couldn't believe what had happened; as if she were waiting for him to wake up. One of the nurses had wanted to give her something for the shock, but she had refused. She simply sat there, his cold hand held in her warm one, her thumb brushing the back of his knuckles as if to comfort him.

Karen, too, felt numb. She stood there, her right hand tucked into her pocket, closed over the letter she had meant to give him. It was a time for sorrow, yet at the same time she felt cheated. Robbed of the chance to make things good between them.

'Why couldn't you wait?' she asked him, whispering the words through the glass of the tiny window in the door to his room. 'Why couldn't you bloody wait?'

And when her brother came, he too seemed stunned. Karen

watched him come down the corridor towards her and knew that someone had already told him. She could see it in his face. She braced herself, but he said nothing. He merely shook his head, then, like a child, gave a great sob of anguish.

Karen reached out, holding him to her, feeling his whole body heave as he sobbed, her own grief not yet ripe. She was still angry with her father. Angry that he hadn't let her explain. He'd never let her explain. And now, it seemed, he'd had the final word by dying.

'There,' she said, patting Jack's shoulder. 'There now, let it all come out.'

But it wouldn't now. It never would.

The thin November light shone through a narrow gap in the curtains, picking out a glass-framed picture on the far wall of the bedroom. Standing in the shadows beside the big double bed, Anna looked down at the sleeping face of her mother, astonished by how changed it was. She looked so frail now, her features pinched and sunken, her skin touched with the pallor of approaching death. In the three weeks since Anna had last come here, she seemed to have aged tremendously as the cancers within ate away at her.

Anna looked up, her eyes going to the picture on the wall. The sunlight winked off the glass, obscuring the old print, but Anna did not need to see it. She knew the photograph from childhood. In it, her father stood beside her mother on the steps of the local church, wearing a morning suit he'd hired the day before, while her mother wore a veil and flowing dress of white, which had been her mother's before her.

Forty-two years had passed since that day. It was, quite literally, a lifetime ago.

Anna turned and quietly left the room, going down the stairs to where her aunt was waiting in the kitchen, a fresh pot of tea resting on a large coaster in the centre of the well-scrubbed pine table.

Her Aunt Charlotte was the youngest of her grandmother's seven children, and when her own mother died, she would be the last. It was a chilling thought.

'I hadn't realised . . .' she began, then saw how the words condemned her. She had been too busy for her own mother. Too busy to come and see her, even though she was dying. What kind of a daughter did that make her? But Charlotte said nothing, merely poured the tea and handed a cup across to her.

'What did the doctor say?'

Charlotte met her eyes. 'It won't be long now.'

It was hard to meet that gaze for very long. It was like a mirror in which Anna saw all her faults: her selfishness especially.

But what did they expect, her mother's generation? They had made their children this way. They had encouraged them to be individuals, to *find* themselves and be free, but they hadn't said anything about the other side of things – the responsibility that went along with all those freedoms.

Well, now it was all catching up with her. She had discovered that her freedom had a price, and that price was loneliness.

Anna sipped at her tea, the minutes passing with a heavy slowness, the silence in the room accusing her. Then, sighing, she glanced at her aunt again.

'I ought to be going. But I'll come tomorrow . . . I'll try and come most evenings.'

Charlotte watched her without comment. Feeling bad, Anna pushed her empty cup away and stood. 'I'll see her before I go.'

Anna went upstairs, expecting to find her mother still asleep, but as she stepped into the room, she saw that she was awake, her eyes staring birdlike across the room at her.

'Mum?'

Her voice was thin, like the faded pattern on old wallpaper. 'Anna? Is that you?'

As she walked across, she realised that her mother could barely see her — that she had reacted to the sound of her footsteps as she came into the room.

She sat, reaching out to hold the frail hand that lay above the blanket, afraid to squeeze it lest she snap the fragile bones she could feel beneath that fine veil of translucent flesh.

'I've been sitting with you,' she said.

'Ahh . . .' And there was a wintry smile. But it didn't last long. It dissolved in a flicker of pain.

Anna looked down, unable to bear the look that had come into her mother's face: a look of startlement, as if she did not understand what was happening to her. Yet when she looked again, that wintry smile was back, as her mother gazed up at her lovingly.

'Are you happy, Anna?' She opened her mouth, but no answer came. 'Are you?'

Anna swallowed, choked suddenly, the waste of her life laid bare before her. What had she done with it? What had *she* created? Nothing but fictions and mounds of rotting paper. Distractions — she had spent her whole life manufacturing distractions.

She looked away, the feel of her mother's hand in her own suddenly so precious that she lifted it to her lips and kissed it.

Yet when she looked again, her mother's eyes were closed, and though her chest gently rose and fell, it was hard to know from her appearance whether she was alive or dead.

'I love you,' she said softly, as if she were speaking to a sleeping child.

Releasing her mother's hand, she gently placed it against that narrow chest, as if she were placing a single flower there. And then she stood, wiping away the tear that had trickled down her cheek.

'Tomorrow,' she said. 'I promise I'll come tomorrow.'

On the following Tuesday evening, Karen waited in the tiny anteroom at the undertakers, her mother and her brother seated across from her, while they prepared her father's coffin.

Tomorrow was the day of the funeral and there would be little time for them to say goodbye. This, then, would be her leavetaking, before they sealed the coffin.

Her mother's face was ashen. This was a torment for her, and she sat there rigidly upright, her hand, where it lay in her son's, limp and lifeless, as if she could somehow die and follow her husband.

As for her brother, Jack, he was silent still, yet broodingly so, and from time to time he would glance at Karen, a strange coldness in his eyes.

Silently, the most senior of the undertakers – a big man with curiously long pale hands – stepped into the room and gave a little bow towards Karen's mother.

'Mrs Turner . . . we're ready for you now.'

Jack helped her to her feet, supporting her lest she give way altogether. Karen followed them through, into a room very much like the one in which they'd waited, only this was decorated with flowers and candles and had a single fake stained-glass window at one end.

There, in the very centre of the narrow room, jutting up out of the plush wine red carpet, was a marble platform on which lay her father's open coffin.

She stepped up to it, standing beside her brother.

Her father lay there, his arms crossed above his chest, like one of those stone carvings one found on ancient tombs. There was colour now in his cheeks and he seemed at peace, yet when she looked at his hands she saw how shockingly pale they were and waxen — as if this were only an imitation of her father and the real man were somewhere else, still alive and vigorous and laughing at this deception.

It was an absurd thought, yet the truth was that, lying there like that, he did not seem real. Whatever a person was, it was not this — not this thing of brittle bone and stone-cold flesh. This was but a puppet, and the moment the animating spirit left it . . . well, it was nothing.

Her mother sniffed, breaking the silence in the room. Then, with a curious awkwardness, Jack stepped forward and tenderly placed a single yellow rose between his father's hands.

Karen felt her throat constrict. Suddenly she too was close to tears. The rose was from her father's garden. One of his roses that he'd cared so much about. How strange that was, that men, when they grew older, seemed to care more for the flowers they tended than for the women who had tended them.

But this was no moment for blame. As Jack stepped back, so she moved forward and, conscious that both her brother and her mother were watching her, placed the letter there beneath the rose, feeling, as she did, how cool her father's hand was, how strange.

He would not read it now. His eyes were blind, his understanding dark. He could not love her now. Could not say sorry. Even so . . .

She stepped back, wiping away the tears that now dripped one after another down her cheek, and as she turned, she saw the surprise in Jack's eyes at those tears. But her mother just stared. She stared and stared, as if some great mistake had been made, and at any moment Karen thought she might raise her arm and point and say, '*Wait! This isn't him!*'

Outside the cold air hit her, making her pull up her collar against the biting wind. Tomorrow seemed a thousand years away but yet she dreaded its coming.

An hour later Karen met Anna in a wine bar just off Upper Street.

The two embraced, Anna holding her a fraction longer than usual and peering into her face.

'Are you OK?' Karen smiled weakly, then shook her head. 'D'you want to talk about it?'

Karen gave a pained laugh. 'What's there to say?' Then, relenting: 'Oh, God, Anna, it's such a mess.'

They sat. Anna stared at her friend a moment, then reached across and took her hands, squeezing them gently. 'It will help to talk, you know.'

'I . . .' Karen stopped as the waiter came across.

'A bottle of house white,' Anna said, barely glancing at him. 'Go on . . .'

Karen smiled apologetically at the young man, then, turning back to Anna, she shrugged. 'Oh, I don't know . . .'

'What?'

Karen's chest rose and fell. 'It's everything!'

'Things not too good at home, then?'

'Well . . .' Karen made a face. 'Lucy didn't come home till Sunday afternoon, and when she did she might as well not have been there.'

Anna looked shocked. 'You didn't tell her?'

'Eventually . . . and then she was all sympathy. But . . . well, it's just so hard. She wants the relationship to be more open and I can't cope with that.'

'Open?'

Karen looked away, real pain in her face. 'Yeah, and we all know what that means, don't we? The freedom to fuck whoever she wants.'

'Maybe she just means she needs a bit of space.'

Karen gave a hollow laugh. 'I don't think so.'

Anna sighed. 'But I'd have thought . . .'

'What?' Karen looked back at her, her eyes clear, no illusions in them. 'That gays were different? Don't you believe it! In fact, if anything it's worse.'

'What d'you mean?'

Karen hesitated, then: 'More promiscuous, I suppose.' She swallowed, then shook her head. 'All I want . . . all I've *ever* wanted is someone I can share things with. Someone who'd be there for me . . . who'd understand me.'

'That's all any of us want.'

'Is it?'

'Deep down.'

'Nah! I think I've dug as deep as it goes. People are pretty shallow when it comes down to it, pretty . . . *selfish*.'

Anna looked away, a faint flush at her neck, then nodded. 'I went to see my mum.'

'Yes? How is she?'

'Dying . . .'

'Oh, Anna, why didn't you say?'

'Because you had enough on your plate. But you're right about people being selfish. Seeing her got me thinking, you see. About myself.'

'But *you're* not selfish, Anna!'

'No?' Anna laughed bitterly. 'I'm your classic nineties girl. I want to have it all: the career, the lifestyle, the . . . Well, all of it. *But* . . .'

Karen was watching her closely now. 'But what?'

Anna looked down, then shrugged. 'We've had this conversation before, remember?'

'You want a baby . . .' Anna nodded. 'So *have* one.'

'Yes, well, just one little problem you seem to have overlooked.'

It was Karen's turn to laugh. Anna looked up at her, surprised. 'And I thought *I* was the naïve one.'

'What do you mean?'

'I mean, Anna, that if you hang about waiting for Mr Right then you're likely to miss the boat. You know what? I reckon nearly half the kids in my form are from single-parent homes. At least you have a great job and your own place and . . . The only thing you need a man for is the actual . . . you know . . . ?'

'But . . .' Anna's lips slowly parted as she understood precisely what Karen was saying. 'I couldn't! I couldn't just have one on my own . . .'

'You wouldn't be on your own. We'd all support you. Listen! In an ideal world you'd be living with Prince Charming and discussing whether to have a netball team or a soccer squad. But the reality is there's no eligible man on the scene, you're as broody as hell and knocking forty.'

'Yes, well, thank you for clarifying things for me, Karen!'

'Sorry.' Karen reached across and squeezed Anna's hand.

'But how would I look after it?'

'You can afford child care, can't you?'

'Yes, but—'

'And your company *has* to give you maternity leave.'

'Six months, yes, but—'

'Well then. I tell you, I see enough at school to know that kids aren't always better off having a father . . .'

As soon as the words passed her lips Karen wanted to bite them back. She looked down, pained.

This time Anna squeezed her hand. 'I know. I know . . . Look, would you like me to come early tomorrow? Provide a bit of moral support?'

Karen looked up at her gratefully. 'Would you?'

Anna smiled. 'Changing the subject, wasn't it good news about Janet?'

*　　*　　*

Anna got home to find Frank parked outside her flat.

She went across as he stepped from the car.

'What do you want, Frank?'

He blew out a long breath. 'She's thrown me out, Anna.'

'So what are you doing here?'

But she could see why he was there. Frank was in a bad way. She'd never seen him cry before, but it looked as if that was going to change at any moment. 'Anna, I . . .'

'Oh, God . . . Look, come in. I'll make you a coffee.'

He made to follow her, grateful as a stray, but she shook her head.

'What?' He looked bewildered, as if she was toying with him. But Anna merely pointed past him.

'For God's sake, lock your car up first.'

She carried the two mugs through and set them down on the coffee table, then took a seat facing him.

'So what happened? She catch you giving *dictation* to your secretary?'

He looked up at that, his eyes flaring briefly. Then, a hangdog expression reaffirming itself on his features, he shook his head. 'Someone must have told her.'

'Told her what?'

'About us.'

Anna sat back, taking that in. '*Us?*'

'Yeah . . .'

'But we were over months ago.'

'Yeah . . .'

He didn't look at her, but she knew what he was thinking.

'So what did she say?'

'What *didn't* she say? She called me everything under the sun!' He sighed heavily. 'Anyway, the upshot is she's filing for divorce. Says she's going to take me to the cleaners.'

'The Sketchley treatment . . .'

'What?' But he clearly didn't see the joke. 'I'd like to know which bastard told her.'

'Well, it wasn't me.'

Frank met her eyes. 'I didn't mean . . .'

'No . . .' Then, more gently: 'No, I know.'

'So,' he said. 'Here I am.'

Yes, she thought. Here you are.

But he was hurting. She could see how much he was hurting, and she could not throw him back out on to the street.

'You can stay,' she said finally.

'Thanks.' He looked at her, his eyes searching hers for something. 'Anna, I . . . I've missed you.' She looked down, then picked up her coffee. 'I sent you flowers.'

Yes, and she had trashed them. But she didn't say that. There was nothing to say. He had ended it. And now he wanted to start over, as if nothing had happened.

'Anna, I . . .'

She met his eyes wearily. 'Leave it, Frank. You can stay tonight. But tomorrow you find yourself a hotel.'

Karen paused outside her mother's room, the murmur of voices from below drifting up to her as she placed her hand on the long brass handle.

'Mum?'

She poked her head round the door and looked inside. Her mother was lying down on the bed in a foetal position, her hands up to her face, and though Karen could not see properly, she knew she had been crying again.

Karen went across and sat beside her, reaching out to draw a strand of hair from across her face. 'Mum . . . you really ought to come down now. It's almost time.'

It was true. The funeral cortège would be here in fifteen minutes.

Her mother sighed heavily. 'How am I gonna manage? I

mean, I can't even change a plug. And your dad always cut the grass.'

'You'll be OK, Mum. Jack'll help out. And I'll pop in now and then. You'll be all right.'

But she was clearly unconvinced. She groaned, then, lifting herself up on one elbow, began to drag herself upright. Karen helped her.

'There,' she said, when her mother was sitting up. 'Let me give you a hand.'

Her mascara was streaked and her eyes puffy, but what did it matter? What did anything matter on a day like this?

Karen looked about her. As the hours passed her sense of unreality grew. She simply could not believe that she was burying her father today. In her mind he was still there in the house, his presence so strong that she expected to turn and see him there in one corner or another, a pint in his hand, laughing at some joke of Uncle Peter's. But Peter would not be telling jokes today.

She helped her mother up, then turned, facing the doorway.

Jack stood there, looking in, his expression sour.

'Get my coat for me, Karen,' her mother said, sensing the tension between them. 'It's in the wardrobe. The long black one.'

'Right . . .' Karen went across and opened the heavy wardrobe door, searching among the endless jackets and coats – her mother's familiar smell filling her nostrils – until she found the one she thought her mother meant.

She turned back.

'I don't know how you had the nerve,' Jack said.

'Jack . . .'

'No, Mum. It has to be said. The reason Dad's in his coffin is because of *her*. You know it and I know it. It killed him to think that his daughter was a fucking freak!'

'A *what*!' Karen took a step towards him, but he pushed her back.

'There was always something *strange* about you. I knew it, even when we were kids, but I never guessed . . .' His features formed into an expression of disgust. 'You just couldn't keep it to yourself, could you, eh? You just had to tell him!'

Then, with an anger she had barely guessed at until that moment, he pushed her hard, thrusting her back into the wardrobe so that she stumbled and fell among the shoes and bags that crowded the floor of it, thick layers of mothballed cloth whipping against her face and neck. She cried out, then tried to get up, but Jack was there, closing the great oak door on her, as if somehow he could shut her away for good.

And above all was her mother's voice, loud now and shrill. 'Jack! Jack! Stop it now!'

There were heavy footsteps on the stairs, and then her Uncle Peter was in the room, pushing past Jack to help her up.

He helped brush her off, then turned to Jack, his rugged face red with anger. 'What's the bloody matter with you? This is your father's funeral, boy! Show some soddin' respect!'

'Don't tell me!' Jack said, glaring at her; like the boy he'd been, always shifting blame. 'She killed him! The little whore!'

Peter's eyes flared. 'That's *enough*! You open your mouth again, Jack, and I'll close it for you!'

'But . . .'

One look from Peter was enough. He was like her father in that; he came from a generation who didn't threaten idly.

Jack scowled, then turned away, almost pulling the door off its hinges as he left. It banged against the wall.

Karen stared after him, her heart beating so hard it felt like it would burst from her chest, the trembling in her so intense that she knew she could not stay there a moment longer. And then, from below, she heard familiar voices. Susie! Yes, and Mandy, too! And, distraught, close now to tears, she hurried from the room, making her way down to them, leaving her mother and her uncle staring after her.

The service in the little chapel was strange, the priest's words so unconnected to the man she'd known, that Karen had been forced to look about her to remind herself that this really was her father's funeral. But that seemed to happen when you died. People lied about you. Nice lies, but lies all the same. Even so, her grief was real, and her sense of loss, and later, when she stood there among her friends, watching as the coffin was slowly lowered into that awful hole, she almost fainted at the thought of its finality.

Jack would not look at her afterwards, and her mother gave her but the briefest glance, as if ashamed of what had happened in her room. But no further mention was made of it; nor did Karen speak of it to any of the girls. It was her secret, a family thing, and she would live with it. But even to think of it brought her to the edge.

'Come on,' Mandy said, touching her arm as the little crowd of friends and relatives began to disperse from the graveside and head back to their cars. 'Let's get back, eh?'

Karen turned and smiled, glad that they were all there, then began to walk back towards the gate, Mandy and Susie to her left, Janet and Anna to her right.

Mandy downed her eighth prawn vol-au-vent, then leaned across to nudge Susie, who was sitting, nursing a half-full glass of wine. There was no one else in the room just then, everyone else having either gone or drifted out into the kitchen.

'You all right, Suse?'

Susie looked up at her distractedly. 'Yeah . . . why?'

'Just that you're a bit quiet, that's all. The baby OK?'

'Yeah . . . yeah, he's great.'

'And Jo?'

'Jo's fine.'

Mandy shrugged and reached out to take a handful of peanuts from one of the nearby bowls. 'Then what is it?'

Susie stared into her glass a moment, then took a large swig of it. 'The bastard made a pass at me.'

Mandy blinked. 'What? I mean . . . *who*?'

'Gus. He came up behind me in the kitchen and put his arms around me.'

Mandy almost spat out her peanuts. 'No! Not Ever-So-Faithful Gus.'

Susie made a face. 'Bloody creep. Had his hands all over me tits, didn't he? And he wouldn't take no for an answer. I had to fight him off!'

'Christ, Suse! That's one for the book!'

'What d'you mean?'

'You, putting up a fight!' Mandy put up a hand. 'Not that I don't think you were right. I mean, there's Jo to think of, ain't there?'

'Right!' Susie glowered with indignation. 'I mean . . . What the bloody hell does he think I am? Some cheap little tart?'

Mandy positively smirked. She reached for her glass and swilled down the peanuts. 'So what did he say?'

Susie looked down, embarrassed. 'Oh, don't!'

'Did he say he loved you?'

Susie jerked her head up. 'Did he, fuck! No . . . he kept going on about how he kept 'aving these dreams about me. Really filthy dreams. I mean, what kind of perv is that?'

'I think it's called a bloke, Suse. Or have you forgotten?'

'Nah, but . . . well, he can see I'm happily married. And then there's Nathan, ain't there?'

'Nathan was in the room, then?'

'No . . . no, Nathan was asleep, as it happened, and his little girl, too.'

'So you two were alone, in your house, with the kids asleep.'

'Yeah. They usually go down for a nap when he comes round. But . . .'

'Well, hats off to the fella, Suse. I mean, it's a wonder he didn't jump you months ago!'

'What d'you mean?'

'Well, just that beneath all that *Guardian* new-man bollocks, he's just like any other bloke!'

Susie raised her glass and drained it, a look of disappointment still clouding her features. 'Anyway . . . I showed him the door, didn't I? Not before I'd given him a piece of my mind, though.'

Mandy was grinning again. 'What d'you say?'

'I told him that if he ever touched me again, I'd shove his Vivaldi CD up his arse, case an' all!'

Mandy grimaced. But she couldn't help a degree of astonishment. In the old days Susie would have eaten Gus alive. Having Nathan had certainly changed her.

'So you're not seeing him again, I take it?' Mandy said, teasingly.

'Too bleedin' right I'm not!'

'Still,' Mandy went on, 'it does prove something.'

'Yeah?'

'Yeah. That all men *are* bastards, after all!'

Susie almost — almost — grinned at that. But at that moment Anna poked her head round the door. 'I'm off. Anyone want a lift?'

'Nah . . .' Mandy and Susie said as one, then laughed.

'Right, well . . . see you Friday, at the launch.'

'See you then!'

''Bye, babe . . .'

When Anna had gone, Mandy and Susie looked to each other, then giggled.

'You know what?' Susie said. 'When he put his hands on me tits, it gave me the shock of my life!'

'Weren't you even a little bit tempted?'

'I was too worried about my milk leaking, I s'pose.' Susie's face broke into a broad smile. 'Mind you, I have thought about it a few times since . . .'

'I bet you have!' Mandy said, reaching out to take her ninth prawn vol-au-vent. 'From what I saw of him, I thought he was bloody gorgeous and he could massage my mammaries any day of the week!'

'You old tart!'

'Yeah . . . I s'pose I am!'

The atmosphere in the kitchen was distinctly frosty. Uncle Peter was talking — telling some story about when he and Karen's dad were boys — but beneath the warm murmur of his voice, there was a definite tension.

Jack sat beside his mother on a low stool, a can of lager in his hands, the base of it resting on his knee. His head was down, but he was glowering. Beside him, Karen's mum sat rigidly upright, barely listening as Peter came to the conclusion of his tale. Her eyes seemed distant and confused.

Karen sat across from her, the kitchen table — which had been pushed against the wall — to her right, Janet beside her now in the seat that Anna had vacated. Janet's hand held hers, its warmth undeniable, yet sitting there, Karen had a vivid sense of the unreality of that moment. It felt like she was embedded in solid glass, or that Time itself had somehow ground to a halt. As she stared at the familiar figures of her mother and brother and uncle, she could not help but think how little she *knew* any of them, these people she had known all her life. They were strangers to her. Total strangers. As she was to them.

How could you know people and not know them? But that was how it was. With friends as with family. And lovers? Lovers were worst of all. You thought you knew them, and then suddenly you were dealing with an absolute stranger. Someone whose love had turned to hate, or . . .

She gave a little shudder, and Janet, feeling it, gave her hand a gentle squeeze.

'D'you want another drink?' she asked, speaking to Karen's ear.

She shook her head. Her uncle had finished his story now and was sitting back, a wistful expression in his eyes. Of all her relatives, he was probably the one she liked the most.

'How's the teaching going, Karen?' he asked, looking at her.

'All right,' she said. Then, because she didn't want to give him nothing, she added, 'I was thinking of changing jobs, actually. Going into primary education.'

'Really?' Janet said.

'Hmm . . .' She glanced at Janet, but then looked back at Peter, speaking to him. 'It's very trying, having to deal with teenagers all the time. It wears you down.'

Jack made a disapproving noise, but Peter glared at him.

'I'm sure it does,' Peter said, turning back to her and giving her a warm, sympathetic look. 'I wouldn't want that job for all the tea in China! Not these days, anyway. There's no bloody discipline!'

'No,' Karen agreed, and smiled faintly for the first time that day. 'I thought I might apply for an assistant head's job. It'll mean retraining, but . . .'

'I'd go for it,' Peter said encouragingly. 'That is, if it's what you want.'

Karen shrugged. 'I think so. I think . . .'

She stopped dead. Jack was staring at her now with an expression of such contempt, such bitterness, that the sight of it took her breath. Calming herself, she stood.

'Look, I'd better go. I . . .'

She stepped across and, allowing him to embrace her, kissed her uncle on the cheek.

'It was lovely seeing you, Karen. Florrie's not well enough to travel, but, well, come and see us sometime. You don't have to be a stranger, you know. You've got our number.'

She smiled. 'I'll try.'

Then, turning to her mother, she stooped down and gave her a brief hug. 'Daisy and Rose are going to clear everything away. I'll see you in the week, Mum.'

Her mother made a hollow, humming sound. Karen kissed her forehead, then began to turn away, Janet getting up from her chair to accompany her.

'Don't *I* get a kiss?'

Karen turned and glared at her brother. He was looking up at her mockingly, so like one of her schoolboys — like the awful Barrett and his ilk — that she felt sickened by it.

'Leave it, Jack,' she said wearily. 'I think you've said enough.'

Susie was pushing Nathan through the park the next day, her mind on all the gossip she had heard at the funeral the day before, when a figure stopped in front of her.

She looked up, squinting against the early-morning sun, then looked away, blushing furiously.

'Susie, I . . .'

'I don't know how you've got the nerve . . .'

'Look, I'm sorry. I don't know what came over me.'

'I think it was bloody obvious what came over you!'

Gus put his hands up in the universal gesture of defence. 'Please. Just listen a minute. I know I screwed up, and it would serve me right if you went and told my wife, but . . . Oh, I don't know. Look! I really respect you, Susie. It's just that, at that moment, looking at you there at the sink, I just . . . *wanted* you.'

Susie glanced at him fleetingly. He had balls, anyway. Most blokes wouldn't come near after they'd been shown the door. And she liked the idea that he respected her.

She sniffed, then. 'If I told Jo, you know what he'd do, don't you?'

'Beat three shades of shit out of me, I know . . .'

'Yeah, well . . . You're lucky I haven't told him. He's got a right temper on him!'

Gus blew out a breath, and pushed his fingers through his hair. 'Look, I really am sorry, Suse. I wish I could put the clock back, I really do. I loved coming round. I . . .'

Susie was glad he didn't say any more. Glad because she'd had the strangest dreams about him last night. Dreams in which she hadn't fought him off.

She looked down, flustered suddenly. 'I'd better go. Things to do . . . you know.'

But the truth was she was flattered by his attention; by the fact that he had made a pass at her. And the fact that he'd been concerned enough to apologise. But it wasn't like the old days. Life was more complicated now.

Susie walked on, pushing the pram hurriedly now, not daring to look back lest it give away how much she had been thrown by what had happened between them.

Jo stood at the window, staring out across the park, his besuited client totally forgotten. He hadn't been sure at first, but that was Nathan's pram, and that *was* Susie. But who the bloke was he didn't know. Only the way they'd talked, the intensity of the way they'd stood there, talking but not looking at each other, was . . . well, it was strange, like they'd had an argument. Only they hadn't had an argument. He'd seen the whole of their exchange and there had been only that strange awkwardness.

Jo frowned, then turned. 'Pardon?'

'I said I'll take it. It's perfect. Tell your vendor that he's got his asking price.'

'Right . . . right, I . . .'

Jo looked back. Susie was hurrying away now, pushing the pram like it was about to explode at any moment.

He turned, giving his client a tight smile. 'OK, we'll . . . er, we'll go back to the office and I'll, er . . . I'll ring my client.'

But his mind was not on the deal. He was looking at the guy standing in the park, pram at his side, staring after *his* wife, and, for the first time since he'd been married, thinking that maybe — just maybe — Susie had been unfaithful to him.

They had taken over the restaurant for the evening, putting up streamers and balloons with *DMZ* emblazoned in bright red lettering. It was a big, two-level venue, and they had cleared away the tables on the lower floor. The caterers had set up the buffet at the far end of the upper level: laying out eight huge tables of food, with everything from vegetarian cuisine to delicious Italian seafood.

On the lower level, a bar ran the length of the back wall, while a couple of roadies busied themselves on the raised platform beside the big double doors, setting up the drums and stands for the band that would play live later on.

All in all, it would knock a huge hole in their promotions budget. Still, launching something like *DMZ* didn't happen every day, and there was a real buzz of excitement as the first few guests began to arrive.

Anna looked about her, slightly nervous now that every-thing was done and there was nothing else to distract her.

Aside from her own staff and their partners, they had invited numerous celebrities, TV soap stars, footballers and the like, and it would be interesting to see who turned up. Photographers from several of the Sunday supplements were already there, hopeful to get their snaps for the 'people' columns, and Anna greeted them warmly, making sure they were looked after by the waiters.

Rose and Jacqui came across to stand with her, clutching their champagne glasses. Jacqui was wearing tight-fitting jeans and a casual black silk shirt beneath a leather flying jacket, whereas Rose had gone for the glam look, with a slinky black minidress and fuck-me shoes. But this was Anna's night and there was no danger of her not being noticed. The fashion department had called in more than a dozen dresses from several top designers and had paraded them through Anna's office before, finally, she had settled on an exclusive little number in bright red from Alexander McQueen.

She had had her hair done specially for the evening and had spent an hour earlier having a makeover from one of the make-up artists she regularly used on shoots.

'Remember,' Anna said, keeping her voice low. 'No bitchiness about our rivals, and no crowing. We're the best but we're modest about it.'

'I'll drink to that!' Rose said enthusiastically, and they clinked glasses.

'I wonder if that bitch Barbara Stannard will turn up,' Jacqui said, speaking out of the side of her mouth.

Anna smiled. 'Oh, I do hope so. I love the sight of envy on a woman's face.'

Rose tutted. 'Now, now, boss. No crowing.' Then, noting the arrival of another car outside the door, she said, 'I hear we're going to meet some old schoolfriends of yours, Anna.'

Anna turned to her. 'God, I hope they behave.'

'How d'you mean?'

'Well, all this free booze and the prospect of meeting up with a few stars.'

'Well, why did you invite them?' Jacqui asked.

Anna shrugged. 'I got a bit carried away, I s'pose. I thought it'd be a laugh. But I'm not so sure now.'

'Relax,' Rose said. 'If they're a bunch of drunken extroverts they'll blend in, no problem!'

'Well . . .' Anna rolled her eyes; then, seeing who was coming through the doors, she started towards them, putting out a hand in farewell to Rose and Jacqui as she went.

'Francesca, Ruth . . . how lovely to see you both again . . .'

Mandy put her plate down on the table next to Susie's, then squeezed into the seat beside her. It was after nine and the lower floor of the restaurant was crowded. Music sounded just beneath the hubbub of talk — a mixture of soul from the sixties and more modern stuff.

'Well, what d'you reckon?' Mandy said, raising her voice a fraction to compete with the noise. 'Brill, eh?'

Susie looked out across the scene, slowly nodding to herself. 'She's done all right, our Anna. You seen who's down there?'

Mandy laughed. 'You're not kidding! There's bloody every-one! Old whatsisname is there . . . you know . . . that Phil Daniels bloke. And Bianca from *EastEnders*. And there's that Damien guy from Blur. I tell you what though, I really fancy that Les Ferdinand. Big Les. I like the sound of that.'

Susie looked back at her. 'Saucy mare. And its Da*mon* from Blur.'

'Damon, Damien, who cares. He could possess me any time!' And with that Mandy began to tuck into her food with gusto.

Susie shook her head. 'Christ! I can remember a time when

you'd 'ave to have dirty jokes explained to you. Now, you're the bleedin' Mata Hari of North London!'

Mandy grinned and, with a half-full mouth, said. 'Talking of which, how's Gus?' Susie glanced at her, her expression reprimanding. 'What did I say?'

Susie shrugged. 'It's just that he came up to me the other day when I was walking Nathan in the park.'

Mandy leaned in close, interested. 'And?'

'Well . . . he apologised, like. Said he didn't know what had come over him.' Mandy snorted. 'No, Mand, I think he really was sorry.' She sighed, then. 'Trouble is, I *do* like him. And ever since he made the pass . . . well, I can't stop thinking about him.'

Mandy picked up her glass. 'It's not worth it, Suse.' She took a long sip of her drink, then, wiping her mouth, leaned close again. 'Look! If you can get back to where you were . . . you know, cosy chats about breast versus bottle, disposables or terries, then hunky dory. But anything more, forget it. You don't want to mess things up between you and Jo, do you? Not if all you're talking about is a quick fumble with an Earth Father!'

'Yeah . . . yeah, I guess you're right.'

Just then Karen arrived. She squeezed in the other side of Susie and put her plate down.

'Smashin' do, ain't it?' Mandy said.

'It's wonderful,' Karen answered. Then, 'Either of you seen Janet?'

Susie pointed across towards the far side, near the loos. 'She was over there last I saw, bending the ear of the magazine doctor.'

'Poor sod,' Mandy said. Then, in a kinder tone: 'You all right, Kar?'

Karen smiled. 'Bit wobbly, but . . . Yeah.'

'Good,' Susie said, elongating the word, her fixed smile

mirroring Mandy's. Both of them stared at Karen a moment longer, then, almost simultaneously, they looked back at their plates, tucking in once again.

For a while the three of them ate in silence. Then Anna's voice broke through the music just behind them.

'Hey, you lot! How's it going?'

Mandy pointed to her plate. 'Just getting me money's worth.'

Anna smiled as if to say 'Ha,ha,' then, leaning over Susie, she confided, 'You'll never guess who's here.'

'Pavarotti?' Mandy asked.

'Madonna?' Susie teased.

Karen just shrugged. She didn't recognise half of the so-called stars anyway.

'Bertolucci,' Anna said, looking about her as if they should be impressed.

'*Who?*' Mandy and Susie said as one.

'Bertolucci. He's a film director,' Karen explained. 'He made *The Last Emperor*.'

They shook their heads, still none the wiser.

'*Last Tango In Paris?*' Anna offered.

Enlightenment — and appreciation — dawned in their faces.

'Ooh! Which one is he?' Mandy asked enthusiastically, wiping her mouth with a napkin.

Susie smiled wistfully. 'I think *I* could have been an actress.'

Mandy pushed out her considerable breasts. 'Yeah, and I could've been a body double for Kate Moss!'

Susie nudged her hard.

But Karen was looking up fondly at Anna. 'It must be wonderful, having all these people turn up. I think it's going to be a great success, Anna.'

'God, I hope so. But it *is* encouraging.' She smiled, then looked from one to the other of them. 'Anyway, eat up, everybody! The band's going to start up in a minute, so I want you all on the dance floor for a bop!'

'Don't worry,' Mandy said. 'We'll get 'em going. Mind you,' she said puffing out her cheeks, 'I feel like a stuffed pig. This lot must've cost a small fortune!'

Anna shrugged. 'It's all PR.'

'Well, whatever it is, I love it!'

'She loves anything she can shove in her gob!' Susie said mischievously.

Mandy went to open her mouth, but the other three shook their heads in unison.

'Anna,' Susie said, putting her hand on her friend's arm. 'You might want to rescue your doctor, only Janet's had him pinned to the wall for the last hour. You know what she's like.'

'Right . . . sure. But remember, you lot, when the band gets going I want you on your feet!'

And with that she was off.

The three women smiled at each other.

'It's lovely, ain't it?' Mandy said. 'I mean . . . she's really done well, ain't she?'

'Yeah,' the other two said and, smiling fondly, turned to watch Anna go down the stairs and begin to cross the crowded floor.

As Anna came closer, she saw that Janet had indeed monopolised her medical expert. Mike was a good socialiser, usually, but right now his eyes looked glazed and he held his empty glass to him forlornly as if he would never ever get a drink again.

Not stopping to find out where they were in their conversation, Anna charged straight in.

'Mike! Listen! Sorry, darling, but do you mind if I drag her away?' And, without waiting for an answer, Anna turned

Janet about. 'Come with me! There's someone I want you to meet.'

'But I was—'

Anna took Janet's arm firmly and marched her off, glimpsing, as she went, the look of pure relief and gratitude on Mike's face as he made a dash for the bar.

'How you feeling?' Anna said into her ear, as they made their way across. 'I think you're looking fatter already.'

'D'you think so?' Janet said gleefully as Anna dragged her on. They stopped before a small group of people. 'Piers, this is my friend, Janet. Janet, this is Piers Crowley. He likes to think of himself as my boss.'

'Ah . . . nice to meet you,' Janet said awkwardly.

'Nice to meet you, Janet,' Piers said, looking to Anna for enlightenment.

'Janet's just found out she's pregnant,' Anna explained. 'But she and her partner had a couple of goes at IVF.'

'Ah . . .' And Piers's face lit up. 'We had both our girls by IVF.'

'Oh . . .' Janet's face broke into a big smile. 'How lovely? How old are they?'

'Five and three. Is this your first?'

Anna left them to it. She turned, making her way back to the bar, stopping to have a word here and there. But halfway across she stopped dead, realising suddenly just who it was standing there at the bar, his profile to her.

Michael . . .

She made to turn away, embarrassed by the memory of that last scene between them in the car showroom. Yet the press of bodies about her was such that she seemed to be carried towards him almost, and as she did he turned and saw her, his eyes widening with recognition.

Even so, she might have turned away and snubbed him, but some spark of curiosity — some vestigial trace of attraction —

urged her on, so that in a moment she was standing beside him, a faint smile on her lips as he grinned at her.

'Hi, Anna!'

'Michael . . . what are *you* doing here?'

'Don't worry. I didn't crash.'

Anna made to say something, but he went on quickly to explain.

'We supply the fleet of cars your company uses.' He smiled. 'So *this* is what I guess you'd call a perk.' He paused, then: 'It's nice to see you again. Congratulations on the launch.'

'Thanks, I . . .' Anna shook her head. 'You must think me a total bitch.'

'Why?'

'The way I laid into you, last time we met. I was *so* out of order.'

'Yeah. You were.'

'And I probably cost you a sale, too.'

His smile broadened. 'Almost.'

'Then you—'

'One hundred and twenty thousand pounds. My commission on that was two and a half per cent.'

'Shit! So I almost cost you three thousand pounds?'

'Almost . . .'

His smile was infectious. It made her legs go weak. Anna found herself smiling back at him and wondering why she had ever, for a moment, let go of him.

'I'd buy you a drink to say sorry,' she said, 'only—'

'Only I've one of these freebies,' he said, raising his glass. She noted he was drinking orange juice.

'Are you driving?' she asked.

'No, but I've an early start. I've got to deliver a car down in Reigate.'

'Ah . . .' Anna swallowed, then, risking being made a fool of, she asked, 'Are you seeing anyone?'

'No. You?'

She hesitated, then: 'No.'

'I'm surprised,' he said. 'Still, I guess you've been run off your feet, what with setting up the magazine.'

'Pretty much . . .'

Anna looked down, feeling gauche and awkward suddenly. Where did she go from here? Why was it she always felt like a schoolgirl in these situations?

She glanced up, trying to read his eyes; to gauge whether he was still interested in her. 'Look, let me give you my number. In case you've lost it.'

'I have it,' he said, his face giving nothing away.

'Ah . . . Of course.' And now she did feel foolish. He clearly wasn't interested, and that bit about her number was a brush-off. Anna swallowed. 'Look, I'd better mingle. I . . . I'll see you.'

''Bye.'

But her face was burning as she turned away and, loath to talk to anyone, she made her way straight for the ladies'.

Stupid! she thought, as she pushed angrily through the door into the echoing marbled interior. How could I have been so bloody stupid!

Janet and Karen stood either side of Mandy as the cab drew up, struggling to keep her upright. Susie, who had hailed the taxi, gave them a hand getting her inside, then turned to give the driver his instructions.

Fortunately Mandy had already been sick, and at some length, so the chances of a repeat performance were low, but the girls watched her carefully, a plastic bag in Janet's hand, ready for an emergency.

'Great do, eh?' Susie said, looking to Karen and Janet and smiling.

'Hmm . . .' Karen agreed, 'but I couldn't do it every night.'

'Nah,' Janet agreed, 'not like some of those celebs. God knows how they manage it! One night on the town and I'm knackered!'

'Yeah, but they don't have proper jobs . . . or kids,' Susie said. 'They can get in at three in the morning, then sleep through to the next afternoon.'

'Like you used to, you mean,' Janet said, a wry smile on her face. 'Still, it's nice to do it now and then.'

'Yeah . . .' Susie agreed.

'You staying round your mum's then, Suse?' Karen asked.

'Not tonight. Jo's looking after Nathan. I expressed some milk into a bottle before I came out. Hopefully the poor sod's coped!'

Just then Mandy groaned, then snuggled into Janet's side, putting her head on Janet's shoulder. Janet looked across at Susie and giggled. 'Talk about put it away! They should have given her a drip!'

'She had one of them,' Susie said, 'remember?'

'Pete, you mean? Yeah, well . . . he's fallen on his feet, ain't he? Waited on hand and foot by some young dolly bird!'

'Hmm,' Susie nodded. 'Must be hard on Mand, though . . .'

'Wassat?' Mandy said slurredly, lifting her head a fraction.

'Nothing,' Janet said. 'Go back to sleep.'

A snore resounded through the cab. The girls giggled.

They were silent a moment, each of them looking out at the late-night West End streets. The cab stopped at the lights at Cambridge Circus, the engine idling.

'Be nice if Anna found herself someone, wouldn't it?' Susie said musingly. 'You know, someone a bit decent.'

Karen, who had been staring out at a couple kissing in a doorway of the theatre — two women, she noted, as they broke from their embrace — looked across at Susie, noting the distinctly wistful look on her face.

'Yeah, it would,' she said, saying nothing of her own desires. Then, looking across at Janet, she asked, 'You OK, Jan?'

Janet grinned. 'Yeah . . . I just can't wait, you know . . .'

Karen looked back at Susie and saw how she was watching Janet and smiling fondly.

'Strange how things turn out, ain't it?' Susie said.

'Yeah,' Karen agreed, and wondered if Lucy would be there when she got home.

They dropped Mandy first, helping her into her house and up the stairs to bed, before Karen and then Janet were taken home. Susie was last, paying the driver from her own purse before stuffing the tenner Karen had thrust into her hand to pay the fare into her handbag, determined to give it back to her next time she saw her.

As the taxi pulled away, Susie clattered up the front steps, her high-heels hurting, realising only now just how much she had drunk.

It was late. She had stayed longer than she'd intended, but it had been a great evening, and as she put her key into the lock, Susie smiled, thinking back on it.

The smile lasted all of two seconds. As she closed the door behind her and turned, the living room door opened and Jo appeared, his face dark with anger.

'What bloody time d'you call this?'

'What!'

'You said you wouldn't be late. It's nearly one o'clock! Where've you been?'

Susie blinked. 'You *know* where I've been.'

'What? All night?'

She kicked her shoes off, then took off her jacket and hung it on the coat stand, feeling suddenly cold-stone sober. 'Look, what is this? I've been at Anna's do. You know that. I'm a bit later than I thought I'd be, but we were having a good time.' She took a long breath. 'Nathan OK?'

There was no sound of him, so she took it Nathan was sleeping.

Jo took a step closer to her. 'Forget Nathan. I want to know where *you've* been.'

'What *is* this?'

She went to walk past him, but he grabbed her arm and turned her, pushing her back against the wall.

'You've been seeing that bloke, haven't you? That *Gus*.'

'No!' she protested. 'I bloody well haven't!' But she blushed at the mention of Gus and at the thoughts she'd been having. Even in the taxi coming back she'd been thinking of him.

Jo stared at her, his eyes wild. 'Well, go on, then! Deny it!'

But suddenly she couldn't meet his gaze.

'You . . .' Jo raised his hand, as if to slap her, then let it fall. Angrily he pushed her away, a look of disgust in his face. 'You bitch! I should have fucking known!'

She reached out to take his arm. 'No, Jo . . . *listen* . . .'

He shook her off. 'What? To you?'

Turning from her, he reached out and took his jacket from the peg, then pulled it on.

Disbelief in her face, Susie took a step towards him. 'Jo? Where you going?'

'Out!' he said, then stepped away from her, pulling open the front door.

It slammed behind him. She heard his footsteps thud down the steps, then the car door slam shut. A moment later the engine started up.

'Jo . . .' She turned and ran for the door, pulling it open even as the car accelerated away from the kerb into the night. 'Jo!'

Her voice echoed down the street. Behind her, in the room upstairs, Nathan began to cry.

'Jo-oh . . .' She slumped down, on to the top step. 'Come back, Jo, please come back . . .'

But the street was dark and silent and the sound of the car had receded into the distance. Jo had gone.

Anna got in just after two. It had been a great evening. Everyone had been so nice, so positive about the new magazine. The only shadow – and it was a minor one – was her meeting with Michael.

She took off her make-up before the mirror, then showered, standing there for ages in that warm, hard flow, wishing that she'd taken up that offer from the young guy from the advertising agency.

Or maybe not. If she had to fire him further down the line it would be more trouble than it was worth. You didn't mix business and pleasure. That was the golden rule.

As she dried herself before the fire in the living room, she thought back over the evening. Mandy had been a bit over the top, otherwise it had been great to have the girls there. Janet, especially, had been in good form. And Susie, too.

She pulled on her silk kimono, then went through to her bedroom, getting into bed. On a whim, she switched on the TV, turning the sound right down, channel-surfing until she found an old black-and-white film from the forties. She was about to turn the sound up, when the phone began to ring. At this time of night it had to be a wrong number. Then she thought of her mother, and sat up straight, her heart pounding.

'Hello?'

'I didn't wake you, did I?'

'Sorry, I . . .' Then she realised who it was. 'Michael?'

'Are you in bed?'

'No. No, I . . .' She tried to sound blasé. 'I was just watching some TV.'

'Ah . . . Look, would you like a bite to eat?'

She looked down, smiling. It was half two and she had been eating bits and pieces all evening. Even so, she wanted to see him again.

'All right. But where?'

'I'll come round to you. I can be there in ten minutes.'

'No, no, erm . . . give me half an hour. I've some faxes to send to the States. I . . .'

'Half an hour, then.' And he rang off.

Anna shivered.

Jumping up, she began to ready herself, applying fresh make-up, then, standing at the wardrobe, she reached in for the dress she had been wearing earlier. She opened her lingerie drawer and stared at the piles of black and white silk, then closed it again.

Anna grinned at herself in the full-length mirror.

Just the dress and nothing else, she thought. Nothing at all.

Anna waited. As the digital readout on the clock showed three a.m., she walked across and, taking her drink from the side, downed it nervously.

What if, after all that, he didn't come? What if he was simply paying her back – making her wait up when he had no intention of coming over?

Besides, she was mad to do this, not only because of the hour, but because she had vowed never to go back into a relationship that had failed. Not after Callum, anyway.

Anna put the glass down, wondering whether to have another, when the phone rang again.

She stiffened. For days now she had been expecting a call. *The* call, as she'd come to think of it. There would be her aunt on the other end and she would have to hear the words she so dreaded.

It rang . . . and rang.

'Oh God . . .'

She went across and picked it up, her face stiffening. 'Yes?'

'It's Michael . . . come downstairs.'

Relief flooded her. 'But I thought—'

'Just come downstairs. Now.'

The phone clicked and went dead. She put it down, then went over to her wardrobe and took out an evening coat – the coat she wore whenever she went to the theatre with friends – and threw it over her shoulders.

She went down, opening the front door tentatively and peering out into the dimly lit street. There was no sign of him . . . and then she saw the Rolls, the glass of its back window dark, parked not a dozen feet away, and even as she saw it the back door swung open.

Pulling the front door shut behind her, Anna hurried across the pavement and, ducking down, slipped into the massive car.

'I thought you had an early start.'

'I did. But I've got one of my boys to do it for me.'

Anna looked about her as he closed the door behind her quietly. There was food on a silver tray – oysters and other dainty bits – and a bottle of champagne was cooling in an ice bucket. But that wasn't what impressed her. The interior of the car was blue leather, with a deep-pile carpet of midnight blue covering the floor. There was a TV and telephone and a miniature bar, but what surprised Anna most was how big the seat was. As big as a bed in a five-star hotel.

Michael pulled her down beside him on that seat and kissed her, a gentle, almost chaste kiss from which he quickly broke; and yet that kiss left Anna's senses inflamed.

She smiled broadly. 'You trying to sell me a car?'

He grinned back at her. 'No. This one's mine.'

'*Yours?*'

'Don't sound *so* surprised.'

Leaning forward a little, he used a tiny remote to turn on the music.

It was Thomas Tallis. His *Spem In Alium*, that most beautiful of all sixteenth-century choral works. The sound of it brought a shiver down her spine.

'Michael, you surprise me.'

'You think that because I sell cars I'm a schmuck?'

'I know you're not dumb, it's just . . .'

He kissed her again. A bedroom kiss this time. Only they weren't in a bedroom, they were in the back of a Rolls-Royce, parked out on the street in front of her flat.

'Michael, I . . .'

'No one can see us. And no one can get in. I've locked the doors. Now we've got music, and warmth and . . .' He patted the seat beside him.

For the briefest moment, the thought that he might do this with endless women crossed her mind. After all, who wouldn't fall for this? Yet there was something about him — the same something she had responded to first time they had met — that allayed those doubts.

She let him kiss her again, her hands moving over his body now, feeling how firm he was beneath the suit, recalling in her mind what a wonderful body he had.

And even as she did, Michael's hand caressed her breast, her nipple hard against his palm as it pushed against the delicate silk of her dress.

His eyes caught hers and held them a moment. 'I'm sorry.'

'Sorry?'

'That we argued. Such a waste. I mean . . . we could have been doing this every night all these months.'

Anna sighed, then reached out to stroke his cheek. 'Still,' she said softly. 'You're here now.'

She pulled his face towards her, and as their lips met she pushed her tongue deep into his mouth. Reaching up, Michael gently pulled at the zip of her dress. The straps fell from her shoulders, revealing her naked breasts, pert and demanding. Michael slipped on to his knees. As he did, Anna wrapped her bare legs about him, enjoying the roughness of his suit against her thighs as her dress rode up. Michael could see now that she was completely naked beneath her dress and, overcome with desire, pushed her back against the seat. As he placed his mouth over Anna's stiff nipple, she groaned and reached out, pushing her fingers back through his hair . . .

Gus lay there, beside his sleeping wife, staring up at the shadowed ceiling of the upstairs bedroom. They had made love not half an hour back. Or tried to.

Oh, it had been all right, and Pat had been quite under-standing about it. She had even insisted that he roll on to his front while she gave him a soothing massage. He, of course, had blamed it on tension and the work he was having to do for his part-time college course, but he knew the real cause, and it disturbed him.

Susie. He could not stop thinking about Susie. Something about her obsessed him. The way she spoke and laughed and smiled, yes, and especially the way she moved her body; the way she would turn in the doorway and look back at him — so *physical*, so . . . *erotic*.

A long sigh escaped him.

'Gus?' she asked sleepily. 'You OK?'

'Yeah . . . I'm just tired, that's all. I'm all right.'

But he knew he wasn't. Seeing her in the park earlier, talking to her, had only made it worse. Not only that, but he kept remembering how she had felt in his arms that time when he'd held her from behind.

He closed his eyes and gritted his teeth.

Let it go . . . let it go.

But he couldn't let it go. He knew he would have to see her again. What made it worse was the thought of hurting Pat and little Katrina. But he could not stop himself. Something drove him: the same thing as — tonight, for the first time ever — had prevented him from making love to the one woman who loved him.

There was a squeal of tyres from the end of the road as a car came speeding round the corner. It slowed, then braked suddenly.

Gus frowned as he heard a car door creak open. There were quick footsteps, then, astonishingly, one of the downstairs windows went with a great crash of glass.

He jumped up and hurried over to the window, even as Pat sat up in bed behind him.

'Gus? *Gus!* What's happening?'

Gus stood there, watching silently as the figure by the car put a finger up to him then climbed back inside and roared away.

'Gus?' She stood beside him now, trying to see past him. There was an edge of hysteria to her voice now. 'Gus? What's going on? Shall I call the police?'

Lights were going on all along the street now and windows and doors opening as neighbours came out to look. But Gus just shrugged and, moving past her, said. 'Just see to the baby. I'll go down and sort it out.'

Part Five

– *Three months later* –

A nna sat in the big leather swivel chair, staring out of the window, watching the snowflakes drift down out of a steel-grey sky. She smiled. Things were going well. She and Michael had been an 'item' now for three months, and he was taking her out tonight to celebrate.

Besides which, she had just had the latest figures for the magazine and sales were up for the second month running. There was a memo from the Big Boss on her desk congratulating her, and the *Standard* had phoned to arrange an interview.

'Anna?'

She swivelled round, facing Rose, who stood there, a folder tucked under her arm.

'Expenses?'

Rose nodded, then placed the folder on the desk in front of Anna.

As Anna checked and signed the forms, Rose waited patiently. The last of them done, Anna closed the folder and looked up, smiling.

'They should publish these. Very creative.'

Rose grinned. 'So where's he taking you tonight?'

Anna shrugged. 'Not sure . . . Michael said he wanted to surprise me.'

'God, I love that. A man who's not utterly predictable.'

'Oh, there are *some* things about Michael that are predictable.'

Rose raised an eyebrow. 'I'm not sure I want to know.'

'But you're right. It is exciting.'

When Rose had gone, she swivelled back round, staring out of the window once again, thinking about Michael. It was true. He was different from the normal run of men, but sometimes, just sometimes, she wished he would relax a little. His energy frightened her. He wanted to be out all the time, partying, burning the candles not only at both ends but in the middle too. And though, right now, it suited her image to be seen about town with a man as handsome and photogenic as Michael, her age forced her to wonder just where this relationship was heading.

There had been a time − with other men − when she had been more than happy to leave things pretty loose, avoiding talk of a *relationship* or *commitment*. But now, before she had admitted even to herself that she and Michael were a couple, she was considering whether he would donate quality sperm for her eggs.

She had raised the subject of children only once, and then in such an obscure fashion − in a conversation about Janet and Susie − that he would not suspect she was sounding him out. If Michael had given any sign that he wanted them, then it might have made it easier, but he had shown not the faintest interest. His sole aim in life, it seemed, was to enjoy himself. Included in that, of course, was pleasing *her* − and in that regard Anna had never had a more attentive lover. But . . .

Anna huffed out a sigh, then, deciding she would not spoil things by brooding, she swivelled round again and, reaching across the desk, picked up her phone.

'Get me Greg in Travel, would you?'

She waited, music playing while the connection was being

made – modern jazz, her choice – and then Greg was on the other end. He was a young American who had impressed her on another magazine, and whom she had poached six weeks back.

'Greg? It's Anna . . .'

'Oh, hi! What can I do for you, Mzz Boss?'

She smiled, enjoying his casual irreverence. 'You can look among your up-coming freebies and see if there's something with white sand beaches and blue skies.'

'You got a writer in mind?'

'Me.'

'Ah . . . got you. Well, there's one comes to mind.'

'Go on.'

'Two weeks in the Grand Bahamas. You know, one of those all-inclusive holidays for couples only. I was thinking of doing a spread on it. A fun-in-the-sun kind of piece, but . . .'

'Come and talk to me about it . . . first thing tomorrow. But it sounds good. What dates?'

'It's just come in, so I'll check. But I think it's pretty much up to us.'

'Find out, will you, and let me know.'

'Will do. Anything else?'

'No . . . oh, yes there is, actually.' She smiled. 'Next time your friend Alex puts in an expenses claim for taxis, tell him to make sure he doesn't have the same handwriting on *all* the receipts!'

'Ah . . . right.'

She put the phone down and sat back again.

Maybe that was what they needed: to get away somewhere. Take time to talk and, well . . .

Anna closed her eyes, imagining it, picturing the two of them walking along a beautiful white-sand beach, the warm sea lapping about their bare feet as the sun slowly set.

What better moment could there be to broach the subject?

And what more flattering thing could a woman ask of a man than he be the father of her child?

She shivered, then opened her eyes again. No good getting carried away, she told herself. No, she was going to be casual about this, not pushy. And she'd choose her moment well.

Anna smiled, then, pushing the thought aside, turned back and reached across for one of the files Jacqui had left for her attention, immersing herself in her work once again. Doing what she was best at.

Less than an hour later, she was sitting beside him in the car — an old fifties Bentley he had borrowed for the occasion — speeding down the M4 at close on a hundred.

She knew better than to lecture him about speeding. Besides, she was intrigued. He had turned up early and demanded that she come at once. Leaving Jacqui to hold the fort, she had slipped on her coat and followed him out into the lift and down.

Now here she was, heading west as the sun slowly set behind them.

She had asked him several times where they were heading, and all he'd said each time was 'Wait and see.'

And so she relaxed, enjoying simply being there beside him. So it had been with Callum once. But Anna didn't let any shadows fall across her happiness. She knew enough now to take each day for what it was; and though she still wanted more, she wasn't going to make the mistake of letting it spoil what she already had.

This was *their* evening, and she was determined that it would be memorable.

As Junction 18 approached, Michael slowed and began to manoeuvre across into the left-hand lane.

'Bath,' she said softly, reading the sign. 'Michael . . . are we going to Bath?'

He glanced at her and smiled, but this time didn't say a word. So Bath it was. Anna stared out through the window and smiled. It was one of her favourite places.

The car had been silent for the motorway journey, but now, as they moved out of the speeding traffic, heading south towards the ancient Roman town, Michael leaned across and switched on the stereo.

The warm, relaxing sound of a modern jazz group filled the car.

If there was one thing she had learned about Michael, it was that he had taste.

He was a reluctant talker. His past was definitely 'history' as far as he was concerned and, though she often elicited tiny clues about it, she knew well enough by now to leave it be. All she knew was that he was estranged from his family. That and the fact that he'd been hurt in love. Badly hurt.

Oddly, it was something that bound them.

'It's years since I last came here,' she said, as they began the descent into the town. Fifteen years, in fact, now that she thought about it. Then she'd been with a guy called Phil. A right prick, now that she recalled it.

'I lived here for a while,' he said, surprising her. 'Back in my student days.'

She looked at him, astonished. But then, why should the fact that he'd been a student surprise her? Only, perhaps, that he seemed to come from a very different background. Working class made good.

Like herself.

'What did you study?'

Michael laughed. 'Young women and the inside of bars, mainly. But that's not what you meant, is it?' He changed down a gear, slowing for a bend. 'My major was psychology.'

Anna raised an eyebrow. 'Useful.'

'Can be. I did a thesis on psychological types. Sometimes it comes in useful, like when I've a new customer walk in. I can generally place them, you see. Know what they want before they want it.'

'It must give you an edge.'

He nodded.

'And with women?' The idea that he had 'placed' her intrigued Anna. It suggested a degree of calculation she hadn't suspected.

'Sometimes. Sometimes I haven't a clue.'

'And with me?'

He glanced at her. 'You I just wanted. First time I saw you.'

It was the right thing to say, and Anna glowed inside. 'And then nearly fucked it up.'

'Nearly. But I guessed I'd meet you again. Counted on it, actually.'

'Yes?'

'Yes.' He reached out and held her hand briefly before returning his own to the gearstick.

'Michael?'

'Yes?'

'Will you come away on holiday with me?'

He smiled. 'I'd love to. What are you talking about? Easter? The summer?'

'Next week, actually.'

He laughed. 'Too busy,' he said. 'My boss would never agree to it.'

'Shame . . .'

They were to the south of the town now and Michael slowed as they entered a roundabout, then accelerated out the other side, beginning to climb now through the Regency-style streets.

'But why not Easter?' he went on. 'We could book

something. Sri Lanka, maybe, or one of the South Sea islands.'

'Maybe . . .'

Coming out of one of the side streets, he slewed the car round, then slowed, even as they emerged on to the Royal Crescent, the Bentley cruising up to the front of the Royal Crescent Hotel and stopping.

'Here?' she asked, surprised despite herself.

'Here,' he answered, putting the car into neutral and pulling on the handbrake. He turned to face her, smiling, his hand resting gently on her thigh. 'You haven't been here before, have you?'

'No,' she said, dazed by just how thoughtful — how romantic — he was. 'It's wonderful.'

He leaned over towards her. 'So are you.'

In fact, it was more than wonderful. Michael had booked a suite, with a bath the size of a small county and a view of the town below. It was beautiful, and that evening they ate in the restaurant just below their room, the elegance of the surroundings quite breathtaking. After dinner they went through into the bar and sat and talked over large brandies. And for once Michael was quite talkative. Anna learned more that evening than she had discovered in three months of being with him.

His father, he'd said, had been a merchant banker, his mother the daughter of a senior partner in the same firm. They were, to put it mildly, rich. Michael, as the eldest of three sons, was his father's favourite and had been groomed to take his place in the family firm. But Michael hadn't wanted that. Michael had grown his hair and rebelled against his father and gone off to be a student.

All well and good. Sons have to learn to be independent of their fathers, and Michael's father was wise enough to recognise that and let his boy sow his wild oats. But even after college, Michael didn't want to get a steady job – perversely, as his father saw it – and the two argued.

Bitterly, as it turned out. Three years passed without the two of them speaking or even seeing each other, and then his father had had a heart attack and died, suddenly, in his office, and so they had never been reconciled.

'That's so sad,' Anna said, reaching across to take his hand.

'Yeah,' Michael said sombrely. 'You see, I was really fond of the old bugger. He was . . . well, he was fun. He had such a joy for living. But I didn't want to *be* him. And I most certainly didn't want to be a merchant banker. But he couldn't see that.'

Anna nodded, watching him closely; loving him at that moment. Wanting, just then, to have his child more than anything she had wanted for some time.

'My brothers, of course, wouldn't talk to me. Nor would my mother for quite some while. I tried, of course, but . . .' He shrugged. 'Well, that's how it is. I try and see them, Christmas and the like, but it's never comfortable. They think I let him down.' He laughed sadly. 'Ironic, really, because as I've grown older I think I've become more and more like him. He'd have liked this, for instance. A good hotel, a decent brandy . . . and a beautiful woman, of course.'

Anna smiled back at him, bewitched by him. Did he know how beautiful he was? How lovely those eyes of his were, especially when they looked so sad?

'Michael?'

'Yes?'

'Can we go to bed?'

'Right!' Mandy said, handing the wine bottle back to Karen. 'So if I book the minibus, you can organise the tickets.'

Karen stared at the empty bottle a moment, then, frowning, set it aside and got up, making her way over to Mandy's fridge. 'I'll pay for them on my credit card, then you can all pay me back.'

'Great!' Mandy said, studying the list Karen had drawn up. 'Susie said she'd get some bits from M & S for on the bus, and Anna's going to book some place she knows for the brunch. The bubbly we can order nearer the time. I mean, we got months yet, ain't we?'

Karen crouched, then removed the bottle of wine she'd brought from the bottom of the fridge. 'What if it rains?'

'Nah . . . it won't rain. Besides, we won't care once we've had a drink!'

'Well, Janet won't be drinking.'

'Nah, I s'pose not. She'll be quite a way along then, won't she? But you don't wanna go draggin' umbrellas and all that along, do you? That'd be asking for bad weather!'

Karen shook her head, amused as ever by Mandy's perverse logic. She began to uncork the bottle. 'I might ask Anna if she could get me a hat for the day. I don't really want to buy one. What d'you reckon?'

'Yeah, I'm sure she could. I mean, she got that dress for her do that time, didn't she? Christ! I'd have shit meself if I'd had to wear it . . . you know, worrying all the time about getting drink spilled over it, or some bastard being sick down the back of it! Five thousand quid it cost. Five thousand! I mean, that'd pay my rent for a year!'

'Hmm. I s'pose you could buy yourself a nice little car for that, couldn't you?

'That's what I mean!' Mandy agreed. 'Five thousand knicker for a dress . . . it's obscene!'

'Well, yes,' Karen said, agreeing for once. She brought the open bottle across and topped up both their glasses, then sat again, taking the list from Mandy to run through it one last time.

It had been Mandy's idea to celebrate her fortieth at Ascot races. With the fourth day of the event falling on her actual birthday, it seemed the ideal venue. She was determined not to let the occasion pass without celebration as the others had chosen to do. A quiet meal wasn't for her!

Mandy was over her 'granny depression' now and was even beginning to get excited by the idea, but the big Four-O remained a psychological barrier. Ascot was designed to get her over that. Susie had suggested a party, but Mandy hadn't wanted it. This — low-key, high-alcohol and a traditional day out for half of upwardly mobile London — was the perfect answer.

'Here . . .' Mandy said, pointing her glass at Karen. 'D'you reckon I'll have to dust off me wedding hat soon?'

'What? Anna and Michael?'

'Yeah, well it ain't me and it ain't you, is it?'

Karen smiled. 'I don't know. But they look good together, don't they?'

'Yeah, and from what Anna says he's like a cross between Errol Flynn and Michael Douglas between the sheets! Lucky cow! Me, I'd be lucky to get Cyril Smith and Benny out of *Crossroads*!'

Karen giggled, more at the wistful expression on Mandy's face than the thought of sharing a bed with a man.

'Yeah,' Mandy went on, 'and I bet it'd be a posh do. Strikes me he's got taste, that Michael. You seen his Roller?'

'Hmm.' But Karen wasn't really interested. 'Look, Mand, do you think we should give Susie some idea of what to buy, foodwise?'

'Nah, Susie'll know,' Mandy said confidently. 'She's quite the little homemaker these days. She's even cut up her Harvey Nicks charge card. But we should all chip in.' Mandy sniffed.

'You don't reckon it's going a bit overboard, do you? I mean, it's not going to be too much for everyone, is it?'

Karen looked down the list and gave a little shrug. 'Nah. It'll be fine.'

'Good! Pity about the stretch limo, though . . . You don't think Anna's Michael could arrange something, do you?'

Karen grinned. 'A minibus will be fine. Honest, Mand. We'll have a great day, I promise you.'

'Yeah . . .'

'Now I must go or I'm going to be late for my date.'

Mandy looked at her, then, teasingly. 'So who is he?'

'*She,*' Karen said. Finishing her wine, she stood, then took her jacket from the back of the chair. 'Her name's Sylvie and I met her at a dinner party last week.'

'So what's she like, then? Long hair? Short hair?' Karen poked her tongue out. 'Well,' Mandy went on. 'I don't know what you go for, do I? I mean, the last few have been so different.'

'Chris and Lucy, you mean?'

'Yeah, well . . . they were like chalk and cheese, weren't they?'

'I s'pose so. Well, Sylvie's older than me and . . . yeah, she's nice. Likes the same things as me.'

'Ah well,' Mandy said, smiling, then coming over to embrace her. 'Enjoy yourself, eh? And don't do anything I wouldn't do?'

'What, like shag fat guys?'

Mandy giggled. 'There's always a first time.'

'You *must* be joking!'

'Yeah, well . . . sometimes I wonder if I'd be better off dating women. In fact, I know I would if it wasn't for the sex!'

Karen smiled, then, kissing Mandy on the cheek, picked up her bag. 'I'll buzz you later in the week, OK?'

'OK. See you, love.'

'See you.'

The play had been interesting — a modern translation of a French play from the eighteenth century — and afterwards, as they sat at the back of the Café Pêche, Karen found herself listening attentively as Sylvie discussed the play's central dilemma: whether the woman should remain in the loveless marriage she found herself in for the sake of the children, or whether she should run away with her new love — her husband's mistress.

To be honest, Karen had found it all rather contrived, and though the playwright — a man, of course! — had tried to write two decent female characters, she had suspected that one of the chief purposes of the play had been to feed an unhealthy male interest in lesbianism.

Men could never write decent women. Not even Shakespeare. They were always adjuncts. Property in all but name.

Sylvie paused a moment and smiled, drawing her dark, bobbed hair back from her eyes as she did. 'Am I losing you, Karen? You look as if you're miles away.'

'I'm sorry,' Karen answered, smiling back at her. 'It's just . . . well, I thought it was all rather . . . unsatisfactory.'

'Unsatisfactory?' Sylvie looked puzzled. She considered the point, then shrugged. 'How do you mean?'

Slowly, hesitantly at first, Karen began to speak, talking not merely of the performance but of other tangential things, drawing examples in from her wide and varied knowledge of plays and books, until, looking up, she saw how Sylvie was looking at her and blushed.

'Well,' Sylvie said, a different kind of smile on her lips now. 'You are a dark horse. I think you'd be wasted teaching primary school kids. You should go for a lecturer's job.'

The blush intensified. Karen looked down. 'I don't think I could. I don't think I'd have the confidence.'

'Oh, nonsense!' Sylvie said. 'You're already teaching at the hardest level of all. Two-thirds of those kids in your classes don't even want to be there! Not only that, but compared to those hormone-riddled hard nuts, university students are as docile as mice! And as malleable as the most innocent four-year-olds! And I should know!'

Sylvie, of course, was a lecturer herself, though in history, not literature. Karen looked up, meeting her deep green eyes.

'Maybe,' she said.

'No maybes about it,' Sylvie said forcefully. 'You should think about it. I'd be happy to give you a reference.'

Again Karen looked down. This was only their first date, but already Sylvie was talking as if she had known Karen all her life. So it was with some of these women. They assumed an immediate intimacy purely on the basis of their sex.

Sylvie sat back a little. 'Shall we order? Or would you like another drink first?'

Karen wasn't sure now that she even wanted to eat. 'Actually, I think I could only manage something small. A starter, perhaps? The, er, mushrooms would be fine.'

'Sure.' Sylvie turned and, spotting a waiter, snapped her fingers. The young man came across at once.

Karen watched Sylvie order — more like a man than a woman in the way she went about things — then smiled as Sylvie turned to her again. 'Another beer?'

She didn't usually drink beer, but this Ice lager was quite nice. 'No, no . . . I'm fine with this,' she said, then looked down again.

'You're quite shy, aren't you?' Sylvie said quietly, leaning closer. 'That surprises me. You were quite outspoken at the dinner party.'

'Was I?'

The truth was, she had been very drunk. Trying-to-forget drunk, as she called it. After all, it was only a month since Lucy walked out on her.

'But I like you like this. It's . . . nice.' And Sylvie placed her hand over Karen's briefly.

Later, while Sylvie was over at the counter paying the bill, Karen sat there in her coat, looking about her, noting the mix of people. Some were clearly gay, others clearly — almost demonstrably — heterosexual, but what was most evident was that no one cared. Here, at the centre of London, it didn't really seem to matter what you were or what you did.

Even so, she wasn't sure she was ready to take the next step and go home with Sylvie. Wasn't even sure if she wanted to see her again. Oh, she had enjoyed the evening — had even, towards the end, relaxed with her — but the next step was a big one, for she wasn't by nature promiscuous and if she slept with Sylvie it would not necessarily be for the sex, but because she wanted to take it further, and she didn't know that yet.

As Sylvie came across again, she stood, slipping her handbag on to her shoulder.

'Ready?'

Karen nodded, nervous suddenly.

Outside, the air was crisp and icy cold, but at least it had stopped snowing now. A faint rime of snow and ice lay on the pavement and as Sylvie hailed a cab, Karen found herself longing for the comfort of her own bed.

The inside of the cab was warm and welcoming, yet once again Karen found herself trembling as she sat beside Sylvie; unsure of herself suddenly. Sylvie gave the driver her address, then sat back, her shoulder and hip pressed against Karen's. And then, even as she had begun to think that nothing might happen, she felt Sylvie's arm go about her shoulder and Sylvie's face come close, her lips pressing against Karen's.

There was a moment's stiffness, a moment's uncertainty, and then she responded, letting her lips part as Sylvie's tongue touched her own and gently brushed against it.

That kiss went on, growing slowly more passionate until, when they broke, Karen found herself staring at the other woman, surprised . . . and aroused, too, her nipples stiff, her groin aching.

Breathing, too, was suddenly difficult. Her body screamed to be touched and held, her flesh caressed and probed by the other woman's fingers, yet something held her back.

'Look, I . . . I don't think I can go through with this. Not tonight, anyway. I . . .'

Sylvie's eyes were understanding. 'You don't want to be rushed, is that it?' Karen nodded gratefully. 'Then don't be.' Sylvie smiled, and put a hand up to Karen's cheek, her fingers lightly caressing her. 'But can I see you again? I enjoyed tonight.'

'So did I.' And it was true now that she looked back on it; now that the pressure to sleep with Sylvie had passed.

'This Friday, maybe?'

'Why not?'

And all the while, Sylvie's hand continued to caress her face, such that eventually she closed her eyes, enjoying the simplicity of that contact.

'You want me to get some tickets for something?'

'Yes . . .' Karen opened her eyes lazily, and as she did so, Sylvie placed her lips against hers once again. This time the kiss went on and on, and when they finally broke, Karen found herself staring at Sylvie, astonished.

'Are you *sure* you won't change your mind?'

She almost – almost – said yes. It would have been easy to. But a faint doubt still nagged at her. Besides, if it was going to happen, it would happen. It was no good letting a few kisses persuade her, as wonderful as those kisses had been.

'You kiss nicely,' she said.

'Ditto.'

Sylvie turned, then, leaning forward, tapped on the glass that divided them from the driver. Reaching back, he pulled it across.

'Yes, love?'

'Just a change of plan . . .' And she gave Karen's address, then sat back, smiling at Karen.

'I can wait,' Sylvie said, a faintly lustful look in her eyes now. 'In fact, things are always best when you have to wait for them, don't you find?'

Karen closed the door behind her, then, not bothering to turn on the light, hung up her coat and bag and walked through into the moonlit living room.

She had almost changed her mind; almost invited Sylvie in. Indeed, now that the cab had gone, she was sure she should have done, for she knew she wouldn't sleep. Now — and she knew it for a certainty — she would toss and turn, in the grip of the most erotic dreams.

Ever since Lucy had gone she had been plagued by sexual thoughts. Dominated by them, almost. Images of how it had been, with Lucy *and* with Chris, returned to haunt her, until, unable to relax, she would have to masturbate.

Perverse, that's what her brother had called her. *Perverse*.

But how could that be so? Had *she* made herself this way? No. This was how nature had fashioned her, and how then could one call it *unnatural*?

She walked through to the bathroom and, switching on the light, turned on the taps, deciding she would run herself a bath, and even as she did the phone rang.

Karen turned, listening. The answerphone was on, and this

once she felt no urge to speak to anyone. No doubt it was one of the girls – Mandy, maybe, wanting to tell her about her latest exploit, or Susie, with her tales of marital woe, or Anna, talking endlessly of Michael and babies and her doubts. But this once she wanted none of it. She wanted only to be left alone.

'Karen? Karen, it's Mummy, I . . .'

Karen started forward, then stopped.

'Look, love, I . . .' She heard the sigh her mother gave and frowned. 'Will you come over? Please, love. We really need to talk.'

There was a silence and then the machine clicked off, the line went dead.

Karen closed her eyes. Now what was *that* about?

She turned back, lazily unbuttoning her blouse, wishing now that she had been braver in the cab. Or weaker, maybe. For a moment she cupped her own breasts, imagining what it might feel like to be touched that way by Sylvie. Then, with a tiny shudder, she reached across and, taking the bottle of lavender oils from the side, uncapped it and let it slowly fall into the water.

Imagination . . . She smiled. What a wonderful thing imagination was.

That evening in Bath had been wonderful, the night so sweet that, had Michael asked her there and then to marry him, she would have done so without a moment's hesitation.

Not that she had expected him to ask. It was too soon – far, far too soon – to be making that kind of commitment. Yet for the first time she had begun to wonder whether she should not, perhaps, set the pace.

Specifically, she had toyed with the idea of coming off the pill. With leaving it all to fate. But that might cause its own problems. She did not want to present Michael with a *fait accompli*, yet the urge to have his child grew stronger every day. He deserved to be consulted about such an important matter — yet Anna could not bring herself even to raise the subject.

Which was why this holiday was so important.

Two days had passed since she'd returned from Bath and, in the glow of that idyllic night, she had gone ahead and arranged things. Now she sat at 'their' table in 'their' favourite restaurant, waiting for Michael to arrive. It was early — just after twelve thirty — and Michael had been surprised to hear from her, but she knew he would come. After all, hadn't she arranged it all with his boss?

She saw him pause in the doorway and look across, his smile as he saw her telling her all she wanted to know.

You're half in love with me already, she thought. And I think I'm falling in love with you.

Which was strange, because you tended to think, as you got older, that that kind of feeling was something adolescent. But each time it struck you was as powerful as the first time.

'Hi,' he said, bending down to kiss her, then taking the chair across from her.

'Hi,' she said. 'Surprised to see me?'

He grinned. 'Yes. What's going on?'

In answer she took the air tickets and the deluxe brochure from her bag and handed them across.

He stared at them a moment, then looked quickly across at her, surprised. 'But these are for Sunday.'

'Uh-huh.' She kept her expression sober, but inside she was smiling broadly. 'We're booked into the Xanadu for a week.'

'But . . .' He shook his head. 'I can't just . . .'

'You can. I've arranged it with your boss.'

'You've *what*?'

'I've spoken to him. I tried for a fortnight but we reached

a compromise. No, actually he thought it was a great idea. Reckons you've been working far too hard.'

'Why you . . .' He was grinning now like a Cheshire cat. Reaching across for her hand, he squeezed it, then leaned forward, pushing his face against hers to kiss her mouth.

Sitting back, Michael stared at the tickets again, slowly shaking his head. 'The Xanadu, eh? Sounds pretty good.'

'Not good. Wonderful. So I'm told.'

He looked at her. 'Anna?'

'Yes?'

'Thank you.'

She shivered. The way he looked at her made her wish they were not in a public place.

'Michael?'

'Yeah?'

'Are you very hungry?'

He smiled, leaning closer. 'Depends what we're talking about here.'

Anna laid her hand over his where it rested on the table. 'It's just that suddenly I feel like going straight for the dessert.'

His smile broadened even further. Bringing her fingers to his lips, Michael looked at Anna through dark lashes. 'OK . . .'

'Good,' she said, 'because I've found a new little hotel. It's not far . . .'

Mandy thought she recognised the voice. Even so she was shocked when Johnson's client turned in his seat and looked up at her.

'*Nick?*'

Nick beamed back at her, his blue eyes wide. 'Mandy!'

Johnson looked from one to the other of them. 'You two know each other, I take it.'

'Oh, a long time ago,' Nick answered, not taking his eyes off Mandy.

Mandy returned the smile, then moved past him to hand the file to her boss.

Back in the main office, sitting at her desk again, Mandy stared across at the door to Johnson's office, lost in thought. After a moment, Tracey leaned towards her across the desk.

'All right . . . don't keep it to yourself, Mand. Who is he?'

Mandy looked back at her. 'Just someone I used to know.'

'Yeah? When was that, then?'

Mandy sighed, then shook her head. 'Oh, a long time ago.'

'So what d'you mean, someone you used to know? Give us the gory details.'

'Get yourself a life, you nosy cow.'

Tracey sat back, a hurt look on her face.

Relenting, Mandy leaned towards her and, in a low voice, said, 'His name's Nick and he was the first boy I ever went out with. My first great love.'

'*No!*'

Mandy nodded, then looked back at the closed door to Johnson's office, remembering how they had parted, that night of the party, more than twenty years ago. They had met again — once, at a bus stop, just before Susie's wedding — but she'd assumed he'd gone back to Australia. But here he was, in Johnson's office.

'You OK, Mand?'

'Yeah?'

'You look a bit off colour.'

'Nah . . . I'm fine.'

But she didn't feel fine. It had been a shock to see Nick sitting there, where she herself had sat so often. As for Nick himself, she hadn't thought of him for ages, but now that he was here, she found she couldn't think of anything else.

And why was he here? Was he working for one of their clients? And did that mean he was back in Islington?

'Mandy?'

Her head jerked up. She hadn't heard him come out of Johnson's office. Hadn't noticed him walking over to her.

She swallowed. 'Yeah. Hi.'

'Small world, eh?' She smiled thinly, feeling awkward. 'What are you doing for lunch?'

'Lunch?' She stared up at him, her mouth open. 'I, er . . .'

'There's a nice little restaurant just round the corner from here. We could go there. I've not got to rush back, so . . .'

Mandy stared. 'But I, er . . .'

'I'll speak to the boss if you like. I'm sure he won't mind you getting away a bit earlier.'

'No, it's OK, I'll . . .' Realising she was acting like a prat, Mandy smiled, forcing herself to relax. 'No, that's great. I mean, it'd be really nice. I'll go and get my coat.'

She paused in the cloakroom, trying to calm herself down. This was silly. Her heart was going like an express train, and she had come over all hot and cold.

Nick, she told herself. It's only Nick.

Yeah, but it wasn't only that. This wasn't just history; this had the feel of unfinished business.

It took a while for her to relax; to get used to him watching her again, and to that smile of his which had not changed a bit over the years.

Nick was still handsome, even if the past few years had seen him put on weight as well as lose a bit of hair on top. But she could talk. She was far from the svelte, shy teenager he had known.

He had lost the tan he'd had when she'd last encountered

him; but then he'd been back from Australia two years now. His mother had died and he'd stayed on to sort out the family's affairs.

'So do you think you'll go back, eventually?' she asked, as the waiter cleared away their plates.

He shrugged. 'I dunno. I mean, it's not as if there's anything out there for me. I thought there was, but . . . Well, all my roots are here. I realised that as soon as I got back. Oh, the weather's shit, but . . .'

Mandy smiled. He was somehow gentler, nicer, than when she'd known him. But then again, adolescent males were not the most subtle of creatures.

'So are you seeing anyone?' she asked; risking the question now that she'd had several glasses of wine.

He shook his head. 'You?'

'Nah,' she said. And she felt that it was the truth. There was no one special in her life.

They had already been through the whole conversation about divorce and its aftermath, but there was an implicit *something* that they hadn't yet got to.

'Coffee?' he asked, as the waiter hovered.

'Yeah . . . yeah, that'd be nice.'

He smiled, then turned and ordered. Looking back, he gazed fondly at her. 'You know, you haven't really changed.'

'You bleedin' liar.'

'No, Mand. Underneath it all, you're still the same. And I was wrong, you know.'

'Wrong?' She felt herself go very still.

He let out a long breath. 'That party. It was stupid of me just to walk out like that. I should have stayed and had it out with you. I should've understood that you were worried about me going off to university. I mean, a good-looking fella like me . . .'

She couldn't help but laugh.

'I've often thought about it, you know,' he said, his voice softer now, more intimate, so that Mandy looked down into her lap. 'I've often thought that what I should've done was take you upstairs and . . .'

He left it unsaid, but there it was.

You should have made love to me, she thought. You should have been the first, not Pete. Yes, and maybe I'd have had a different life from this. Maybe I'd have been happy all these years.

She shivered. Even to think about it hurt.

'So what now?' he asked.

Mandy shrugged. She wasn't sure that turning back the clock was wise. She wasn't who he thought she was. She had changed too much. He still had this vision of a younger, more innocent girl in his head, and she wasn't like that any more.

'I don't know,' she said finally.

'Well . . . can I see you again? Take you out to dinner, maybe? Or the theatre?'

She laughed at that.

'Sorry . . . what did I say?'

'The theatre . . . I hate the bloody theatre!'

'Ah . . .' And he smiled, as if it were amusing. But that too was part of it. He was from another world. Anna's world. Karen's world, too. But not hers.

Mandy sighed. She could see now how it wouldn't have worked. How, even if he'd had her all those years ago, they would have slowly drifted apart.

'You always were a clever sod, weren't you?' she said, apropos of nothing.

'If you say so . . .' Reaching across, he put his hand over hers. 'Look, Mand. I would like to see you again. I . . . I've often thought about you.'

'Yeah?' But she couldn't meet his eyes. Couldn't honestly

say that she had thought about him that much, not once the initial wave of pain had passed. Oh, from time to time something might spark off a memory, but she had been too busy raising two kids to brood over past mistakes.

'OK,' she said finally. 'Dinner. But not tonight.'

'Saturday?' He gave her hand a little squeeze.

'Yeah . . . yeah, Saturday'll be fine.'

'Shall I call for you? At seven, say?'

Mandy swallowed, her mouth dry now. 'Make it eight.'

'All right. You're at the same place?'

She looked up at him, surprised that he knew. Then again, everyone knew everyone else's business. Always had done.

'So,' she said, as the waiter set the coffees down before them, 'tell me what you did after university. I never did find out where you got to.'

Karen looked up as her mother came back into the room, then smiled, accepting the cup of tea she was offered.

'Ta . . .'

Her mother stared at her a moment, that same faint, distant smile still on her face. Then she sat, cradling her own tea on her lap.

This was hard for her. Karen could see that. Her mother was hunched into herself, trying to find where to start. Yet when she looked up again, Karen was surprised to find that she had tears in the corners of her eyes.

'I'm so sorry, sweetheart. I don't know . . .' She stopped, taking a moment to control herself, then went on. 'It's been hard for you, I know. And Jack . . . well, Jack was wrong . . .'

'Mum, you don't have to . . .'

'But I do. I should have said something before now, but . . .' She sighed. 'I went to the doctor's the other day. Not for me, but . . . well, to talk about your dad and everything. And she said Jack was wrong to blame you. It wasn't you: she said, it was his own fault. Sixty fags a day and a heavy fat diet, that's what killed him. It was his veins, you see. They were too thin. All clogged up and, well . . .' Karen looked down, unable to speak. 'It's just that . . . I wanted you to know, that's all.'

Karen flashed a grateful smile at her mum, then sipped at the too sweet tea.

She heard her mother sip from her own cup. Then, 'So how's Chris?'

'We're . . .' Karen looked up, meeting her mother's eyes. 'She left me, Mum. Months back. I . . . I'm seeing some one else.'

'Ah . . .' But her mother didn't ask.

'Have you seen Jack recently?'

Her mother nodded. 'He pops over once a week to see how I am. He's taken it very badly.'

'Yeah . . .'

'Oh, but he'll come round, Karen. Eventually.'

'You'll speak to him, will you?' But it wasn't fair, and she regretted saying it at once. 'I'm sorry, I . . .' She blew out a breath. 'It's been hard, Mum. So hard. I wanted so much for dad to understand.'

'Yes . . .' Her mother watched her, her grey eyes trying hard to understand her only daughter. Trying, but not understanding. Not ever understanding, for all that she loved her.

Mandy slipped the old photo album back into the drawer, then sat again, huffing loudly, annoyed with herself for being so silly about this whole thing. He was just a bloke, after all. Just another bloke. So what if she hadn't spoken to him properly for a quarter of a century? So what if she'd made a promise? Was it *her* fault she'd never been able to keep it? Anyway, what had he expected? That she'd wait for *ever* for him?

No, the bugger should have rung her. But he didn't. So it was all history. She'd had another life, and so had he.

Even so . . .

She stood, then marched out into the kitchen and, picking up the phone, dialled Karen.

'Come on . . . *Come on* . . .'

It rang and rang and rang.

'Shit!'

Mandy slammed the phone down, then picked it up again, this time dialling Susie.

Susie answered at once. 'Hello?'

'That was quick! You waiting for a call?'

'Oh, hi, Mand, how's things?'

'Can I come round?'

'Round? Sure. Why, what's up?'

'I'll tell you when I see you. Ten minutes, eh? I'll stop for a bottle on the way, OK?'

'OK, babes. See you then!'

Ten minutes later she was handing Susie the litre bottle of Liebfraumilch she'd bought and pulling off her coat.

'So?' Susie said, staring at her. 'Spill the beans. You're not up the duff, are you?'

Mandy opened her mouth, then, indignantly. 'Certainly bloody not!'

'I just thought—'

'Look, Suse, I may be daft but I ain't stupid.'

'Nah . . . anyway, come through and plant your bum down. It's been a while since we 'ad a good natter.'

'So what you're saying is . . .' Susie paused, then giggled.

'What?' Mandy said. 'What's so bleedin' funny?'

'Just the thought of you and Nick, finally . . . well, you know, *doing* it.'

'Oh, thanks! And what's so funny about that?'

'Just that you took your time . . .' Susie sniggered. 'Twenty-four years! I mean, I've heard of foreplay, but . . .'

'Yeah, well we haven't *done* it yet, have we? And I'm not so sure I want to.'

'I don't see your problem, Mand. He's good-looking, employed, he likes you and, well, he's *available*. Christ! He's a lot better bet than some of the dogs you've been going with!'

'Oh, cheers!' She raised her glass. 'My best mate!'

'Cheers!' Susie said, and clinked her glass against Mandy's.

Little Nathan had been asleep for the best part of two hours now and they were both well on the way to being drunk. The Liebfraumilch was long gone, along with a bottle of Black Tower and half a bottle of Bulgarian red they'd found in one of the cupboards. Now they were on to the spirits. A bottle of Vladivar vodka to be precise.

'So what do you want from Nick if it ain't his body?' Susie asked, getting herself more comfortable in her chair.

'I dunno . . . I mean, he's nice.'

'Yuk!' Susie said, making a face. 'Who wants *nice*. They always turn out to be creeps.'

'What, like Gus, you mean?'

'Not particularly . . .'

'You seen him recently?'

'Nah . . .'

'So things are all right, then . . . between you and Jo, I mean?' Susie hesitated; the kind of hesitation Mandy knew all too well. 'Suse?'

Susie shrugged. 'I dunno . . . I guess things haven't been right for some time. I mean, we still do it, now and then, but . . . well, truth is the sparkle's gone out of it. Know what I mean?'

Mandy sighed. 'And Jo . . . what does Jo think about it?'

'I dunno. We can't seem to talk about it. You don't, do you? But he stays out a lot these days. And the drinking . . .'

Mandy stared at her a while, then shook her head. 'Why didn't you say?'

'What's there to say? It's life, ain't it? You get on with it. And there's Nathan . . .'

Mandy understood that well enough. It was how her life had been. A trade-off. One happiness for another. And no chance, it seemed, of having it all – a loving husband *and* a grateful child.

'You still love him though, don't you?'

Susie looked down, then, softly: 'Yeah.'

'Then you've got to make an effort. You know, hand the baby over to your mum for the night, put on the sexy underwear and . . .'

Mandy gave a little jiggle of her body, making Susie splutter with laughter. Then, more seriously, she said. 'Yeah . . . maybe.'

'No maybes, Suse. Do it. Don't lose him. It's a phase, that's all. You'll be all right.'

'Yeah?'

'Yeah,' Mandy said, holding out her glass. 'Now splash a bit of vodka in there.'

When Jo crept in, just after midnight, he could see that Susie had had a visitor. There were plates and empty bottles and glasses all over the living room, and the CD player was still on, even though the disc had finished playing.

He slipped his shoes off, then tiptoed through, stopping in the doorway to the bedroom, astonished by the sight that met his eyes.

'Fuck me . . .' he whispered, noting the two female forms that lay there in the double bed. And Nathan?

He looked across, making out the tiny shape asleep in the cot.

Jo pinched himself. No, he wasn't asleep in some urinal in

a pub and dreaming this – that was *his* bed, and in it were the two women he had been sleeping with not two years back.

Pulling off his tie, he threw it aside, then began to unbutton his shirt. He threw it off, then unzipped his trousers and peeled them off. He was standing there now in his boxers and socks. Reaching down, he pulled them off one at a time, then straightened up, grinning at the thought of what he was about to do next.

He stepped over to the foot of the bed, pausing a moment to note that Mandy was wearing one of Susie's nightshirts, the thin cloth pulled tight over those voluptuous breasts.

God, he remembered those well . . .

Jo crouched, about to slip into the narrow space between them, when Mandy lifted her head a little.

An eye flicked open, freezing him with its steely gaze.

'Don't you even think about it.'

He straightened. Then, sheepishly, he backed away. 'Mand . . .'

'Night!' Susie called. And the two women dissolved into giggles.

Jo turned angrily, and stomped from the room.

'Poor boy,' Mandy said quietly 'Maybe you should . . .'

'Not tonight,' Susie said, and yawned heavily. 'Night, Mand.'

'Night, Suse.'

And, with another snort of laughter, they turned away from each other, each of them staring thoughtfully away, as Jo thumped and banged about in the spare room, swearing and muttering to himself.

Karen had stayed with her mother until late, looking through the old photo albums with her and reminiscing about the past. It had been good for both of them and she felt better than she had in months. Her mother, too, had seemed livelier, happier even, now that things had been resolved between them.

And maybe she was right. Maybe Jack would come round. In time.

She put the key in the lock and turned it. The flat was dark and silent. Closing the door behind her, she switched on the light, noticing at once the envelope that lay on the mat, no stamp on it, only her Christian name.

She bent down and picked it up, then slit it open.

It was from Sylvie. She had been passing by and had called in on the off-chance. She was going to have a quick drink in the wine bar round the corner.

Karen hesitated. She would have gone by now, surely? It was well after twelve. Then again, what harm would it do to look?

Leaving the light switched on, she went outside again, locking the door behind her, then paused to listen.

She didn't like walking these streets this late at night, but it wasn't far. Just round the corner and fifty yards along.

Karen was breathless when she got there. She had half run the distance, looking this way and that, scared in case some shadow should leap out at her. Now she stood there, getting her breath and peering through the etched glass of the window, trying to see if Sylvie was still there.

She didn't see her at first, then, as someone stood, she glimpsed her, there by the bar. She had put on her coat and was clearly about to leave.

Karen pushed inside, standing there as Sylvie got up from her stool and turned. Seeing Karen, she smiled. Putting down her bag, she waited as Karen went across to her.

'So you came?' Sylvie watched her all the while, smiling, her hand reaching up to touch Karen's arm. 'I didn't know if you would.'

'I've only just got back. I went to see my mother.'

'Ah . . .' But Sylvie didn't seem interested in that. Her hand stroked Karen's arm. 'Sit down. I'll buy you a drink. What do you want?'

Karen really didn't want anything. She had had about a dozen cups of tea at her mother's and felt bloated.

'Just a white wine and soda.'

Sylvie turned and ordered two, then looked back at Karen. 'I didn't sleep, you know.'

Karen knew what she meant. She hadn't slept either, not even after she had made herself come. And the dreams she'd had . . .

Wanting to change the subject, she noticed that Sylvie had a book poking from the top of her bag. 'What are you reading?'

'Oh, this? You'd like this . . . it's a murder mystery, but it's written as poetry . . .'

'Really?' Karen took the book from her and looked at its cover a moment, reading the title aloud, '*The Monkey's Mask* . . .'

'Raymond Chandler for dykes!' Sylvie said, and gave a low, raucous laugh.

Karen looked at her, surprised by that laugh, then smiled. Up until that moment – and the kiss aside – she had been thinking Sylvie something of a cold fish. But that laugh showed a strong sense of humour.

Their drinks came, and Sylvie handed one to Karen, chinking her glass against hers.

'To us!' she toasted.

Karen shivered, then sipped her wine, knowing suddenly that, this time, she would not send Sylvie home on her own.

Karen woke to find Sylvie sleeping peacefully beside her. For a while Karen lay there, staring at her, at the delicate femininity of her – at her almost childlike breasts and the soft lines of her face in sleep — and wondered why she hadn't slept with her that first time.

It had been fantastic. So gentle at first and then so intense, rough almost. And afterwards, Sylvie had held her and stroked her until, aroused once more, they had made love again.

Karen shivered, surprised by how much she already felt for this woman who, until a few hours ago, had, for all their talk, been a stranger to her.

And that was the weird thing about sexual intimacy. How much of the person it revealed. Things that no amount of talk — however intimate — could ever unveil.

She smiled, amazed by the situation she found herself in. Just three years ago she had never slept with a woman, but now she was on her third lover. And each time it was different, a new experience.

Karen raised herself up on to one elbow, studying Sylvie for a time, intrigued by the play of moonlight and shadow on her naked form, by the gentle rise and fall of her breasts as she slept. She wanted to touch her, to run her fingers over that soft, almost silken flesh, yet it would be a shame to wake her. Not yet, anyway. Let her sleep. After all, the whole morning lay ahead of them.

Again she smiled, then lay once more, one hand beneath her cheek as she faced Sylvie, studying her face — her nose and lips, the delicate shape of her ears and the soft down beneath her chin. How old was she? Forty-five, maybe. Yet her body seemed much younger. And those years had clearly not been wasted. Sylvie made love with an experience that neither Chris nor Lucy had ever matched — and with a consideration for her needs that neither of those others had ever displayed.

Even so, she was determined this time not to make the same mistakes: to become either too possessive or too demanding.

This time she would relax. This time she would take each day as it came.

Jo got to the house with five minutes to spare. There was no one hanging about, either in front of the house or in any of the cars, so he took the opportunity to ring Simon on his mobile.

'Simon? You fancy a drink lunchtime? . . . The Albion? . . . Quarter past one? . . . Great! See you there.'

Jo snapped the mobile shut and slipped it into his jacket pocket even as a rather tasty-looking red BMW pulled up just in front of his car. P-reg, and as clean as the minute it came out of the showroom.

He watched the woman slide from the car. Mid-thirties, he guessed. Smart business suit and black tights. Neat shoulder-length hair and her sunglasses up on top of her head.

Divorced, he knew at once, with the instinct of his trade.

Tightening his tie, he climbed out and locked the door, then turned to face the woman.

'Mrs Jacobson?'

She smiled and came across, offering her hand. 'Sorry I'm a bit late. Meeting ran over.'

The accent was neatly clipped. Middle-class.

'That's all right.'

Was he mistaken or was that the old glint of interest in her eyes? He looked away, staring straight ahead through the etched-glass panel of the front door.

'Well . . . it's a nice little property. Well maintained. Tastefully decorated. Not really a family house, but perfect if you're looking for this kind of thing.'

He looked back at her and saw she was watching him, the faintest smile of amusement on her lips.

'You want me to sign now, or do I get to look at it first?'

He smiled. 'Sorry. Of course.' And, taking the keys from his pocket, he started towards the door, conscious of her walking just behind him.

He felt old reflexes wake in him. Old responses. He felt that vague tingle of anticipation . . .

Yeah, but he was married now. He had a kid to think of.

As he fitted the key into the lock and turned, she was right there beside him, so close that her face almost touched his own.

'Sorry . . .'

Jo pushed the door open, embarrassed suddenly, not looking at the woman as she walked past him into the hallway.

'Nice,' she said, looking about her. 'Shall we start upstairs?'

He swallowed. 'Yeah . . . yeah, of course.'

She was gagging for it. He knew it without any shade of doubt. He'd been here before, and not just with Mandy. Christ! He'd had dozens of women like her, on floors and in strange beds, on kitchen tables, even in a bath!

He watched her walk up the stairs. Christ, she had a lovely arse. Tight and firm. And the short business skirt she wore seemed like a come-and-get-me beacon.

Jo closed his eyes and counted to ten, then followed her up the stairs.

Susie sat at the kitchen table, cradling the coffee mug and staring out of the window at the back garden. Nathan was asleep finally, and for a moment she could relax. There was hoovering to do, and washing, but for once she shut them out of her mind.

Jo. What was she going to do about Jo?

The sound of the downstairs door slamming had woken her, and she had gone across to the window in time to see him climb into his car and drive off. Leaving the baby asleep in his cot, she had gone downstairs, to find the blankets and a pillow stacked neatly on a chair in the front room, a used plate scattered with toast crumbs on the drainer beside the sink in the kitchen.

And not even a goodbye.

'Shit!' she said, remembering what had happened in the night. 'Shit! Shit! Shit!'

She stood, then went across and took the phone down from the cradle, walking over to the back door as she tapped in the number.

It rang a moment, then. 'Hello?'

'Mum? It's me. Susie.'

'Hello, love. How's my little cracker?'

'He's fine . . . Look, Mum, will you do me a big favour?'

A faintly hesitant tone crept into Doreen's voice. 'Yeah?'

'Will you have Nathan for a couple of hours tonight? It's just that Jo and I could do with spending a bit of time together, and so I thought I might do him a meal and—'

'You think two hours'll be enough then?'

Susie laughed, surprised. 'Mum!'

'Well, you ain't talking about watching *The Waltons* together, are you?'

Susie giggled. 'Mum! Behave yourself!'

'I've got no bleedin' choice, 'ave I! But of course I'll look after him. When do you want to bring him round?'

'About eight?'

'And what about bottles and all that?'

'I'll express some breast milk for him.' Then: 'Look, Mum, are you sure?'

'Sure I'm sure. Now you sort yourself out.'

'Thanks, Ma. You're an angel.'

She'd given Jo every opportunity to make his move. She'd sat on the bed and looked at him. She'd stood at the window, looking out at the garden, flaunting that lovely arse at him. And then she'd sat back in the sofa in the lounge, her legs slightly parted as she'd stared up at him, all wide-eyed and smiling. A dozen or more clear signals, and he'd ignored them all.

And so here they were, half an hour later, standing on the doorstep once again, and he'd kept his knob in his trousers. Susie ought to be proud of him. Only Susie didn't give a shit right now. Susie wouldn't have cared if he'd been shagging the Dagenham Girl Pipers three at a time as long as she wasn't one of them!

He locked the door, then turned. 'Well? What do you think?'

'It's nice, but I'm not sure.' She looked up at him through a veil of dark lashes. 'Perhaps you'd like to persuade me over a drink?'

'I . . . Look, I'm sorry, I've got a lunch appointment.'

'Ah . . . Another time, perhaps?'

Jo looked aside. 'I'm not sure that's a good idea.'

'No?' She was still staring at him, and he could almost feel himself blushing. 'You don't indulge, then? Wife at home and all that?'

'And all that.' He forced himself to look at her again. 'You're a nice woman, Mrs Jacobson—'

'Jean.'

He swallowed, then: 'Look . . . maybe someone else ought to see you next time.'

She smiled. 'You know, you surprise me.'

'Surprise you?'

'Just that you look the type. You know . . .'

He grinned. 'I was.'

'And then?'

'Then I met the right woman.'

She looked him up and down, then leaned forward and

kissed his cheek. 'Shame. Still . . . if you ever change your mind . . .'

'I won't.'

Even so, she took a card from her bag and handed it to him, smiling. 'If you come up with something you think I should see . . .'

'Yeah . . .'

He watched her walk over to the BMW and slide in, those long legs disappearing out of sight.

Christ! he thought. I could have fucked her senseless!

Yeah, but it was only trouble. And he'd had enough of that to last him a lifetime.

Susie stood before the full-length mirror, admiring herself. The lingerie she had bought for their honeymoon still fitted. Despite the baby, she had kept her weight down and got back into shape pretty quickly. There were dark rings under the eyes, but a bit of make-up would do wonders. Besides, if she knew Jo, he wouldn't necessarily be looking in her eyes.

She turned away, looking about her, then walked over to the wardrobe and opened the door. All of Jo's suits hung there, neatly pressed, including his wedding suit, dry-cleaned since *that* debacle. His shoes lay in a neat row at the bottom of the wardrobe. The sight of them made her realise how much she liked living with him.

Poor sod. It must be hard for him sometimes. Especially recently. But she'd make it up to him tonight. She'd make him remember why he'd married her.

Slipping on her kimono, Susie went downstairs to the kitchen. She had prepared a casserole — one of Jo's favourites — and even gone to the trouble of making him a crumble. The question now was whether to splash out on a bottle of bubbly or get him a couple of beers. Becks. Or maybe one of those big cans of Sapporo that he liked.

Susie stood there a moment, resting against the clean-scrubbed pine table, smiling to herself. She liked it when he'd had a few beers. He was very mellow then. Not only that, but it made him last longer, and she always used to like it when he took his time.

She shivered, realising suddenly how much she'd missed him making love to her. Trouble was, she was always done in by the end of the day. No one had told her how demanding it would be. And when she wasn't knackered – that was, when she was just ordinarily tired – then Jo was at work. Like now.

A thought came to her. Maybe she shouldn't wait. Maybe she should phone him now and tell him to come home for lunch. Not that he'd get to eat anything . . .

'No,' she said decisively. If the baby woke he'd be twice as pissed off as he was now, and that was no good. She'd stick to her plan. Get Nathan round to her mum's and then enjoy having a bit of time together.

Smiling to herself, Susie went through into the dining room and began to set the table, with candles and place mats and everything.

'No, I'm serious. I'm really proud of you!' Simon said raising his pint to Jo. 'Most men wouldn't have thought twice about giving her one.'

'That's just it,' Jo said, staring down into his pint. 'I *did* think twice. And then twice again. In fact, I had to turn away from her at one stage. It was like having a friggin' steel bar in me pocket!'

'Then you were a saint, my friend,' Simon said, slapping Jo on the back.

'That's what I keep telling myself.'

'Things no better, then?'

'Things are fucking disastrous. She's either too tired or

she's not in the mood. And her tits are completely off limits. Nathan's taken over in that department. She used to like me touching her, but now . . . well, it's like going to bed with me mum.' Simon frowned. 'Oh, don't get me wrong. I love Nathan right enough. He's a darling. But sometimes . . .'

'What?'

'Oh, I don't know. I find myself . . . *resenting* him. Resenting just how much of Susie he's taken away from me.'

'It's just frustration, man.'

'Yeah. I know. But it doesn't help. It's like . . . well, the stronger the bond gets between *them*, the weaker the link between *us*. It's as if all her love is being used up now on the baby, and there's none for me.'

'Hmm. It must be hard, though.'

'Hard?'

'For Susie, I mean. They're demanding little things, babies.'

'And you'd know about that?'

'I can read.'

'Amazing what they publish in *Gay Times* these days!'

Simon smiled, then looked down. 'Don't be hard on her, Jo. She needs your support. Show her that you're there for her. She'll come round. You know she will.'

'It's all right saying that, but you don't have to live with it!'

'Then maybe you ought to go and see a prostitute . . .'

'What?'

Simon looked up and met his eyes. 'You heard. Go see a whore once a week. Get it out of your system. But no affairs. Think of the kid, Jo. You need to be there for him, while he's growing up, and if you blow it now you won't get a second chance.'

Jo brooded for a while, then shook his head. 'Trouble is, I don't think she really loves me any more. Maybe it was that thing with Mandy . . .'

'Bollocks! 'Course she loves you. She wouldn't have taken you back if she didn't. It's just that she's tired, that's all. Give her time. Be patient. It'll all come good. You'll see.'

'I don't know . . .'

'Snap out of it. Would Uncle Simon ever lie to you? Now get the rest of that pint down your neck and I'll buy you another.'

'You off, Jo?'

Jo looked up from his desk. 'I've just got a few things to finish, Grace, then I'll be on my way.'

'We'll be in the Slug and Lettuce if you fancy a drink.'

'I dunno, I . . . hell, I ought to be going home.'

'Just one, eh? Or you got other plans?'

Jo considered a moment, then. 'No. Don't reckon I have.'

'Well? You working or drinking?'

He looked at the open file, then shut it and slipped it away in the drawer. 'Looks like I'm drinking.'

Islington on a Saturday night was as busy as the West End, the pavements crowded, even at the end of February, with strolling couples, looking for a restaurant, or a pub to sit and have a drink in.

While Nick was in the loo, Mandy sat at the table by the window in Granita's, staring out at the passers-by and wishing she were somewhere else. Granita's was a bit posh for her, the menu rather too *nouvelle* for her taste, and Nick had made much of the fact that the Blairs had used to frequent it. Personally she preferred the Sarcan, the Turkish restaurant just round the corner, where meat and more meat was the order of the day.

She looked up as Nick came back and took his seat.

'Decided yet?' he asked.

Mandy sighed. 'No. I can't make up my mind.'

Nick looked down the list of main courses, then looked back at her, smiling. 'The lamb's always good here. It's what I'm having.'

'OK . . .'

Well, why fight it? She was so nervous about this that she'd lost her appetite anyway.

'So,' he began, as the waiter brought the drinks they'd ordered, 'what have you been up to since the divorce?'

Mandy shrugged. 'Not a lot till I got the job. That changed everything.'

'Yeah . . . I guess it must have.' And he smiled at her fondly. 'And your two boys. You said they're not living at home any longer.'

'Luke was, but he's moved out now. Sharing a flat with some mates. Jason's well settled. His girlfriend Gemma's having a baby in the summer.'

She glanced at him as she finished, watching his reaction, but Nick seemed to take it in his stride.

'So you're all alone in the house? It must get lonely at times.'

'Yeah . . . yeah, sometimes.'

Mandy looked down, thinking about what Susie had said the other night. Was Nick really looking to take things up where they'd been left off all those years ago, or was he just another guy looking for a shag?

'It's like my mum's place,' he went on. 'While we were all at home – you know, when we were kids – it seemed a tiny little place, cramped as hell, but now that there's only me . . . well, I rattle around a bit.'

'You wouldn't sell it, though, would you?' And as she said it, the thought of her and Nick on the bed in his room came back to her from across the years. Her first sexual fumblings had been in that old house.

'I've thought about it,' he said. 'And God knows, now's

the time to sell in Islington. The prices have gone through the roof!'

'Yeah . . .' She'd always rented. House prices had never interested her.

'You never thought of moving away, Mand?'

'What, from Islington? Nah. I mean, where would I go? All me mates are here.'

'Yeah, but, don't you ever get a hankering to travel? You know, see places, do things.'

Mandy thought about it a moment, then shrugged. 'No. Oh, don't get me wrong, I like a bit of sun and sand . . . in fact, me and the girls from work have got a holiday lined up at Easter. A week in Malaga, swimming pool and everything.'

Nick smiled. 'You'd have liked Australia. Great weather, great beaches.'

'Yeah, but I'd 'ave got homesick, wouldn't I?'

'Not necessarily.'

'You mean, you didn't?'

Nick shrugged. 'Sometimes, but . . . well, there are compensations, so you make the best of things.'

That much was true. She raised her glass and clinked it against his.

He frowned. 'What was that for?'

'Making the best of things. I know all about that.'

Mandy looked away. She hadn't meant to sound so bitter.

'I'm sorry,' he said.

She looked back at him. 'You broke my heart, you know that, don't you?'

He looked at her for a long moment before Mandy averted her eyes.

'But . . .' She looked down at her glass, then smiled. 'It was all a long time ago, wasn't it?'

He, too, was smiling now. 'Yeah. Even so, I am sorry. You

should have come and visited me, you know. At college. Who knows what would have happened?'

She met his eyes. 'You should have asked me.'

'Yeah . . .' For a moment he stared at her, very serious, then, more quietly, he said, 'It's not too late, you know.'

'No?' But a little tremor went through her, and her stomach felt suddenly uneasy. She was meant to be cool about all this.

'Look,' she said, after a moment. 'Let's take things step by step, eh? It's been a long time and we're not the people we were.'

'Aren't we?'

'No,' she said, knowing it was only half true; that inside she still felt fifteen most of the time. 'No, we ain't.'

Nick paid the bill, then turned to Mandy. 'You want a drink somewhere before you get back? Or would you like to come back to my place for a coffee?'

She was feeling a little tipsy now. 'A *coffee*?' Mandy laughed. 'Not exactly original, is it?'

As soon as it came out of her mouth, she realised that it was the wrong thing to say.

'Mandy, I . . .'

'Look, I'm sorry. I . . .' She blushed. 'No . . . no, I'd love a coffee. Really. But why don't we go back to my place? I've only got instant, but it's only round the corner. I could show you those old pictures I was talking about.'

Nick smiled at that, everything back on a more normal footing suddenly. But Mandy found herself confused. If not sex, then just what *did* Nick want from her? For months now she had got used to going out with blokes who, come the end of the evening, were guaranteed to want one thing and one thing only, and it didn't come in a coffee jar! But with Nick she was suddenly on quicksand, unsure how to read things.

Nick still seemed to have this glowing vision in his head of how things had been, before the both of them had had lives. He still had this romantic notion about the two of them, whereas she saw things more pragmatically these days. Oh, it was flattering, certainly, to know that he still cared after all these years, and he wasn't a bad-looking bloke, but Mandy wasn't sure whether she was ready yet for anything more than a strictly sexual relationship.

She glanced at him, then swallowed deeply. Even the way he looked at her, with that distant smile of his, seemed to suggest that he saw someone other than the Mandy Evans who was there before his eyes. Someone younger and more innocent. But how long would that last? How long before that roseate glow faded and he saw her for what she really was?

And did she want to have that happen? To get involved and then be dumped? Wasn't it better not to take the risk? To go on as she was and have a bit of a laugh, a bit of fun. Wasn't that why her life had been so empty before – because she had tied herself down to a single man and made herself his woman, there to do *his* chores and be *his* bed mate?

Did she really want to do *that* again?

It made her think of the awful chat-up line some bloke had tried on her a few weeks back. Some beefy red-necked guy with a double chin, as it happened. 'Here, love,' he'd said, putting his hand firmly on her arse. 'You fancy coming home with me? I'm looking for someone to do me housework!'

Nick had stood and was pulling his jacket on. Seeing her amusement, he smiled and asked. 'What's the joke?'

'Oh, nothing . . . just thinking about something someone said, that's all.'

She smiled at him, then stood, even as the waiter came up with her coat. 'Look,' she said. 'We ain't sixteen, right? And we've both been through the mill, so . . .' He went to speak, but she raised a hand. 'No, listen to me, Nick. Please.

I gotta say this. I'm almost forty. I may not have travelled the world, or done a lot in your eyes, but I'm not naïve, and I'm not looking for the same things out of life that I wanted when I was a kid. Can you understand that?'

'I . . . think so.'

'Good . . .' She half turned and gave the waiter a smile, letting him help her on with her coat, then turned back to Nick. 'OK, then. I'm ready for that coffee.'

Susie sat there staring at the open doorway of the dining room. She had drunk the whole bottle of Sauvignon and then polished off all three of the beers she had bought for Jo. The casserole was in the bin, where she'd dumped it an hour past, with the crumble on top of it. The candles had burned down and there was only the hiss of static from the hi-fi in the corner.

There was the click of a key in the lock and the sound of the door creaking open. She heard him sniff and put his case down on the hall floor.

The door clicked shut.

He thinks I'm in bed, she thought; all of the anger she'd been feeling welling up in her again.

His footsteps came on up the hallway then stopped.

'Suse?'

He peered round the door, confused. Drunk, too.

'Where the fuck have you been?'

Jo blinked. 'What?' Then, focusing on the candles, the dinner plates, he asked. 'Who's been round?'

She shook her head. 'You arsehole.'

'What?' He straightened up, then shook his head as if to clear it. 'Hang on . . . are you talking about me?'

'Yeah, *you*, you bastard! Where the fucking hell have you been?'

'Drinking, if it makes any bloody difference. *Why?*'

'Because I've been sitting here waiting for you, that's why!'

'Waiting? Don't make me laugh! The only reason I'm still here is 'cause you need someone to pay the bills!'

Susie leapt up at that. 'Is that what you think? Is that what you really think? 'Cause if it is you can piss off right now!'

'Oh, I will! There's plenty of *real* women out there, who'd—'

The doorbell rang. Jo wheeled about unsteadily. 'Who the fuck . . . ?'

Susie pushed past him and opened the front door. 'Mum . . .'

'Hello love, had a nice time?'

Doreen stopped dead, so that Bobby almost cannoned into her. She looked to Jo, then back at Susie, then set the baby's carrycot down. 'Oh, er . . . we'd best be off.'

'Don't bother on my account,' Jo said, taking his coat from the coatstand. 'I'm off anyway!'

As he pushed through, Susie made a grab for his arm. 'Jo . . . *Jo!*'

But he was gone, into the night. Susie stared after him a moment, then turned, distraught.

'Where's he off to?' Bobby asked.

'Oh, shut up!' Doreen said, opening her arms and holding her daughter to her as she dissolved into floods of tears.

It had been a disaster. The worst sex she'd had since . . . well, since Pete. And as for the embarrassment . . .

Mandy lay there, watching Nick dress, noting how he couldn't even look at her, and felt all of the subdued anger and irritation bubble up in her. It was probably her fault, for rushing things, for asking too much of him – or the wrong things – yet if the sex was no good, what future had they anyway?

'I'd better go,' he said quietly, pushing first one foot and then the other into his slip-ons.

'Yeah. You'd better, hadn't you?'

Nick glanced at her, surprised by the hardness in her voice, a flicker of annoyance in his eyes. The sight of it set her off. She sat up, leaning towards him accusingly.

'What the bleedin' hell did you think I was? Did you think I hadn't changed after all these years?'

'Mandy, I . . .'

'Piss off! Go on! It wouldn't be the first time, would it?'

That did it. He straightened, his expression sour, then, snatching at his jacket, tugged the door open and went out. The front door slammed a moment later.

'Oh, shit . . .'

Mandy lay down again and closed her eyes. She hadn't meant to get angry, but it was as if the mere sight of Nick set her off. And maybe it always had. They'd always rowed, even when things were good between them. So maybe it was fated after all. Maybe it had all been for the best.

She got up and padded through to the bathroom, sitting there naked on the loo seat while the water cascaded into the bath.

Nick wouldn't be back. Not after that performance. Twenty-four years he'd waited, and the poor bugger couldn't even get it up!

Seeing the funny side of it, Mandy smiled thinly. Maybe she should have given it mouth-to-mouth. Then again, Nick had been shocked enough already by how 'forward' she had been.

She shook her head, surprised. She'd never thought of Nick as prudish. Then again, thinking back, he'd never been that pushy when it came to sex. If he'd really wanted to, he could have been the first. Christ, she'd fantasised about it often enough!

A little later, lounging there in the warm tub, Mandy felt relaxed, her body flooded with an unexpected relief. There she'd been, wondering absurdly if this wasn't, perhaps, her last chance at happiness, when all the time it had been merely another chance to get into a rut.

Well, that was that. She wouldn't be seeing Nick again!

The doorbell rang.

'Oh, shit! It can't be.'

Mandy sat up, a worried expression on her face, listening, telling herself to stay where she was and not answer it, but as it rang a second time, she knew she would have to.

Hauling herself up, she stepped out of the bath and pulled her bathrobe on, then hurried through, leaving a trail of wet footprints, even as the doorbell rang again.

She threw the door open, taking a breath as she did, irritable now. But it wasn't Nick.

'Hello, Mand,' Alex said, his eyes lustfully taking in her state of half-undress. 'Any chance of a coffee?'

They knew him at the club from years back, and a tenner was enough to sweeten the bouncer at the door. He sat in a corner, alone, cradling a beer, letting the music wash over him. There weren't many people in yet, and none he knew, but that didn't matter much. He didn't really want company. Not yet, anyway.

He'd thought about going home to his mum's, and that was still an option. He had a key, and he could sleep on the sofa. But one thing was certain: he wasn't going back. Not tonight, and maybe never again. That was it. He wasn't going to be called an arsehole just because he'd been out for a drink.

He took a long deep breath, then swigged at the bottle.

'Hello again.'

Jo looked up, then registered surprise. 'Oh, hi . . .'

She smiled down at him. 'On your own?'

- 442 -

He looked about him exaggeratedly, then shrugged. 'Looks like it.'

'Mind if I sit down?'

'It's a free country.'

She sat. For a moment she was silent, watching him, then. 'It's Jean.'

'I know. I've got your card.'

'You're out late, aren't you?'

'I'm a big boy now.'

'And Mrs Right?'

He raised his bottle in a mock salute. 'Back home.'

'Doesn't sound like a lot of fun.'

He looked down. 'It ain't.'

'You gonna buy me a drink, then?'

Jo looked up. Slowly his face seemed to sober up. 'All right,' he said. 'What would you like?'

She laughed. 'I'll have the drink first. Brandy and coke. And easy on the coke.'

Susie woke to the sound of the baby crying. She lay there a moment, trying to remember what had happened, then sat up.

Only then did she register the empty space beside her in the bed.

She got up and went over to the cot, picking Nathan up gently and cradling him to her breast.

'There, there . . . it's all right now, sweetie, Mummy's got you.'

That little mouth puckered, tiny hands grasped; feet kicked in a repetitive motion. Nathan's tiny face wore an expression of petulance and need.

Sitting on the edge of the bed, she undid the top two buttons of her top with practised ease and placed him to her breast, directing her swollen nipple into his eager mouth.

At once the crying ceased. At the same time Susie felt the release in her milk-full breast; that pleasant relief it always brought her.

She closed her eyes and sighed. No doubt Jo was downstairs, sleeping on the floor again. Well, serve him right this once! He shouldn't have been such a prat.

Even so . . .

Susie stiffened, reminding herself of the wasted dinner, the hours she'd waited. Indignation filled her once again.

'Arsehole . . .'

Surprised, Nathan jerked and lost the nipple briefly, howling until he had it back again, then snuffling contentedly as he sucked and sucked.

Susie smiled, watching him, recalling how Nathan looked in sleep sometimes; how he would continue sucking in his dreams, the fingers of one hand blindly opening and searching the air, then settling again. If only Jo would take more time to watch Nathan the way she watched him, then maybe he might understand. Or begin to. As it was . . .

Things were bad. She wasn't kidding herself. But sod it, she'd tried and he'd pissed on her. What did he expect?

Yeah, but maybe she'd make him breakfast and a cup of tea, as a peace offering.

She smiled again, and stroked Nathan's chin with her little finger. 'Come on you, drink up . . .'

There was no sign of him downstairs. And then she realised. She had locked and bolted the door. He couldn't have got back in, not without waking her. So where the hell was he? At his mum's?

Susie waited until eight to phone. Mrs Ball answered with that stiff, rather lah-di-dah voice of hers. No, she said. I haven't seen Jonathan for a couple of weeks.

Next she tried Simon's.

'Suse? . . . Jo? . . . No, not here I'm afraid. . . . Yeah, if he phones I'll get him to ring you. . . . OK. 'Bye.'

Leaving the baby to cry in his bouncer, Susie threw on a dressing gown and went out on to the street. The car wasn't there. Not that she could see, anyway. It would serve him right if he'd been pulled by the police, the amount he'd drunk.

She went back inside and put the kettle on, then picked up Nathan and cuddled him, soothing him until he was quiet again.

Where was he? Where the sodding hell was he?

At nine she phoned the estate agents. They were open Sunday mornings, but Jo wasn't there. At least, he hadn't arrived yet. She put the phone down, angry now, but worried too.

And as she did there was the sound of the key in the lock.

Susie froze, tense with resentment.

Nathan began to cry.

The door clicked shut. There were footsteps in the hallway. They paused briefly outside the door, then continued, then there was a thud, thud, thud as he went upstairs.

The bastard!

She went out and stood at the foot of the steps, holding the baby to her shoulder as she shouted up at him.

'Where the hell d'you think you've been?'

A pause. The door to the wardrobe in their bedroom creaked open. There was the sound of hangars being moved on rails, then a muffled response.

'At my mum's.'

'Liar! I phoned her. She hasn't seen you in weeks!'

'It was late,' he shouted down. 'I didn't want to wake her, so I slept in my car outside.'

'Fuckin' liar . . .' But this time it was under her breath.

She knew now. Knew for certain. She didn't even have to look for clues.

'You fuckin' liar!' she screamed. 'Who is she? Who the fucking hell is she?'

The wardrobe door slammed shut. The footsteps returned. Jo's face appeared over the top of the stairs.

'What do you care?'

'I care 'cos I don't wanna catch something. If you've been stickin' your dick up some—'

'Oh, don't worry, it wasn't a whore! She was classy. A *real* friggin' woman!'

Susie could feel her face burning: could almost hear the thumping in her chest.

'You shit! You fuckin' little shit!'

He came down the stairs towards her, a change of clothes over his arm. As he passed her, Jo reached up and squeezed the baby's hand.

The door slammed shut.

They had spent the day in a huge white motor cruiser fitted with a glass viewing hull, sailing the shallow aquamarine waters a mile offshore. They had swum in an idyllic bay, diving off the side of the boat into the cool, clear water, and afterwards had sat there beneath the pale yellow awning in the heat of the day, eating barbecued shark fresh from the spit, followed by the freshest pineapple she'd ever tasted, washed down with rum that was as strong as the Bahamian accent of the boat's skipper.

It was enchanting, like a dream after the cold greyness of London, and Anna had never been happier. She felt reborn, and that evening, in the huge, mahogany-panelled dining room, as a steel band played, she and Michael drank a rum punch toast to 'the future'.

That was the first time Anna had heard Michael speak of

any kind of future. For all she knew, he lived for the day, as if 'now' were tattooed into his every cell. But even the way he looked at her seemed suddenly different — seemed *charged* with meaning, and she wondered vaguely if he might not propose to her on this holiday.

She watched as he joined in with a limbo competition, his enthusiastic efforts being pipped finally only by a six-year-old local girl. Michael was delighted for her, and picked her up and danced around with her until the girl shrieked with delight.

In the bar, later on, they reacquainted themselves with some of the other residents of the luxurious hotel, where, so she discovered, a matted-haired Howard Hughes had spent his last years as a recluse in the penthouse suite, walking on newspapers so as not to scratch the beautiful parquet floor with his overlong toenails.

One of those at their table was a Texan who, so he claimed, was a multimillionaire. And who was she to doubt it? The man had a massive yacht moored in the hotel's marina, and as the night drew on, she and Michael were invited to a party on it later in the week.

As they stepped into the lift, ready to go back to their suite near the top of the hotel, Michael drew her close and kissed her. It was a surprisingly tender kiss, and she looked at him afterwards — he was not normally so restrained, so gentle.

'Michael, I . . .'

'Shh . . .' he whispered, his hands reaching up to rest either side of her neck, his fingers gently stroking the flesh behind her ears. 'Quiet, now . . .'

And again he kissed her. So chaste, so delicate a kiss — and at the same time so erotic.

He could have had her there in the lift, but he was patient, waiting until they were back in their room. There he unzipped her dress and pulled it from her, then slowly kissed her hips and stomach, his hands gently caressing her nakedness, making her body scream at him to end this torment and take her. But Michael was not going to be rushed.

Picking her up, he gently laid her on the bed, then slowly undressed, watching her all the time, the faintest of smiles on his lips.

The only light in the room was from the harbour below. Sounds drifted up to them — drunken calls and laughter — but they were scarcely aware of them. As he kicked off his shorts and stepped across, she could see how much he wanted her, and as he lay beside her she reached down to gently touch and hold his hot stiff penis.

'Gently,' he said. 'I want this to last.'

And so, slowly, they began, caressing each other with their hands and planting tiny moist kisses on each other's flesh. Limb slid against limb and then he was inside her, Anna crying out as he pushed deep into her sex, the feeling so good that she again found herself close to orgasm. But Michael slowed things once again, gently, delicately teasing her, brushing the tip of his penis against her sex as his teeth pulled at her nipple, playing her like an instrument until, gasping, he released himself into her. And this time she did let go, the sensation so intense she gave a little shriek which turned into a strange kind of whimpering noise.

Afterwards, lying there, he laughed softly.

'What?' she said, enjoying his amusement.

'That noise you made.'

She hit him playfully. 'Well, you weren't so quiet yourself, were you?'

'Yeah,' he said, raising himself up on his elbow and grinning down at her, 'but at least I sounded normal.'

'What, normal for a gorilla having a heart attack, you mean?'

'At least I didn't do chicken impressions!'

'Chicken impressions!' Anna sat up. 'When did I do chicken impressions?'

'Well, OK . . . a partridge maybe . . .'

She hit him again, less playfully this time. Catching her wrist, he pulled her to him and kissed her.

'D'you fancy a midnight swim?'

Anna grinned. 'What, like this?'

'It would be nice, wouldn't it? But no. I don't think they'd take kindly to us running through the hotel in the nude, do you?'

She shrugged. 'Spoilsport. I don't think anyone would care.'

'Well . . .' He rolled over and stood, then walked over to the french windows and stepped out on to the balcony. She joined him there a moment later. It was warm, a crescent moon throwing its light across the scene. Michael put his arm about her shoulders and pulled her close.

'It's beautiful, isn't it?'

They had a view of the marina some eight floors below. Many of the yachts still had their lights on and there were people out on deck, partying into the morning. They heard the chink of a bottle against a glass and laughter.

'Imagine living like this for ever,' Michael said.

Anna sighed. It was lovely, but . . . 'It would bore me,' she said truthfully.

'Bore you?' He seemed astonished. 'How could you be bored? I mean, you could fish, swim, travel about. I'd love a yacht. Christ, I'd take a whole year off and sail the islands!'

'And what about me?'

He looked down at her and grinned. 'You'd be with me. You could be my cabin girl.'

'Oh, thanks a lot! Doing the cooking and washing, no doubt!'

'The washing, yes . . .'

She gave him a little punch in the side.

'Ouch! The idea doesn't grab you, then?'

'For a month, maybe. Any longer and I'd go doolally. I have to work, Michael. It's how I am.'

'Pity . . .'

Anna looked down. Was this the moment? Certainly she had never felt more natural with him. And Michael . . . Michael seemed to have relaxed for the first time since she'd known him. Oh, he always enjoyed himself, but tonight . . . well, tonight it was as if he'd opened up. As if whatever had happened to him in his past — that thing that made him so cautious about commitment — had suddenly ceased to hold him.

'Michael . . .'

'Yes?'

'Michael, what if I said I wanted something from you? Something . . . well, something really important.'

He stared out into the night, smiling. 'Well, first of all I'd ask, can I afford it? And if the answer to that were yes, then it'd be yours. Why, what do you want?'

She hesitated, her mouth dry, then asked. 'I'd like a child, Michael. Your child.'

He was silent. Very silent. His arm still lay across her shoulder, but suddenly it was as if he wasn't holding her. It lay there passively against her flesh, still warm, the same as it had been a moment before, but now she could feel a difference in the way it pressed against the top of her back.

Michael let out a long, weary breath. 'Anna, I . . .'

His arm slid away. He turned, facing her, his back to the landscape — to the marina and the trees and the sea beyond. His eyes met hers, an expression of sadness in them, of regret that she had ever raised the subject. Suddenly Anna wished that she was dressed; their very nakedness seemed somehow wrong now.

'Don't spoil it, Anna.'

'Spoil it? But . . .'

He put a finger to her lips. His touch was gentle, yet it was also quite brutal.

'*Don't*. It's been such a perfect evening.'

She made to speak again, then fell silent, her head going down, the disappointment she felt showing clearly in her face.

How could it spoil things? *How*?

Michael reached out and held her, his hands resting lightly on her hips, but the magic of his touch had gone now. Her words had killed it. A little shudder went through her and she realised she was going to cry. She had been so sure . . .

'Anna, I . . .'

She turned away abruptly, making her way quickly to the bathroom where she closed the door and bolted it behind her.

There, slumped down on the floor, her back against the cold tiles of the wall, Anna let the disappointment wash from her in a flood of tears, while outside the man she'd hoped would be the father of her child stood naked at the balcony, looking out into the Caribbean night, a sigh of exasperation escaping him.

A perfect evening . . .

Anna spent the night on the huge sofa in the living room. Sleep was fitful, yet she woke early, even as the dawn broke, her mind clear, knowing what she had to do.

Michael too had clearly not slept well, for she heard him almost at once, moving about inside the bathroom, running the water to wash, then shaving, the buzz of the shaver drifting out to where she lay.

She closed her eyes, pained by her memories of the night. It had begun so well, so promisingly, and then . . .

She let her breathing calm.

What was wrong with her wanting his child? Didn't he love her?

Clearly not.

She sighed, and even as she did, the door linking the rooms slid open. She opened her eyes and turned, seeing him in the doorway.

He stood there, naked but for his boxers, looking at her. 'Anna, I . . .' He shrugged. 'I don't know what to say. I thought . . .'

'Right! Girls just wanna have fun, eh?'

He was silent a moment, then he nodded. 'Yes. I guess that's it. I got it wrong, didn't I? I didn't realise you had a plan.'

She sat up, facing him. 'A *plan*? You make it sound so . . . *calculated*!'

'Wasn't it?'

'No . . . no, I . . .' She took a long breath, trying to control herself. 'You don't know much about women, do you, Michael?'

'If you say so.'

It was such a *weak* thing to say. She glared at him. 'You arsehole!'

'*What*?' He stared at her uncomprehendingly. 'Let me get this straight. You spring this baby stuff on me, and I'm supposed to . . . to *what*? To just go along with it? To see my whole life transformed just because of some *whim* of yours? It's a big thing, Anna. A huge fucking big thing!'

'D'you think I don't know that?'

'Then what *was* that crap?'

She stared at him, understanding in that instant that she had made a huge mistake. She saw herself suddenly as one of a long line of Michael's conquests. Part of his mysterious past. But beyond that she was nothing.

'Do you love me, Michael?'

'Do I *what*?'

'It's just that I thought . . .' She laughed. A pained, awful laugh.

Oh God, she thought, how could I have read the signs so wrong?

'Anna?'

She stood, then walked across. It was as if she did not exist. Slowly, methodically, she took the clothes she was to wear from her case and pulled them on, then repacked her two cases, knowing he was watching her all the while.

Only when the cases were closed and locked did she turn to him again. 'You'll never know what you missed, will you, Michael?'

But he said nothing; simply stared.

She turned away. 'I'm going home.'

'Don't be silly, Anna.'

'No. I'm going home. You stay if you want. It's all paid for.'

'Anna, you don't have to do this. We had a good thing going. We were *good* together.'

'No.' She smiled bleakly. 'It was just surfaces, Michael. Skin-to-skin stuff. Anything deeper . . .'

Anna grimaced. She had really cared for him. She had really pinned her hopes on him.

'I'm sorry,' he said quietly.

'Yeah, well . . .'

'At least let me carry your cases.'

'Like that?'

He looked down, realising he was wearing only his boxers, then looked back at her, sighing.

'Shit, Anna, what went wrong?'

Chapel Market that Wednesday lunchtime was packed with shoppers and, steering the heavily laden pushchair through that throng, Susie began to wish, as she so often did these days, that she'd won the lottery and was one of those rich bitches who could afford to hire help to do this kind of thing. As it was, she had to do the lot: shop, cook and look after Nathan, not to mention cleaning the house and doing the washing! From one handle of the buggy hung a super-size plastic bag of Pampers, while from the other hung a Boots plastic bag containing endless jars of juice and baby mush.

Nathan himself was asleep in the buggy, spark out with his little head to one side and his mouth wide open – fly-catching, as Jo liked to call it.

The thought of Jo put a worried frown on Susie's face. Things still weren't good, and though they had patched things up, a state of an uneasy truce still existed between them.

Jo had come home straight from work every night since the 'incident', and she, for her part, hadn't said another thing about that tart he'd been with, but . . .

Susie pushed the buggy on aggressively, just missing some bloke's leg by a fraction. Trouble was, Jo thought only about himself. He didn't give a monkey's for *her* problems. He thought because he brought home the pay cheque he was the only one who worked, but he was a lazy bastard when it came down to it. He didn't do a sodding thing about the house.

And the more she thought about things, the more angry she got.

The crowd thinned and she found herself out in Liverpool Road, the Angel just to her right. Susie looked right, then left, then hurried across the road, struggling to get the buggy up on to the pavement. Turning left into Upper Street, she glanced about her, wondering what she had forgotten – for she always forgot something when she went shopping – then, on whim, decided she would pay a visit to Body Shop. It would do her good to spoil herself for once.

It was coming out of there – a new lipstick and mascara

in her bag — that she ran bang into another buggy, and behind it . . .

'Gus!'

Gus had been about to yell at her to be careful, but seeing who it was, his face lit up in a huge beam of a smile. 'Susie! Hi! How are you?'

'I, er . . .' Susie looked down, embarrassed. She had had a dream about Gus the other night, and running into him reminded her of it. She blushed. 'Hi . . .'

'He's coming on, isn't he?' Gus said, referring to the sleeping Nathan. 'You can tell he's going to be a real lady's man.'

Susie looked up at that, then smiled. Like all women, she was a sucker for compliments to her child.

'He's like his dad.' Then, realising just what she'd said, and hoping it wasn't altogether true, she quickly repaid the compliment.

'Katrina's grown.'

Katrina, five months Nathan's elder, was also fast asleep.

'Yeah . . . yeah, it's my week with her.'

Susie frowned, not understanding.

'Oh, we've split up, Pat and I . . . a month or two back, actually. We . . .' He sighed, then. 'Look, Susie, can we talk? I . . .'

Susie looked down hurriedly. 'I should be getting back . . .'

'Yeah, but . . .' He put out his hand then drew it back before he touched her. 'Well, how about a quick drink? While the kids are asleep.'

A little shiver went through Susie. She hesitated.

'Just one,' he coaxed. 'I can't stay long either.'

'OK . . .' she said. 'A quickie.'

'Sure. Then I'll let you go.'

'Well?' Susie asked, as Gus sat down and handed her across her drink. 'What happened?'

The two children were still fast asleep in their buggies, side by side next to the narrow table.

'I told her about us.'

Susie had been about to sip her drink. Now her head jerked up. 'You *what*?'

'I told her everything. About how I made a pass at you that time and how I made a fool of myself and—'

'But nothing *happened*.'

He was staring at her now. 'Didn't it?' Gus sighed. 'Well, it did for me. I think I fell in love with you.'

Susie stared down at her drink a moment, stunned. Then, pushing it away from her, she stood. 'Look, I'd better go. This—'

Gus reached out and took her hand. 'Susie . . . I . . . look, I don't want to make things difficult for you. Believe me. I want what's best for you. But I felt you should know.'

Slowly, so as not to offend him, she withdrew her hand. Then, 'Sorry, Gus, but I . . .'

He had taken out a pad and, even as she spoke, began to write down his address and telephone number. A new address, she realised. Looking up at her, he handed it across. 'Here. If you change your mind and want to talk.'

Susie swallowed, then, afraid to say another word, she edged past him and, slipping off the brake, began to wheel the pushchair out down the narrow aisle between the tables. Yet even as she made her way along, she was conscious of Gus's eyes on her, and felt a warm flush colour her neck and cheeks.

Outside she paused, getting her breath. Christ! That was all she bloody needed! She glanced at the piece of paper in her hand and went to crunch it up and throw it away, then, changing her mind, tucked it into her pocket.

In love . . . how could he be in love with her, the bloody idiot!

But the thought of it was like a fly buzzing in a silent room, distracting her, and as she hurried along the busy street, she kept remembering what it had felt like to have his arms about her, his hands caressing her breasts.

'Come on,' Mandy cajoled, '*tell* us! It can't be *such* a big secret!'

It was halfway through the evening and Karen and Anna had got into a conversation in the kitchen. Mandy had joined them there, all ears.

'Mand . . .' Karen pleaded, sensing Anna's embarrassment. 'Leave it.'

Anna shrugged, then picked up the tray of nibbles. 'It's not a big deal, Mand, really.'

'Nah, it looks like it.' Mandy made a face. 'Still, if you can't trust your friends . . .'

They went through, into the living room, where Susie and Janet were sitting, chatting.

'I mean,' Mandy went on, 'I tell *you* everything, don't I? All the gory little details . . .'

'Look, if you *must* know,' Anna said, putting the tray down and turning to her, 'we were talking about me having a baby. There! Happy now?'

Mandy put a hand to her mouth. 'You don't mean . . .'

'No. I *don't* mean. I was talking about *getting* pregnant, not *being* pregnant.'

Janet and Susie both looked up, Janet with a broad smile on her face. 'Well, I think it's a *great* idea.'

'Yeah,' Susie agreed, a slight confusion in her face, 'but don't you need a fella first?'

Karen and Janet exchanged troubled looks. A week and a half had passed since Anna had returned from the Bahamas, and all of them knew that things hadn't worked out with Michael. But tonight they had steered well clear of the subject, because tonight was Anna's night – an informal celebration of her fortieth birthday. Anna, however, didn't seem too put out by the remark.

'I used to think like that, but maybe I was wrong. Maybe I just can't have the whole package.'

'What d'you mean?' Mandy asked, taking a handful of peanuts and perching on the arm of the sofa.

'I mean, maybe I should forget about finding a father for my child. Maybe I should just *have* it.'

'What?' Mandy laughed. 'You and the Virgin Mary, you mean?'

'I don't think Anna means that,' Janet interposed. 'And I don't think she's talking about artificial insemination, either!'

Susie and Mandy both looked to Anna, astonished. Anna herself looked down, a faint flush at her neck. 'Well, it isn't as if I'll be looking to him to support the baby. Just provide the sperm.'

'You're *serious*, ain't you?' Susie said.

Anna met her eyes, then nodded, the smallest smile creeping into the corners of her mouth.

'Well, good luck to you, Annie!' Mandy said. 'Mind you, I wouldn't want to be starting a family again at my age.'

'Well, thanks Mand, *there's* encouragement!' Janet said. She turned awkwardly and smiled at Anna. 'No, I think it's a wonderful idea. We'd all have little 'uns together . . . you thought of that?'

Anna hadn't, but it wasn't such an awful idea. After all, she might only have a chance at one child, and it would be nice if she – or he – had some ready-made friends.

'So who's the lucky fella?' Mandy asked. 'Or haven't you met him yet?'

Anna glanced at Karen, then shrugged. 'I don't know. I haven't really decided yet.'

'But you must have *some* idea . . .'

'Mand,' Karen said, exasperated by her friend. 'Leave the poor girl alone!'

'No, it's OK,' Anna said, gesturing to Karen to pass the wine bottle across. 'But it's true. I haven't really considered that aspect of things. I have done *one* thing, however . . .'

Anna looked about her, as the others gazed at her, curiosity burning in every face.

'I stopped . . .'

'Stopped?'

'You know. Taking the pill.'

'So you *are* serious,' Susie said. 'But what if the fella insists on using condoms?'

'How many blokes do you know who *insist* on wearing a rubber?' Mandy said and reached for her wineglass.

'Yes, but that's not what I meant . . .' Susie tilted her head slightly sideways, as she always did when a difficult matter came up. 'What I mean is . . . some fellas are wise to that kind of thing these days, what with that Child Support Agency and all. They don't want to be lumbered paying for some kid for the rest of their life. So . . . well, how are you gonna pull it off, so to speak?'

'What? Make sure he *comes* inside me?'

'Oh, delicately put!' Janet said, sitting up straight.

'Well . . . I've got to be practical,' Anna said. She smiled. 'You see, I don't want to be too calculating about it, but—'

'Why not?' Karen butted in.

All four of them looked to her.

'Well,' she went on, 'it's not as if you want any old baby, is it? If you're going to have a child, it might as well be the best child you can have. And that means choosing the father carefully.'

Mandy shuddered. 'I dunno. It all seems a bit too *deliberate* for me.'

'No, but she's right,' Janet said. 'I mean, it's different for me and Susie. We've got men we love, and our babies are an expression of that love. But if there's no one special . . .'

Susie looked down, making no comment.

'Well what about that guy you used to see,' Mandy said, gesturing towards Anna with her glass. 'What was his name? Frank.'

'The one I told to fuck off? Yeah?'

'Yeah,' Karen said, 'but he did turn up on your doorstep, didn't he?'

'Did he?' Janet said, and she, Mandy and Susie all looked to Anna for further enlightenment. This was something they hadn't heard about.'

'It was nothing,' Anna said. 'He'd left his wife, that was all, and . . .'

'Well, there you go!' Mandy said. 'Unless he's gone back to her, he'll be desperate for a shag. And I thought you said he made you laugh.'

Susie looked to her, raising her eyebrows. 'That ain't exactly the kind of thing Anna'd be looking for . . .'

But Karen interrupted her. 'No, no . . . Mandy's right. Frank would be a great choice. He's intelligent, healthy . . .'

'And not bad-looking . . .' Mandy chipped in.

'Hmm . . .' Anna said dubiously. 'I don't know. Besides, I as good as told him to fuck off a second time. I made him sleep on the sofa and slung him out in the morning.'

'Yeah, but the fact he turned up shows he was willing.'

Susie snorted. 'I've never met a man yet who wasn't *willing*.'

'You know what I think?' Janet said. 'I think you ought to advertise.'

'Oh, yeah,' Mandy said. 'I can just see it. Wanted: Prime-Quality Sperm.'

Susie giggled. 'I can see the T-shirt now! It'd be all the rage in the clubs!'

'Leave off!' Anna said, grinning.

'Well, why don't you make a list?' Janet said. 'You know . . . of the men you know.'

'Jan . . .'

'No, Jan's right,' Mandy said. 'You could work your way through them one at a time!'

'Mand . . .'

'You could have 'em queuing up, couldn't you? I tell you, I'd come to the audition. In fact, if you need any help, I could be your official taster.'

Anna giggled into her glass. 'Oh, so you get the cream and I get the dregs? Yeah, thanks, Mand!'

Karen stood up and, picking up one of the bottles they had opened earlier, began to go round, topping up their glasses. 'Well, I still think Frank's your best bet.'

'I'm not sure . . .' Anna said, making a face.

'That's not what you used to say.'

'Yes, but . . .'

'Well, personally, I'd have come off the pill months back,' Mandy said. 'You should have got yourself pregnant, *then* told him . . .'

Anna looked down, while the others glared at Mandy.

'*What?*' she mouthed.

'You're probably right,' Anna said. 'But Michael's not an option. Not any more.'

'Sorry . . .' Mandy smiled apologetically. 'It's just that sometimes blokes react differently once it's a fact. I don't s'pose there's many that'd want one, given the choice!'

'Well, Steve did!' Janet said indignantly.

'Yeah, but that's Steve!'

Janet smiled, knowing how lucky she was.

'Well, if it was up to me,' Karen began, and all four of

the others burst out laughing. '*What?*' Karen said, looking about her, a look of bewilderment on her face. 'What did I say?'

'Yeah, let's listen,' Mandy said, wiping a tear from her cheek, 'this'll be interesting . . .'

'Yeah,' Susie said. 'You would know what you were looking for, wouldn't you, Kar? A bit hairy, with one of those big purply veiny things!'

Karen smiled. 'Well I didn't actually mean . . . *me*.'

'Yeah, but it's a thought, though, ain't it?' Janet said. 'I mean . . . just 'cos you're gay, Kar, doesn't mean you mightn't want to have a baby, does it?'

'Oh, leave her alone,' Anna said, going across and putting her arm about Karen's shoulders. 'Anyway, we're talking about me and my dilemma. It's *me* who's forty and it's *me* who's . . .'

'Desperate!'

Anna poked her tongue out at Susie.

'What about the bloke downstairs,' Janet suggested. 'Be handy for baby-sitting an' all.'

'*Gerry!*' Anna shrieked, appalled by the suggestion. 'Have you seen him? I'd have to get a hoist put up just to get him on the bed. He's about eighty!'

'Yeah, but you know what they say,' Susie offered. 'There might be snow on the roof, but there's a fire in the grate!'

The others roared, but Anna merely shook her head. 'In Gerry's case there's nothing on the roof. He's as bald as a badger . . .'

Mandy grinned as she raised her eyebrows. 'Something to slide around on.'

'Mandy!' Janet was holding her belly as she laughed.

'And I shouldn't think there's much in the grate other than cold ashes!'

'Ah, bless 'im,' Mandy cooed, her face all sympathy.

'Mandy! He's eighty. It's all over by the time you're that age.' Janet was practicality itself.

Mandy slowly shook her head. 'I can't imagine it.'

'Yeah, but that's because you're on overdrive, ain't it?' Susie said. 'You'll burn yourself out.' She laughed at a sudden thought. ''Ere . . . d'you remember that woman, years ago, who won the football pools. She suddenly had money after being hard up all her life and she couldn't cope. They made a film about her – *Spend, Spend, Spend.* Well, that's you, Mand, only in your case it's *Shag, Shag, Shag.*'

The girls hooted with laughter as Mandy threw a cushion across the room at Susie. Then Janet farted loudly and set them all off again.

'Yes, well, thank you for all your invaluable advice,' Anna said sarcastically. 'I'll keep you informed of any developments.'

Karen reached across and squeezed her hand.

'Good luck to you, that's what I say!' Mandy said. 'Here,' she added, looking about her, 'let's have a toast. To Anna . . . and to her search for super sperm!'

'To Anna . . . and super sperm!'

Doreen opened the door, her face breaking into a grin as she saw who it was.

'Oh, hello, Suse. You didn't say you were coming round.'

Susie edged the pushchair past her, then turned. 'Can you do us a favour, Mum? Could you look after Nathan for an hour?'

'Yeah, sure. Why, what's up?'

'There's just something I've gotta do. If Jo phones, tell him I'm in the bath and that I'll phone him back.'

Doreen narrowed her eyes suspiciously. 'Suse?'

'Look, it's nothing. Just something I'm trying to arrange for his birthday, that's all. I want it to be a surprise.'

Doreen's face cleared. 'Oh . . . OK, love.' She bent over the pushchair, beginning to unfasten Nathan's straps. 'And how's my handsome boy, then? Nan's got something special for you . . .'

'Thanks, Mum,' Susie said, watching them a moment. 'I'll be as quick as I can.'

'All right,' Doreen said, not even looking at her. 'You shoot off. We'll be OK.'

Susie stopped, her left hand resting lightly on the iron railing as she stared down the lamplit terraced street towards the house. Her heart was beating fast, and her breath steamed in the cold early-evening air. She didn't have to look at the piece of paper; even so, she slipped her right hand into her pocket to touch it, as if to remind herself why she was there.

In the old days she wouldn't have stopped for a second to think about what she was doing. But things were different now. More complicated. Now she had Nathan to think of . . . and Jo.

Susie looked down. In a sense, Jo was the reason she had come. If he'd only tried, she'd have been at home right now. But he hadn't.

The bitterness she felt made her pull her coat tighter about her and walk on, her high heels clicking on the pavement. Glancing to either side, she quickly crossed the road, then stopped, seeing the big, three-storey house just ahead. The light was on in the hallway, and in one of the rooms on the first floor.

Susie walked on, stopping before the door. There was an intercom at eye level on the wall to her right. Labels beside the three buttons gave the owners' names. Gus's was in the middle.

She pressed it, then, after a moment, pressed again.

There was a hissing and then a scratchy voice said, 'Who is it?'

'It's me,' she said, hoping he didn't have company. 'Susie.'

There was a pause, then. 'I'll be down.'

Susie turned away, looking back down the street, embarrassed suddenly. What if someone saw her? But the street was empty.

She turned back, waiting as a shadow appeared behind the glass panels of the door.

The door swung open, and Gus stood there, in a pair of scruffy jeans and a T-shirt.

'Susie, I . . .'

She stepped past him hurriedly, then turned as he closed the door. He looked at her, then stepped across.

'I can't stay long,' she said quickly, before her nerve failed her. 'Mum's got the baby for an hour. I . . .'

Reaching out, he took her in his arms and drew her close, kissing her. At first she held back a little, then, with a little shudder, let go, her hands moving up until they held his shoulders.

As they broke from the kiss, he stared at her, his eyes wide with surprise. 'I didn't think—'

'An hour,' she said. 'That's all we have.'

His flat was remarkably neat and tidy, the bedroom tiny.

Susie stood there, looking about her. The room's walls were bare. A single wardrobe stood against the right-hand wall, while on a tiny bedside table stood an alarm clock and a picture of Katrina.

Gus's life had shrunk to this. And all because of her.

She shivered and turned. Gus was in the kitchen, opening a bottle of wine. That, too, was so like him. Another man would have gone straight for it, but not Gus. In fact, now that she thought of it, it was amazing he had ever made that pass.

Susie closed her eyes. She had not yet even taken off her coat. If she turned now and walked out of the door, everything would be OK. She had come here, true, but she had yet to do anything.

'Here,' Gus said, coming alongside and offering her a glass.

'Thanks . . .'

She took it, feeling awkward suddenly. Where did they go from here?

If he had taken her and fucked her in the hallway, it might have been OK . . . but then, these *were* flats and who knew who might come in?

She almost laughed. It would not have stopped her in the past.

Gus smiled, noting her amusement. 'What is it?'

'Nothing. I was just . . .'

She realised that she couldn't tell him. Her past — her awful, sordid past — was as alien to him as anything could be. He could not imagine who she was, or what she had been. How could he be in love with her? He didn't even know her.

She stared down into her glass. Jo, on the other hand, understood what she was. He *knew* her. He had seen those photos of her Max had taken. And she knew him. Even his weaknesses.

A tiny tremor went through her.

Gus reached out and took her hand.

'Gus, I . . .'

'Don't say anything, just—'

'No. No, it's . . .' She looked up, tears in her eyes suddenly. This was a mistake. And though she was going to hurt him, it was better that she did it now than later.

'I've got to go,' she said, squeezing his hand.

'Why?'

'I shouldn't have come. I . . .'

The look of pain in his eyes was awful, but it wasn't her fault. He shouldn't have fallen in love with her. And what kind of idiot told his wife when there was no cause?

She turned and hurried out, setting the glass down on the side as she went.

Outside she stopped, then turned, looking back. She was sorry. Very sorry. But she was not responsible for Gus. Jo was her husband, her man, her lover, and she knew that she wanted him back.

Susie shivered, then, pulling her coat tighter about her, walked on.

Jo was waiting for her when she got in. As she pushed Nathan's pram through into the kitchen, she saw that he had bought her flowers.

'Suse?'

Nathan had fallen asleep on the way home. Clicking the pushchair's brake on with her foot, Susie smiled at him, then turned to look at Jo.

Jo was sitting there at the kitchen table, still in his suit, his loosened tie the only sign that he maybe wasn't going out again.

That and the flowers.

'They for me?'

'Yeah . . .' His smile was uncertain. They had barely spoken the last few days and it seemed an age since he had touched her. 'Look, Suse, I'm sorry. I've been behaving like a pig.'

She almost said yes — almost started on him again — but checked herself just in time. This was not the time to fight old battles. If they were going to start again, this was the time to do it.

Susie picked up the flowers and lifted them to her face,

drinking in the sweet fragrance. They were lilies. Her favourite. Looking to Jo, she smiled. 'They're lovely.'

Jo stood, awkward still, like it was difficult to take the next step.

Susie put the flowers down, then stepped across to him. 'We've made a real soddin' mess of this, ain't we?'

Jo stared back at her, his eyes moist now, and nodded. 'Suse . . . I don't wanna lose you. But I need you to help me. What have I got to do?'

Susie smiled, touched by the tears that were forming in his eyes. 'Just hold me,' she said, burying her face into his neck. 'Just hold me like you used to hold me.'

Part Six

Two and a half months later

Janet lay on her back on the bed, the swollen hump of her belly exposed as the doctor smeared on the special jelly. Beside her, Steve stared past her at the small black-and-white screen of the ultrasound scanner, waiting for something to appear.

She was well over six months on now, and while the baby had been kicking a lot recently, seeing it on the scanner always made it seem more real for them. It was only six weeks since the last scan, but they were hoping to see real changes in their baby – signs of growth. This would be the last scan before it was due and they wanted reassurance that everything was all right.

As the doctor reached for the transducer, Janet gritted her teeth, not because it hurt – you hardly felt a thing as it slid across your flesh – but because she wanted to pee. As instructed, she hadn't been for at least two hours before the scan and now the pressure on her bladder was quite painful.

'Look, Jan!' Steve said excitedly, as the chaos on the tiny screen resolved itself into the outline of their baby. 'Look! God, hasn't he got big!'

They didn't know it was a boy, but Steve tended to assume as much when he got excited. Watching the screen, Janet grinned like her head would split in two, as the doctor pushed the transducer this way and that to identify first a little arm and hand — the fingers perfectly formed — and then the chest with the tiny heart beating away for all it was worth.

Seeing that, Janet felt her own heart beat furiously. Already she loved this child. Even without seeing its face, she knew it would be the most beautiful thing she'd ever seen.

After the last session, she had confessed to Steve that she would rather watch that tiny screen all day than a feast of the best TV. To see that little miracle of theirs moving about inside her filled her not just with joy but with real euphoria.

This was their reward for being patient. For persisting.

Janet looked to Steve and squeezed his hand, then looked back at the screen as the doctor took his measurements.

'Well,' he said, leaving the transducer where it was for a moment. 'Baby's coming along just fine. Twenty-eight weeks, aren't you?'

'Just,' Janet said.

'Right. Well, that checks out perfectly. And as far as I can see there appear to be no problems whatsoever. Your child looks perfectly formed, I'm pleased to say.'

'You hear that, Jan?' Steve said, as if she'd suddenly gone deaf. But she didn't mind. She loved the way he got excited over such things.

'Do you want a couple of prints before I finish?' the doctor asked, looking to Janet, then to Steve.

'Yeah, that'd be great,' Steve said, grinning once more. He had several in his wallet already.

'Right, well I'll just do those, and then we can clean you up and get you home.'

Janet smiled at him. 'Take your time. We're in no hurry.'

Steve had parked the car up near Regents Park and they decided to have a little walk before they went back. It was a beautiful afternoon and though it was only the second week in May, already it felt like summer.

They bought ice cream from a van parked beside the road then sat on a bench by the boating lake, watching young couples walk slowly, arm in arm, along the path. For a time they were silent, enjoying the day; then Janet turned slightly.

'Steve?'

'Yeah?'

'I think it's safe now.'

'Safe?'

'You know . . . to decorate the baby's room.'

'Yeah?' He looked at her uncertainly. Up until now they had refrained from doing anything, buying anything, just in case it felt like tempting fate. But after this morning Janet felt confident at last. She'd seen how strong its little heart was, and the very fact that the doctor had taken her off the high-risk category was encouraging to say the least.

'Yeah,' she said, after a moment. 'In fact, we could stop on the way back. You know, get some paint and paper and—'

'Jan?'

'Yeah?'

Steve leaned across and kissed her; a slobbery ice-creamy kiss.

'Eeyuk! Get off!' But she was laughing now. 'Well? What do you think?'

Steve considered a moment, then, enthused by the idea, nodded emphatically. 'All right. I could do it over the weekend. But I'll need some new brushes, and I'm not sure that that primer we bought when we did the kitchen's still OK, but—'

'Steve?' He stopped, then turned, looking at her again. 'I love you.'

* * *

Anna sat at her mother's bedside as the doctor clicked his case shut and looked across at her.

'Are you OK?' he asked. 'Would you like me to prescribe something?' Anna shook her head. 'If you change your mind . . .'

'Thanks,' she said gratefully. Then, because it seemed strange not to be doing something, she asked, 'Is there anything I've got to do?'

He considered, then. 'No . . . I think your aunt's dealing with the arrangements.'

'Right . . .'

When he was gone, Anna looked back at her mother. She was so peaceful now you could almost imagine she was sleeping. Except that she was no longer making that awful noise – that bronchial rattle that she had read about in old novels and never thought to hear.

Reaching out, Anna drew back the strand of grey hair that had slipped out of place as the doctor had examined her.

The flesh of her brow was still warm.

For a moment Anna let her hand rest there. This death was for the best. Her mother had suffered awfully these last few weeks, but now she was at rest.

Anna understood that now. Knew now how death could be preferable to life. And that struggle had taken its physical toll on her mother. But now she *looked* peaceful. That awful pained weariness had gone from her features. Even so . . .

Anna felt numb. All of the grief she ought to have been feeling wouldn't come. It was as if something was shutting it out. Instead what she felt was fear. A fear of being alone in the world.

Her mother had loved her, whatever she had done. Had been proud of her achievements, small and large. And now she was gone, and that love and that pride had gone with her.

Oh, there was her aunt, yet her aunt was childless. A

road not taken. And she herself, was she to end that way? Childless. One of nature's cul-de-sacs.

If so then the killing of her child – that awful termination of the baby she had carried briefly – took on an even greater significance.

She had thought of it often recently, and each time she did it grew clearer to her just how huge a mistake it had been not to have that child. It would have been – what? – two by now, and whether Callum had stayed with her or not, at least she would have had that, whereas right now she had nothing.

The road lay straight and bare before her. And it led nowhere.

Unless . . .

Anna sighed, then stood, walking over to the window and looking out. She had been off the pill almost four months now, but in all that time she had done nothing to further that scheme she'd hatched. Instead, and perhaps for the first time in her life, she had become quite celibate. Nor had she really missed the sex – though sometimes the thought of it had kept her awake long into the night. No, what troubled her was something Mandy had said that night of her fortieth – something about the *deliberateness* of the act.

She hadn't commented at the time, but it was how she herself felt about it. To use a man and then discard him, just to have a baby, seemed somehow wrong. Calculating. And she didn't want to be thought of as calculating, even if – to get what she wanted – it was a necessity. And so she had waited, hoping that Fate would intervene and send a man her way. But Fate was a stubborn bastard. Or simply malicious, perhaps. She even thought of advertising again, and leaving it all to chance, but then what Karen had said would come to mind – about how she ought to have the best baby she could, and how that meant she ought to choose the best man she could to have it by.

And then, of course, there'd been her mother's illness.

That, more than anything, had kept her from thinking about her own problems. For weeks now she had come every night to sit with her mother, talking quietly to her or reading the poetry that she so loved. And now that was done with, and she could go back to the business of living.

Anna turned slightly, looking at the figure on the bed then spoke quietly. 'So it's me now, is it?'

She walked across, stopping to look at the wedding picture on the wall. Then, knowing there was nothing more for her to do here, she left the room and went downstairs.

Aunt Charlotte was sitting in the kitchen, a pot of tea before her. She had poured two cups, and as Anna came into the room, she pushed one of them towards her.

'Thanks . . .'

Anna sat, finding herself wordless for once. What did you say when your mother had just died?

'It's all taken care of,' Charlotte said, looking down at her tea. 'They'll come and take her later on.'

'Oh . . .' She hadn't thought. 'I guess that's . . . usual?'

Her aunt nodded. 'The funeral's Friday. I'll let every-one know.'

'Right . . . er . . . thanks.'

'It's for the best, Anna,' her aunt said after a moment. 'The poor love was suffering so much.'

'Yes . . .' And Anna smiled. A smile that broke. And suddenly, unexpectedly, she was crying.

Charlotte stood and came round the table, then crouched beside her, holding her, her own tears flowing freely down her face.

'There, there,' the older woman said, as if to a child. 'There, there . . .'

* * *

She phoned Frank from the office. He was surprised to hear from her, but delighted. He wanted to see her straight away – that evening – but then she told him about her mother and he grew quiet.

'I'm sorry, Anna,' he said, all sympathy suddenly. 'I know she meant a lot to you.'

In the end, they arranged to meet for lunch on Thursday. Yet even as she put the phone down, she burst into tears again. Jacqui, seeing her through the glass window of the office, came in after a moment with a box of tissues.

'Are you OK, Anna? I mean . . . if you want to go home I'll cover . . .'

Anna shook her head. 'No . . . it'll do me good to be here. Stop me thinking too much about it.'

'Well, if it gets too much . . .' And, smiling sweetly, Jacqui left her.

Strange, Anna thought, turning in her swivel chair to look out over the London skyline. Why is it you never understand how much you need someone until they're gone from your life?

It was like some perverse law of nature.

And now Frank. Did she need Frank? And could she go through with this with him – this genetic hijack – and not tell him what she was doing, or why she had bothered to contact him again. It seemed cruel. But maybe cruelty was the only answer to her predicament.

She let out a long, long breath, then turned back to her desk.

'Work,' she told herself, reaching out to take the first of the files from her in-tray. 'Distract your bloody self, woman!'

But her mind was elsewhere. Was standing in a quiet room, staring at a wedding photo on a wall, while behind her the woman in the photo lay dead, her story told.

*   *   *

Mandy had barely pulled off her coat and switched the kettle on when the doorbell rang. Smiling, she went back out and opened the door, standing back as Susie pushed past her with the pram.

'Hi, Suse! Thanks for coming round. Just that I've been getting meself in a bit of a stew about the arrangements.'

'S'all right,' Susie answered, slipping off her jacket, then giving Mandy a quick peck.

'And how's my little monkey?' Mandy asked, bending down to grin at Nathan. He was eleven months now and almost walking. Grinning back at Mandy, he reached up to her, and, old softie that she was, she undid his straps and picked him up, cuddling him to her as she walked through to the living room.

'I can't stay long,' Susie said, following her in. 'Me and Jo are goin' out tonight.'

Mandy, who had sat with Nathan in the middle of the carpet, looked up at her. 'Anywhere nice?'

'Not really. We're just going up the pub for a few hours. But it's good just to get out. Bit like being on a date. Jo loves it.'

Mandy smiled, pleased that things were finally working out for them.

Susie watched her a moment, then, hearing the kettle click, made towards the kitchen. Mandy went to get up.

'No, Mand, you stay where you are. I'll make the tea.'

As she pottered about in the kitchen, getting down cups and taking the milk from the fridge, they continued their conversation, their voices raised to carry across the hallway.

'So what's the problem, Mand?'

'Well, I thought I had the minibus booked, but the bloody company's gone bust, ain't it? And what with it being only six weeks away, I was worried we might not find another one.'

'Have you phoned any other companies yet?'

'One or two, but they've got nothing. I just wondered if you knew anyone. Or whether Jo might know someone. I mean, there's lots from round here who go, ain't there, so it might be hard finding someone to take us.'

Susie plumped two teabags down into the pot, then poured the boiling water in. 'Nah . . . we'll be all right. We'll have a cup of tea and a chat, then I'll make a few calls.'

Methodically, Susie laid out the tea things on a tray, then carried them through, putting them up on the sideboard where Nathan couldn't get to them and pull them down on top of him. He was crawling everywhere these days, yes, and climbing up on things. She'd learned to her cost not to put treasured nick-nacks where he could get at them, and they'd already had to have the video repaired where Nathan had systematically stuffed a dozen plastic farm animals into the cassette slot.

As she turned, she saw how Mandy was gazing at Nathan fondly, and smiled. 'Won't be long before you've got one of your own to play with.'

'*What?*' Mandy turned, a moment's shock in her face; then she understood what Susie was saying. 'Oh . . . yeah,' she said proudly. 'Not long now. Late July, Gemma reckons. Same time as Janet's.'

'Jason must be getting excited.'

'Yeah, well . . . he don't know what's gonna hit him, does he?'

Susie nodded sagely, then turned away, pouring Mandy a cup, which she placed high up on the mantelpiece. 'So how's things apart from that? How's that fella you were seeing? Fireman Sam?'

Mandy grinned, wagging her finger at Susie. 'I don't want no greasy-pole jokes, thanks very much. I have enough of that lot at work taking the piss.'

Susie laughed. Picking up her own tea, she raised it to her lips. 'So,' she said, looking down at Mandy over the rim of the cup, 'has he let you try his helmet on yet?'

Mandy picked up the small cuddly pig Nathan had dropped and threw it at Susie, who was now giggling helplessly.

'Sorry, sorry,' she was saying, bending down to pick up the soft pink toy, dropping it on the sofa and flopping down beside it. 'No, seriously. How's it going?'

Mandy's face broke into a grin. 'Yeah,' she said thoughtfully. 'It's nice.'

'What's that s'posed to mean?'

Mandy gave a little shrug of her shoulders. 'Well, we just get on. You know. We talk to one another . . .'

'That makes a change!'

'Yeah, it does,' Mandy said, nodding. 'I'd be the first to admit it. I think it's 'cos we've got a lot in common. He's got three kids, although his are a bit younger than mine. And he split up from his wife about six months ago, so we both know what it's like being on your own.'

'So how often d'you see him?'

'Dunno. Three times a week, I s'pose. He sees his kids a couple of days, and then it depends on his shifts.' Nathan pulled away from Mandy, steadying himself on all fours before making off across the room.

Susie grinned. 'I've always found firemen a bit sexy, actually. Has he ever put his uniform on for you?'

'Get off!' Mandy laughed, slapping Susie's leg as it stretched out beside her.

'No, I'm serious. I can just imagine it. That uniform, all rough and heavy, with nothing underneath the jacket.' She shuddered. 'Go on. Has he?'

Mandy's mouth curved upwards in the most enormous smile, so that Susie leaned forward and punched her playfully on the arm.

'You lucky cow!' she screeched.

'No, it's not like that,' Mandy was saying, trying not to laugh.

'No?'

'No! We didn't sleep together for ages, and then when we did it just felt right. D'you know what I mean?'

Susie gave a brief smile.

Mandy turned, resting her arm on Susie's knee and looking up into her friend's face. 'D'you remember, you said to me once that the difference between a bloke fucking you and making love to you was in whether he held you afterwards?'

Susie gave a quick nod, remembering the occasion too well.

'Well, Sam holds me afterwards. And I tell you what, Suse. It feels bloody good.'

Susie reached down and squeezed Mandy's arm and there was a moment of understanding that passed between them. Susie had always known that Mandy had been in love with Jo, and in some strange way *she* had borne the burden of guilt that her friend had been so badly hurt. Now, she felt that lifted from her shoulders and it was a good feeling.

'Oh, my God!' Susie shouted suddenly. 'Look!'

Mandy followed Susie's gaze across to a small side table where Nathan had pulled himself to his feet, and had taken one step away from it, his arms flapping in mid-air.

Susie dropped to her knees beside Mandy and held out her arms. 'Come on, darling. Come to Mummy.'

Nathan wrinkled his brow, giggled and took one more step before falling on to the cushion of a full nappy.

Susie screamed with delight and rushed forward, lifting her son into the air so that he laughed noisily. 'You clever, *clever* boy!' she said, beaming with pride.

Mandy looked on indulgently, recalling the joy of such

moments. The phone rang and she struggled to her feet, walking across the room to answer it.

'Hello.'

'Hi, Mand. It's me.'

'Oh, hi, Kar.'

'Listen! I just thought you'd want to know. Anna's mum's died.'

'Oh . . . shit!'

'Yeah. Anyway, I can't stop. I've got a meeting. Listen! If I tell Janet would you call Susie?'

'It's OK she's here!' Mandy looked across to make eye contact with Susie.

'Good. I'll call you later, OK?'

'Yeah. How's Anna?'

'Bearing up, I think. Speak to you later. 'Bye.'

'Yeah. 'Bye.'

Mandy replaced the receiver. Bending forward, Susie placed Nathan on the floor and looked across expectantly.

'Anna's mum?'

Mandy nodded. 'Yeah.'

'Poor Anna.'

'Yeah . . .'

Susie sat at the round wooden table, watching Jo as he stood at the bar, ordering their drinks. It felt strange, as it always did, not to have Nathan with her, but it was liberating too, as though she were suddenly free to be a *woman* and not bound by the self-imposed constraints of being a *mother*. And the woman in her looked across at Jo and felt a sudden surge of excitement that this man belonged to her, that she knew what his body looked like beneath those jeans and that shirt, and that later they would make love.

Thinking back over the past year it seemed crazy now to think that they might have thrown it all away, that there had been a time when she couldn't bear the thought of making love, and when she had considered — albeit it fleetingly — that someone else could have taken Jo's place.

She hadn't noticed Jo walk across so that when he placed her drink on the table before her, Susie jumped.

'Where were you?' he said, sliding into the seat opposite her.

'What?'

'You were miles away.'

'Oh,' she said, grinning. 'I was just thinking about how lucky I am.'

'I'll drink to that,' he said, raising his glass in a toast.

'Cheeky bugger!' And with that she tapped his shin playfully with her foot.

Reaching under the table, Jo found Susie's knee, pressing the soft flesh above it. 'Don't start something you can't finish,' he said grinning.

'Nor you!' she said, parting her legs slightly, so that he leaned back in his chair, laughing.

'I popped round to see Mandy today,' she said, raising the bottle of Becks to her mouth.

'Yeah?'

'She's got herself a new bloke.'

'Good,' he said, placing his glass of beer on the table and wiping a hand across his mouth. There was no eye contact. He looked away, across the pub, at the menu on the wall.

'D'you fancy something to eat?'

Susie shook her head. 'I thought we might get a take-away.'

Jo looked up at her and grinned. He understood what she was saying and as she returned his smile, he felt his penis go stiff.

Then suddenly Susie's expression changed to one of sadness. 'Did I tell you Anna's mum's died?'

Jo shook his head. 'It was expected, though, wasn't it?'

'Yeah, but it don't make it any easier, does it? And it must be weird being completely on your own. I mean, I know Lyndsay's a pain in the arse, but I'd hate to be an only child with both me parents gone.'

Jo looked at her across the table a moment, then leaned forward, his elbows resting on the wooden surface.

'So how many d'you reckon we'll end up with, then?' he said, holding her eyes.

Susie shrugged, embarrassed almost. Did he sense she wanted another child? Did she dare say how she felt and run the risk of his refusing? She hadn't meant for them to discuss it like this. She had wanted to choose her moment.

''Cos I think,' he said, reaching across the table for her hand, 'that if we're going to have another then the gap shouldn't be too big. I mean, it'd be nice for Nathan to have someone to play with.'

Slowly, she allowed her face to break into a smile; not afraid now to show her feelings.

'I thought you wouldn't want any more,' she said quietly, stroking the outside of his hand with her thumb.

'I love you. I love Nathan. The worst has gotta be behind us now. 'Course I want us to have another one. If that's what you want.'

Susie nodded enthusiastically.

Jo reached for his glass. 'A toast,' he said, raising it towards Susie as she, too, lifted her bottle of beer into the air. 'To us!'

'To us!' she repeated, tipping back her head and draining the remains of the bottle.

Jo was half out of his seat, his empty glass in his hand. 'Another?'

Susie reached across and grabbed hold of his sleeve. 'I'd

sooner go for that takeaway,' she said, her mouth curling at the corners into a mischievous grin.

Walking across the dimly lit car park hand in hand, Susie felt like a teenager, her body tingling with anticipation. Standing by the passenger door, she followed Jo with her eyes as he walked round to the other side of the car. Stopping at the door, he looked across at her, the width of the car between them, his lust barely concealed.

The door lock clicked open on the passenger side as Jo turned the key. Sliding inside, Susie allowed her skirt to ride up her legs and almost immediately Jo's hand was on her bare flesh, stroking the soft skin on her inner thigh so that she groaned, the sound of her pleasure inflaming him further.

Reaching down the side of his seat, Jo pulled the lever sending it into recline, then reached across to do the same to Susie's, so that he rolled over on top of her, a desperation in the way he kissed her face and neck.

Susie pulled at the buttons on her skimpy black shirt, and it fell away from her, revealing the white lace bra beneath. His breathing heavy now, Jo pulled at the cup, releasing her breast. Squeezing the soft flesh between his fingers, teasing the nipple so that it stood hard and erect, he lowered his mouth towards it as Susie arched her back to meet him.

She could feel his penis pressing into her through his jeans and moved her groin against it, grinding her sex against him. She knew that at any moment she would come, and she wanted to have him inside her when she did; wanted him to orgasm with her. She pulled at his zip, and together they pushed his jeans and boxers over his buttocks, and without removing her knickers, she guided his hot stiff penis inside her, crying out as he thrust into her, coming almost at once.

And as he did, she had a fleeting thought that this could turn out to be a momentous occasion . . .

Mandy lay on the sofa flicking through the TV channels with the remote control, settling finally on *Newsnight*. Not that she really liked *Newsnight*, only the rest was so dull. She listened with only vague interest and even vaguer understanding as the pros and cons of monetary union were debated, depressed as always by the sight of pundits looking no older than Jason.

Licking the chocolate-chip ice cream off her spoon, she looked into the half-empty tub and replaced the lid. This was going to signal the start of her diet. She had decided that it was time to get into shape. It had often struck her as perverse that she found it easier to lose weight when she was feeling good about life. When she was depressed she ate.

At the moment she was feeling very good about life. And more than a little of that was down to Sam. For the first time since her break-up with Pete she had found someone who understood what she was going through; someone who could empathise. Not even the girls had fully appreciated what had gone on in her head, and how could they? None of them had ever experienced it, that sense of floundering in the water, reaching for a line that wasn't there, and the feeling that you're slowly drowning.

Walking through to the kitchen, Mandy went across to the freezer and replaced the tub of ice cream, dropping the dirty spoon into the washing-up bowl before reaching up to flick on the kettle for a final cup of tea before she turned in. Standing with her back to the sink, waiting for it to boil, she looked across at the vase of flowers in the middle of the kitchen table and smiled to herself. Luke had called in earlier, to have a bite to eat and to ask her to mend the zip on his favourite pair of Levis, and he'd brought her the flowers. He'd bought them from a garage on the way and they looked half dead, but she'd been deeply moved. She couldn't remember the last time *anyone* bought her flowers.

There was a click as the water boiled and the kettle switched itself off. Mandy turned and dropped a tea bag into the mug. She was just about to lift the kettle when she heard a sound at the front door. Glancing at the clock, she walked out into the hallway. Stopping at the kitchen door, she peered through the glass panels of the front door but there was no sign of anybody. She was about to turn back, deciding it must have been the wind, when she noticed the white envelope on the mat. Her brow furrowing, she walked across and picked it up.

Turning it over, she read aloud her name, Mandy – nothing else, no surname – written in biro. Gingerly, she pulled at the flap, taking out the letter as she made her way back to the kitchen. Glancing at the foot of the page she saw Sam's name, followed by a solitary kiss, and her heart sank. There wasn't much to read. The letter was brief and to the point. He had decided, for the sake of the kids, that he was going to give it another go with his wife. She wanted him back, it seemed. He thought a lot of Mandy, so he said, and he was sorry to hurt her like this, but . . .

Mandy dropped the letter on to the table and it skimmed across the surface, coming to rest against the vase of flowers. Stepping across, she lifted the kettle and poured the boiled water into the mug, staring into it, watching the tea bag bobbing on the surface. Turning, she stepped across to the fridge and pulled out an opened carton of milk. She carried the milk over to the cup, but as she raised it to pour it into the tea, she turned and – her features breaking into a grimace – threw the carton across the room so that it burst open as it hit the cupboard door, milk splashing everywhere.

Her back against the worktop, and with her hands reaching out on either side, gripping the edge for support, she stared unseeing at the white streaks running down the cupboard, forming droplets that fell on to the work surface below, mirroring the tears that fell unchecked from her eyes.

Stepping through the door of the restaurant, Anna saw Frank an instant before he saw her, and had time to adjust the preoccupied frown she wore for a tentative smile.

Frank got up from his seat and stepped round the table to greet her. He was beaming.

'Anna . . .' It was close to a whisper, and as he leaned close, she felt his lips brush her cheek.

They sat, facing each other awkwardly across the narrow table.

It was almost six months since she had last seen him and he seemed to have aged. Or was that only her faulty memory? After all, there had always been a trace of grey in his hair, and that thickness in his neck . . .

No. Looking at him, she saw that he *had* aged. Living on his own had taken its toll, and he was not the man she'd known. Even so, something of his charm – his attractiveness – remained. It would not be hard to sleep with him, even after all this time.

Anna looked down, the brutality of that reminder of why she was here bringing a flush to her neck.

'Shall I order some wine?' Frank asked, seeming not to notice her embarrassment.

'Yes . . . that would be nice,' she said, looking up; noting how his eyes drank in the sight of her. She smiled. A more genuine smile than before. 'So how are things?'

He laughed gruffly. 'Things are shit. Or were . . .'

Anna felt a little flutter in her belly at that. She didn't want this to get too heavy. Already she had the sense that Frank was half in love with her, and that might make this awkward.

More awkward, she corrected herself, for, God knew, it was awkward enough to start with.

'I keep hearing nothing but good things about you,' he said, turning to summon a waiter. 'The magazine just goes from strength to strength.'

'Yes . . .' But for once she wasn't interested in shop talk.

Frank ordered the wine, then turned back to her. 'I was sorry to hear about your mother, though. When's the funeral?'

'Tomorrow.'

'Ah . . .' Frank looked away a moment, then met her eyes again. 'I've missed you, Anna. I . . .' He shrugged. 'I came close to phoning you a number of times. I . . . well, I was a bit of a shit to you, wasn't I?'

Anna considered that a moment, then shrugged. 'I wouldn't say that. It was what we both wanted at the time.'

'But now?'

Again, she didn't want to build his hopes. Didn't want him to think this was more than it was.

'Look, Frank, I think we should take this one step at a time, eh? See how it goes.'

'Sure . . . look, I'm fine with that. We've changed, both of us. I know that.' He reached out to hold her hand. 'But things could be different this time.'

He paused significantly, then: 'I'm divorcing Mary.'

Anna found herself staring fixedly at where his hand covered her own. Jerking her head up, she met his eyes. 'I . . . I hope I wasn't to blame for that.'

'No, no . . .' He shook his head, a hint of pain in his eyes suddenly. 'Things had been wrong for a long time. My neglect, her indifference. The old, old story.'

'And the kids . . .'

He sighed and then squeezed her hand. 'Well . . . I'm trying to see them as much as I can, but it's difficult. I can't stand to be with her any more, and we row so much. I've tried having

– 489 –

them with me, but she doesn't like that, and besides, there's so little space where I am. It's . . .'

Messy, Anna thought, and decided that she didn't want to get involved. Frank as a lover had been one thing; Frank as a prospective husband, complete with all his emotional baggage, was quite another.

'Look,' she said, 'I can't stay long today. I've got a lot to do as I'm off tomorrow, so . . .'

'No, no, I understand. Let's order, eh?'

She smiled, then squeezed his hand back. 'Maybe we can meet up next week, one evening. When I'm feeling more . . . *sociable*.'

And now his smile, which had faded, returned. 'Sure. No . . . that would be great. Just great.'

Karen stepped down from the ladder, propped the roller against the paint tray, and stood back to admire the wall she had just painted. The colour wasn't *her* at all; in fact she'd always been rather afraid of colour and had decorated the whole place in magnolia when she'd moved in. So this, a dazzling deep lilac, was completely out of character. With its literary connotations, she had been attracted to its name, Hubble Bubble, but had blanched rather on opening the tin and seeing just how vivid it was.

In the past her thinking had always been that a room's colour was best provided by its adornments – books, cushions, rugs – but now, determined to become more adventurous, she was splashing out. Literally.

The wall stood in stark contrast to the other three and, encouraged now, she stepped across to the paint tin, eager to crack on and complete the job. As she tilted the tin over the tray, filling it with fresh paint, the phone rang. Karen glanced across at it and, checking that the red light on the answerphone was flashing, carried on with the job in hand.

The ringing stopped and after a moment or two a familiar voice filled the room.

'Hi, Karen. It's Sylvie. You didn't mention it but I guess you might be away. In fact your tape's probably full of messages from me. Sorry. It's just that I've been wanting to see you. I thought I'd get tickets for us to go to—'

'Hi, Sylvie. It's Karen.'

'Oh!' Sylvie said, unable to conceal the surprise and disappointment in her voice. 'I've left about ten messages!'

'I know. Sorry.'

'What's going on?'

There was a heavy silence.

'Karen?'

'I think we should cool it for a while.'

'Cool it? What d'you mean, cool it?'

Karen shrugged. 'I just think it would be better if things didn't get too . . . heavy. If we kept it a bit more casual.'

The anger in Sylvie's voice was evident. 'Oh, so you want casual sex now, is that it?'

Karen didn't answer. She glanced up at the painted wall, and down at the dollop of paint that had dripped from the roller on to the leg of her jeans.

'Look, I'm sorry, Sylvie, but I have to go,' she said, a renewed confidence in her voice. 'I'm in the middle of painting a room.'

'Anna?'

'Oh, hi, Kar . . . hang on a second.' Anna gestured to her secretary that she was done with dictating, then, as the girl left the room, swivelled about, putting the back of the chair between her and the door. 'Sorry, I had someone with me . . . How's things?'

'Great. I was just phoning to see how it went . . . you know, with Frank.'

'Hmm . . . I don't know.'

'What d'you mean, you don't know?'

'Whether I can go through with it. He's getting a divorce.'

'Ah . . .'

'Precisely . . . and to cap it all, I still think he holds a candle for me.'

Karen laughed. 'A candle's no bloody good!'

'No . . .' Anna laughed too. 'No, I guess it isn't. But it doesn't feel right.'

'Then choose someone else from your list.'

'Oh, yes . . . that great long list of men I know!' She sniffed. 'No. It has to be Frank. But I've got to be careful. I don't want to hurt him. He's been through enough this past year, and whether it's his fault or not, I don't want to feel guilty about what I'm doing.'

'Then tell him.'

'I can't tell him! Be serious, Karen. The guy's lonely, vulnerable, and very low on self-confidence right now. I tell him I want his child, then he'll be wanting to move in with me, and thinking I want the whole package.'

'And don't you?'

'No, I bloody well don't! I knew that the moment I sat down facing him today. In fact, I very nearly got up and walked straight out again. It was just *so* embarrassing.'

Karen was silent a moment, then, speaking slowly, deliberately, she said: 'If you are going to do it, then I think you should do it soon. The more you hesitate, the worse it'll get. Sleep with him then dump him straight away. It'll hurt him, sure, but at least it'll give him a chance to get over it quickly. He might hate you, but he won't mope over you.'

Anna smiled. 'Is this really the timid Miss Karen Turner I'm talking to?'

Karen laughed. 'You think I'm getting tough, then?'

'No . . . just sensible in your old age.'

'Less of the old . . .' Karen hesitated, then. 'I gave Sylvie the elbow today.'

'Sylvie! Really?'

'I said we should cool things for a while. She was getting too demanding.'

'And are you OK?'

'I'm fine. Finishing my decorating, actually. And I thought I might take a holiday. I need one.'

'You and me both. Maybe I'll come with you.'

'After you've shagged Frank.'

'Oh, God . . . don't remind me.' Anna stared into the distance a moment, then laughed. 'Kar . . . I think it's a great idea. I mean, I need to get away. Mum's death . . . well, you understand, what with your dad. So don't book anything. Not till you've spoken to me, OK?'

'OK. Now I'll let you get on. But suss out the best time to shag Frank, and get it out of the way. You'll feel better once it's done, I guarantee.'

'All right. 'Bye, Kar.'

''Bye, Anna.'

Anna sat there for a while after Karen had hung up, staring at nothing. She had looked at her diary only yesterday and had worked out that these next few days were when she would be ovulating. She sighed. Then, knowing that she wouldn't relax until this was over, she spun the chair round and, picking up the phone again, dialled Frank. Karen was right. It was no good waiting.

As he picked up the phone Anna spoke quickly, before her courage failed her, arranging to see him at nine o'clock that night. And as she replaced the receiver she closed her mind to the surprise and delight she had heard in Frank's voice.

Anna emerged from the shop, the large green bag with its exclusive name hanging over her wrist. She had hoped it would make her feel better — that it might have helped her enter into the spirit of things — but as she carried the ridiculously expensive lingerie from the store, Anna was not merely two hundred pounds poorer, but filled with the same doubts concerning the evening ahead as she had harboured earlier.

There was, admittedly, a part of her that was intrigued to know what sex with Frank would be like after all this time. Indeed, there was no getting away from the fact that she could do with a good screw, and he had always been pretty damn good in that department. And having made the decision that he would be her ideal sperm donor, she knew that it was now or never; that if she prevaricated for another month she would never go through with it. And then she would be back to square one.

She had left work early knowing that, under the circum-stances, her colleagues would be understanding, bearing in mind her mother's funeral the next day. The image of her face flitted into Anna's head and she closed her eyes tight, as though to erase the picture from her mind. Her mother would *never* have understood what she was doing.

Making her way along Bond Street towards the junction where she knew she could pick up a cab, Anna glanced idly at the window displays as she passed by, feeling like a truant schoolgirl being out while the shops were still open.

Amid all the noise of late afternoon traffic, Anna had paid little attention to the sound of a car horn from the road alongside her, and had merely tutted with mild irritation as it sounded a second time, making her jump a little. But out of the corner of her eye she became aware of the Rolls-Royce, and when the horn sounded a third time she turned towards it, ready to give the driver a mouthful.

Slowly, the black glass of the passenger window glided

down and as Anna leaned forward, looking into the car, the sight of Michael sitting there, smiling out at her, literally took her breath away. It was only a split second before she regained her composure, at least outwardly, but he had clearly taken delight in his effect on her.

'I didn't *frighten* you, did I?' he said, grinning.

Anna shook her head. 'I was just wondering who the prick in the car was.'

He laughed out loud, so that she was forced to smile too.

'And now you know,' he said, his eyes moving over her face. 'Can I offer you a lift?'

'You don't know where I'm going,' she said, grinning.

He shrugged. 'The offer's there.'

Behind Michael's, another car hooted, the driver impatient to get going.

'OK,' she said, and, opening the door, she slid on to the wide leather seat. Turning, she placed her shopping in the back, then glanced at him. 'Just drive!'

They had exchanged pleasantries, and Anna had told Michael about her mother, but it was all oddly strained, as though they had never been anything more than casual acquaintances and, as she sat there, Anna wished that she had never got into the car.

But as they drove up through Regents Park, Michael suddenly slowed, then pulled over to the side of the road. For a moment he sat there, his hands poised over the wheel, staring out through the windscreen. Anna sat silently, listening to the sound of her own breathing, her heart pounding as she waited for him to speak. Watching him, his profile even more beautiful than she had allowed herself to remember, she felt that old familiar desire to touch him.

'I've always felt,' he started suddenly, still not looking at her, 'that we were unfinished business.'

When she did not respond, Michael turned to look at her. 'Really?' She tried to sound businesslike. 'In what way?'

He shrugged. 'Just the way it ended, I guess. It was like, one minute we were lovers . . . and the next . . .'

'Don't tell me you didn't enjoy the rest of your holiday.'

He couldn't help smiling, and Anna was surprised by the momentary flicker of jealousy. 'Boys just wanna have fun, eh?'

This time it was he who didn't answer. For a moment he looked down, then, as he raised his eyes, he took hold of her hand from where it lay in her lap. 'I really cared for you, Anna. You do know that, don't you?'

But she couldn't answer. There was a tightness in her chest and she gave the briefest of nods. Reaching round with his other hand, Michael gently stroked her cheek and Anna shivered.

And as she heard the words fill the car, she could barely believe that she had uttered them.

'Michael, I want to make love to you . . .'

Frank must have been watching from an upstairs window and seen her step out of the cab, for as she climbed the steps, the big front door swung open and he stepped aside, letting her walk past him into the massive hallway.

His apartment was upstairs, on the second floor, and as she stepped inside, she was reminded that Frank was a man of considerable taste. The flat was beautifully decorated. Fine prints hung on the walls, and the whole place had an air of refinement, not so unlike her own flat. Even so, she felt awkward being there. For her to have come at all at this hour meant that in all probability she would stay; and if she stayed, it would mean sleeping with him. Frank knew that; or, at least, he surely hoped it would be so.

He took her coat, then, as she made herself comfortable

on the leather sofa in the living room, brought her a glass of chilled wine. An expensive one, she could tell from the taste of it.

They had not spoken yet, but his eyes never seemed to leave her. Finally, feeling uncomfortable with the silence, she spoke.

'You have to forgive me, Frank, but I'm in a funny mood. My mother's death, I . . .'

'It's all right,' he said. 'I understand. When my father died, I . . . well, it took me ages to get over it. Like you're suddenly right there, in the firing line.'

'Yes . . .' And she was suddenly glad that he understood that much. But the rest of it? No, Karen was wrong there. She couldn't even begin to tell him *why* she was there.

She looked down, swallowing deeply. Then, in a tiny, yet oddly husky voice, she asked, 'Will you hold me, Frank?'

He set his glass down, then came across and, sitting beside her, awkwardly put his arm about her.

Anna leaned in to him, closing her eyes, refamiliarising herself with the feel and smell of him.

There, she thought, that isn't so bad, after all.

His hand slowly caressed her back. 'Do you want to talk?'

She thought about that, then realised that it would be too dangerous. There would be a temptation to be open with him, and where would that get her? No. It was best to be direct. To get what she came for and go.

'Frank . . . can we go to bed?'

She felt the slight tremor of surprise in his body. His hand slowed. Then, as if in afterthought, he squeezed her gently.

'OK,' he said quietly, and sat back a little from her.

She met his eyes and smiled, seeing the faint ghost of past lust in his.

'Are you sure?' he asked, more serious than she'd expected. 'I don't want to rush you.'

Anna looked down. 'I just need to be with someone tonight. I need . . .'

Her voice broke — genuinely — as she thought of what tomorrow held for her. She could still remember how she'd felt, standing at Karen's side at Karen's father's funeral. Now it was her turn.

'Come on,' Frank said, gently taking her hands and helping her up.

They went through, into his bedroom, where a single lamp burned on the far side of the bed. She was surprised to see a double bed there, and a TV in one corner, as if this were a marital bedroom. He had clearly changed the sheets, too.

A bathroom led off. She went through and began to undress, even as she heard him moving about in the bedroom, kicking off his shoes and unbuckling his belt. Her mouth was dry now, and as she looked at herself in the over-bright light above the mirror, she wondered idly if she would ever tell her child about this night.

That was, if she conceived a child.

As she removed her dress, she noted the faint mark on her neck, where Michael had nipped her in the midst of their passion. And as she thought of it, so images of their coupling filled her mind, making her smooth her hand down over her breasts.

She had not meant to let Michael fuck her. At least, not like that. But she hadn't been able to help herself. And when he'd come, she had felt a strange tingling in her head, and down her spine, unlike anything she had ever felt before.

'Anna?'

She turned, guiltily, and looked at him in the doorway. He had noticed nothing, it seemed. Stepping across to her, he finished unbuttoning her dress, then, as it fell, reached behind her to unfasten her bra.

She gazed at him a moment, uneasy at the way he looked at her, then, reaching out, unfastened his trousers and, unzipping them, let them fall.

They were almost naked now.

Taking her hands, he drew her to him and kissed her. That kiss surprised her, arousing her so that her nipples were stiff.

Yet what did that say about her? For only a few hours ago she had been making love to Michael. Was it only lust, then? Was all of this love business only a charade, to mask this darker need in them all?

She reached down and held him through the thin cloth of his pants, hearing him groan as she did, and for a moment she was tempted to kneel down and take him in her mouth, as she used to do, but there was a reason for her being here, and she remembered it now.

'Fuck me,' she said, whispering it urgently in his ear, easing down his pants so that his prick sprang free. 'Fuck me!'

His eyes were inflamed with lust now, and as he pushed her down on to the bed and entered her, she cried out — almost a yell of pain. That cry pushed him to the edge and over, and in three, maybe four thrusts at most, Frank came, holding himself rigid against her, his whole body shuddering, as he buried his seed deep inside her.

It was after two and Frank was sleeping now. They had rested, her body nestled against his, then made love a second time. And then he'd held her, his left hand caressing her until, exhausted, it fell still.

She had waited until she was certain, then, carefully lifting his arm from about her, had slipped from the bed and gone through to the bathroom, closing the door behind her before she switched on the light. She had then dressed quickly, the sight of his sperm dripping from her as she stood there waking her to the reality of what she'd done.

Anna had thought about taking the day off after the funeral, but had decided she'd be better off at work. She didn't want to have too much time to think. Yesterday had been pretty awful and she was feeling a little raw, to put it mildly. Work! That was what she needed right now.

She did not look up as the door opened, knowing instinctively that it would be Jacqui standing there.

'Anna,' she said in unnecessarily hushed tones, 'it's Frank on the phone again.'

Anna placed her pen on the desk and looked up. Resting back in her seat she thought for a moment, deciding her response.

'It's the fourth time he's called,' Jacqui said and Anna noted the pity in her voice.

Sighing, and with an air of resignation, Anna told her to put the call through. She knew she would have to speak to him sometime, but, feeling a little fragile, she had been hoping to put off the inevitable for a little longer.

The phone rang only once before Anna picked up the receiver.

'Hello.'

'Anna! Hi, it's me. Frank.'

'Yeah. Hi, Frank.' Her voice was cold, unfriendly almost.

'Er, I've tried you a few times but you've been busy.'

'Yeah. Jacqui said. Sorry.'

'No. No problem.'

He sounded so pathetic that Anna was torn between irritation and pity.

'Look, Frank,' she said. 'I really am pretty busy today, so . . .'

'Anna! I need to see you. I . . .'

'It's a bit difficult. I've got meetings and then—'

'What about tonight? We could have dinner.'

'I'm tired, Frank.'

'Yeah, sure. I'm sorry. It's just that there's something I want to . . .'

She knew what he was trying to say; she had known it as he had made love to her. It had been different from all those times he'd screwed her when they'd been having an affair. Now he was in love with her. She couldn't help but smile at the irony of it all.

'*Anna?*'

'OK,' she said finally. 'But I can't do dinner. I'll come by your place for a drink. About seven thirty.'

'*Great!*' he said, and so gratefully that Anna winced.

''Bye, Frank.'

She did not wait for him to say goodbye before she replaced the receiver, annoyed with herself for allowing Frank to make her feel so guilty.

Anna waited outside the door to his apartment. Even now she was unsure how she wanted the evening to end, as her mind swam in a confusion of emotions. She was fond of Frank but she knew the moment had passed for them; he had had his chance a long time ago and had failed to take it. She preferred not to think about Michael and what it was she felt for him, but one certainty was she could not have made love to him the way she had, with the kind of passion she had shown, if she had felt anything approaching love for Frank.

The door opened and he stood there, beaming out at her. She smiled thinly and made to move past him into the hallway, and as she did so he leaned forward and kissed her awkwardly on the side of the head.

'Go through,' he said, indicating the living room up ahead. 'I'll fix you a drink.'

Anna avoided making eye contact, though she was aware of him looking at her.

Frank walked over to a sideboard and poured two glasses of wine from the half-empty bottle, then returned, handing one to Anna.

'Cheers!' he said, raising his glass.

'Cheers!'

'Sorry about the calls,' he said, perching beside her on the arm of the sofa. She fidgeted uncomfortably, edging away a little. 'And I know it was your mother's funeral and all but . . . well, it's just that I *had* to see you.'

'Frank . . .'

'No! Anna! Let me finish. Please.'

She lowered her eyes, looking into her lap where her hands lay.

'Ever since you called me the other day, I've been on cloud nine. I know it's a cliché,' he said, holding up his hand apologetically, 'but it's true. I've felt like a lovesick schoolboy. And when we made love, it was . . .' He shook his head, searching for words to describe it. 'It was *amazing*.'

The sudden touch of his fingers on her neck sent a shudder through her, so that he pulled away, shocked by her reaction.

'What is it?' he said softly.

'Look, Frank, it's no good,' she said, not wanting to look at him, to see the pain in his eyes and then not go through with it. 'I'm not in love with you. There's nothing between us any more.'

His laugh was hollow. 'You can't say that.'

'I can. I don't love you, Frank.'

He was on his feet now, towering over her. 'You called me! Remember?'

'I know,' she said, ashamed of herself and of her deception. 'I'm sorry. It was a mistake.'

'A *mistake*! You say it as though you dialled a wrong fucking number!'

Leaning forward, she placed her glass on the coffee table and rose to her feet. 'Look, I'd better go.'

She made to edge past the table but he stood in her way, immovable, his face cold and angry.

'Please, Frank,' she said quietly.

Lifting his foot on to the edge of the table, he pushed it with sufficient force to send it hurtling across the room, glasses, ashtrays and magazines flying off in all directions.

'Yes. You'd better go.'

Anna rushed from the flat, clinging to the memory of the countless times in the past when he had left her to go home to his wife, leaving her in her flat alone, holding on to that in order to stop the tears from coming.

Because she had to think about the future now. It was no good looking back.

Part Seven

– Ascot – four weeks later –

Edging her way along the aisle of the minibus, Mandy glanced sideways through the long window towards Janet's flat.

'Give 'er another hoot, will you, handsome,' she said smiling at the driver, who physically swelled in his seat from the unexpected and wholly undeserved compliment.

Squatting between the two front seats, Mandy reached into the small fridge, running her hand along the row of champagne bottles to find the coldest of them. Her selection made, she pulled it off the shelf, took a fresh carton of orange juice from the rack on the fridge door, and pulled herself upright.

''Ere, make yourself useful,' she said, handing the driver the bottle of champagne, while she busied herself with the carton, struggling with her false nails. The driver popped his cork with disappointing restraint and handed the bottle to Mandy.

'Right! A little top-up before we move off?'

Karen shook her head and placed her hand over the half-full glass of Buck's Fizz in her hand.

'Just a splash of orange juice for me, thanks,' Anna said, offering up her glass, 'otherwise I'll be drunk before we get there.'

'That's the idea!' Mandy grinned. 'Suse?'

'Yeah, go on, then! I'll keep you company!'

'Good girl!' Mandy beamed, making her way towards the rear of the bus. The champagne fizzed as it hit the bottom of Susie's glass, rising up over the rim and dripping down on to the floor. Mandy glanced over her shoulder and mouthed an apology to the driver.

'At this rate we'll arrive just in time for the last race,' she moaned, glancing through the window yet again as she made her way back to her seat.

'Yeah, but better she goes now than we have to find her a bush on the way,' Anna reasoned. 'The size of Janet, if she got down there I don't know we'd ever manage to haul her up again.'

'Ah, bless 'er!' Susie smiled. 'I remember what I was like with Nathan. I only 'ad to sneeze and I'd feel it all running down me leg.'

Karen's lip curled with distaste. 'Lovely!'

'Actually, I remember when I was heavily pregnant – with Jason I think it was – and I had to have a wee on a bucket 'cos something 'ad 'appened to the toilet. I was so big. There was just flesh everywhere. Anyway, Pete said it looked like the bucket had disappeared up me arse!'

'Here she is!' Karen announced and all four girls turned to watch Janet as she waddled towards the bus. A cheer went up as she neared the open door.

'Sorry!' she said, pulling herself up the steps on to the bus.

'C'mon, Nellie!' Mandy teased. 'Get that big butt of yours on 'ere! I've saved a couple of seats for you.'

Clutching her hat in one hand and her handbag in the other, Janet looked down the narrow aisle to the back of the bus. 'It's not very big, is it?'

'Not very big!' Mandy exclaimed. 'If it wasn't for you we'd

have been able to manage in a mini! Anyway, what was you expecting? A stretch limo?'

'Ooh, I'd love to ride in a stretch limo,' Susie said dreamily.

Anna turned in her seat. 'You should've said. I could've got one of my people to fix us up.'

'Now she tells us!' Karen said, as she took Janet's hat and bag and began stowing them in the overhead rack.

'Right! Little drink, Jan?' Mandy said, reaching across for the champagne bottle.

Janet considered a moment before shaking her head. 'Better not. It'll only start me off again.'

'Yeah. Maybe you're right,' Mandy said, dropping into her seat and gripping the bottle between her knees.

Anna glanced across and laughed to herself.

'What's so funny?' Karen was smiling.

Anna shook her head, then nodded in Mandy's direction. 'Nothing. I was just wondering if that was the latest in contraception.'

Susie peered over the top of the seat in front. 'She used to prefer a nice cup of tea to rumpy-pumpy, but she's gone a bit upmarket. Now she won't open her legs for anything less than a bottle of Moët, will you, Mand?'

'Cheeky cow! Anyway, you lot are only jealous,' she said smugly.

'I think I could lose a bottle up mine and not even notice,' Janet said flatly, shifting uncomfortably on her seat.

The girls' laughter mingled with the sound of the bus's engine as Rob, the driver, turned the key in the ignition.

'Right! Ascot here we come!' Mandy shouted, and the cheers that followed could be heard from the street as the bus pulled out into the flow of morning traffic.

They chatted noisily as they sat round the table they had

prebooked for brunch, plates of kedgeree, hunks of crusty bread and glasses of champagne littering the starched white cloth. And in the middle of it all, one of the saddest sights Mandy had ever seen: a birthday cake decorated with forty candles arranged around the uncompromisingly cruel dedication HAPPY BIRTHDAY GRANNY! In spite of being full up on the kedgeree, Mandy had insisted on cutting herself a slice for no other reason than to consume the much-hated title that would shortly be hers.

It had taken some time to negotiate the London traffic so that when, finally, they had arrived at the Robin Hood Inn, they had been travelling for well over an hour. Janet had made a desperate penguin-like dash for the loo, while Anna was deputised to sweet-talk the manager into giving them a table even though they were half an hour late for their booking. She had dropped a few names, flashed her press card, and they had suddenly found themselves in a wonderful corner table flanked by a window so that they could watch the comings and goings in the busy car park.

From where they sat they could see Rob sitting alone in the bus, his flask of tea perched on the dashboard. Mandy had been all for inviting him in, but the others had protested. After all, they'd argued, this was *their* day, and besides, they were paying him enough for him *not* to mind eating on his own.

The restaurant was packed out and reminiscent of a wedding reception, with everyone dressed in their finery: the women in silk and exotic hats, the men in morning suits and toppers. But the loudness and coarseness of their voices was strangely incongruous with those symbols of a forgotten aristocracy with which they had disguised themselves. To Anna they seemed like children who'd been let loose with a dressing-up box.

At a nearby table, a group of six men were laughing

raucously at some shared joke. The girls turned as one as the noise level soared.

'All right, girls?' one of them called over. 'Off to the races?'

'Nah,' Susie responded with a straight face. 'We're on our way to our cleaning job.'

'Yeah? What are you, then?' He looked at his friends around the table. 'Moppers, hooverers . . . scrubbers?'

With their laughter ringing in her ears Mandy leaned in to Susie. 'You laid yourself open to that one.'

'Wankers!' Susie hissed.

''Ere!' another of the men called over. When the girls failed to respond, he raised his voice. ''Ere, darling,' he called trying to attract Janet's attention. 'You out looking for a husband, are you?'

'You out looking for a penis, are you?' she spat.

'Oooh, feisty. I like a girl with a bit of go in 'er.'

'Huh! I would've thought the only kind of girl you'd like was blind, no sense of smell and with an IQ smaller than her shoe size.'

The men roared with laughter and, slowly, the girls allowed themselves to join in the joke, the banter good-natured but with that ever-present sexual undertone.

Unable to shake off her profession's propensity for eavesdropping, Anna became fascinated by the exchanges between two couples at a table just off to her right. The guys — mid-thirties, well suited and booted — sat opposite two women who, to Anna's expert eye, were clearly older, though she imagined the men had been easily fooled by the slim figures, facelifts and designer suits.

'So what exactly *is* a commodities broker, then?' the blonde streaked one asked, her accent unmistakably working-class London.

'A broker who handles commodities.'

'Yeah, I know that,' she giggled. 'But what exactly do you do?'

'What? Apart from worrying whether to drive the BMW or the Porsche, you mean?'

The two girls made brief eye contact.

'Oh, yeah. So you earn a lot of money, then, do you?'

'A *lot*.'

Placing her elbows on the table, she leaned a little closer so that he could see her cleavage beneath her Chanel jacket. ''Cos I've got expensive taste.'

'I can imagine,' he said, pouring the last of the champagne into his glass.

'Have we got time for another bottle before we go?' the dark-haired girl asked, draining her own glass.

This time it was the men who made eye contact.

'I'm just gonna nip to the ladies',' blondie said, pushing back her chair. 'You comin', Jen?'

Jenny raised herself out of her chair, brushing against the silent man's arm as she eased herself away from the table. 'If you're ordering coffee as well,' she said, 'I'll 'ave a cappuccino.'

Anna watched, fascinated, as the two women wove their way through the maze of tables, their arses wiggling beneath their painfully tight miniskirts, their fake-tanned legs impossibly perched on strappy sandals that were so high they looked as though they would topple forward at any moment.

As the women disappeared through the door into the ladies', the commodities broker caught hold of the manager's arm. There was a hurried, whispered conversation, whereupon the guy pulled out two fifty-pound notes and stuffed them into the manager's hand. Their chairs screeched as they pushed them away from the table, and before you could say 'little shits', they were out the door and racing across the car park. Anna watched as they jumped into a dark green BMW and, laughing like children, roared across the tarmac and out on to the road.

Moments later, the two girls reappeared and seated themselves at the table. Anna turned to the others and in hushed tones explained what she had witnessed.

'D'you think I should tell them?'

Mandy's lip curled downward. 'Sounds like they were taking the piss a bit, though.'

'Yeah, but look at 'em,' Susie said. 'You gotta feel a bit sorry for 'em, ain't you?' The two girls were obviously beginning to feel a little awkward now, as the two seats at the table remained empty.

'I can't believe women can be that stupid!' Karen sat back in her chair, prepared to let the others decide what to do.

'I'm gonna tell them.' Anna was on her feet before anyone could argue. She went across and, leaning between the two women, explained that the blokes had done a runner. The others watched as the two women gazed out of the window as though they somehow imagined they would see the green BMW there.

The words 'Fucking oiks!' floated across from their table, and after a few more minutes' conversation Anna returned to the others.

'Would you lot mind if we gave them a lift to Ascot? Only they're up shit creek without a sugar daddy.'

'Sugar daddy!' Mandy spat. 'That blonde one's forty if she's a day. Her skin's been pulled so tight over her face she's got fucking nasal hair growing on her head.'

Mandy, Karen, Susie and Janet looked across to the two girls, who smiled sweetly.

'What they like?' Janet asked.

'Seem nice enough.'

'A bit common, though,' Mandy protested, returning their smile.

'Oh, unlike us, you mean?' Susie laughed.

'Yeah, well, there's common and there's *common*.'

'Well, what shall I say? Yes or no?'

'A bit mean to leave them stranded.' Karen was a sucker for a lame duck.

'Yes?'

The girls nodded and Anna looked across to the other table, beckoning them across.

'And anyway, Mand, you never know. You might have met a couple of soulmates.'

Glancing over, Mandy grimaced as she watched the girls hook their Gucci bags over their shoulders. 'Who? Nip and Tuck? I tell you, if I ever get like them, do me a favour and have me put down.'

The others avoided making eye contact with Mandy and had turned to greet their two new travelling companions.

The drizzle had begun just as they had pulled off the road and into the racecourse, eliciting groans throughout the bus. But Janet was just grateful that they had arrived in one piece. While the others, having consumed vast quantities of champagne, had been oblivious to Rob's often erratic driving, she, clinging nervously to her tumbler of warm orange juice, had pressed her foot into the floor at every bend in the road.

Jen, their dark-haired hitchhiker, had perched herself on the seat beside the driver with almost catastrophic effect, so that whenever she would turn in her seat to talk to the rest of the girls seated behind her, her tiny skirt would ride up her thighs revealing the delicate black lace around the leg of her panties.

Had the karaoke machine not been on and the laughter not been so loud, they would probably have heard him pant. As it was, the only other physical sign of his growing excitement was the way his hand kept jerking on the steering wheel, sending them on more than one occasion on to the wrong side of the road.

'Thank fuck for that!' Janet said as Rob stepped outside the bus.

The others looked at her, mystified.

'Well, if her skirt had gone any fucking higher he'd have let go of the bloody wheel and yelled Geronimo!'

'*What?*' Jen's attempt at soft, wide-eyed innocence was almost impossible to achieve on a face tighter than a homophobic's arse on a gay-rights march.

'Ah, poor sod probably ain't had it in years,' Susie said, watching him through the window as he lit a cigarette. 'I mean. Look at 'im!'

All seven girls gazed through the window at the pathetic specimen leaning against the side of the bus, and could only guess at what was going through his head.

'Almost makes you feel sorry for 'im, don't it?'

The six other voices rose, unanimous. 'No!'

Having made their way across the soft grass, their heels sinking into the sodden turf, the girls had refused several invitations to join impromptu parties beneath umbrellas and canvas gazebos. Hampers and picnic tables stood beside stretch limos, minibuses and cars, and the alcohol was flowing freely and with indiscriminate generosity.

Karen had been the only one organised enough to bring along an umbrella, and as she held it above her and Janet, the two of them walking arm in arm, people were forced to make way, the others falling in behind them as they created a channel through the press of bodies heading for the turnstile.

'I'm not sure this was such a good idea,' Janet said, looking ahead to the impossibly narrow entrance.

Karen squeezed her arm. 'You'll be all right. If you get wedged I'll just pretend you're not with me.'

Behind them, heavy negotiations were in progress.

'Listen! If we stick together, they won't notice we're two tickets short. Just give 'em in as a bundle and we'll push through.' The way Jen said it made it sound pretty straightforward.

'I don't think . . .' Anna began politely.

'We ain't total fucking mugs,' Mandy interrupted, though there was no malice in her voice. 'Thing is, girls, *we've* got our tickets. And we don't know you from Adam.'

Jen's blonde friend decided to have another go. 'Yeah, but—'

'No "Yeah, but" anything. We've got tickets. You ain't.' Susie gave a tight-lipped smile.

'Try a tout,' Anna suggested helpfully. 'Look! There's loads of 'em over there.'

The crowd slowed almost to a standstill as it neared the entrance. Quickly distributing the tickets among the girls, Anna glanced over to her right to see Jen and her mate laughing with a heavy-looking fella, each with a hand on one of his arms.

'I feel a bit guilty,' Anna said, nodding in their direction. Susie and Mandy followed her gaze.

'Don't worry about them,' Susie said matter-of-factly. 'If those two fell in shit they'd come up smelling of roses.'

'Yeah,' Mandy said solemnly, still staring after them. 'But there'd always be a little bit of a pong hanging about 'em, wouldn't there.'

Anna and Susie caught one another's eye, then pushed through the turnstile, while behind them Janet, who had decided there was no way she was going to squeeze through that tiny gap, looked about her for another way in.

''Ere! 'Ang on!' she yelled, as Anna and Susie began to walk away. 'There ain't no bleedin' way I'm gonna get through that, is there?'

'S'all right,' Mandy said, coming up behind her. 'Look, there's a gate over there for the disabled . . . and very fat ladies!'

Janet's heart sank when she turned the corner at the end of the bar to find the queue for the ladies' stretching out through the door and fifteen feet along the wall. Sighing heavily, she shuffled to the end of the queue, desperately hoping that she would be able to hold on long enough to avoid a puddle on the floor. Five minutes later and having moved no more than a few feet, she caught the eye of one of a group of girls some way ahead. She was several inches taller than every other woman in the queue so that Janet could easily see her as she leaned forward and muttered to her friends. Straightening up, she called over their heads to Janet.

'Here, love. You go ahead if you're desperate.'

Janet was filled with a mixture of gratitude and embarrassment as everyone looked round.

'Would anyone mind?' she said in a quiet voice.

Most people said nothing while others encouraged her to walk straight to the front, so that she felt elevated suddenly, enjoying a position of rare privilege bearing in mind the British intolerance of queue-jumpers.

Sitting on the loo, she welcomed not only the obvious relief to her bloated bladder, but the opportunity to take the weight off her feet. Reaching down for her handbag, she lifted it on to her knee and, unzipping the side pocket, pulled out her wallet. In spite of Mandy paying for brunch, and Anna refusing to accept anything towards the birthday cake, Janet's contribution towards the bus, the champagne, a tip for Rob (which she had handed over begrudgingly bearing in mind his wanky driving) and her entrance ticket had set her back well over a hundred pounds and far more than she had anticipated. Thank God the girls had refused to let her join in the whip-round for the bar as she was only on orange juice.

Opening her wallet, Janet emptied out the contents — a solitary five-pound note. She knew she could always borrow money from from one of the girls — Anna was bound to have plenty on her — but that wasn't the problem. She was meant to be economising. She had told Steve that she wanted more than the statutory maternity leave; that if she was going to have only one baby then she wanted to spend as much time with it as possible. Of course he had been sympathetic, but he was also a practical creature, and knew there was no way they could afford for her to take unpaid leave, unless they cut back drastically. The IVF had cost them dearly; that was the irony of it.

Janet pushed the fiver into the back of her wallet, in case of an emergency, dropped it into the bag and levered herself off the pan.

The first bottle of champagne had been devoured in one round, so that before Janet had even emerged from the loo, Mandy was easing her way through the press of bodies towards the bar on a mission to purchase two more.

Along the far side of the room a row of bored-looking women sat behind glass panels, issuing tickets as punters passed across their bets; on the wall above them, television screens listed the runners and showed the latest odds. Mandy had never been to a racetrack before, which was curious considering her dad had been a serious gambler. Perhaps that's why, she mused. Perhaps he had always wanted to go alone; or perhaps her mum hadn't wanted them to become addicted to the same drug as had, finally, been his ruin.

As a teenager she had landed herself a Saturday job in the local bookies, which at the time had seemed rather sophisticated compared with the ones she had had in the baker's and the shoe shop. But she could remember still the earnest concentration on the faces of the men as they peered up at the screen, willing their horse home. And could remember too the haunting desperation on those same features as, defeated, they tore the useless slip in half, treading it underfoot as they contemplated the misery of returning home without their week's wages.

But this! This was different! This was a social occasion and the racing – judging by the enormous queue at the bar compared with the one at the betting section – was incidental. All about her people were laughing and joking, so that Mandy felt high from the atmosphere alone.

Squeezing her way through, she turned her head slightly to apologise to a woman whose hat she had managed to tip off, much to the amusement of her friends, and as she looked up she saw Pete's unmistakable profile. He was standing a little way ahead of her, by the bar. He looked happy. But in the split second of recognition Mandy decided that she didn't want to see him; not today.

She tried to turn about, but the woman's hat had been repositioned and presented a barrier. She attempted to shuffle sideways, but a bitch with an arse like a sofa bed was determined not to budge and Mandy found herself being carried forward by bodies following in her wake, eager for a drink. Turning abruptly, she inadvertently knocked a drink from a guy's hand and as it fell to the floor and smashed into pieces, it splashed up his girlfriend's legs, and she let out a squeal. Heads turned in her direction. And one of those heads was Pete's.

'Oh, Jesus!' the guy said. 'Watch what you're doing!'

'You stupid cow!' the girlfriend began, but Pete, who had stepped across, raised his hand to defuse the situation.

'It's all right,' Pete said, his voice calm but firm. 'No need

to make a song and dance. It was an accident, OK? Here . . .'
And he stuffed a twenty-pound note into the guy's top pocket.
'Buy yourself another bottle on me, all right, mate?'

'Yeah, right . . .' the guy said, weighing up his chances
against Pete and deciding he didn't really want to push
things.

Mandy smiled sheepishly. 'Thanks.'

'S'all right.' Then, smiling at her as if he was genuinely
pleased to see her: 'I didn't expect to see you here, Mand.
Come on over . . . there's a few of us.'

Mandy went across, but it wasn't until she was among Pete's
little group – most of whom she knew – that she realised that
Emmy was there, too.

'Look who's here,' Pete said, introducing Mandy.

'Yeah. I'm with the girls.' She glanced at Emmy. 'Hello
again.'

'Hiya!'

'You usually come at the beginning of the week,' Mandy
said, turning to Pete again, a slightly accusing tone in her
voice.

'Yeah, I know, but Emmy wanted to come, so I thought . . .'

'I've never been before,' Emmy said, with the enthusiasm
of a child on a treat.

'No,' Mandy said flatly, glancing at Pete. 'Neither have
I.'

'You want a drink?' Pete said, oblivious of the undertones.

'No, it's all right. I've gotta get a couple of bottles for
the others.'

'Pushing the boat out, eh?'

Mandy looked at him a moment. 'Yeah, I thought I would.
What with it *being my birthday*.'

'Oh, happy birthday,' Emmy was saying, but Mandy's eyes
were still on Pete.

'Shit, Mand! Sorry! Happy birthday!' And he leaned forward and gave her a kiss on the cheek.

'Dare we ask which one?' Emmy giggled.

Not if you want to keep those caps on your front teeth, darling. Mandy thought. But she simply smiled.

'Privileged information, eh, Mand?'

'I don't know why men think women don't want no one to know their age. I mean, it don't worry me. By the time the baby's born I'll be nearly *thirty*!'

'You seen Jason lately?' Mandy said turning to Pete, grateful for an opportunity to change the subject.

But before Pete could answer, Emmy stepped in. 'Oh, I don't mean Jason's and Gemma's. I mean *ours*.'

Mandy stared at her gormlessly. 'Sorry?'

'Oh, don't tell me he ain't told you yet.' And Emmy gave Pete an affectionate jab on the arm with her tiny fist. 'He's terrible.'

Mandy looked to Pete but he would not meet her eye and was staring at his shoes. With no concession to subtlety, she turned to glare openly at Emmy's tummy. There was a gentle swell over the abdomen and as Emmy placed her hand upon it, stroking it through the thin black lycra, Mandy forced herself to look away.

'We thought it'd be lovely for 'em. You know, our daughter and Jason's little one, 'cos there'll only be a few months between 'em. He's dead excited, ain't you Pete?'

Pete nodded without looking up.

'Daughter?'

'Yeah. I had one of them tests, didn't I? It was great. We got a little picture and everything. Don't s'pose they had them in your day, did they?'

Mandy's smile was so thin it looked like a scar splitting her features.

'Look! I'd better be going.'

'Mand . . . let me get you a drink.' Pete had looked up finally, a pleading look on his face. His hand gripped her elbow.

'I told you. No thanks.' Their eyes met for a brief moment. 'In fact I think I'll leave it. It's a bit crowded in here.'

Mandy turned to go, pulling her arm out of his grasp.

''Bye, Mandy!'

'I'll call you, Mand.'

But Mandy could not answer either of them. There was a searing pain across the bridge of her nose and the tears were clinging to her lashes.

Having woven their way across the rain-drenched courtyard from the Lawn Bar to the Tryon Bar, negotiating umbrella spokes and overlarge hats, the girls were relieved to find the place a little less crowded. Mandy had literally dragged them out of the other one and as they waited for her to be served at the bar, Anna wandered back clutching five cream-coloured booklets.

'I s'pose we should back some horse flesh while we're here,' she said, handing them out. 'The race cards are inside.'

Susie slipped her handbag into the crook of her arm and flicked through enthusiastically. 'My dad gave me a couple of tips, actually.' The others laughed. 'Yeah, all right, all right.' Susie's dad's propensity for backing losers was renowned.

Karen glanced over to where Mandy stood at the bar, wearing the anxious look of a woman in need of a drink.

'Does anyone know what's the matter with Mandy?'

The others shook their heads.

'Probably to do with it being her birthday, and that,' Janet offered, transferring her weight from one leg to the other.

'D'you think I should have a word?'

'I'd leave it if I were you, Karen,' Anna advised. 'She'll snap out of it once she's had another drink.'

Janet was beginning to feel uncomfortable. The standing around was making her legs ache and her bump had begun to feel incredibly heavy. Casting an eye round the bar, she noticed an empty stool near the betting booths over to the left.

'Listen!' she said, already moving away in order not to miss the opportunity. 'I'm gonna sit meself over there for a bit. Give me legs a rest.'

Perched there, a solitary pregnant woman, it was as though people were drawn to her like filings to a magnet. No longer seen as a threat, women would stop and talk, the mothers among them relating stories of their own pregnancies and labours, while others — the childless — would touch her swollen belly as though it were a talisman. Men, too, would stop and chat. Not in a flirtatious way, but often as a father to a mother, eagerly relating stories of their own youngsters which were never discussed with their friends and were taboo with women whose knickers they were hoping to dive inside. It was as though she were suddenly sexless.

She had got into conversation with two pleasant fellas — Jimmy and Kevin — when she'd dropped her racecard on the floor. The thought of making the effort to leave her stool and retrieve it had defeated her and, in her highly superstitious condition, she had decided that it was probably Fate. In any case, she couldn't afford to place a bet.

So when Kevin handed her the racecard she had smiled weakly, nervous suddenly that she might be flying in the face of Fate. But they had got talking and had discovered that she and his mate, Jimmy, had friends in common.

''Ere, Jim!' Kevin said suddenly, nodding towards the overhead screen. 'The odds are looking good for the three o'clock!'

Jimmy looked up, concentrating for a moment, then reached inside his trouser pocket, pulling out a thick wallet.

'Not a bad bet at sixteen to one. How much d'you reckon?'

Jimmy shrugged. 'Twenty?'

'Yeah, all right. Gi's your money, then.'

Jimmy pulled a tenner from the wad of notes and handed it across to Kevin.

'You having a bet, love?' Kevin said, pulling a ten-pound note from his own wallet.

Janet shook her head and wrinkled her nose. 'I don't really bet.'

Jimmy laughed. 'You can't come to Ascot and not have a bet!'

'Listen!' Kevin said, pulling a five-pound note from his wallet. 'I'll put this on for you.'

'No! You can't do that.'

''Course I can. For luck.'

'No, I can't let you.'

But, laughing, Kevin had already turned away.

'What's it called?' Janet shouted after him.

'What?' he said, over his shoulder.

'The horse. What's it called?'

'Lucky Jim.'

'Bound to be a winner, ain't it?' Jimmy said, laughing.

Janet quickly reached inside her bag and pulled out her wallet. 'Here!' she called to Kevin, waving a five-pound note in the air. 'I'll only let you put it on for me if you use this.'

'Put it away!'

'I mean it!'

Even without knowing her he could hear the determination in Janet's voice. Shaking his head, he stepped back and took the note from her hand before turning once again towards the betting booth.

'And it had better win!' she called after him, only half joking.

'Win? It's a dead cert!'

*   *   *

"'Ere y'are, ladies. Get this down you!'

Terry, a porter at Smithfield, poured champagne into Anna's and Susie's glasses before bringing the bottle up to his mouth and draining what remained in one gulp.

'So,' his mate began, 'what do you girls do for a living?'

Susie grinned. 'Well, I'm a domestic help, and she's a—'

'Secretary!' Anna interrupted. 'With a firm of accountants.'

'Well,' Terry schmoozed, 'we should get on, then.'

'Yeah?' Anna looked sceptical.

He edged a little closer so that his shoulder rubbed against hers. 'I'm red-hot with figures.'

Anna fought to avoid Susie's eye. 'Yeah, right,' she said, trying to keep a straight face.

All around the bar groups of men and women were engaged in similar banter; the lies outrageous, the compliments a load of bollocks for the most part. Anna had run a poll in the first issue of her magazine in which men were asked to list their favourite places for making love. The findings had made fascinating reading, with the golf course topping the chart, and for several days the office was awash with appalling jokes of the 'hole in one' and 'putting the pink' variety. Anna could imagine that there would be a fair amount of rumpy on the racecourse that afternoon and was only grateful that it hadn't figured in the survey: 'winning by a length' and 'goes well on soft ground' would have been too much to put up with.

While Anna and Susie played the game, Karen stood slightly aloof from the small group, feeling a little awkward. She couldn't help but wonder whether people could tell she was a dyke, and in spite of herself felt self-conscious in these unfamiliar surroundings. Across the other side of the bar she could see Janet in conversation with a couple of women.

Glancing across at Mandy, who stood there like a spare part between Susie and Anna and the two blokes, she mouthed the message that she was going over to check on Janet. Mandy acknowledged with a brief nod, her eyes dropping down once again to look into the empty, smeared glass she had been clutching now for close on twenty minutes.

'So you're Terry,' Susie was saying, laying her hand on the porter's shoulder. 'And what's your name?' she said, turning to his friend.

'Richard.'

'Big bastard, ain't he?' Terry said fondly. Reaching across, he took hold of his friend's hand and held it out towards Susie. 'Look at that!' he said.

Susie and Anna stared down into the vast palm of Richard's extended hand.

'Go on,' Terry urged. 'Get hold of it.'

'What?'

'Go on,' he said, nudging Susie.

Cautiously, Susie held out her hand, gripping the other in an ill-matched handshake.

Terry could barely contain himself. ''Cos you look like the kind of girl who likes a Big Dick in her hand!' He roared at his own joke, while Richard wore the faintly bored smile of someone who had been there many times before.

On another day and in other circumstances it was the kind of repartee that Mandy thrived on, but right now she felt like a teetotaller at a piss-up, the Virgin Mary in a brothel, and, smiling an unnoticed apology, she made her way across to the bar and ordered a glass of champagne.

This wasn't at all what she had in mind for her birthday. Bumping into Pete like that had ruined everything. He had looked so well, so happy, and she tried to recall whether he had ever looked like that with her, wondering at the same time whether he had ever wanted her as much as he seemed to want Emmy. She knew that anything they might have had was dead now, but suddenly it became important — essential, even — for her to know that once upon a time he had loved her, too.

And she wished, too, that Luke and Jason were there with her, to comfort her, and as a reminder that something good had come out of that marriage. She didn't envy Pete starting parenthood again, but a part of her envied Emmy's swollen belly, the irrational part that made her wish she and Pete had met later, once they had both lived a little and so avoided all that destructive *resentment*. It wasn't fair.

She hated the thought that part of Pete would live on through a child other than one of hers, but at least she had been there first. At least she had that.

Mandy reached for her glass and drained it in one go. Turning back to the bar, she pulled a five-pound note from her bag and waved it in the air to attract the barman's attention. Suddenly, she felt warm breath on the back of her neck.

''Ere, doll, I'm for hire if you fancy a quick one under the arches!'

Mandy swivelled round, her face only inches from that of her randy taxi driver. She opened her mouth to speak but his hands were either side of her face. 'Give us a kiss!' he said, his lips over hers before she had time to utter a syllable.

And before she had recovered, the sound of his friends' cheers still ringing in her ears, he had caught the barman's attention and ordered three bottles of champagne.

'Now, if I remember correctly,' he said, grinning as he turned to face her, 'it's your birthday. Am I right?'

Mandy grinned and nodded.

'All the more reason to celebrate,' he said, handing Mandy a glass from the bar. Then, leaning close, he whispered in her ear. 'And I'll give you your present later if you're a good girl.'

*   *   *

Karen stood among the small group of women, facing Janet, who was still perched precariously on her stool. Away from the crowd at the bar, it was easier to talk without being barged aside or shouted over, a relief not to feel the press of hot bodies. The two women – Fiona and Kim – had got into conversation with Janet as they struggled with the racecard; like her, they had never placed a bet in their lives, but with the benefit of Jimmy's and Kevin's coaching, Janet offered what little advice she could.

'It's not how I imagined it,' Fiona was saying, wrinkling her nose. 'I mean, I thought it was going to be full of toffs, but, well . . . it's all a bit common, don't you think?'

Karen smiled politely.

'Where do you come from, then?' Janet shifted from one cheek to the other then back again.

'Hackney,' Fiona said proudly.

'Ah,' Janet said. 'Ah, right.'

Karen smiled to herself as she watched Janet explain the complexities of the betting system to the women, not entirely convinced that she had a complete grasp on the subject herself.

'So, because it's been raining, then that one should be a better bet. See . . .' Janet leaned forward, indicating the form under number three. 'He likes it when the going's soft.'

Fiona put a ring round number three.

'Aren't you having a bet?' Karen said, turning to Kim. The dark-haired woman was in her mid-thirties and, along with her friend, was here with colleagues from the firm of solicitors where they both worked. She glanced up at Karen from beneath a black raffia sombrero, and wrinkled her nose.

'I don't really bet. Silly though, isn't it? Coming here and not having a little flutter.' Karen smiled. 'So. What do you do? For a living I mean?'

'Teacher.'

'Really?' She seemed surprised. 'Primary or secondary?'

'Secondary. But I'm thinking of changing.'

'Yeah?'

'Mm. I've just applied for a deputy head's job in a local primary.'

'Well, I admire you. I'm not sure I could hack it.'

'It's not too bad once you work out how to seize control.'

'You make it sound like a battleground!' Kim laughed and Karen found herself staring at the woman's mouth, fascinated by the way her dark red lips curved around her teeth.

As though suddenly aware of the intensity of her gaze, Karen jerked her head round to where Janet and Fiona were laughing at some shared joke.

'Did you hear that, Kar?' Janet said.

But Karen's thoughts were elsewhere. 'Sorry?'

'Did you hear what Fiona just said?'

'Er, no. Sorry. What was that?'

'She's got two kids. A boy and a girl. Guess how old they are.'

Karen shrugged. 'No idea.'

'Eighteen and sixteen. She don't look old enough, does she?'

Karen smiled. Genuinely surprised, she shook her head.

'How 'bout you, Kim? You got any kids?' Janet shifted uncomfortably on her stool.

Karen watched Kim's reaction out of the corner of her eye as she briefly shook her head.

'Kim had the good sense to get out of her marriage before kids came along to complicate matters,' Fiona explained. 'It took me fourteen years.'

And as Fiona and Janet fell back into conversation about the raising of offspring, Karen turned once again to Kim.

'So you're divorced?'

'Mm.'

'A long time ago?'

'About three years.'

Karen had felt attracted to straight women before, but it had always felt like window shopping with an empty wallet. However, standing there, talking to Kim, she felt a compulsion to push things a little, just to see where it might lead.

'How about you?' Kim asked. Karen pursed her lips and shook her head. 'Is that no husband or no kids?'

'Neither.'

Beside them a group of lads had become a little boisterous, overexcited by too much alcohol and a big win on the last race. As two of them tussled good-naturedly one fell against Kim, pushing her forward. Profuse apologies followed, including the offer of a drink.

'No, no, I . . .'

'Let me save you,' Karen whispered in her ear and, laying her hand on Kim's back, she guided her round the corner so that they stood alone in a darkened nook.

'Thanks.'

Karen smiled. Kim had her back to the wall as Karen stood facing her. For a moment she felt a mixture of power and trepidation as she wondered what to do next. She wanted to lean across and kiss those glistening red lips, wanted to push her tongue between them and press her body against the other woman's, to feel Kim's breasts against her own.

Perhaps sensing this, Kim reached up and removed her hat, pushing the fingers of her other hand through her hair.

'They get on your nerves after a while, don't they? Hats!' she said, her voice breaking as she looked up to meet Karen's gaze, nervous but excited too.

Karen slowly nodded.

'I was wondering,' she said, reaching up to push away a

strand of Kim's hair that was hanging over her eye, 'if you'd like to meet up some time. Up in town.'

Kim's eyes had closed for a moment as Karen's fingers brushed across her forehead. She swallowed. Finally, unable to speak, she nodded.

Karen's face broke into a broad, triumphant grin. She stared into Kim's eyes and saw something there of the fear she had once seen reflected in her mirror.

Leaning in, her mouth on Kim's ear, she whispered hoarsely. 'I can't wait.' And before she pulled away the tip of her tongue stroked Kim's lobe and she felt the tiny shudder of excitement that passed through her.

The sound of Janet shrieking broke the spell and they both rushed forward to see what the matter was.

Kevin was grinning from ear to ear, delighting in the effect he was having as he continued to count notes into the palm of Janet's hand.

'. . . sixty, seventy, eighty, and your five-pound note!'

'Oh, my God! I can't believe it!'

'Didn't you listen to the race?' Jimmy laughed.

'I was chatting. Aw, this is fantastic,' she said, holding the wad of money to her lips and kissing it. 'Come 'ere, the pair of you!'

Like bashful schoolboys, Jimmy and Kevin leaned closer and Janet kissed each of them on the cheek.

'Christ!' Kevin complained. 'I wish all the women I met were as grateful as you!'

'The ones you give money to are, Kev!' Jimmy joked, then roared with laughter.

'Yeah, yeah, yeah. C'mon, comedian, let's go down on the course.' He turned to Janet, and squeezed her hand. 'Listen! If we don't see you again, babe, I hope it all goes well.'

Janet couldn't stop grinning. Pushing her money into her

bag, she pulled out her racing card. ''Ere, not so fast!' she said. 'You got a tip for the last two races?'

'Cheeky cow, ain't she?' Kevin said to his friend even as he reached across for Janet's card. Pulling a biro from his top pocket, he flicked through and made a mark against the names of two horses before handing it back to her.

'And if they come up trumps I'll expect you to call it Kevin, all right?'

Susie and Anna stood either side of their Smithfield porter and smiled for the camera.

'Oh, fuck! I forgot to put the flash on!' Terry said, fiddling with dials on the complicated-looking camera. His three subjects groaned.

'Right! Back in position!' he called finally.

Richard placed an arm around Susie's and Anna's shoulders; then, suddenly, his hand was over Susie's left breast. She spoke out of the corner of her mouth while maintaining her fixed smile for the camera.

'Unless you wanna remove your balls from the end of my stiletto, you better shift your fucking hand!'

'Oops! Sorry, darling,' he said, snatching it away. 'It must've slipped. Got no control over me limbs, you see. Got injured fighting for my country, didn't I?'

'Oh, yeah?' Anna laughed doubtfully. 'Where was that, then? Wembley Stadium?'

Susie snorted.

'No, don't laugh, girls. I'm serious. I'm a war veteran.'

The girls howled with laughter.

'I *am*! I was in the Falklands.'

Terry's voice came from behind the camera. 'Say bollocks!'

'He's already said it,' Anna screeched and they were off again.

Richard, however, was indignant. 'Oi, Terry! Tell 'em. I was in the Falklands, wasn't I?'

'Yeah . . .'

Richard took on a superior air. 'See!'

'. . . as a cook!'

This time all three of them laughed at Richard's expense.

Anna wiped the tears from her eyes. 'Did you do your wrist in, peeling all them spuds?'

But before he could answer, Susie stepped in. 'Nah, that's just 'cos he's a wanker!'

The two girls clung to one another, helpless; their hats clashing so that they perched at a comical angle. Susie dabbed at her eyes with a tissue, removing mascara from where it had run beneath her lashes.

'Oh, look at this,' she said, inspecting the black-smudged tissue. 'I'd better go to the loo. I must look a right state.'

'Yeah. You do,' Anna said flatly.

'Piss off!'

Anna clutched her side in mock pain, where Susie had nudged her with her elbow.

'Listen! I'm coming with you!' she said, catching hold of Susie's arm as she turned to leave.

'We'll see you later,' Susie called sweetly over her shoulder.

'You're coming back, ain't you?'

'Yeah. 'Course.' Susie's sincerity almost convinced Anna.

'You are joking, I hope,' she whispered as they wove their way towards the loo.

'Too fucking true I am,' Susie said. 'Those two were doin' my head in.'

As the raucous laughter of Mandy's taxi driver and his mates rang out after yet another obscene story, Anna made her excuses and left. For a long time she had stood on her own at one end of the bar, while Susie chatted to an old girlfriend she had bumped into, and then Mandy had come along and 'rescued' her, dragging her across to meet her new bosom buddies.

Oh, they had been welcoming enough, and generous with their champagne to the point where Anna was beginning to feel a bit squiffy, but as she stood back a little from them, watching Mandy, she couldn't help thinking that her friend deserved more. Not better: there was nothing *wrong* with these people. She just deserved *more*.

Susie was still deep in conversation, looking more relaxed and more radiant than she had for some time. And Anna noted, with a wry smile, that this was probably the first occasion since Nathan was born that they had been out and she hadn't spent most of the time boring them with the minutest detail of the baby's latest achievements. Oh, she loved Nathan as much as she loved Susie, but she could only muster just so much enthusiasm about his eating habits, teething problems and his recent attempts to master the art of walking.

As she looked about her, it occurred to Anna that many of the people here were rapidly reverting to a childlike state as they swayed precariously, suffering from the advanced effects of alcoholic overindulgence.

Janet was sitting in the same place she'd been almost since they'd arrived, her swollen belly resting on her thighs as she perched on the stool. She was talking animatedly to a couple of women, looking glorious and completely happy, wallowing in the sheer achievement of her pregnancy and the promise it held for the future.

And looking at her, Anna felt a flutter in her stomach at what the future might hold for her. All day long she had suppressed her excitement; denied the urge to tell everyone the news. But at the back of her mind had been the pregnancy test she had carried out that morning. Sitting alone, on the edge of the bath, she had gasped as the result showed positive, barely able to take in its ramifications. But she could not allow herself to get carried away; not yet. It was too early. The test could be wrong . . .

She thought of the second test she had bought, saw it in her mind's eye where she had left it, standing in the middle of the kitchen table, awaiting her return. There was a moment too when she thought of Frank, and of Michael, but she quickly shook them from her mind. This was about her, not them.

Glancing across at Janet, watching her hands as they caressed her belly and the child growing within her, Anna smiled to herself, no longer filled with envy but with hope.

Karen was standing just beside Janet. Anna watched as she took a racing card from the woman beside her. She wrote something on the front of the card and handed it back, their hands jointly holding the small booklet until the moment of eye contact was broken as the woman pushed the card hurriedly into her shoulder bag.

Somewhere up ahead the door opened, allowing a cool breeze to wash through the bar. Anna drank it in and, as the door closed again, she pushed her way towards it, thirsting for more. The air was heavy inside and she was feeling increasingly nauseous from the clouds of smoke circling overhead.

The rain had stopped and the sun was out, transforming the place suddenly into a beautiful canvas created from the most dazzling palette. Hats and dresses in the most exquisite colours paraded before her, lifting her spirits. Raindrops dripped from the guttering overhead, splashing on her Chanel-covered shoulder as, smiling now, she moved away, towards the small stone staircase leading up to the VIP terrace.

It suddenly occurred to Anna that, had she not been so preoccupied, she might have thought to arrange press passes for them all and taken the girls into one or other of the exclusive parties taking place up there. They meant nothing to her, but the girls might have enjoyed it.

At the sound of laughter overhead, Anna glanced up to see the two girls – Jen and her mate – to whom they had given a lift. They were sporting large VIP badges, holding a glass of champagne in one hand and a canapé in the other. Anna almost laughed out loud when she saw their male companions, but instead tucked herself beneath the cover of the steps to avoid detection. They were making a play for Mark Hadley – her erstwhile colleague – and another yuppie-looking bloke she vaguely recognised from her days at *Smash Hits*. They both had reputations as leg-over merchants, and Anna vaguely wondered whether she ought to warn the girls that if it was expensive wedding bells they were after, they were stoking the wrong fire. But, when it came down to it, she knew that they deserved each other.

Still, there was something sad about them, and as she listened to their drunken laughter she wondered how these two women would end up once their beauty had finally faded. What would they have once that was gone?

'There you are!' Janet said, making her jump. 'We're going down on the course.'

'What for?'

'To see some greyhounds!' Janet made a face. 'What d'you think we're going down there for?'

'Yeah. I mean, I can't go home and tell me dad I came all the way to Ascot and never saw a bleedin' horse, can I?' Susie reasoned.

'And anyway,' Karen added, 'Janet thinks she's an expert tipster now, don't you, Jan?'

Janet nodded, all serious. 'You behave yourself and I just might give you a tip for the next race.'

Anna laughed. 'Where's Mandy?'

Susie said, barely containing her amusement. 'She

said she was nipping off to 'ave a look at what's-his-name's new cab.'

The girls snorted with laughter.

'Yeah,' Janet said. 'I bet you he's showing her his gear stick right now!'

'Yeah, well all I hope is he's got a bit of clutch control!' Susie said, joining in the game. 'Mind you, you can wipe those taxi seats over with a damp cloth, can't you!'

'Suse!' Anna protested.

'Well,' Susie said, looking to her. 'The back of a cab at Ascot . . . I ask you!'

'Hark at Miss Prim!' Karen laughed. 'Have you forgotten the roof of that bus shelter in Holloway Road with Billy Hall?'

Susie covered her face with her hand.

'Anyway,' Janet said, beginning to push through the crowd, leading the way, her bloated body waddling from side to side like Mr Wobbly. 'Let's get down there before we miss the race.'

Susie pulled the two plastic carrier bags from her handbag and placed them side by side on the rough concrete step high up in the grandstand.

'Right!' she said, looking up at Janet as she placed a palm over each of them so they didn't blow away. 'Get your bum on those!'

With difficulty, Janet lowered herself on to the bags, so that by the time she was seated, no evidence of their existence remained.

Janet looked at her. 'I daren't ask why you had those in your bag,' she said, as Susie sat down beside her.

'You'd be surprised what you carry round with you once you've got a kid. I've probably got a nappy and a bib in there, an' all,' she said, nodding towards her voluminous handbag.

'Yeah, well they might come in handy. Me bladder's bulging a bit!'

Susie glanced briefly at Janet, a brief sigh escaping her as she felt a moment's nostalgia for the pregnancy she had so much enjoyed.

'You getting excited now?'

Janet grinned. 'Yeah. But sometimes I look at the size of me stomach and I wonder how the hell I'm gonna get it out. I mean, look at me! It can't all be water, can it?'

The two of them gazed at her dress, draped like a marquee over her knees, and burst out laughing.

'I've told Steve I wanna have it naturally,' Janet said, shaking her head as she slowly stroked her belly, 'but I don't know.'

'Fuck that!' Susie said emphatically. 'All you wanna worry about is getting it out. Bollocks to all them veggies that bang on about the beauty of natural childbirth. I mean, there's gotta be something wrong with 'em, ain't there? How can *anyone* enjoy having your tonsils removed through your arse? 'Cos that's how painful it is.'

Looking to Janet, Susie noticed that the colour had drained from her face. Reaching across for her hand, Susie took her it inside her own and squeezed her fingers.

'You'll be all right,' she said quietly.

They sat there in silence for a couple of minutes, watching Anna and Karen down on the course placing Janet's bet as instructed, then followed them as they made their way back up the stand towards them.

'I felt like a proper punter putting your bet on,' Anna laughed as she handed the ticket to Janet. 'You sure fifty quid was such a good idea?'

' o late now!' Janet said. 'Anyway, it's only money I've   't's a bit like what you ain't had, you don't miss.'   'ed.

'Did you put some money on it yourself?'

'*I* did!' Karen said, waving her ticket. 'Five pounds to win!'

'I went for number one,' Anna said, checking her racecard.

'No comment!' Susie giggled.

'Thank you, bitch!'

'Ooh, look! They're lining up,' Karen said excitedly, peering across to the other side of the racecourse, where the horses were trotting up to the starting line.

Janet struggled to her feet, hanging on Susie's arm. 'Pity Mandy ain't here. Fancy going to Ascot and not seeing a bit of horse flesh.'

'She's probably grappling with another kind of meat at the moment,' Susie said with a straight face.

'Yuk!' And Karen pulled a grimace.

Susie leaned in towards them. 'He was a big bugger, an' all. It's probably like climbing up a drainpipe!'

All of a sudden a roar rose around the stand and their laughter was lost in the sounds of people cheering on their particular horse. Arms waved in the air, bodies jumped up and down with excitement as the horses galloped down the first straight, with little space between the six runners. Bunched together on the rails, the jockeys' colours were indistinct at such a distance.

'Where's my one? Where's number five?' Janet shouted anxiously, jogging up and down on the spot.

'He's laying third on the rails,' a man shouted from behind them.

As her horse headed towards the next bend, Janet could just make out the purple and lilac silk on its rider's cap, and could see clearly for the first time the handsome grey gelding beneath him.

'There he is!' she screamed, as though surprised. 'Come on Court Jester! Come on Court Jester!'

On either side of her the other girls, too, were shrieking, possessed suddenly. Karen was jumping up and down while Anna was clapping wildly. Susie, beside her, stood with her hands poised over imaginary reins and, with knees bent, and a thrusting movement to her hips, willed Court Jester home.

As the horses moved into the final straight, the roar of the crowd became deafening as three horses battled it out ahead of the field. Janet was screeching for all she was worth, her fingers digging into Karen's shoulder. And when, at the line, Court Jester stuck his nose out in front to take the prize, she almost collapsed.

'Oh, my God! Oh, my God!' she panted, her voice croaking.

'We won! We won!' Karen was shouting, hugging her.

The others, too, were laughing, exhilarated by it.

'You must've won a bleedin' fortune!' Susie said, squeezing Janet's arm. 'What odds did you get?'

Janet looked to Anna, whose face broke into a broad grin. 'Sixteen to one!'

Janet's eyes widened. 'Oh, my God! That's . . . eight hundred quid! Suddenly she looked unsteady on her feet and grabbed hold of one of the metal rails along the stand.

'D'you wanna sit down, babe?' Susie said, placing her arm round Janet's shoulders.

But she was shaking her head. 'I'd never get up again. I'll be all right in a minute.' Reaching inside her pocket, she pulled out the ticket and handed it to Anna. 'Would you mind getting it for us, Annie?'

Anna smiled and took the ticket from her.

'You'd better take Karen as bodyguard,' Janet said. 'I don't want you getting mugged and losing all my winnings.'

'Nice to know you're so concerned about our wellbeing,' she called over her shoulder as she and Karen descended the steps.

But Janet did not take in Anna's words. At first she thought her bladder had given way under the strain, yet as the liquid continued to run down her legs, soaking into her shoes and creating a mustard-coloured streak down the front of her yellow dress, she realised that something was wrong. Looking down, she saw a dark pool forming round her feet and, in a moment of panic, Janet pushed her fingers beneath her dress, smearing them with the warm liquid. As she held her hand out before her, her relief at seeing that there was no blood was quickly followed by panic.

Susie was staring away, across the stand, taking in the spectacle.

'Suse!'

'What?'

'*Susie!*' she yelled, a real urgency there now, so that Susie immediately turned. Following Janet's gaze, she saw the problem straight away and burst out laughing.

'Aw, Jan, I told you I had a nappy in me bag.'

'I ain't pissed meself, you silly cow! I've started! Me waters have gone!'

'Oh, fucking hell!' Susie craned her neck to locate Anna and Karen in the crowd, and then, above the hubbub of noise, their names rang out loud and clear.

'A-nna! Ka-ren!'

Anna and Karen turned and seeing Susie's waving arms and Janet's obvious distress, ran back up the stand towards them.

'She's started!' Susie shouted as they got closer.

Janet was standing, legs apart, watching in horror as the waters continued to flow, running down the steps like some man-made waterfall.

Susie reached inside her bag for her mobile. 'I'll phone nine nine nine.'

'No!' Karen said, taking charge. 'There has to be an ambulance on the course. I'll find a steward. It'll be quicker.'

'I'll come with you,' Anna said, making to follow Karen down the steps.

'No!' Janet insisted through gritted teeth. 'No. Get my fucking winnings!'

Susie and Anna couldn't help laughing, relieved that she was sufficiently in control to get her priorities sorted.

'OK,' Anna said, patting her hand before making off down the steps two at a time. 'Don't panic . . .'

By now a small crowd was forming around Susie and Janet as they stood there, helpless, waiting for help to arrive.

'Oh, shit . . .' Janet said, putting her hand over her mouth.

'What?' Susie said, her face etched with concern.

'It won,' Janet said, staring at her.

'Yeah,' Susie said, grinning. 'Sixteen to one! Great, eh?'

'Yeah, but now I'm gonna have to call it Kevin!'

Janet was beyond caring now. As she raised her foot to step up inside the ambulance a fresh gush of water splashed down her leg.

She groaned.

'Hang on a minute,' the paramedic said to her colleague, leaving Janet stranded there with one foot inside the vehicle and the other sinking into the soft turf of the racecourse. Opening a small cabinet, she brought out a couple of small white towels and placed them on the seat running along the inside of the ambulance. 'Sit on these, will you, love?'

Janet pulled herself up the step and quickly lowered her bottom on to the rough towelling. The nappy Susie had given her hung sodden and useless inside her knickers, and as she felt the water soak into the seat beneath her she marvelled at how much of it there was. She had expected enough to fill a milk bottle, but it felt as though she'd shed a barrel load . . . and still it came!

Karen followed Janet into the ambulance, sitting beside her and taking hold of her hand.

'You'll get soaked if you sit there,' Janet said miserably.

Karen squeezed her hand. 'Don't worry about that.'

Standing just outside, Susie hitched up her skirt and raised a foot on to the step.

'Sorry, my love,' the male paramedic said, holding up his hand, unable to resist a quick glance at Susie's thigh. 'Not enough room, I'm afraid.'

'But we've got to go with her. We're her mates.'

He smiled, reaching round the side of the door frame for one of the doors. 'Don't worry. She's in safe hands.'

'But which hospital are you taking her to?' Anna called, from just beyond Susie.

'The Royal Ascot. It's not far.' And even as he spoke he fastened shut the first of the doors.

Inside, Janet let out a deep moan.

'Just remember your breathing, my love,' the female paramedic called back to her as she climbed into the driver's seat. 'You ready, Stu?'

Stuart, the ambulanceman, reached for the other door.

'Aw, c'mon, mate,' Susie pleaded. 'We won't get in the way.'

He smiled thinly. 'Sorry.' And with that he closed the door.

'We'll get there as soon as we can, Jan!' Anna shouted through the closed doors, jumping back as the engine started up.

'Mean bastard!' Susie shouted as the ambulance pulled away along the empty racetrack.

The stands were still full as the crowds awaited the last race. Looking up at them, Anna sighed.

'It's going to take us ages to fight our way through that lot. And fuck knows where we left the minibus. Do you remember?'

Susie shook her head. 'I told Janet to. As she wasn't drinking.'

Anna glanced along the track at the receding ambulance. Suddenly, her face broke into a grin. 'Come on,' she said, kicking off her shoes.

'What?'

Stooping down, she picked up the shoes and hooked the slingbacks over her forefinger. 'We're going to have to leg it.'

As understanding dawned, Susie kicked off her shoes and did the same.

'Hat!' they said simultaneously, and whipping them off their heads, they raced off through the wet grass in pursuit of the disappearing ambulance. A cheer rose through the stands as they laboured along the track, mud spattering their legs and skirts as they ran.

A steward stepped on to the track to jeers from the crowd but the girls split up, one swerving either side of him to leave the poor man floundering as they stumbled on, laughing and gasping for breath.

Out of the corner of her eye Anna could see a vehicle tracking them. It tooted but she and Susie ignored it and carried on. They had lost sight of the ambulance by now but could see an exit from the course up in the distance. The car hooted again and as Susie turned to stick her finger up at it, she could see Mandy hanging out of the back window of the taxi, her face looking strained as she shrieked unheard into that open space.

Susie grabbed hold of Anna's arm and as they stopped so the cab stopped just ahead of them. Out of breath, they waited for it to reverse so that it was alongside them, just the other side of the barrier.

'What the fuck are you two doing?' Mandy's expression was priceless.

Anna and Susie clung to one another, fighting for breath.

'Janet . . . gone to . . . hospital.'

Anna nodded.

'What? What hospital? Why?'

'She's . . . having . . . the baby.' Anna pulled herself upright.

'Shit!' Mandy shouted, flinging open the door. 'Quick! Get in!'

The two girls stumbled across to the cab, barely able to lift their legs over the rail, they were so exhausted.

'Come on . . . come on!' Mandy urged.

As they fell into the cab, cheers rose once more from the stands and as they pulled away, Anna and Susie managed to raise their arms sufficiently to wave through the open window.

Slumping back into the long seat, the three of them sat side by side, grinning.

'So where've they taken her?' Mandy asked finally.

'The Royal Ascot.'

'D'you hear that, cabbie?' she called jokingly and her friend nodded, turning off the course and on to the road leading towards the exit.

'Steve meeting us there, is he?' Mandy said, reaching forward to slide shut the glass panel between them and the driver.

Anna and Susie stared at one another behind her back.

'Oh, fuck! Steve!'

On a chair in the corner of the birthing room, five battered hats formed a mound, while five pairs of mud-caked shoes had been carefully stowed out of sight beneath the seat.

Janet lay prostrate on the bed, a monitor round her belly and another on the end of a thin wire that had been inserted up her fanny and attached to the baby's scalp. Beside her, a screen registered the intensity of each contraction.

Karen and Mandy stood on one side of the bed, facing Anna and Susie on the other.

Mandy cast about the room. 'It's all changed since I had my two. I mean, they wouldn't have allowed us lot in back then. And look! She's got her own little bathroom and everything.' She slowly shook her head, impressed.

Janet was barely conscious of what she was saying as she fought her way through another contraction; stronger than the last so that it took her breath away. Only as the pain subsided and normal breathing resumed was she aware of Karen stroking her hand, and smiled up at her pathetically.

'Did you tell Steve to go home for my bag?' she said, turning wearily to Susie.

'Sorry. I didn't think you'd have packed one, with it being so early.'

Mandy laughed. 'She's had it ready for the past six months, ain't you, Jan?'

'I mean, look at this!' Janet answered, pulling at the floral nightgown the hospital had lent her. I look like Granny Bleedin' Grunt.'

'Don't worry,' Anna said, leaning over and squeezing her arm. 'When it's all over I'll nip to Marks and buy you a couple of new ones.

'Would you?'

Anna smiled reassuringly. ''Course. And I'll get stuff for the baby. Just don't worry.'

'Anyway,' Mandy said, 'afterwards is when you want something nice. I mean this is only gonna get covered in blood, ain't it?'

Janet's shoulders sagged.

'Yeah,' Susie added enthusiastically. 'And at least you had your legs waxed. I mean, imagine having to have all them doctors standing round you and you look like a gorilla from the waist down.'

'Oh, don't!' Mandy said, animated suddenly. 'Did I tell you about that bloke I went with? Well, I'd been out with him a couple of times, just for a drink like, and then the third time we went back to my place. Well there I was, laying in bed in me birthday suit, waiting for him to come out the bathroom. But when he walks in I get the shock of me life! He's covered all over in this horrible black hair. It was even on his bum! I didn't like to hurt his feelings so I tried to go through with it, but whenever I opened me mouth I was having to fish hairs off me tongue! I felt sick. It was like shagging a fur coat!'

'What happened?' Karen asked, her brow deeply furrowed, intrigued despite herself.

'I had to tell him, didn't I? I felt a bit mean, but, well you've got to be cruel to be kind, ain't you?'

'Except you can hardly expect the guy to do a body shave every day.'

'No. No, I know that. But, well, maybe he has to look for women who *like* that sort of thing . . .'

'What d'you mean, advertise?' Susie laughed, the words already formed in her head. "Hairy fucker seeks animal lover for ticklish relationship" . . .'

Janet squirmed in agony.

'"King Kong seeks gentle female to stroke his fur and for meaningful friendship" . . .'

Her lips rolled in on one another as she fought to contain the pain.

'How about, "Big Bad Wolf looking for Little Red Riding Hood to gobble him up, enjoys theatre and intelligent conversation" . . . ?'

Gradually, Janet's pain subsided and her head slumped back against the pillow.

'All right, Jan?' Karen asked cheerfully, smoothing Janet's

hair from her forehead, surprised to find it damp with sweat.

'Steve should've been here by now,' she said anxiously.

'There's probably a lot of traffic,' she said, smiling. 'Don't worry. He'll be here.'

'Mind you, Jan,' Susie said rubbing a hand over Janet's bare shin, 'once he is, all you'll do is shout at him. I remember when I had Nathan. Jo had claw marks right down his arm by the time I'd finished.'

'Was Pete there when you had the boys?' Anna asked.

Mandy's lip curled disdainfully. 'Was he heck! When I had Jason he was watching Arsenal up in Sunderland or somewhere, and with Luke . . .' She shrugged. 'Well . . . he just wasn't into it, I s'pose.'

There was a moment's awkward silence, broken finally by the distant sound of a woman screaming.

'Ooh fuck!' Janet said, a look of horror on her face, and the girls erupted into laughter.

'Did I tell you he's having a baby?' Mandy said calmly, as though announcing she was going to have her hair trimmed.

'Who?' Susie said, turning to face her as she perched one cheek on the edge of the bed.

'Pete. Him and his little cheerleader.'

'You're joking!' Anna gasped. 'When did you find out about this?'

'Today. He was there. You know . . . at Ascot.'

'Bloody hell! No wonder you looked pissed off,' Susie said, slipping from the bed and stepping across to put her arm round Mandy's shoulders.

Janet braced herself to cope with the contraction about to engulf her . . .

'You don't want him back, though, do you, Mand?' Anna's head was tilted to one side as she sought to understand the emotions her friend was experiencing.

'You must be joking!' she answered without hesitation. Sighing heavily, she reached up and began fiddling self-consciously with the cannister of gas and air propped beside her. 'I don't know. It just made me feel a bit depressed for some reason.'

Janet's knees rose up so that her heels pressed against her buttocks; her eyes clenched tight as the wave of pain washed through her . . .

'It just felt like he was starting out all over again — you know, making a fresh start — while here I am . . .'

The other three made eye contact around the bed.

'So it wasn't that she can fit into a size ten and was born the year we left school, then?' Susie said quietly, her voice serious.

Anna and Karen looked at them, and then all four burst out laughing.

'You prats!' she cried. 'There I am baring my soul and all you can do is take the piss!'

Janet shuddered as the pain reached its height and, slowly, began to subside . . .

'But you've got to look at these things practically, Mandy,' Anna said, pressing a knuckle to the corner of her eye to soak up a tear. 'You don't want Pete, you don't want another baby, you don't want the kind of life you had with him. So there you are.'

'Yeah,' she said quietly. 'I know.' She looked up to see them all looking at her. 'And I hope he gets one who cries all fucking night!'

With laughter still filling the room, the midwife entered through the swing doors. 'How're we doing?' she said, walking across to the foot of the bed and unhooking Janet's notes from where they hung. Having taken in the information, she replaced the notes and pulled on a pair of sterilised gloves.

''Ere, Mand, you could do with a supply of those,' Susie said, snorting.

Mandy dug her in the ribs as Anna glared across at them like they were two naughty children.

'I'm just going to have a look. OK, dear?' Clare, the midwife, smiled at Janet up the length of her body.

Janet nodded and her knees parted beneath the floral nightie.

Two hours later Janet had entered second stage. She lay there, her eyes closed for a moment as she struggled to regain the strength to cope with the next onslaught. Around the bed the girls still stood, exhausted now by the emotional strain of it all.

Her hand aching inside Janet's vicelike grip, Anna gently peeled back her fingers and changed places with Karen.

'Sorry,' Janet sobbed, her speech slurred from the inhalation of too much gas and air.

Anna smiled and stroked her cheek.

Across the other side of the bed Mandy glanced at her watch. Janet's head swivelled at the movement.

'He should've been here by now,' she wailed. 'Where is he?'

'Just try and relax, Jan,' Susie soothed.

'I can't relax!' she screamed. 'I'm dying!'

'I told her she should have had an epidural,' Susie said out of the corner of her mouth.

At the foot of the bed, the midwife prepared her instruments in readiness for the delivery.

'Now, Janet,' she began, laying her palm over Janet's belly, 'when you feel the next contraction I want you to push. OK?'

Her teeth clenched and her eyes closed, Janet nodded blindly, her face contorting as the excruciating pain dragged at her innards. Looking on, the girls winced, impotent to ease her suffering.

'D'you want some gas and air?' Mandy said, releasing the mask from its hook and offering it to her. She shook her head and as her screams rang out, Mandy pressed the mask to her own face and breathed deeply.

'Lovely!' the midwife announced, peering between Janet's legs. 'One more push and we should see the head. You're doing brilliantly, my dear.'

A flicker of a smile passed over Janet's face, but as the pain resumed all too soon she yelled so that her voice could be heard down the end of the corridor.

'*Steve!*'

It was the first thing Steve heard as he rushed from the lift and raced along to the reception desk of the labour ward. Having no need for directions, he followed the sound of that unmistakable voice, pushing through the doors, shaking and breathless, just in time to hear a cheer rise up at the appearance of the baby's head.

Jo's arrival in the waiting room, although totally unexpected, had been readily accepted as just another of the day's unusual little turn-ups. In fact, with Steve's car in the garage for a service, he had been called upon to drive Steve to the hospital, and had delighted in a genuine excuse to break the speed limit.

Susie sat on Jo's lap and draped herself about him, her fingers playing through his hair, tensing occasionally when a wail went up along the corridor.

The other three wandered nervously round the waiting room, as anxious as any expectant father. Through the wall they could hear Janet's screams.

Anna winced. She had been shocked by the brutality of it all; at how primitive the whole thing was in spite of the monitors and equipment. But how wonderful, too, to be able to produce another life from your own body, to have created something that made your own mortality pale into insignificance.

Anna looked about her. They were all silent, listening now to Janet, her cries sounding barely human as they were drawn up from somewhere deep inside her. Then, all of a sudden, the birthing room fell silent too. The girls listened, leaning in, the sound of their breathing filling the air. And then it came. The searing, catlike mewl of a newborn baby. As one, they screeched with joy, rushing together and hugging one another with pure delight and a euphoria born of relief.

And that was how they stood, laughing and joking, Jo looking on indulgently, when, some five minutes later, the midwife came in and asked if they would like to see the baby. Grinning broadly, they filed into the room, entering with an almost reverential air.

Janet lay on the bed looking exhausted but deliriously happy, with tears streaming down her face. The baby, wrapped in a white blanket, suckled at her breast and Steve had his arm about them both, his scratched and bleeding limb holding them to him. He, too, had been crying.

Looking up, Janet beamed from ear to ear. 'It's a boy!'

Susie gazed up into Jo's face. Smiling, he placed his arm about her and squeezed her arm, burying his face in her hair.

Mandy leading the way, they rushed forward to kiss the proud parents, hugging them, everyone in tears now. Then, gathering round the bed, they peered in at the tiny bundle of flesh and blood that their two friends had so desperately fought for, and who in the end had been created through the power of their love.

Leaning over, Karen placed her little finger inside the baby's tiny fist.

'Hello, Kevin,' she whispered.

'*Kevin?*' Steve said, leaning away from them.

All five women burst out laughing.

Lovingly, Janet looked up into Steve's face. 'It's all right, Steve. I'll explain later!' She grinned. 'It's a long story.'